Vengeance

Patrick Knight

Vengeance

ISBN 9798846336650

Vengeance

For my cousins, Dark and Moon.
Meet The Reaper…I think you'll like him.

"But my dreams, they aren't as empty
As my conscience seems to be
I have hours, only lonely
My love is vengeance, that's never free."
The Who – Behind Blue Eyes

"Show me a hero and I'll write you a tragedy."
F. Scott Fitzgerald—The Crack-Up

Prologue

This was the part he had come to love. No, love wasn't the right word. Crave. It was a craving. It was like the craving he used to have for cigarettes. He had tried a thousand times to quit, and he knew there would be guilt afterward, but the scream of the nicotine won out every time. He would always light up, and deal with his conscience later.

Yes, this was exactly like that.

David stood silently in a nameless alleyway in Oakland. He pressed his body close to the wall of the dingy gray building closest to the street. Although he had just sprinted into the alley, his breathing was barely perceptible.

He turned his predatory gaze to the street. Ancient streetlights rose from cracked holes in the sidewalk. Only the ground directly below each lamp was lit by their pale glow. The waning moon cast more light than these feeble sentinels, but even the moonlight was yellowed by the impoverished landscape. It was as if the very concrete that formed the streets and buildings absorbed the moon's luminescence, leaving behind only a faded husk.

No light at all, however, penetrated David's alley. It stood like the gaping, black maw of some colossal beast. If there had been anyone on the street watching him, they would have sworn that the opening had somehow darkened when he entered it, as if a shadow had passed over the moon.

He watched his pursuer. He often wished he could thank Hollywood personally for the images portrayed in the movies and on television. One rule that he felt he could count on was this: When a person is faced with an unfamiliar situation, he will behave like a character he has seen on TV. Television was predictable, and so were the villains he preyed upon.

Tonight was no exception. The young man he had toyed with for the last 15 minutes was edging along the sidewalk toward him. A composite of every cop and criminal on every bad TV show, he made for the corner slowly, his back to the wall. In his right hand he held a gun. A Glock, David thought, maybe .40 caliber. Ugly gun. The boy held it pointing toward the street, his fingers constantly searching for a comfortable grip. The young man's left shoulder intermittently rubbed against the brick, whispering the secret of his approach.

That sound alone would have been enough for David to time his attack, but, as it turned out, it would not be necessary. The young man had failed to realize that his movements were being broadcast by a plate-glass window across the street. This was almost unfair, but it was getting late, and David was tired. It would end here and now, and not for him.

His pursuer reached the edge of the building and paused. David's fingertips began to tingle. His pulse quickened, and the familiar red cloud rolled through his body. He felt the warm rush of blood starting near his ears and moving slowly toward the center of his face. When the wave reached his eyes they narrowed...focused. His muscles coiled like a cobra preparing to strike. He inched his right arm up to the level of his opponent's head, holding it out straight, fist clenched. His left hand grasped his right wrist, thumb on top, fingers toward the street.

He watched in the window as the young man brought his weapon into both hands and raised it to within inches of his face. *Just like in the script,* David thought.

Then, as predicted, the young man awkwardly thrust his head around the corner into the alleyway. He had a split-second to comprehend what was about to happen, and he screamed. But the scream lasted only that same split-second.

David timed the movement perfectly, and two 14-inch steel blades shot from their housing on his right arm. They were thick, but razor sharp. About six inches along their path, they struck their target, entering the young man's skull with a dull *THOCK*. When they did, his scream ended abruptly in a squeak that faded into a guttural groan.

There was no blood, at least not yet. The young man's now lifeless body collapsed, first buckling at the knees and then toppling backward. He ended up in a grotesque pantomime of the hurdler stretch.

"Maybe if you'd tried running track instead of..." David began under his breath, but the look on the boy's face stopped him. The terror that had filled the last moment of his life remained etched there. As the blades remained locked in the boy's skull, David was currently mortally connected to him, his right fist fixed just inches from the child's face. And he was a child, David now saw. Maybe 17 or 18 years old at most. His eyes were still open, his face still frozen in a look of horror. It was the look of a child who had bolted upright in his bed after waking from a nightmare. Unfortunately for this boy, the cold asphalt took the place of his bedsheets, and his mother would not arrive in time to ease his fears.

Guilt washed over David. This wasn't the cigarette guilt of old. His heart, coming down from pumping venom into his veins, now felt as if it were going to shatter. Tears filled his eyes as he placed his left foot on the child's face. With a great tug, he pulled the steel blades free. He let out one great sob as he did this, probably loud enough for anyone nearby to hear. David was unaware of the sound. Time stood still as David pictured this child's mother caressing her baby boy's head as he drank hungrily from his bottle, and again caressing his head as he lay here dead in the street.

David moved to the wall of the nearest building, his tears flowing freely now. He didn't even bother to wipe the boy's blood and gray matter from his weapon. If he were apprehended tonight, the boy's DNA would write him a ticket to Death Row. But at least then he could rest.

Moving on instinct alone, David continued with his routine. He placed the two lethal points against the brick, and forced his weight against them. The heavy springs inside the blades' housing resisted his efforts, but he was able to force them home with a sharp, metallic snap.

As they set back in their resting place, there was a screech of metal on metal as the blade scraped across the housing. This was a sound that he recognized. It was, in fact, a regular part of his nightly ritual just five years prior, in a time before monsters such as the one at his feet had taken his life away from him.

A deathly cold stoicism took the place of his grief. His heart, in its third role in as many minutes, turned as black as the alley in which he now stood. He looked down at his victim. He saw that blood was now seeping out from behind the boy's head, spreading away in a black circle, enveloping and swallowing the moonlight on the street as it moved. Blood had welled to the surface of the two wounds on the boy's forehead, but hadn't spilled over yet. The wounds looked like a pair of vacant black eyes above the boy's own, which were wide open and equally vacant.

David saw again the evil he had meant to silence. For a second time, David's left foot met the boy's face. This time, he brought it down with enough force and malice to shatter the boy's cheekbone. Blood shot up from the wounds and then flowed freely across the boy's face and into the street.

His thirst for vengeance momentarily satisfied, David turned into the alley, letting the darkness envelop him like a mother's embrace.

Part I—The Fall

1

That incessant screeching was coming from underneath the bed again. David had thought many times that he should get under there and see if he could do something about it. If nothing else, he could see if WD-40 would do the trick.

It did serve a purpose, though, which probably kept him from getting around to it. It gave him something to think about other than what was going on above him. He had never liked baseball, so this helped keep things from ending…well…*prematurely.*

He opened his eyes. Karen had both hands on his chest, supporting her as she moved her hips rhythmically. Her long hair hung forward, mostly obscuring her face. A thin film of perspiration glistened on her brown skin, which, combined with the chill in the room, made her nipples as hard as bullets. Moving together, their bodies rocked the bed, creating a steady, screeching backbeat to the Pink Floyd on the stereo.

Karen pushed off of his chest and arched her back, lengthening and flattening her stomach and thrusting her breasts up and out. David loved it when she did this. Caught by surprise, he felt his orgasm become suddenly urgent and unavoidable. Luckily, she was also moving toward hers. She thrust herself faster and faster into him as he rose up to meet her. She began to moan, first softly, but soon escalating into hard-breathing ecstasy. That was enough to push David over the edge. It didn't happen every night, but tonight they came together, both of them gasping with a mixture of pleasure, release and relief. Karen fell down on top of David, and they stayed that way for a time, breathing heavily and letting "Comfortably Numb" wash over them.

It was a Tuesday, and they had work in the morning. More importantly, neither wanted to revisit the events of the past week. They had already been around that plenty, and, in their relationship anyway, sex was meant to be a period or exclamation point, never a comma. There was not to be much conversation tonight.

"I love you, David," Karen breathed.

"I love you too."

Karen moved over against him. David raised his arm to accept her, holding her close to him, relishing the weight of her head upon his chest. She was so familiar, yet he still loved her as much as he had when their love was as fresh and new as spring rain. He couldn't imagine sharing his life with anyone else, and he certainly couldn't imagine a life without her.

Karen was asleep less than a minute after her last word. David wasn't as fortunate. The situation Karen had gotten herself into with this kid Darius weighed heavily on his mind. He had a feeling he might be up for awhile. He reached for the remote control and turned on Leno. He kept the volume so low he could barely hear it. It didn't matter—he had plenty to think about. As Jay began his monologue, David let his mind slip back over years and miles, remembering the life he had known with Karen--the only person other than his parents and grandmother that he had ever really loved.

2

David met Karen in 1992, at the beginning of the second quarter of their Junior year at Stanford University.

The first time David saw her, Karen was sitting in the third row of "History 161, The Roman Empire--Augustus to Aurelius." David, who was double majoring in chemical and mechanical engineering, was taking the class to fill one of the fuzzy course requirements the University thought he needed to ensure a well-rounded education.

David was a back-row guy...always had been. He couldn't stand the thought that someone might be looking at him when he couldn't look back. He supposed that was a bit self-centered thinking that anyone behind him would be interested in the back of his head, but one never knew.

Professor Marian Van Wolde waddled to the front of the class, introduced herself, and began to go over the syllabus. David would later learn that she was widely known as Professor VW, not only because of the initials in her last name, but also because she was roughly the size of a Volkswagen bus and tended to wear flowery clothing. David immediately tuned her out and allowed his eyes wander about the room. He was taking this class Pass/Fail, so he didn't intend to be here much. He would show up once or twice a week, read enough of the required material to slam together a term paper, show up for the midterm and final, and take his "Pass," thank you very much. The other engineers in the room would do the same, so this was his last chance to check out who else was in the class in case he needed to borrow notes.

He looked around the lecture hall. Seated around him was the usual mix of characters. There were the back row guys, like him, who usually looked like they just rolled out of bed but were quite often a hell of a lot smarter than they looked. In the front row sat the serious-note-taking-kiss-asses. They would furiously scribble down every word Professor VW uttered and then quickly look back up at her to demonstrate how captivated they were by her lecture, nodding with the put-on exuberance of child actors on the Barney show. These people were nearly always a hell of a lot dumber than they looked. In between were a few jocks, a few sorority girls, a few engineers that David recognized, and a whole lot of History-types. History types were almost normal—not quite bathed, sometimes, and usually a little high-strung, but overall they were OK to hang out with. They were certainly not as geeky as the engineers in most of David's classes.

Just as he was finishing his sweep of the class and mentally confirming that he would spend no more time there than absolutely necessary, he noticed The Girl in the Third Row. She had dark hair that was pulled back in a ponytail, and she wore jeans and a pale yellow sweatshirt. Although he could only see her profile from his position across the lecture hall, he suspected that she might be worthy of further attention.

He was fairly sure he had never seen her before. Stanford, quite frankly, is known for its academics and not for appearances by its co-eds in Playboy's "Girls of the Pac-10." Therefore, the good-looking girls on campus were fairly well known by name and current residence hall by most of the male population. David checked his mental catalogue and found no immediate matches. He became intrigued.

He feigned tying his shoe so he could lean forward and get a better viewing angle. He was right about two things. First, she was definitely attractive. Second, she had definitely somehow escaped his previous attention.

As Professor VW finished her synopsis of the quarter and moved into an overview of Rome prior to the ascension of Augustus, David decided that he clearly would need to investigate the mystery of The Girl in the Third Row further.

Contrary to his original expectation, he showed up at the very next lecture and began the mating dance of the male college student. The Girl in the Third Row was now The Girl in the Fifth Row. She was still alone, which was promising as he carefully planned an introduction that would not appear carefully planned. The fact that she didn't seem to favor a particular row would make it difficult to pull off a plan that involved sitting next to her. He couldn't just sit down next to her; that would be too obvious. And he couldn't just plant himself in that general vicinity and hope she would sit next to him; that left too much to chance and would take too long. It seemed the next step would be to casually follow her out and find out what she did after class. She would likely have a bike, which would be ideal, but she might be a walker, which would present another challenge.

As he waited for the incessant ramblings about the First Triumvirate to end so he could move on with his plan, he reflected on what he was doing. Why not just go up and introduce himself? He knew the answer to that question, and at least he could admit it. He was quite shy when it came to meeting new people, especially in a one on one situation. In addition to being shy, he was also obsessive in his need to plan things out to the minutest detail well before taking action. He was pretty sure he over thought most things, but that had served him well academically. In matters of the heart, however, this combined with his shyness had kept him from acting on quite a few possible love interests.

Now that he thought about it, David had never really had a serious girlfriend. He had dated a few girls in high school, one for about four months. He had had maybe half a dozen abbreviated relationships in college that started with alcohol consumption and ended with nothing to talk about. It seemed that both the obsessive planning and his shyness went away when he was drunk, but so, of course, did his judgment. What he really needed was to pick the right girl and somehow end up drinking with her. Fat chance. He'd stick with his current strategy.

The lecture was over. He quickly got up and tried to cross traffic to the other side of the lecture hall. He normally entered from the opposite side she had, and he was taking quite a chance exiting the other. If he did happen into conversation, he would have to abandon his bike on the other side of the building and walk. Better that than to appear to have forgotten where he parked it. Or, even worse, to confess the truth.

He finally reached the exit and looked around for The Girl (her unfaithfulness to a particular row had forced him to shorten her moniker). He was just in time to see her riding away in the direction of the main quad. She was on a blue 10-speed bike, but he couldn't see any distinguishing features of the bike from his angle. What he did see, however, was the fact that her sweatshirt was riding slightly up, allowing him, and probably others, to see about two inches of bare skin on her lower back and a hint of lavender underwear peaking up above her jeans.

He felt two emotions at that moment, both strong enough that he was startled by them. First, he felt an overwhelming need to once again change her nickname from THE Girl to HIS Girl. Second, he was suddenly beset by a protective jealousy that someone else may be looking at HIS Girl's lacy panties.   He looked around and didn't see anyone looking in her direction…lucky for them.

David actually started to sweat. His face was flushed, and there was a hint of activity in his nether regions. He felt he had to sit down and did so on the steps of the lecture hall. He had never talked to this girl, and had really only seen the side of her face from across a lecture hall and the small of her back from 40 feet away. He couldn't describe it, but he knew what he felt was not solely because of her physical appearance. She was pretty, and seemed to have a nice body under her jeans and sweatshirt (sky blue this time), but that wasn't even half of it. He had a good idea that this girl was not like others. She wasn't one of those prissy sorority girls waiting for the next kegger at the Sigma Chi house in order to find a boy willing to help her earn her M.R.S. Degree. She wasn't one of the ridiculously career-driven girls who spent every night in the library and every morning at the career center looking at the morning's postings for summer internships. She wasn't even one of the nondescript girls drifting aimlessly through school because Daddy was paying for it. This girl was here on her own terms, and would graduate with a degree that served her own purpose and no one else's. He didn't know how he knew this, but in his mind there was no doubt that it was a fact.

The next day, David arrived at class early and parked his bike on her side of the hall. He entered the lecture hall and sat in the back row. There were only a few other students in class already, and she wasn't one of them.

The class slowly began to fill up. Many came in twos and threes, some alone and a few in larger groups. They all filed in to more or less the same seats they always did. He kept watching the door that The Girl normally used. She was nowhere to be seen.

Eventually, Professor VW ambled in, spread a notebook open on the podium and attached a remote microphone to her blouse. She hadn't caught her breath yet (although it was only a 30 foot walk from her office to the lecture hall) so the microphone broadcast her labored breathing quite conspicuously over the hall's sound system. She became conscious of this fact and tried to quiet her breathing. Her efforts quickly spiraled down into a cycle of her holding her breath and then briefly gasping even louder for air. Realizing her efforts would be futile, she detached the microphone and pretended to untangle the cord.

David watched this display with amusement. While she fumbled with the microphone cords, he scanned the lecture hall again. The Girl was not in her usual area, and he hadn't seen her come in her normal way. He looked across the class, eventually ending up with the back row on the other side of the lecture hall where he normally sat. He nearly dropped his pencil when he saw The Girl sitting in the aisle seat he normally occupied. Not only that, she was looking right at him!

He snapped his head back down toward Professor VW, who seemed to finally have her breathing under control. That, however, was now the furthest thing from David's mind. What could this mean? Clearly this must be an accident. Maybe she had come from the library before class and had been running late. That would explain her parking on that side of the building and sitting in the seat he left open. But she was looking at him, wasn't she? How was that to be explained?

He knew one thing. He couldn't look over at her for the rest of class. He wasn't prepared for this, and if she saw him looking at her again she might put two and two together and realize the truth. He had planned to either talk to her after class by their bikes, or possibly follow her today and see where she went. But now, everything was up in the air.

The 50 minutes that followed were possibly the longest of his life. He had an undeniable sense that she was looking at him, and he was dying to glance over and confirm that fact. But his will to conform to the plan was strong, and he kept his focus on the front of the room. He didn't hear a word of the lecture…couldn't remember even a hint of the content.

Finally Professor VW wrapped up, and he got up to leave, careful not to glance her way. He walked out into the cool January sun. Arriving early meant his bike was basically landlocked—it was against the only bike rack and surrounded by about 60 other bikes. He wove through bikes and their owners as they unlocked, pushed, lifted and backed their bikes from the logjam.

Just as he reached his bike, he felt a hand lightly grasp his elbow. The hand slipped away as he turned to face its owner.

"Excuse me," said The Girl, "I wasn't sure if you were ever going to introduce yourself, so I thought I would. I'm Karen."

David was speechless. So much for planning.

3

As David would later find out, The Girl, now known as Karen, had also noticed David and had spent nearly as much time planning a "chance" meeting.

Karen explained to David not long after they met that she was not normally the type of person to get worked up over such a situation. First of all, she didn't spend a whole lot of time worrying about her social status at all. She had more important objectives than making new friends, and she certainly was not looking for romance. She did have a small group of friends and she did spend time with them socially, she just didn't see the point of complicating matters with more friends or a boyfriend. Her friends provided enough of a diversion from her studies when necessary, but were rarely a distraction, which suited her perfectly.

Secondly, if Karen did find herself in a position where she wished to make a person's acquaintance, she would just do it. She had done so with the chair of the history department (who subsequently became her academic advisor), with Colin Powell when he was speaking on campus, and with the mother of her last boyfriend.

Mildred was her name, and she found Karen "fresh." Chad was Karen's boyfriend, and turned out to be quite the momma's boy. Mildred quickly convinced Chad (whether financial pressure was brought to bear was never verified) that Karen was much too forward for him, and besides, what did he want with a "Mexican girl from East L.A.?" Chad didn't put up much of a fight, and allowed his mother to introduce him to some Delta Gamma girl whose mother was in Mildred's country club in Boston. Chad, seeing the error of his ways, told Karen that he didn't think it was working out and he needed some time to himself. As it turned out, he apparently needed approximately 6 hours to himself, and then he hooked up with Lynette of Beantown at that night's party at his frat house. Lynette was seen leaving the house at about 6 a.m., executing the "walk of shame" with flawless perfection. But she had left Chad a present. He was now the proud owner of a nice case of the clap. Instant Karma's gonna get you, baby.

It seemed that when Karen first noticed David across the lecture hall, she was not able to walk over and follow her customary introductory procedure. She actually started to think about what the best way to meet him would be, and whether he would think her forward if she just walked up to him and said "Hi" (God Damn that Mildred for making her doubt herself). She wasn't exactly sure why she was hesitating…she just knew she wanted it to go right with The Back Row Guy.

To complicate matters, she began to suspect that he was watching her as well. What was his problem that he didn't just come up to her? This was why she didn't need a boyfriend…too much of a headache…too many games to play.

The day he parked his bike on the other side of the building made her snap out of her haze and regain her normal control. After all, she had done the same thing, and again they were on opposite sides of the class. If she didn't do something, they were likely going to waste the entire quarter trying to park or sit in the right place. The Back Row Guy sure didn't look like he was going to make a move any time soon. Karen had no more time for this, so she decided to get it over with and introduce herself.

David assured her that the same was true of him. That is, that he normally wouldn't have spent so much time planning their meeting (a lie), and that he was thinking of introducing himself to her after their next class (probably another lie). Karen didn't really buy his explanation, but she found it cute just the same.

David and Karen met on a Thursday. They ended their first encounter by agreeing to meet for lunch at 11 a.m. on Friday at the Student Union Cafeteria. Neither had an 11:00 class, so they would be able to get in ahead of the noontime crowd.

The cafeteria offered pretty standard fare. David had a turkey sandwich and Karen had a salad. Both noted to themselves without much surprise that their choice of food was far from what they would normally have chosen. David would have normally gone with pizza or one of those big burritos, but he was afraid he would drip sauce on his shirt or shorts. Karen would have normally gone with pizza or one of those big burritos, but she was afraid those choices would give the impression that she did not eat like a "lady."

It was unseasonably warm, probably about 70 degrees. They sat on the patio under a leafless oak tree. The mottled sunlight that shone through the tree's dense branches was just enough to provide warmth without making the couple squint or shade their eyes. There was only a whisper of a breeze, which carried the perfume of the eucalyptus trees behind the next building. It made the day seem alive, yet was not even enough to cause them to place their cups of soda on top of their napkins to keep them from blowing away. There were very few other people on the patio, and those were several tables away. David and Karen were able to speak in normal voice, without asking the other to repeat themselves amid the din of several other conversations.

As much as they both had worried about their choice of meal, they had worried more about what they would say to the other during this first real meeting. To the pleasant surprise of both parties, however, the conversation was easy and natural, and at no time needed to be forced. During the time they had, each spent almost equal time filling in a rough timeline of his or her life to date.

Karen went first. "I grew up just outside of Los Angeles," she began.

Karen Chavez, for the record, was technically not a "Mexican from East L.A." as Mildred had so eloquently (and derisively) put it. Karen's paternal grandparents moved to Los Angeles from Guadalajara before her father was born. Francisco Chavez did, in fact, grow up in East Los Angeles. After raising an appropriate amount of hell in his teens and early twenties, he settled down and landed a job driving a school bus for the Glendale school district. He met and eventually married his "Irish Rose," Kathryn O'Neill. Kate was an English teacher at Glendale High, and was a native of the Los Angeles suburb.

Karen, their first child, was born on Thanksgiving Day, 1970. Francisco and Kate had three sons after Karen. Francisco Jr. was born in 1973, Michael in 1975, and Nicholas in 1981. They were aware that their children would face prejudice and other challenges growing up with parents of different races. The took care to teach their children about their Mexican and Irish heritage, and to emphasize the importance of the children being caring and responsible individuals. Francisco and Kate provided a warm and loving home environment, and they hoped to be rewarded with intelligent, well-behaved, and independent thinking children.

And, in fact, that was the case with Karen. Karen excelled through her school years in her studies and in other activities. She attended Glendale High, and she was never embarrassed of having her parents so close. Growing up the daughter of an interracial marriage had forced Karen to develop very thick skin, and she was able to shrug off adolescent insults easily. In fact, her indifferent reaction to teasing was so effective that her would-be ridiculers quickly gave up in favor of preying on more interesting and rewarding targets.

Karen loved her parents, loved her brothers, and really loved her life. In fact, she was inspired by her parents to become an educator herself. Both Francisco and Kate were very popular with the students. Most parents were simply tolerated by children and their friends. Some were actually liked. Very few parents, let alone parents who were also teachers, were popular enough that their children and their children's friends liked to stay home and be around them or invite them to go out. Karen's parents were the proud owners of a full-size van, and it was always full of kids. Francisco and Kate were the preferred escorts to Magic Mountain, the mall, or the pizza restaurant. One could say that Francisco and Kate's good nature and understanding of children were the reasons for their popularity. That, however, was only part of the truth. Karen herself was at least partially to thank. She set the tone for her brothers and friends by treating her parents not as the social albatross that other kids did their own, but as actual people, and fun people at that.

Karen saw that her parents had a positive effect on their students and her friends, and she could think of nothing more noble for her own life than to be a teacher as well. She studied hard and maintained a 4.0 GPA. She scored 1420 on her SATs—740 verbal and 680 math. She was on the student council, ran track, and volunteered at a group home for young children on weekends. When the time came, she applied to Stanford, was accepted, and made it her first choice.

Karen's parents had saved what they could for her education. Francisco also studied the Financial Aid process, and was able to get a good deal of funding from the government in the form of grants and loans. It was touch and go for awhile, but in the end Karen was able to go to Stanford.

Karen entered Stanford in the fall of 1989. She was 18. Francisco Jr. was 16, Michael was almost 14, and Nicky was 8. Karen had always made it her business to keep her brothers on the right track. She kept her eye on Francisco Jr. at school and did her best to intervene when trouble came looking for him. Michael and Nicky were in Junior High and Elementary, respectively, but she still took a close interest in their lives. She knew the pressures they would face growing up, and she suspected the boys would have a more difficult time of it than she had. They would be faced with pressure to drink, smoke, take drugs, steal, race cars, join gangs, and have sex early and often with as many partners as possible. Maybe worst of all, they would feel the need to sacrifice their own identities in order to "fit in." If they chose to embrace their father's heritage, there were Mexican gangs and thugs that would welcome them into the fold. If the boys tended toward their mother's side, there were pot-smokers, headbangers, wastoids, and, worst of all, the quiet, anti-social misfits that exist in pairs or small groups and stockpile firearms and plan for the eventual reckoning they will visit upon the jocks, pretty girls, and oppressive faculty.

She knew that her brothers were good kids, and she encouraged them to recognize and embrace their dual cultures. She also knew that most Latino kids were good kids, as were most white kids. There were predators on both sides, though, and they looked for kids of the same race to prey upon. All you need is one thing in common to get someone to take the first drink, the first drag, the first Raiders jacket from the store.

By her own estimation, Karen had been successful with Francisco Jr. He excelled at soccer and baseball, and was a solid B+ student. He was independent and confident, and he kept focused on school, sports and family. She knew he'd had run-ins with some undesirable elements in her school, and she felt he had handled himself admirably. He was already 6 feet tall and was a fit and strong 175 pounds. He was much bigger than most of the thugs in his class and he made it pretty clear that he wasn't interested in a life of crime, so they didn't mess with him much. He knew Karen was keeping her eye on him and his younger brothers, but he didn't mind. He was proud of her and admired and loved her. Karen loved him back.

Michael, however, was another story. Mike was small for his age, and even smaller for his grade as he was one of the youngest in his class. He was less resistant to teasing than his older siblings, and had come home crying many times throughout elementary school. Karen tried to talk to him and encourage him, but she didn't feel like she was getting through. On top of being small, Mike wasn't very coordinated and therefore was a very poor athlete. He was a smart kid, but didn't take a great interest in school. Knowing that he was intelligent made it difficult for their parents to accept the C's and D's he brought home on his report card. After having a fairly easy time getting Karen and Francisco to study, they were frustrated by their third child. Mike sensed his parents' frustration, and it made him withdraw more and resent them and his perfect siblings. By the time Karen left for college, Mike spent almost all of his time locked in his room. He had a friend named Wayne that slunk in and out of the house with Mike, each carrying an overstuffed backpack and neither saying a word to anyone.

Karen and her parents worried after him and wondered what was in the bags and what was hidden behind his locked bedroom door. There were secrets behind that door, they feared, and there were secrets behind his eyes as well.

Perhaps the thing that disturbed his parents the most were the moments of happiness that were sprinkled throughout Mike's life. There were days when Mike was happy…really happy. Usually it was on a day with no school, when the family was together either at home or out somewhere. For no apparent reason, Mike would start making jokes, acting silly, hitting and play wrestling with his brothers, and hugging his sister and parents. He would also carry on conversations with his family about current events, politics, and other fairly weighty subjects. Karen was often astounded at his clarity and depth of thought, and of the amount he knew about certain subjects, especially those concerning politics and government affairs. It was on these days when either Kate or Francisco Sr. would attempt to talk to Mike about what was going on with him, and to ascertain what he did in his room alone or with Wayne. Inevitably, these conversations would drive Mike back into himself, like a snake that has been poked with a stick. Mike's entire family was distressed by his behavior, but seemed powerless to change it.

If Francisco Jr. was one bookend that offset Mike from the family, then Nicholas was the other. Nicky was starting third grade when Karen left for Stanford. Although it was too early to be sure, indications were that Nicky would be much more like Karen and Francisco Jr. than Mike. Nicky was almost a head taller than most of the boys in his grade. He was a natural athlete, and he spent hours practicing soccer in the family's backyard with his dad and oldest brother. He was big enough to be a bully in school, but instead he was kind and helpful. In fact, his presence in school to this point had, as strange as it may sound, set a tone of tolerance and peace. When bigger kids were picking on smaller ones, Nicky applied some muscle and reason to the situation, causing the bigger kids (who were still smaller than he was) to see the error of their ways. Instead of avoiding girls like they had cooties, Nicky was polite and held doors for them and helped them lift and carry things when appropriate. He was friendly with everyone, and his classmates, instead of resenting the strange power he had over them, loved him for it. He was the world's first elementary school demagogue. His teachers talked about him in the lounge, relating one story after another that brought surprised chuckles and shaking heads.

Incidentally, it appeared that Nicky was going to be brilliant. Unlike many smart kids, he wasn't ashamed of his intelligence. It never occurred to Nicky that good grades would be something to hide from the other kids. He won several math and spelling contests in his early years of elementary school. His A+ papers covered every square inch of the refrigerator.

Nicky's parents loved him. Karen loved him. Francisco Jr. loved him. To Mike, Nicky was a demon sent from hell to steal the love that should have been his. But Mike kept that secret to himself.

And so in the fall of 1989, with assurances from her parents and Francisco Jr. that Mike and Nicky would be well looked after, Karen left her parents and three brothers behind and traveled 400 miles to the north, ready to make mom and dad proud and demonstrate to her brothers that they could be whatever they wanted to be.

"My gosh, listen to me. I'm not letting you get a word in edgewise. I've been talking for half an hour. You must be bored to tears!"

Actually, David was not bored. He was fascinated by the way her mouth moved, the way the January sun glimmered in her hair, the way her eyes sparkled when she talked about her family.

Karen had related most of her story to David, although she skipped most of the details about Michael. David thought it was a great story. She was exactly the opposite of most of the girls he had met since coming to Stanford. His heart was beating strangely. It felt like an unseen hand was inside his chest giving it a little extra squeeze now and then.

"No, not at all. Your family sounds great. I'd like to meet them."

As soon as he said it he wanted to take it back. He could see the words floating across the table to Karen's ears and attempted to will them back. It was way too early to be volunteering to meet her family. He was going to scare her away.

"Maybe you can. I'm sure they would like you. But why don't you tell me about your family now?"

Maybe you can. What did that mean? He couldn't think about that now. He hadn't expected to have to give his life story, but he figured he should at least attempt to follow her lead. His mind was swimming from fascination to nervousness to panic. She seemed so relaxed and calm. She was just looking at him, waiting for him to start. A smile danced around her lips. Was she secretly laughing at him? Shit, he better say something. He took a drag on the straw in his Coke, even though it had been empty for at least 10 minutes. He got a little bit of slightly sweet water from the melting ice. He hoped that would be enough to keep his throat from clicking. Taking a deep breath, he began his story.

4

"Well, I'm from South Dakota."

"No way! Did you grow up on a farm?"

"Kind of. You know there are actually towns in South Dakota too."

"Oh, I know. Sorry. What was the name of your town?"

"I spent most of my life in a little town called Red Rock, but I was pretty much born on a ranch. It belonged to my grandparents, but my parents lived there too when they got out of college."

"Did they meet in college?"

His parents had, in fact met in college. They both went to Northern Black Hills University in White Falls, South Dakota.

David's mom, Mary Duncan, was from nearby Rapid City. His dad, William McGuire, grew up on his father's cattle ranch near a much smaller town about 60 miles south of Rapid City called Red Rock. Bill went to NBHU to study Agri-business, fully expecting to return to his father's ranch and claim his birthright. He wasn't at all excited about the prospect, but one didn't question certain things in his family. He was an only child, and his father Daniel "Red" McGuire left no doubt in anyone's mind that Bill was to be the third generation of the McGuire family to work the 6,000 acres known as the "Running M". Bill's mother, Lena, was a dutiful ranch wife. She was good to Bill, but certainly made no move to question the destiny his father had lain out for him.

Mary went to NBHU because she had nothing else to do after high school. Her father was a dentist in Rapid City and her mother stayed home with her and her older sister, Ann. Her parents insisted that she go to college, if for no better reason than to find an educated man to marry instead of someone she met in a shit-kicking bar outside of town. Ann had done that, and she had the bruises to show for it.

Bill and Mary met early in their Freshman year, which was the fall of 1964. They dated throughout college, and were married one month after they both graduated in June of 1968. Bill graduated with his Agri-business degree, Mary with a degree in sociology. Mary knew from the beginning that life with Bill would include his working on his father's ranch, and she was amenable to that. She didn't particularly want to be close to her parents, or to her sister and her asshole husband. She suspected the 50-mile drive down the two-lane highway followed by the 7 mile stretch of winding gravel road that led to the McGuire ranch house would preclude frequent visits, and she was correct.

So they moved into Bill's parents' house right after college. Not long afterward, Bill and Mary bought an airstream mobile home and parked it about a quarter mile back up the road from his parents' house, which provided a welcome buffer from the elder McGuires.

That buffer, however, soon began to border on isolation for Mary. Bill worked with his father from dawn to dusk, and Lena was not one to go out of her way to come down the road and pay a social visit to Mary. The crackling AM radio wasn't much company, and there was only so much cleaning she could do in their small mobile home. Mary soon convinced Bill that they should try for a child.

Much to Mary's joy, their efforts to start a family were successful almost at once. David was conceived on New Years' Eve, 1969, after his parents had shared a pot roast and most of a bottle of Thunderbird to toast the New Year. Bill woke up on New Years' Day, 1970, with one hell of a hangover. Mary woke up with somewhat more than that.

5

David was born about 36 weeks later, in September of 1970. His birth came earlier than expected, and for no apparent reason. The labor took Mary by complete surprise, and the birth occurred in the McGuire farmhouse, with the assistance only of David's grandmother. The ambulance arrived minutes after, and David and Mary were taken to Rapid City Regional Hospital, where David spent the first three days of his life.

After the doctors gave clearance for both mother and child to leave the hospital, the entire McGuire family returned to the ranch, where David began his life much like his father had 24 years earlier.

David's first five years were spent mainly in the company of his mother and grandmother. He only left the ranch on Sundays to go to church. His parents had some friends who had kids around his age, but they visited infrequently. David found himself generally playing alone in the yard, sitting in the kitchen watching the activity, or reading in his room. His mother taught him to read quite early, and he took to it like a fish to water.

In the winter after David's fifth birthday, his Grandpa Red got very sick with what was first thought to be a chest cold. When he didn't improve after three days, Lena began to press him to see a doctor. Red, of course, "didn't need a goddamn doctor." A few days later, Red began to cough up small amounts of blood, and Bill and Lena wrestled him out of bed and into the truck.

Red, as it turned out, had an advanced case of lung cancer. The unfiltered Marlboros had apparently won a tight race with the red meat in his colon and the beer in his liver. He died a month later, in January, 1976.

As the ground began to thaw that spring, Lena and Bill happened into a conversation that revealed neither had a real desire to carry on in the ranching business without Red. After some hesitation due to guilt caused by Red spinning in his grave, Lena and Bill decided to sell the ranch.

They did pretty well in the sale. With the proceeds, they built a large home in the hills just east of Red Rock. Bill used most of the rest of the money to purchase the local hardware store for a song from its retiring proprietor, Harley Hanson, on the condition that he would keep the original name for a minimum of 10 years.

"Harley's Hardware" had done a fair business over the years simply because it was the only hardware store in town. Moreover, it was the best place in town for the old-timers to go to escape their wives and bullshit over coffee and cigarettes.

Over the past few years, however, Harley's own lowered energy level (he was in his 70's) combined with his always limited business sense had caused him to fall behind the times. Most people in town had taken to driving to Rapid City to make any major hardware purchases. They still came in when they needed some nails, duct tape or a hammer, but nearly everything else could be found cheaper and with a much greater selection in the big city chain stores.

Bill set out to change that. He was careful not to alienate the regular, coffee-drinking clientele, but he changed almost everything else. He brought in a full line of tools, including the newest electric ones. He also began to carry farm and ranch supplies, which brought in a great deal of business from out of town. Soon, most of the town's hardware needs were again available at Harley's Hardware.

Times weren't always easy in the mid-70's. Red Rock depended on ranching, tourism, and a local VA hospital for most of its economic health. All three hit a soft spot just as Bill was getting started, and the town felt the pinch. The sale of his father's ranch allowed Bill some flexibility in accepting payment for his wares, so he extended credit to just about anyone who needed it. Soon, most of the businesses, ranchers and homeowners in the area had a credit line with Bill. He kept track of what everyone owed him, but he was too big-hearted to say anything about it. He ended up accepting homemade rhubarb pies, boysenberry preserves and chokecherry jam in payment, as well as myriad goods and services he didn't especially need.

Bill was a good enough businessman to realize that he was running himself right into the ground. His store was doing a booming business, but very little money was actually finding its way into the register. By the summer of 1978, two years after he bought the store, Bill had almost run completely through the money from the sale of the ranch. He crunched the numbers every way he could, and he realized that the only way to stay open was to stop extending credit to his neighbors.

While Bill was figuring out how to break the news to his customers and friends, the luck of the whole town suddenly changed for the better. A VA hospital in Nebraska was closed by the government, and the majority of its permanent residents and its budget were transferred to the Red Rock VA. In turn, the Red Rock VA was able to staff up to accommodate the new guests, in addition to lifting a pay freeze for current employees. In a town of less than 5,000 people, adding over 100 jobs is a big deal, and that's what happened in the fall of 1978.

The ripple effect on the town was immediate and dramatic. The stores that supported the VA workers began to see business pick up right away. They, in turn, were able to increase wages and hire a few more folks. By the beginning of 1979, the town was enjoying a bona fide economic boom.

The people in town didn't forget their friend Bill McGuire, whose generosity had helped them get by when times were tough. It happened slowly at first, but soon everyone in town was coming into Harley's to ask Bill what they owed him, ready with their checkbooks. Smiling, Bill would pull out his notebook, where he had dutifully recorded all purchases and payments. The townsfolk (especially the women) were aglow when they found out that he had recorded every pie, preserve and jam as a payment. Most insisted on paying the entire bill anyway, saying that the foodstuffs could count as interest, as Bill otherwise had asked for none.

By the summer of 1979, Bill was rolling. The town was building, and they were using tools from Harley's Hardware, paint from Bill's new paint department, and lumber from the new yard he had opened behind the store. Not one person would dare to drive to Rapid City for hardware, ranch or building supplies anymore, mainly out of loyalty to Bill, but also for fear the rest of the town would be waiting with pitchforks upon his or her return.

When the Red Rock mayoral election rolled around in 1980, the town was ready for a change. Mayor Clayton "Sonny" McFarland Jr. had decided not to seek re-election after 12 years as mayor. Several of the businessmen in town approached Bill to run. Bill refused at first, but eventually broke under pressure and agreed. It was rumored that the same group had actually "encouraged" Mayor McFarland to step aside. Sonny often fancied himself as an effective and well-loved mayor, but the business leaders and most of the other folks in town felt differently. He had run uncontested in all but his first election. He thought this was because no one thought they could do a better job. The reality, of course, was that no one else wanted to deal with the bullshit. He probably would have been surprised to know, in fact, that he was known alternately as "Spanky," "Mayor McCheese" and "Mayor McFatass" behind his back. The townsfolk didn't so much dislike him as they just disregarded him. With the emergence of Bill McGuire as a potential leader, the town jumped at the chance to affect a change at the top.

And so, in the fall of 1980, Bill McGuire was sworn in as mayor of Red Rock, South Dakota. He would remain mayor until 1993.

Bill did not disappoint the people of Red Rock. Bill's first term focused on keeping the money at home. He asked the people in town to let him know when they felt they had to go to Rapid City for something, and then he figured out a way to supply the same thing in Red Rock for a fair price and with a reasonably comparable selection.

He worked through other businesses when he could, and encouraged folks to start their own businesses when it made sense. He also found that sometimes the best way to accomplish his goal was to expand his own business. In 1981, he bought the empty building next door to Harley's and started the only real furniture store in Red Rock. In 1982, he reorganized the old hardware store and built an addition to connect the hardware and furniture stores. He brought in household products, toys, and a limited selection of practical clothing.

By the time he was up for re-election in 1983, there was no question that the town was enjoying its most prosperous time ever. The local merchants, grocery stores, restaurants and hotels had all the business they could handle. Wages were up, and unemployment was almost non-existent. The local contractors couldn't keep up with the demands for new houses and remodels on the old ones. Bill was re-elected without opposition.

6

While his dad was building his businesses and building the town, David was enjoying a happy and fairly normal childhood. His mom was able to stay home with him and make sure he ate his vegetables and learned his manners. He got straight A's from kindergarten all the way through sixth grade. He was also a decent athlete. He played little league baseball and soccer starting when he was eight years old. He was slightly above average in size, and he was fairly well coordinated. His success in sports, however, was more due to the fact that he was much smarter than the other kids his age and grasped the concepts of each sport in much greater detail.

Being the mayor's kid isn't the easiest thing to live down as a child, especially in a small town. When his dad first became mayor, his friends actually thought it was pretty cool. The older he got, however, the more ribbing (good-natured and otherwise) he had to withstand. By the time he entered middle school, he had been in more than one fist fight that started with some smartass kid saying "My dad says your dad is a…" David could take friendly barbs, but when anyone insulted his dad and meant it, they were going to get a fat lip or a bloody nose at a minimum. He also took his share of punches to the mouth, and he found that he had a pretty high tolerance for pain. After awhile, David gained the reputation of someone you didn't want to mess around with. Even if you got the drop on him, he would take your best shot and then knock you flat on your ass.

By the time he started middle school, David had become a bit introverted as a result of his dad's station in the community. Most kids that age don't want anyone to even know their parents exist. David's dad was in the paper almost every week, whether it was turning the first shovel of dirt at the new community center or handing over the "First Dollar of Clear Profit" to the new chiropractor in town. David still loved his parents and made no apologies for anything. In fact, he was proud as hell of what his dad did for the town and the people who lived there. As he entered adolescence, however, his dad's position meant he had at least one more thing to worry about than the other kids.

As he navigated the sometimes treacherous waters of middle school, David found a new passion in football. Football started in seventh grade, and David signed up with the rest of his friends. As in other sports, David's intelligence gave him a head start, and his physical size and toughness completed the picture. David's fearless and sometimes reckless play in the linebacker position caught the attention of the high school football coach. Red Rock High had a proud football tradition, although the low student population made depth a problem. When the star varsity linebacker went down with a knee injury in David's eighth grade year, the high school coach made the unprecedented move of bringing David up to dress as a reserve on the varsity team. David quickly picked up the defensive schemes better than the older players, and his size and strength combined with his natural instincts for the game soon earned him a starting role as middle linebacker for the varsity team.

While his premature success on the football field served to make him almost universally popular in both middle school and high school, it also made him somewhat of a man without a country.

David's friends were essentially the same ones he had had throughout elementary and middle school. Most of them played football and other sports also. Of course none of them enjoyed David's early success, nor did they ever catch up. When David was called up to the big show, his early ascension was met with understandable consternation among his old buddies. While they remained his friends, there was a wrinkle in their relationship that had never been there before. It was somewhat like an undiscovered fault in the earth's crust, lying hidden and unknown, yet weakening the surface just the same.

Nor did David find new friends in his high school teammates. They did respect him and treat him essentially as an equal on the football field. They were also civil and cordial to him off the field, but they certainly were not interested in being an everyday friend to David.

David soon found that he didn't really have friends in whom he could confide, mainly because there was no one who could really empathize with a football star/genius/mayor's kid. Socially, he still hung around with the friends he had in middle school, but the rift was always there.

This point was driven home to David one weekend in the spring of his Junior year in high school, when he was attending Bobby Harper's wedding. Bobby, who had graduated four years prior but had never left town or stopped hanging out at high school parties, had knocked up Deana DeBusse, a sophomore, in the cab of his pickup after a keg party at the lake. Fred DeBusse, Deana's dad, ran the Red Rock Shooting and Archery Range, so Bobby was "doing the right thing" and saving his own ass at the same time.

As David watched Bobby's best man hand over the $200 speck of a diamond on a microscopic, gold-plated band, David began to muse about who his best man would be should he ever have the misfortune of finding himself in Bobby's shoes. There was no clear choice, but he could narrow it down to one of four of his close friends. This fact led to a more sobering realization; that none of the four would choose him. His friend Brett would choose John and vice versa, and his friend Bob would choose Chuck and vice versa. For the first time, David realized what a fifth wheel he really was in his pentagon of friends.

And so it was that David progressed through high school without really forming any anchoring attachments to anyone. Each year he become more dominant in football, winning all-state honors beginning his sophomore year. Likewise, he was not just on a different page than his classmates academically, he was in a whole different library. Despite his success in both areas, David, for all intents and purposes, was a loner, hiding in plain sight disguised as a small-town football hero.

Lacking any real binding ties to Red Rock other than his family, it was very easy for David to consider going to college far away, where he didn't know anyone. He had both athletic and academic avenues open to him, and he investigated both. By the end of his junior year, he had decided that he would like to play football in college, but that he would go to a school with fine academics as well in case football didn't work out. He was smart enough to know that being All-State in South Dakota didn't exactly mean you were NFL material. He was 6'2" and about 220 pounds, which was nothing to make the scouts drool, especially since he wasn't particularly fleet of foot.

The schools that met his criteria were Stanford, UCLA, University of Washington and Notre Dame. While Stanford was certainly the weakest in football, it was by far the strongest academically, and the football program was recognized enough to get NFL attention if he deserved it. With that in mind, Stanford was his first choice.

As it turned out, football would not even be a consideration for David going forward. The week after he took his SAT tests, in the final football game of his senior season, David suffered a devastating knee injury when one of his own teammates fell onto his planted leg. He had surgery a few weeks later, which doctors pronounced a limited success. That is, David's knee would function properly and serve him well in normal life, but the loss of cartilage and damage to ligaments would likely prevent him from continuing with competitive football.

Coincidentally, his SAT scores came back the same day he returned home from knee surgery. His disappointment over his loss of his future as a football player was at least partially mollified by his score of 1520, which would combine with his grades and multiple activities to allow him to gain acceptance to each college to which he applied, Stanford University first among them, of course.

7

In September of 1989, David left Bill and Mary with an empty house, left behind his friends, left behind the town in which every resident knew his name, left behind his small pond, and moved 1400 miles west to the San Francisco Bay area and Stanford University.

For his first two years at Stanford, David relished his newfound anonymity. He found it incredibly relaxing to be able to come and go without thinking in the back of his mind that whatever he did would get back to his parents as quickly as if they had lived in a Little House on the Prairie and had to make all of their calls through a nosy switchboard operator.

Most of David's early friends resided in his Freshman dorm, and they quickly became better friends than he had ever really had in high school. Most notably, David became very close with his Freshman roommate, Bartholomew Saint John.

Mr. Saint John was going by Bart when David met him. He was quite the opposite of David socially when sober. Bart was outgoing almost to the point of obnoxiousness, but most people found him charming and forgave his raucous, bawdy humor. David liked him immediately. Bart liked David too, and he also saw what he had in this shy kid from South Dakota…he had a pet project.

Bart was from New York City, although he had been born in London. He moved to New York when he was 5 years old with his mom and dad. His dad worked for a big Madison Avenue advertising agency. His specialty was marketing American products to the British. He was the best, and he was paid handsomely for his talents.

Bart grew up in a two-story apartment on 68th and Park. He went to an expensive private school which required ties of the boys and required that girls not apply. Due to frequent travel and incredibly long hours by his father and addictions to shopping and prescription pain killers by his mother, Bart was quite self-sufficient. He had a fake I.D., and he knew how to carry himself in order to pass it off.

David had no idea how, but within 30 minutes of his arrival to Stanford Bart knew of three fraternities throwing keggers. Bart made it very clear that David would accompany him to each that evening.

The two boys, along with several other boys and girls from neighboring rooms, went out that night and staggered from one party to another, imbibing more alcohol than most of them ever had before. For some, it was the first time they had partaken of this Nectar of the University Gods. At least half decorated the bathroom stalls, the sinks in their rooms, or various trash receptacles and bushes with large quantities of vomit.

David found the liberation of drunkenness exhilarating. He and Bart walked with arms over shoulders back from the third party, stopping once when Bart saw a Mercedes parked in the student parking lot of a dorm down the street from their own. "No college kid should be driving a goddam Mercedes," Bart said as he unzipped his fly and pissed a long stream of pale urine all over the driver's door. Laughing and following his new friend's lead, David similarly christened the hood, radiator, and the shiny hood ornament…not something he could do in a million years back in Red Rock.

When they got back to their room, David had an epiphany. "Hey, man. Do you like Aerosmith?"

"I'm more into the Pixies. You ever heard "Monkey Gone to Heaven?" replied Bart.

"The what? Man, we just listen to hard rock and metal in South Dakota. Except a little country, but that's just the ranch kids."

"The Pixies. Here, I'll play it for you."

Bart walked over to his Aiwa sound system and loaded up a CD. In a moment, Black Francis and Kim Deal took over the airwaves in their small dorm room.

"What the fuck is this? Turn that shit off. I need you to hear something," said David, grimacing at the screaming fat man's voice coming from Bart's speakers.

Laughing, Bart pushed a button and cut the Pixies off in mid-sentence. "It'll grow on you, trust me," Bart said. And it turned out he was right, oddly enough.

David was standing at his boombox, fast-forwarding a cassette tape he had pulled from a red and black case that sported a yellow Aerosmith logo. After a few tries, he got to the song he was looking for.

"David, you're going to have to invest in a CD player if you're going to want me to listen to your redneck music," said Bart.

"Don't call me a redneck. Now listen."

In spite of all he had seen in his teenage years in New York City, Bart found himself grow uneasy at David's tone of voice and the look on his face when he expressed his displeasure in Bart's use of the colorful euphemism. David's face and voice said, "Look, I like you, but if you call me that again I'll beat your Yankee ass until everything but your neck is red."

As Stephen Tyler began to deliver his gutteral performance of "John, Saint John," Bart felt the unease pass away, and he chalked it up to the alcohol. His new roommate was standing in front of him smiling like an innocent child. He must have imagined the murderous gleam in his eye.

"Bart sounds like an old-West villain or a quarterback for the Packers. I'm gonna call you John Saint John like the song. That OK with you?" asked David.

It was OK. In fact, Bart hated the name Bart only slightly less than Bartholomew, and both only slightly less than having a name that started with Saint. Going by John Saint John only addressed his hatred for his first name, but it was a start.

The name stuck, and so did the friendship. John and David were inseparable. They were both engineers, so they took most of the same classes for the first year and for the first part of the second. David was a good deal better student than John, and he helped him immensely. In the second quarter of their Sophomore year, David began taking course requirements for Electrical, Mechanical and Chemical Engineering, not having decided which would be his eventual major. John quit engineering and started taking Political Science classes. He had given up on his dream of being any different from his dad, and figured that either Law School or advertising would be his future.

And so, along with a small group of good friends, David and John progressed happily through the first two years of college. Large quantities of alcohol were consumed by all, and, unfortunately for David's lungs, so were large quantities of cigarettes. John offered David his first cigarette just after David had given him his new name. At first, David only smoked when he drank. By Christmas break his Freshman year, his casual habit had grown to a full-scale addiction. David and John were often seen sitting in their side-by-side bedroom windows, smoking like chimneys while they took a study break. David told himself that he could quit at any time, but that was no more true for him than any other smoker. It would be a few years before he could quit, and he never would have been able to do so if he had to do it alone. It's hard for an introvert to break the momentum of an addiction without help from outside. Since his few real friends were in the same nicotine-flavored boat as he was, it would take a force of nature to get him to quit. As it turned out, he met that force of nature about two years later, and she had been as interested in his story as he was in hers.

8

David had finished his story, and their first date on the student union patio should have ended there. But it didn't. Something held them there, lost in each other, Karen's brown eyes never leaving David's blue eyes. They each skipped their afternoon classes and walked together to the oval, where they sat in the grass and talked as they watched the pick-up volleyball games and dodged Frisbees. Neither had ever felt more comfortable and content than they did that day, and they didn't want it to ever end.

David and Karen spent the rest of winter quarter falling in love. To be more accurate, they spent the rest of the week falling in love, and the rest of the quarter falling ever more deeply in love. They spent most of their time together, including spending most nights together, usually in David's room.

John, David's ever-faithful roommate, basically took all of this in stride. John had a girlfriend of his own, and the four of them got together quite often. David didn't spend time with Karen because it was required of him, as is the case in many relationships. He was with her almost all of the time because he wanted to be. Karen was not at all possessive, but it turned out that his friends liked her so well that she usually ended up coming along whenever he went out with them.

The only thing Karen did that gave John any ammunition in the argument over who was more pussy-whipped was that she encouraged…no, required…David to quit smoking. David had tried a couple of times and had failed miserably. Once Karen made it known that she wasn't a fan of cigarettes or of kissing men who used them, David quit cold turkey, and really didn't ever have another craving.

Such was the totality of the transformation in David's life once Karen was in it. David came to a realization not long after they were together that his obsessive nature, the nature that was in charge when he was figuring out how to meet Karen, was really close to an addiction in and of itself. With

Karen around, he was able to relax, and the obsessions and addictions melted away.

It was nearly impossible for them to split up for the summer between their junior and senior years, but each had to return to their respective homes for the summer. Their reunion in the fall was sweet, and they vowed that they would never be apart again.

David and John got an off-campus apartment for their final year, and Karen, who nominally had a dorm room on campus, essentially lived with David, John, and John's girlfriend, Caroline. Their senior year was even better than their junior year, and each knew that they had met "The One." As graduation neared, John determined he would be moving back to New York, and David and Karen planned to remain in their apartment as they started their post-college lives together. While the future was normally frightening for college grads, David and Karen were thrilled at the prospect of beginning this journey together. They were young, in love, and perfectly content with their lives.

And they might have stayed that way forever, had it not been for a wrong turn, and a man named LaShon Jackson.

9

"Hello?"

"David, it's dad."

"Hey dad, where are you?"

"We're in Reno. We ended up having breakfast with Bob and Judy, so we didn't get out of Salt Lake until about 10."

"Are you still coming tonight?"

"No, we figured we'd stay here and get an early start in the morning. We're going to try to leave at about six, but you know your mom."

"I know…it's about four hours so I'll expect you around noon."

"I hope sooner, but you're right…she'll probably cost us a couple hours."

"You guys gonna gamble tonight?"

"I'll probably hit the tables a little, and I'm sure your mom will drop about two bucks on the nickel slots before she starts to feel guilty and comes to stand over my shoulder."

Bill and David McGuire shared a laugh at Mary's expense before David asked, "Is she there?"

"She's in the bathroom. Don't tell her what I said."

"Don't worry. You got the directions to my place?"

"Yep. Just stick around until we get there in case we need to call you."

"OK, but be careful if you have to stop. You can get turned around pretty easy and end up on the other side of 101. That's East Palo Alto. If you find yourself crossing the freeway, don't stop or get out. Just get out of there. Get back on the freeway if you have to and go up a few exits and turn around in Redwood City and come back and try again."

"Don't worry, we'll find you," Bill chuckled.

"Dad, I'm serious! It's not safe over there, especially for Ma and Pa Kettle."

"Hey, watch it! Your mom and I are much more cosmopolitan than you give us credit for."

"Whatever dad, just be careful, OK?"

"OK buddy, thanks for the advice."

Bill McGuire paused for a moment, and then added another thought, "You know, you've grown up awfully fast. It seems like just yesterday you were a little squirt in the back seat…"

"I thought I was conceived in the trailer," David interrupted.

"Allright smartass, watch your mouth. If your mom heard you say that she'd have a stroke."

"I know…sorry."

"Anyway, now you're giving me advice. I was going to say how proud I was of you until that comment."

The McGuire men shared another short laugh, then Bill continued, "Just kidding. You know how proud I am of you, don't you son?"

"Sure, dad. Now cut it out before you make me cry."

"Got it. Your mom's out now. You wanna say 'hi'?"

"Sure. See you tomorrow, dad."

"OK. I love you, buddy."

"Love you too dad."

There was a pause as Bill handed the phone over to Mary. A moment later, his mom's voice blasted into his ear, giddy with excitement.

"David?"

"Jesus mom, I'm right here."

"Sorry. Is Karen there?"

"Yep, she's right here," David replied. Coincidentally, Karen had just walked into the kitchen and put her arms around his waist, looking up at him slyly. David switched the phone to his left hand and put his right arm back and around her shoulders. She was wearing a cream-colored terry cloth robe. For some reason, she felt too tall, but he'd investigate that when he finished what would surely be an emotional roller-coaster with his mom.

"I'm so excited to finally meet her!" his mom exclaimed, back to the too-loud-for-the-phone voice.

"I'm excited for you to meet her too. Go easy on the gambling tonight, OK mom?"

"Oh, we aren't going to gamble. We'll just get some dinner and go to bed."

"OK mom, whatever you say."

"Oh David, you're such a character. I can't believe you're already graduating from college. With honors, too! We're so proud of you!"

"I know mom, dad told me."

"I doubt if he told you with the right amount of enthusiasm, though!"

"Well, that's probably true. Thanks, mom."

"You're welcome. We'll see you tomorrow. We love you so much, David!" David's mom sounded close to tears.

"You OK mom?"

"Yes, I'm just so happy! I just can't wait to see you and Karen," she said, clearly beginning to break down.

"OK mom. I'll see you tomorrow. I love you."

"We love you too," she said, trailing off at the end of each word, trying to hold back the dam that was about to burst.

"Bye Mom," David said and hung up quickly.

"They're not coming?" asked Karen.

"Nope. They stopped in Reno. They'll be here around noon tomorrow," David replied.

He looked down at Karen and took in her radiance. Her eyes sparkled back into his, giving him a view into her soul and mirroring his own. He couldn't imagine his life being any better. He was graduating from Stanford in two days with a double engineering major (and with honors in both, no less). Then he was taking Karen to Cabo San Lucas for two weeks to blow off some steam before he started his new job at BioMech in South San

Francisco. His starting salary of $55,000 was the highest of any Bachelor's degree engineer in his class.

You'd better enjoy this moment, he thought as he pulled Karen close, *because it won't last forever.*

"Where's John and Caroline?" asked Karen.

David sensed both playfulness and seduction dancing around the edges of Karen's question. Some of the blood checked out of the penthouse and headed south. "They went out. They won't be back for awhile."

"Good," Karen whispered, as she pulled back from him a few steps.

As it turned out, life could get better. David watched as Karen dropped her terry-cloth robe to reveal a lacy red bra and panties combination. On her feet were strappy, red pumps with at least three-inch heels. Karen let him drink her in for a few moments, and then she turned and walked toward the bedroom, trailing her robe behind her. David's eyes ran from the spike heels up the thin line of her lower leg, over the tightly defined bulge of her calf muscles, past her firm, tan upper legs to her perfect ass. Her red lace panties were so thin that they were almost non-existent. He watched her ass as it moved steadily from side to side. There was no jiggle at all, just a slight shimmer from bottom to top when each of her feet hit the floor.

He watched her walk all the way to the bedroom, and then he turned over the reins to his fully erect penis to drive for the rest of the night.

David's life got better three times that night. The last time was slightly before midnight. Lying in bed, gazing at the ceiling, his left arm around the naked body of his lover, David paused again to think that his life surely would never be any better than this.

This time, unfortunately, he was right.

10

Bill and Mary McGuire pulled out of the parking lot of the El Dorado Hotel and Casino at 6:53 a.m., although the clock on the dashboard of Bill's tan Dodge Caravan still showed Mountain Time of 7:53.

11

At 6:55 a.m., almost 200 miles to the south and west, LaShon Jackson pushed open his bedroom window, hoisted himself up, and pulled his 155 pound frame through onto a small desk that was positioned under the window. He edged across the desk, not wanting to wake his mother in the next room. Carefully, carefully, he turned around and eased his window closed. He had drunk at least 320 ounces of malt liquor in the last eight hours, not to mention at least a dozen hits off the joints that were being passed around at the party he had left 20 minutes earlier. Thanks to lots of practice, however, LaShon was able to creep across his room, avoiding the filthy clothing, alcohol and food containers strewn across the floor, and into his spongy twin-sized bed. He pulled a grimy bedsheet over his head, and dropped quickly off to sleep.

12

Bill and Mary McGuire were making excellent time. They had stopped for gas and food in Reno, so they were not planning to stop until they reached David's rented house, which was just off of University Avenue in Palo Alto. They paid their toll on the Bay Bridge at 10:14 a.m., and rolled across the mighty structure toward San Francisco.

Bill had driven David to school this way, but this was Mary's first time to the West Coast.

"Wait until you see this view of San Francisco, honey," he said as they drove through the tunnel at Treasure Island.

Mary wasn't disappointed. "Oh my god, Bill, it's beautiful. It's the biggest thing I've ever seen."

"I know. Sometimes I forget how much there is in the world that we haven't seen. I've spent so much of my time working I've never taken you on a nice vacation. We've never even been back to Ireland," Bill said.

"'There are greater things on heaven and earth than are dreamt of in your philosophy,'" Mary replied.

"What?"

"Shakespeare."

"Oh," Bill thought for a moment. "Hey that's pretty good."

"I know. Maybe you should start reading a little bit more, darlin'."

"Funny. I'm serious, though, Mary."

"Well then, maybe we should take some time and go to Europe. Now that David's out of school and on his own, we can maybe relax a little bit and try to enjoy life," Mary said.

"You know what, you're right. Let's go to Europe this summer. Ireland and Italy for sure. Maybe Spain and England too. Anywhere but France."

"You don't want to see Paris?" Mary asked.

"If I want to be insulted by a waiter, I'll go to the Red Rock Tap and ask Ed for a Lite Beer. That's as close to French hospitality as I need to get."

"Agreed. So are we serious?"

"I think we are. Let's see if we can do it this summer."

"Sounds good to me. I love you honey."

Bill glanced over at his wife, seeing that she had that misty look in her eyes. "I love you too," he replied, smiling.

Mary gazed at her husband, her lifelong friend, for a few more moments, and then she looked back over her shoulder at San Francisco skyline. In another minute, they crested the hill that leads south to the peninsula. A few seconds later, the city was hidden from view by the hillside.

"It goes by fast, doesn't it?" she said.

"I know. It looks so big when you first see it, but it really only takes a few minutes for it to go right by," Bill replied.

"I was actually talking about life, honey."

"Oh, well, that too, I guess," he said wryly.

Bill put his right hand on Mary's left knee. Mary dropped her left hand down and took his. Hand in hand, they motored south along the 101 Freeway to see their son.

13

At 10:21 a.m., Dolores Hayes unceremoniously opened the door to her son's room. "LaShon," she said, "LaShon, you get up now. You got to be to work at 'leven."

Dolores crossed the mine-field that was her son's bedroom floor. As she approached the heaving lump in her son's bed, the smell of alcohol and marijuana became unmistakable.

"BOY, DID YOU SNEAK OUT AGAIN LAST NIGHT!? YOU TWENTY-SIX YEARS OLD! YOU TOO OLD TO BE FUCKIN' AROUND WITH THAT CROWD."

The mass on the bed stirred for a moment, and then was still.

Fuming, Dolores grabbed the filthy sheets that covered her good-for-nothing son (who took after his good-for-nothing father, who she hadn't seen since LaShon was two years old) and tore them away. The smell of pot and malt liquor was fanned up into her face by the sheets. It burned her nose, but, moreover, it stoked the fire in her eyes.

Dolores reached across LaShon and grabbed an empty King Cobra can that was lying on his bed next to him. With malice intended more for his father than him, she raised it in the air and brought it down on top of his head with a crunch. Before he could cover up, she pistoned the black and gold can again, smacking him on the head.

Out of instinct more than anything else, LaShon curled into a fetal position, covering his face and head with his arms. Dolores brought the can down at least a half a dozen more times on his shoulders and hands, finally giving up and hurling the crumpled can against the opposite wall.

"I had to beg Mr. Grimes to keep you on the last time you wuz late! You late agin and he gonna drop you, you ungrateful little shit!"

LaShon peaked one eye out from behind his hand. "Ma, I hate that motherfuckin' job," he stammered, barely intelligible.

"BOY, DON'T YOU USE THAT FUCKIN' LANGUAGE WITH ME, YOU UNGRATEFUL LITTLE MOTHERFUCKER. IF YOU LOSE THIS JOB, I'M KICKIN' YOUR NO GOOD ASS OUT OF HERE FOR THE LAST TIME."

With that, she whirled her ample frame about and trudged out of his room, lifting her knees up like she was walking with snowshoes. When she reached the door, she said in an even, almost conversational tone, "I'm not going to tell you again, LaShon. You've got a half an hour to get down there. If you're late, I'm gonna tell Mr. Grimes to fire you. If he does that, you're on your own."

She closed the door firmly behind her.

It was probably the quiet tone that got LaShon moving. She yelled about 96% of the time, so he wasn't worried when she was yelling. It was when she was calm that he knew she meant business. As long as she was yelling, he felt, it meant she still loved him. When she stopped yelling, it was like she had given up on him. He had been able to test this theory the previous three times she had kicked him out. This time, she said it was for the last time. He was pretty sure she'd take him back, but he figured he'd better not tempt fate.

LaShon rolled off of his bed, one foot landing on an empty Old English bottle. It rolled out from under his foot and he crashed down on the floor. Shit, this wasn't going to work. He was still way too fucked up to work, or to drive for that matter. He needed a little pick-me-up to get going.

He rolled onto his hands and knees and fished under his bed. He pulled out an old Nike shoebox (nothing but the best when it comes to footwear) and removed some random newspaper clippings (Raiders football articles mostly, but he had never read any of them). With the camouflage removed, LaShon gazed down into his own private apothecary. There were pipes, papers, hypodermic needles, a rubber strap, three lighters, two bent spoons, and various other paraphernalia, not to mention baggies and balloons filled with various types and grades of illicit drugs.

LaShon lifted the box onto his bed. He remained on his knees and reached into the box, choosing his poison for the day. He lifted his choice up in front of his face, both elbows resting on the bed. From behind, it would appear that his bed was an altar, and that LaShon was preparing to pray. This, of course, was exactly what was happening.

14

At 10:54 a.m., Bill McGuire flipped up his right turn signal and eased off the 101 at the University Avenue exit. The exit was a little different than he had pictured it.

"Isn't this exciting, Bill?" Mary squealed.

"Sure, honey."

"I really can't wait to meet Karen. David has been so happy since she came along. She's such a sweet girl."

"Uh-huh."

"Is everything OK?" Mary asked.

"I think I made a wrong turn. We're going back across the freeway. David said that wasn't right."

"Do you have the directions?" Mary asked.

"I left them in my bag. I thought I'd remember. They seemed pretty simple."

"I can reach back and get them," Mary offered.

"We're coming up to a red light," Bill said, "You can get them when we stop, if you don't mind. My bag is kind of jammed down behind my seat."

"OK honey."

Bill coasted to a stop at the red light. He was the first car. With a glance around, he noticed two things. One was that he was at the corner of University and Grand Avenues. Second was that David was correct in his admonishment; this was not where he and his wife wanted to be in their tan minivan, middle of the morning or not. He decided the best thing would be to keep his eyes straight ahead. Looking from side to side could draw attention he didn't want. He glanced down at the dashboard clock, seeing that it read 11:58, he decided now was a good time to change it to Pacific time. As long as his eyes were inside the car, he felt things would be OK.

Mary unbuckled her seatbelt and got on her knees to reach behind Bill's seat. She wrestled with his bag for a moment. Realizing it was jammed in too tight, she unzipped the top and began to dig around for the yellow scrap of paper on which Bill had scribbled the directions to David's house.

15

LaShon was in his car, a 1972 green Cadillac Eldorado that had definitely seen its better days. He was jamming down Grand toward Mr. Grimes' shitty little liquor store at about 60 miles an hour. It was 10:59. Shit, he had one minute and he'd be late. If he missed the light at University, he was fucked.

When he was a block from the light, it turned yellow. When he was a half a block away, it turned red.

Fuck it, he thought, and stepped down on the accelerator.

16

Bill was still changing the dashboard clock when the light changed to green. About one millisecond after it changed, the cars behind him began to blast their horns. Instinctively, his foot slipped from the brake onto the gas pedal. Bill's adrenaline was already pumping from David's stern warning and the appearance of the area outside of his car. The sudden fury of the horns behind him gave him another shot. When his foot hit the gas pedal, it stepped down hard. The McGuire's Caravan shot out into the intersection, throwing Mary off balance in the back seat. Startled, she looked out the drivers' side window.

"BILL, LOOK OUT!" she screamed.

17

LaShon had it up to 70 by the time he hit the intersection. If he didn't have at least three controlled substances racing around his bloodstream, he might have been able to avoid the tan minivan that flashed into the narrow tunnel that was his field of perception. As it stood, his body was able to do nothing to avoid plowing into them. His foot didn't even leave the accelerator.

"What the fuck is a minivan doing in EPA?" he had time to think before his head smashed into the windshield of his old Cadillac.

18

As promised, Bill had kept his eyes straight ahead when he took off from the intersection. He didn't even see the evil-looking grill of the Cadillac bearing down on him until his wife screamed. He turned his head to the left and saw the old boat. It was close enough to see the vacant look in its driver's bloodshot eyes.

"I think we're going to miss David's graduation," he thought, just before his body was obliterated by a ton and a half of speeding steel.

19

David's pain was nearly unbearable. His Grandma McGuire had passed away two years ago, and his mother had drifted almost completely apart from her parents and sister, so his parents were his only real family. His mom's parents came to the funeral and sat next to him in the front row, but his parents' friends were more familiar to him and provided much greater comfort. In fact, he resented the role his grandparents took in grieving so openly for a daughter they had only seen a few times a year since David was born. As soon as the funeral was over, David turned his back on them and never spoke to them again.

Had it not been for Karen and John, David would have been lost. John had completely taken care of the grisly task of getting David's parents back to South Dakota for burial. Karen had taken on the much more difficult task of keeping David from completely falling apart with grief. She was there when the police knocked on the apartment door, and she never left his side even for a moment. She flew back to South Dakota with him, and she held his hand as he walked into his parents' empty house. She held him as he sobbed in the kitchen, remembering his mom cutting the crusts off of his PB&Js, she caressed him as he stood in the back yard, picturing his dad tossing him the football. She was there for him to lean on at the funeral, and she provided the grace and dignity that the situation required as nearly everyone in town filed past him afterward to profess their sincere condolences for his loss.

In the days after the funeral, David's grief began to break, but not in favor of acceptance. David began to get angry…very angry.

Karen had risked a quick shower the second day after the funeral, and when she turned off the water, she heard glass breaking in the kitchen. She wrapped a towel around herself and ran down the hall toward the cacophony. She rounded the corner into the kitchen, and stopped short just in time to avoid being hit in the head by a flying plate. Her wet feet slipped out from under her and she fell sprawling on the hardwood floor.

David didn't stop, but he did adjust his angle and began throwing plates against the opposite wall. Karen lay quiet for a moment, realizing she was lying in a minefield of broken glass and china. She didn't move, but instead raised her voice above the crashes.

"DAVID, STOP IT RIGHT NOW!"

For a wonder, he did. He looked at her, and what she saw was not her boyfriend. His eyes were shot with blood and were glowing with flat murder. For the first time since she had met him, she was afraid, but she instinctively knew she couldn't back down.

"WHAT ARE YOU DOING?!" she yelled at him.

He didn't answer right away, but his eyes softened just slightly and he stepped through the glass and scooped her up off the floor. He held her steady in one arm and brushed his other over the counter, clearing it of debris. He set her down and scanned her back and legs for cuts, seeming to gather himself as he did so.

"David..." she began, but he cut her off.

"Karen, I want to kill him. I think I have to kill him. How can I let him get away with this...with killing my..."

David couldn't finish his sentence. He had a catch in his throat that he couldn't get past.

Karen wanted to hold him, wanted to tell him it was OK, but something told her this was something she had to nip in the bud. The look in his eyes was not something she wanted to allow to ever return.

"David," she said firmly, "I will not allow you to talk that way. He's going to go to jail for a long time for what he did, maybe forever. If you go after him and end up in jail yourself, what good will that do? Would your parents want that for you? No...it would kill them all over again to know their death lead to the end of your life."

"How do you know he'll go to jail, Karen? Criminals get off all the time with a slap on the wrist. He's probably going to get some bleeding-heart lawyer who will get him off on some sort of technicality, or some kind of argument like he had a bad childhood or something. If that happens, and if he goes free after a few years, I...I don't think I could live with myself if I didn't get revenge for my parents. What happened to "an eye for an eye?" How can he take two lives and not lose his own?"

"This isn't the Old West, David! You're not some cowboy out for vengeance. This society does not allow for vigilantism, and you'll get caught and go to jail and that will be the end of our lives together. Is that what you want? Do you not even care about me any more?"

"Of course I care about you, Karen. But...he killed my parents. How can I just live with that, or let him live with that?"

"David, you're just going to have to live with it. And I'll be here for you every minute to help you move on, but only if you promise to let it go."

David was silent, and couldn't meet Karen's eyes.

Karen grabbed his face roughly and pulled it toward hers so he would meet her eyes. He resisted, but then let go and met her unwavering gaze. He was steady for a moment, and then he broke.

Great racking sobs erupted from deep within David. The loss poured out of him, and he buried his eyes in her neck and she held him tightly until he began to gain control.

"I promise, Karen. I will learn to live with it, but you can't leave. You're all I've got now."

"I know, David. I won't leave, as long as you keep your promise"

He pulled away and looked in her eyes again. A fresh wave of tears erupted from him, like poison being ejected from his body. She held him longer, and eventually he was able to bring himself under control.

20

That was the last time David cried. The dam had broken, and afterward he seemed better able to move on. Karen's relief was immeasurable, and oddly enough, the next few weeks they spent in Red Rock closing out his parents' affairs were actually somewhat enjoyable. David had his melancholy moments, but he got better each day, and they spent a good amount of time going fondly though his parents' possessions and driving around Red Rock to show Karen his old stomping grounds. David's healing was off to a good start, now, and as it turned out, there was so much to take care of that his mind barely had time to wander back to his parents or their murderer.

One of David's first visitors after the funeral was his father's New York Life agent, Steve Cochran. After that meeting, David learned at least that money was not going to be a problem for him and Karen when they got back to California.

It seemed that several years ago, in order to help Steve out of a tough spell, Bill McGuire had purchased a $1 million policy on himself and $500,000 on Mary. This was about triple what was necessary by convention, but Steve was in danger of having to leave town to look for work elsewhere if he didn't pick up the pace. Of course Bill never expected the policies to be used so soon, or both at the same time.

David, therefore, put the Bekins charges on his credit card in anticipation of the insurance payment. And, being raised on practical Midwestern values, he intended to purchase a house immediately upon returning to California.

David and Karen went through everything in the house, deciding whether to keep, sell or donate each item they encountered. The donate pile was by far the largest. David intended to give all the clothes as well as many of the other everyday items in the house to various local charities. The Catholic Daughters, Knights of Columbus, Rotarians, Shriners, Lions, Elks, and

Lakota Friends League were each asked what types of items they could use. In the end, the Catholic Daughters and the Lakota Friends walked away with the majority of the loot.

The largest items...furniture and appliances mostly...were to be sold along with the house and the store (and all of its assets and inventory) at a public auction on the Saturday following the funeral. David made himself scarce when the auction actually took place. He didn't really want to be a witness as his parents' lives work was sold to the highest bidder.

As it turned out, the house and furniture went to a couple from Rapid City who intended to retire in Red Rock. Since they didn't know the McGuires, they didn't feel as ghoulish living in their house, and were therefore willing to go up to $180,000 for the place. This was only about $20,000 below market value, and Bill's lawyer told David he should be very happy with that. The business, with all of its assets, liabilities and inventory, was purchased by a group of businessmen from Red Rock for $650,000. They were up against Ace Hardware, who wished to purchase it and turn it into a franchise. They went a little higher than they had originally planned to keep Bill McGuire's business local. It was a symbol for them of the town's heart, spirit and pride, and they would be damned if it was going to go to some big corporation.

Although the sale price was legally binding, David asked his dad's lawyer to figure out a way for him to give back $150,000 to the group to keep them closer to their budget. It took some doing, lots of paperwork and some convenient oversights by the county recorder (not to mention around $5,000 in legal fees), but in the end David ended up buying in to the group for $151,000 and then selling his share for $1,000 back to them. The group and the town never forgot David's generosity, and he was enthusiastically invited to return home whenever he could, although he never took them up on the offer.

When all was said and done, after all taxes, fees and disbursements, David cleared just under two million dollars through the death of his parents.

And, of all the lawyers who set out to do good but ended up representing big evil corporations against people who had gotten cancer from their products, of all the landowners who had gotten rich by evicting low-income families to develop high-end condos, of all the politicians who had started out with high ideals but realized that the only way to advance was to take bribes from special interests, of all the people in the world who felt guilty for the money they had, none of them could hold a candle the guilt David felt over becoming a multi-millionaire at the expense of his parents' lives.

David rolled his guilt up with his anger and thirst for vengeance, and packed it down deep inside where it was hidden even from him. This was the cost of keeping Karen, and it was a cost he would gladly pay. And as they flew back to California, he felt the anger and guilt and pain receding. He felt Karen's cool hand in his, he smelled her sweet perfume, looked in her lovely face, and he began to feel at ease. The more miles he put between himself and his parents graves, the more he felt rejuvenated...almost back to normal. He knew there would be an ebb and flow of feelings in the coming months, especially during LaShon Jackson's trial, but he really felt he could get through it. As long as Karen was by his side, he really felt he could get through anything, no matter what punishment the law deemed fit for his parents' murderer.

Little did he know, that theory was about to be put to the test.

21

David's new employer, BioMech, had been very understanding about the time he needed to take care of his parents' final arrangements. They also knew about the upcoming trial, and had told him that he could take whatever time he needed for that. They had recruited David very heavily (as had several other companies) and they seemed to genuinely care about him and their other employees.

"We want you as part of our family, David," said his boss, Mr. Greer, "and we want you to do whatever you need to do to get these matters settled. We want you here for the long haul. We've got high hopes for you. If we need to be patient for you to get started, then we're OK with that."

As it turned out, David wasn't going to need any time off for the trial.

John Kleinfeldt, the Assistant District Attorney assigned to prosecute LaShon Jackson, had asked David to call him when he returned to town. David did as he was asked and called the morning after he and Karen arrived back in the Bay Area.

"David, thanks for calling. How are you doing?" John Kleinfeldt asked after David identified himself.

"OK, I guess," David answered.

"Good. Now, I don't know if you know this, but Mr. Jackson is still in a coma.

"No, I just got back to town last night and you're the first person I've talked to. What does that mean?"

"Well, legally, we can't try him if he can't participate in his own defense. So, until he comes out of the coma, everything's on hold."

"What?" David asked incredulously. If he weren't so close to the case, this would probably have made sense. As it was, David felt he should be tried and sent to prison for life, conscious or not.

"That's the law, David. I'm sorry, I know it doesn't seem fair. As soon as he wakes from the coma, if he wakes from the coma, that is, I'll call you and let you know what comes next."

"What if he doesn't come out of it?"

"Then there won't be a trial."

David was silent. He had been geared up to deal with this trial, get it over with and move on with his life. His mind scrambled to come up with a rational thought, but none came.

"David, I'm sure this isn't what you were expecting. In my line of work, I see this kind of thing all the time. You're looking for closure, and it's just not going to come right away. My best advice is to go to work, live your life, and do your best not to think about this. I know you want justice, and it will come one way or the other. If he dies or stays in the coma, that's a pretty steep penalty for his crime. If he wakes up, we'll go to trial and I'll do everything I can to make sure he does hard time. Either way, he'll pay for what he did. Until then, though, you should try to put it out of your mind."

"That's easier said than done," David managed.

"I know, David. You call me any time you want to talk about this. Otherwise, I'll call you as soon as there is any news."

"Where is he, by the way," David asked.

"Stanford Med Center."

"Jesus," David breathed, "My last tuition check is probably keeping him alive."

"I don't think they're linked..." John began.

"I know, bad joke."

"Oh, OK. Well, I'll call you when I have news."

"OK. Thanks, Mr. Kleinfeldt."

"David please, call me John."

"OK. Goodbye."

"Goodbye, David."

David hung up and related the conversation to Karen.

"He's right, you know," she said, "You should try not to think about it."

"Are you serious?" he asked.

"Well, what else can you do?"

"Nothing, I guess. I just feel so…impotent. I was all ready for a trial…now I may never get one."

"Well, if he dies, that's kind of the ultimate punishment. If that happens, are you going to be OK?"

"Only if I kill him myself," David said coldly.

"DAVID! You promised!"

"I know, I was just kidding," David said, even though he wasn't. The conversation with Kleinfeldt had stirred up the feelings he had spent the last two weeks trying to quell.

He looked at Karen. She clearly found no humor in his comment. The look on her face made it clear that he would need to keep his desire for revenge buried and well out of sight…especially out of Karen's sight.

"Karen, come on, I know I promised. I'll promise again. I'm not going to do anything like that. I'll just try to forget about it until he either dies or wakes up. Either way, I'll be OK."

"Are you sure?" she asked.

"Don't worry, I'll be fine," he said, with enough sincerity to win the Academy Award.

And he was able to keep up his performance for the next several months. By the time Lashon Jackson woke from his coma almost four months after the accident, David and Karen were settled into their post-college lives.

David paid about three-quarters of a million in cash for a house on the hill in Millbrae, an upscale city on the peninsula about 15 miles south of San Francisco. He knew that financing the house was probably a better idea, but the interest rates were relatively high and his father had always taught him that an 8% return with no risk was about the best investment you could get.

The house was about 15 minutes from BioMech, where David began work the same week he found out that the trial would be delayed. His performance at work was as convincing as with Karen. After his training period, Mr. Greer assigned him to a fairly low-priority project, and gave him limited responsibility. David, however, quickly proved that he was capable of much more. About three weeks in, David was assigned to the most important project in the history of the company, a move which raised both eyebrows and expectations.

BioMech was a privately-owned research company whose major contract was with the U.S. Military. Their charge was to come up with innovative products to aid the United States soldier on the battlefield. The products, specifically, were chemical or mechanical in nature, or sometimes a combination of both. They worked on nutritional supplements, antidotes to chemical and biological weapons, and lighter and more efficient ways to carry and deliver the appropriate doses of each to the soldiers.

They had also come up with many military uses for lightweight plastic and other hybrid materials that had been invented or modified in their own labs. The project David was assigned to was along these lines. It was the biggest and most ambitious project ever accepted by the company, and the military gave them a blank check for development. If they were successful, the company, and the employees involved in the project, would be wealthy beyond any of their dreams.

Meanwhile, Karen was one of thousands of Californians who studied for and was awarded an emergency teaching credential to combat the shortage of qualified teachers in the state. She then quickly landed a position teaching Freshman and Sophomore History at Edison Academy in ultra-wealthy Atherton.

Edison was a private preparatory school that catered to the children of San Francisco and Silicon Valley's wealthiest families. Children arrived daily in limousines from as far north as San Rafael and as far south as Monterrey. There were also boarding facilities available, where students from all over the Bay Area spent weeknights and then went home on the weekends to catch a moment with their busy parents between meetings and tennis lessons.

It was Karen's good fortune that the headmaster of Edison Academy belonged to the same country club as her academic advisor at Stanford. When Karen expressed her desire to teach, it only took one phone call to set her up with a job. So, when most first-year teachers were faced with classrooms packed with 35 students and 20 year-old desks and textbooks, Karen taught classes with fewer than 20 students and all the brand new materials she could wish for.

By October of 1993, David was almost three months into his project with BioMech. He was enjoying the challenge of it, and was working long hours by choice. His team very quickly grew to respect his knowledge of both chemistry and mechanics, as well as what his boss called "the Midwest work ethic."

While David's long hours did keep him away from Karen, they also served to push LaShon Jackson to the back of his mind. So, when the phone rang at their house on the night of October 17, 1993, David picked it up without hesitation or trepidation.

"Hello," David said.

"David? John Kleinfeldt. How are you tonight?"

David set his wine glass down and sat forward on his lounge chair. He and Karen had been enjoying a fairly expensive bottle of Cabernet on their balcony as they looked out over first the multitude of lights that dotted the land below them, and then the huge black comma that was the San Francisco Bay.

"Hey Mr. Kleinfeldt...I mean, John. How are you?"

"I'm OK David. I have news on the Jackson case."

"OK."

"Well, he's out of the coma. In fact, he woke up about a week ago."

"A week? Why didn't you call then?"

"Even though he woke up, his prognosis was still unclear. We had to wait until yesterday to get back the opinions of his doctors and two psychologists."

"Why did you have to wait?"

"Well, David, it's complicated."

There was a long pause…long enough for David to realize he was about to be fucked. His blood began to boil.

"If you remember, I told you he had to be able to participate in his own defense. Along the same lines, he also has to be found by a judge to be mentally fit to stand trial. The consensus among the doctors and psychologists is that Mr. Jackson will never fully recover. In fact, they are saying that the very best hope for him is for him to eventually have the mental capacity of a nine-year-old."

John paused again, waiting for a question or some sort of indication that David was understanding where he was going. None came, so John continued.

"So my boss and colleagues and I had to decide what to do. It's standard on all cases and, anyway, we decided that the odds of a judge ruling that he is both able to participate in his own defense and that he is mentally fit to stand trial is very low. Then we have to get a jury to convict a guy that's basically a child now. Not only that, the trial will be in East Palo Alto, and it's pretty likely that the jury will be...uh...sympathetic toward him. His attorney will have him testify and exploit his injuries and mental state to prove that he's been punished enough and, in fact, that he's not even the same person who committed the crime."

"Murdered my parents, you mean?" David interrupted harshly.

"David, I'm so sorry to have to be the one to tell you this, but we all agreed that this trial is not one we can win. Our duty to the public is to prosecute cases where the investment in time and money is commensurate with the probability of conviction. In this case, considering the fact that he truly has been punished quite severely and the fact that the odds are very low

Vengeance

that any judge or jury would send someone of his mental state to prison, we've decided not to prosecute."

"So he gets away with murder, then?"

"I guess if you want to call having the mental capacity of a nine-year-old getting away with it, then yes. I'm so sorry, David."

David's anger became rage. He could feel control slipping away with every breath. Without another word, David pushed the off button on the cordless phone and set it down on the table next to his wine glass. He stared at a spot just above the railing, his eyes well out of focus, trying to center himself.

"David," Karen asked, "was that Mr. Kleinfeldt?"

"Yeah," David said dismissively.

"What did he say?" she asked.

David didn't answer. He didn't even move.

After a minute or so, Karen started to ask the question again. "David, what did…"

The rest of Karen's question went unasked. If she had continued, it would have been unheard anyway. People in Pompeii who were in conversation when Mount Vesuvius erupted would have understood what Karen was feeling when her words died in her throat.

David burst up off the lounge chair with surreal suddenness. Karen couldn't tell how he got his legs under himself so quickly. All she knew is that before she could blink, David was grabbing onto the balcony railing with both hands bellowing a wordless scream into the night sky. Then, just as suddenly, he was back at the small table between their chairs. From Karen's perspective, he was coming directly at her. In spite of herself, she shrunk away from him as if he might strike her.

Instead of striking her, however, he grabbed the phone, turned back around and hurled it with all his might off of the balcony. Karen followed the unlikely path of the phone as it spun about all three axes and arced out of sight into the night sky.

71

David wasn't done. He pivoted back around to the table and grabbed first one wine glass, then the other, and then the wine bottle, casting each off the balcony in the same general direction as the phone. Still not satisfied, David finally picked up the small table itself and swung it over the balcony like an Olympic discus thrower.

The crashing glass and clanging metal as David's unwitting projectiles landed on the rocks and trees of the hillside below their balcony started Karen out of her stunned silence.

"DAVID!" she screamed. "David, stop it!"

She had yelled his name at the top of her lungs, but he showed no signs of hearing her. His rampage continued without missing a beat. As he reached down to pick up the chaise lounge chair he had been sitting on sipping wine ten minutes earlier, Karen launched herself at him, intending to grab and restrain him from behind. In her distress, she misjudged the distance between them and hit David from behind at full speed. She knocked him forward into the low lounge chair. His shins banged into it, and their combined momentum forced him forward over the chair with Karen, who was now hanging on to his back and shoulders, along for the ride.

Most of David's weight came down on the chair, and then he bounced and rolled off the other side. Still hanging on to his back, Karen was now between David and the balcony floor. They both crashed to the floor, David's full weight falling on top of Karen. David heard a thick thud as her head banged against the floor. Suddenly thinking clearly, David scrambled to his feet and turned around to face Karen.

She wasn't moving. Cursing himself, his temper, ADA Kleinfeldt, and mostly LaShon Jackson, David gently scooped Karen up and carried her through the open sliding glass door into the bedroom. He lay her on the bed and carefully tipped her up on her side to check the back of her head. He didn't see any blood. He slid his hand across her hair, pulled it away, and was relieved to see that there was no blood there. He let her roll onto her back.

While he was debating whether to call an ambulance, Karen began to stir.

"Karen? Karen, can you hear me? Are you OK?"

Karen continued to stir, and then grunted softly. Over the next 60 seconds, the longest of David's life thus far, Karen became more and more animated, eventually opening her eyes. At first, she appeared not to know where she was or what happened. For a moment, David wasn't even sure she knew who he was. Soon, however, David could see in her eyes that everything was coming back to her…and it was very clear that she was not impressed with his behavior.

"Karen, are you OK?" he asked again.

Karen closed her eyes again, and then said with some effort, "David, my arm hurts a lot. My head and my back too. I think I need to go to the hospital."

"I'm so sorry…" David said, close to tears.

"David, I don't want to talk to you right now. Just help me up and drive me down to the hospital."

David complied with her wishes. He moved quickly and efficiently, despite a pall of guilt and anger that hung over him. He was exceedingly gentle with Karen as he helped her down the stairs and into the car, but he didn't speak another word until they arrived at the hospital. The next words spoken between them, in fact, were from Karen when she asked David to stay in the waiting room while she followed a tired-looking nurse to the examination area of the Mercy Hospital Emergency Room.

Karen emerged two hours later. Her right arm was in a cast, and she was moving very gingerly due to a bruised tailbone and a concussion.

David stood up and rushed across the waiting room to her side. "What did…" he began.

"David, I really think it's best if we still don't talk for awhile. I don't want to say anything I don't mean, and I really have a lot of thinking to do to figure out what it is that I want to say to you."

"OK, Karen. I just want to say that I'm so sorry."

"I'm sure you are, but I really don't know if that changes anything. Now please, drive me home. When I'm ready to talk to you, I'll let you know."

David drove her home and wordlessly helped her out of the car and up the stairs. He got her up to their room, and then broke the rules by saying, "I'll sleep in the other room, but if you need anything, just call me."

"No, David, why don't you stay. I think I'm ready to talk," she replied. David didn't like the look of resignation in her eyes.

"OK," he replied quietly, trying to make his eyes look as weepy and apologetic as he could.

"David, I know you've been through a lot, and I've tried to be there for you and overlook your mood swings and your wild temper. And…well, you know I love you…more than anything in the world. But…"

She paused for what seemed like eternity, staring out at the place on the patio where the table used to be.

"But?" David finally prompted.

"But I don't know if I can go on with you anymore. I know you didn't mean to do this," she said, holding up her casted arm, "but I almost have the feeling I'm lucky this is all that happened. I thought you were going to hit me. And if you didn't do that, you could've accidentally knocked me off the balcony or fallen off yourself. This is like the fourth or fifth time that I've really been scared to be around you. And…I just can't live in fear of you. I love you too much and it just tears me apart to have to live in fear of someone I love. I got enough of that with Michael and I don't need it with my boyfriend and I really don't need it with my husband."

David's heart hurt to hear this coming from his lover, his best friend, and the closest thing he had in the world to family. He could no longer control the tears that had threatened behind his eyes. One at a time, they began to slip down his cheeks.

"So," she continued, "I thought a lot about leaving you after this. But…I've decided to give you one last chance."

David, who had been holding his breath for some time, let it out in a breathy gasp that bordered on a sob. "Oh Karen, I'm…"

"Wait, I'm not done. I'm going to stay, but you have to make me some promises. First, you need to get over this LaShon Jackson thing. I could hear enough of what Mr. Kleinfeldt was saying to figure out he isn't going to trial because he's not going to recover from his injuries. You know, that's probably worse than going to jail. Whatever your opinion is, you need to live with the fact that his punishment is not going to include him going to jail. You have to promise me that you're not going to try to take the law into your own hands, and you also have to promise that you're going to take care of this temper of yours and go back to the David McGuire I fell in love with. If you have to go to therapy, go to therapy. I'll even come with you if you want. If you can control it without therapy, that's fine. But I'll promise you this…if you ever go off like that again, or if you ever raise a hand to hit me or anyone else, I'll leave you and move back to LA and you'll never see me again. And it's not just the temper. If you let this thing hang over your head and you're going to be moping around here all the time feeling sorry for yourself that you didn't get your revenge on him, I'll leave too. We have a chance for a great life, David. A really great life. You have a girlfriend here who loves you and will do anything for you…anything but watch you destroy yourself with bitterness and self-loathing. If you can control that, then you've got me for life. If not, it will break my heart, but I'll leave. So, David, can you make me those promises?"

Without hesitation, David said, "Yes of course I promise. Just don't leave me. Please don't ever leave me. You're the only thing that matters to me in this world. I promise…"

He went to her, and she accepted him with her uninjured arm.

Karen stayed, and, as far as she knew, David kept his promises.

22

David chose not to go to therapy. Instead, he did what men do, and he buried his feelings deep inside. The anger, the guilt, the unrequited need for revenge, all of it he packed down in the pit of his stomach and kept it there. That was the price to keep Karen, and, in David's mind, that was a small price to pay.

His mind, however, did not speak for his soul. While outwardly he very soon had performed a very slick act of magic and transformed himself into what Karen referred to as "the David McGuire I fell in love with," inside his heart and soul swirled a maelstrom of discontent. Within a few short weeks, he realized he wouldn't be able to keep up his act for long if he didn't do something.

That something, he soon realized, was to keep a certain door open. That door led to revenge, and if he didn't allow it to close completely, he could relax and settle into the lie that was his life. As long as, if necessary, he could kick down the door and visit a reckoning upon LaShon Jackson, he would be fine.

With an apologetic call to John Kleinfeldt (made from work, of course), David learned that LaShon would soon be released into the care of his mother, whose name was Dolores Hayes. David also learned that he would likely spend the next several months in an inpatient mental care facility to help him learn to live again. When he hung up the phone, it took no more than a phone book and a Thomas Guide to find the home of Dolores Hayes, and the future home of LaShon Jackson.

So, approximately two weeks after he broke Karen's arm on the balcony, David McGuire sat in his car outside of a run-down shack in East Palo Alto. It took him about a half an hour to get there from work. He and the other members of his team worked long hours, but the hours were flexible, and long lunches were not uncommon. He told his boss that he would be back in a couple of hours...had some errands to run. After a quick spin through the McDonald's drive-thru, David headed down the peninsula to EPA. He figured he could spend an hour in front of the house and then head back. Karen wouldn't call him at work. She was teaching and would only call after 3:30, unless it was an emergency. Karen would never know. And what she didn't know wouldn't hurt her.

He didn't know what he expected to see, or even what he hoped to see, but sitting there at least made him feel like he was doing something. As he munched on his quarter pounder with cheese and large order of fries, he surveyed the shitty little dwelling that had spawned a murderer.

The house, if you could call it that, was in the same state of disrepair as the others on the street. It was very small. David guessed maybe 700 or 800 square feet. The house was an ancient shade of tan. David could see paint peeling and flaking off in chunks up around the eves. There was no garage, just two dirty lines through the weeds in the front yard where Mrs. Hayes must park her car. The yard was bordered by a rusty chain link fence. The front of the house showed only a front door and one window. The door boasted a screen that was attached only by the bottom hinge. It leaned drunkenly to the right, resting on the cracked concrete stoop. The window was covered with rusty iron bars. The rain gutter above the window was detached at the corner of the house and sagged halfway down to the ground. Many houses are named. Monticello, Tara, Tipperary. This house had no name, but if it did, only one would be appropriate...Despair.

Chewing slowly, David's eyes traveled around the house and yard, memorizing every detail. He frequently checked the street in front and behind him as well. A white man sitting in his car eating McDonald's was not a normal sight in this neighborhood. He was thankful that he hadn't traded in his old Accord for a Mercedes or BMW. Karen and his co-workers had urged him to do so, but the car had never had an operational problem when he didn't have money, so it didn't deserve to be cast aside now that he did.

Traffic on the street was light, and none of the people who walked or drove gave him more than a second look. It seemed that the folks who were out and about had better things to do than to bother with him. Just as he was getting ready to pack it in, he noticed an old, brown Cutlass pull up behind him and stop. In spite of himself, his pulse quickened and sweat quickly broke out on his back, arms and forehead.

The door of the car opened, and a middle-aged black man got out. He was wearing gray slacks and a short-sleeved blue shirt. He wore a gray cap on his head which bore a red, white and blue patch depicting an eagle taking flight. In his right hand was a bundle of letters and magazines.

Relieved, David watched the mailman make his rounds as his heart rate slowly came back to earth. He was efficient with his deliveries and covered eight houses and was back in his car and gone in less than five minutes.

Watching him flip open the ancient, charcoal-colored mailbox in front of Dolores Hayes' home, it came to David that there may be some very interesting information about Mrs. Hayes or her son therein. So, after the mailman pulled away, David checked the street carefully, fired up his Honda, and pulled across the street. He was able to drive up on the shallow curb and reach the mailbox through his driver's window. He quickly opened it, grabbed the contents, threw them on the passenger seat, and sped off down the street toward the freeway.

He was vaguely aware he had just committed a federal crime, but that thought was well in the back of his mind. The overwhelming emotion in David's mind was exhilaration. He had done something. Something concrete that he could hold in his hands. And, what's more, he felt he could do it again and again until he found out all he needed to know. David sped up the 101 back toward work. Something bordering on joy danced around his psyche. He had his resolution. It wasn't closure in and of itself, but it was close, and it kept the door open for more definitive closure should the need arise.

Over the next year, David visited East Palo Alto several times. He went at different times of the day and week. Each time, he helped himself to the contents of the mailbox. He soon knew Mrs. Hayes' place of employment, work schedule, her bank and account number, and her meager checking account balance. More importantly, he knew approximately when her son had been transferred from Stanford Med Center to a state hospital northeast of Sacramento in the Sierra Foothills. He had even taken a day off of work and driven up to the El Dorado State Rehabilitation Center to see where LaShon was sent to recover from his injuries.

Another year later, David was parked well down the block when LaShon arrived back home to live with his mother. A few weeks later, David watched LaShon climb into his mother's orange Pinto and go with her to the office building in Redwood City where she performed some sort of data-entry task. Once there, she held his hand and walked him into the Jack In the Box across the street. LaShon was apparently given a uniform and a wet towel, and he embarked on what would now be his life's work; cheerfully keeping Jack's red-plastic tables clean and free of debris.

David no longer found it necessary to visit the Hayes home. He now made periodic visits to LaShon's Jack in the Box, ordering food in the drive through and then eating it in his car in the parking lot. He didn't dare go in. As much as he felt he was at peace with his life, he didn't want to tempt fate and place himself in the same room as LaShon. Instead, he watched through the window as LaShon dutifully picked up every scrap of wrapper and every errant French fry and wiped up every bit of spilled ketchup, soda and milkshake, smiling the entire time.

David expertly kept his secret from Karen. In a sense, he even kept it from himself. When he wasn't feeding his obsession with LaShon Jackson, he was completely at peace with his life. For long periods of time, he wouldn't think about Dolores or LaShon, or even his parents. All other parts of his life were completely separate from the part that had him skulking in his car in East Palo Alto and Redwood City. That part of him, the part that still wanted to keep the possibility of revenge within arm's reach, lived in a completely separate room within his soul. Sometimes, the door to that room would open up a crack. He didn't plan it and couldn't predict it, but when it did, David would go in. He would do what he needed to do to assure that he could still find his parents' killer whenever necessary, and then he would shut the door and re-enter his everyday life. Sometimes the door would stay shut for weeks, sometimes months. But as long as it was shut, David was only peripherally aware of its existence.

As such, the years after their fateful night on the balcony were good ones for David and Karen. They both worked hard at their jobs and found them very fulfilling. To them, it seemed that they didn't have to work at all on their relationship and found that even more fulfilling.

In a real sense, they didn't really even have to work either, as David had invested the $1.5 million he had remaining after purchasing the house in Microsoft, Intel, Netscape, and several other technology stocks that went through the roof in the 1990's. As they moved into the latter part of the decade, David's fortune had grown to well over $4 million. As in their relationship, they both continued with their jobs because they loved them - worth doing just for the pure joy.

Through it all, they traveled widely, lived richly and loved completely. Neither could imagine any greater happiness than they had found together.

Over the years, David spent less and less time watching LaShon Jackson. By 1997, four years after the accident, he quit going completely. He truly believed that he was finally at peace. Having closed that chapter of his life, he felt ready to open another.

23

In December of 1997, David took Karen to New York City for Christmas and New Years. As they watched the ball drop, David got down on one knee and proposed marriage. Karen accepted without a moment's hesitation.

As do many men, David found that Karen had already planned most of their wedding before he had even proposed. Karen took steps to conceal this fact by asking David's opinion on various ideas she had for the wedding. For example, she said, "I was thinking we should have Calla Lilies as the focal point of the flowers. What do you think?"

The fact that most of these ideas were presented to him less than eight hours after he proposed gave David a pretty good idea as to the extent his wedding had already been planned for him. He was actually just fine with that. In fact, he was relieved. He had no idea what to do for a wedding, and, while he was happy to help with the arrangements, he was counting on Karen to take care of the ideas.

David very soon learned that Karen had always wanted a June wedding, and she wanted it to take place on a beach in southern Los Angeles County that was available for such events. She had seen it in a magazine, and just happened to have cut out the article and placed it in her purse in case she might need it. The wedding would be a simple one, with an elegant but unassuming dress for Karen and a halo of white flowers in her hair, and a loose fitting white shirt and linen pants for David. The reception would be a much more elaborate event, and Karen would find a suitable hotel or other facility for that.

After some extensive calculations and some consternation on the part of both the bride- and groom-to-be, they decided to wait a year and a half for the wedding. Considering their work schedules and the logistics of planning a wedding in Southern California from Northern California, there just wasn't enough time to plan it properly or reserve the necessary venues before the coming June. Not wanting to budge from her June dream, Karen suggested and David agreed to a wedding in the third week of June, 1999.

The eighteen months they had to plan the wedding allowed the process to fold neatly into their everyday lives. Both of them were now in their fourth year of employment, and they were working harder than ever at the jobs they had grown to love.

David had been promoted to the position of assistant project manager of the same critical project he and the company had undertaken four years earlier. Very much due to David's involvement, the team had progressed faster than the company or the military had hoped. Their challenge, however, presented them with many complex, intertwined and even conflicting problems to solve. It seemed that it would be another two to three years before they had a deliverable product. Just prior to David's trip to New York, they had performed a successful demonstration of their current prototype to a Colonel Gates, who was the officer in charge of the project on the Military's side. He was extremely impressed, and informed them that the military was willing to provide any further funding necessary to expedite the completion of the project. BioMech did require additional funding, they said, and they funneled that funding directly to David and his teammates in the form of huge bonuses and salary increases of nearly 50%. They could see the gravy train coming around the bend, and they needed to keep their team together until it arrived. David was now pulling in about $90,000 a year.

Karen was enjoying similar success at Edison Academy. She was incredibly popular with the majority of the students, faculty and staff. The students saw her as a refreshing change from many of the stodgy old professorial types that pontificated from behind their podiums in the other classrooms. Oddly enough, the stodgy old professorial types found her refreshing as well. She brought a new energy and attitude to both the classroom and the faculty lounge that everyone at the venerable institution seemed to appreciate. Even the headmaster, Dr. Hollingsworth, who had given her the chance at the behest of Karen's academic advisor, came to think of her as "the new blood." He felt that she provided an infusion of life into the school, and he had hired three other young teachers in the subsequent four years to try to continue along that path.

Unfortunately, however, the stodgy old professorial-types, the headmaster and the alumni of the venerable institution subscribed to a set of rules that needed to be followed. These rules were unwritten and unspoken, only implied and alluded to. Teachers who didn't follow the program as prescribed by 100 years of tradition could find themselves in trouble.

Karen had never had occasion to be informed of any of these rules. She had been luckier than she could have known in having four years of students who were generally diligent and capable, and she had not had the occasion to fail any of them. If any of them had deserved it, however, she would have done so without hesitation. She certainly had never been given a free pass, and she was not about to start cheating these kids out of their education by giving them out.

Everything changed for Karen in the fall of 1998. When her second-period Sophomore English class filed in, she was disappointed to note that John McNamara, Douglas Weinstein and Truman Nakimura were on the roster. As Freshmen, they had been in her friend Stacy Ling's class for history. They were disrespectful and disruptive in class, and they refused to study or take their assignments seriously. They were also prone to make crude sexual comments about Ms. Ling, and some of the other students in class.

Stacy had come to Karen for advice on handling the boys, and Karen tried her best to help her. They didn't respond to any disciplinary action she took, so she went to the headmaster for help. He replied by saying, "They are good boys, Ms. Ling. I think you need to try harder to get through to them. I don't think discipline is the answer here. The year is almost over anyway, so if you can't make any progress, just move them along and we won't have to worry about it anymore."

"But Mr. Hollingsworth," she replied, "all three of them are failing my class. I can't move them along. John McNamara is carrying a 39% average, and the other two aren't much higher."

Mr. Hollingsworth stiffened and looked up from the papers he had been perusing during their conversation. He fixed her with a stern gaze, and said, "Now Ms. Ling, Walter McNamara, Barry Weinstein and Ishiro Nakimura are alumni of this school and are our three largest donors. Combined, we receive more than 35% of our annual donations from those three families. Do you think it would be a good idea if we held back their sons?"

Ms. Ling caught the tone, and realized she had come precariously close to violating the program. She was in her first year, and she needed the job quite badly. So, in spite of her moral objections, she promoted the three troublemakers along to the tenth grade.

Karen, of course, was violently offended by the old-boy network that allowed, even encouraged, three promising young men to waste the educational opportunity that millions of children around the world would love to have. She hadn't said anything at the time, but she had stewed silently over the summer over the injustice that had been done to Ms. Ling and children everywhere. She promised herself that, if any of those three or any others like them ended up in her class, they would receive treatment equal to all the other students, even if that meant she had to give them failing grades and hold them back.

Now here they were, sauntering into her class like the kings of the world. John McNamara even had the audacity to stop and look her up and down on his way in. It made her skin crawl.

As she wrote her name on the board, she was sure she heard someone behind her whisper something which might have been, "Look at that fucking ass!"

She ignored the comment for the moment, but took care not to take her eyes off the students for the rest of the class, especially the three suspects,

Vengeance

who were sprawled in the back row like lions who had just eaten a Zebra for lunch.

As the bell rang and the class stirred into life, Karen called out over the din, "Mr. McNamara, Weinstein and Nakimura, please stay a moment."

The three boys looked at each other, grinned, rolled their eyes, and strode to the front of the class. They weren't frightened or nervous in any way. They were all very big boys for their age, and they purposely stood close enough to make her look up at them. They arrogantly looked her right in the eye, when they weren't stealing a glance at her breasts, that is.

"Gentlemen, I know you are accustomed to behaving however you wish and not meeting class requirements in order to pass. I just wanted you to know that I will not tolerate such behavior in my class. If you disrupt the class, I will send you to the headmaster's office immediately. If you don't keep your average above 70%, I'll report you to the athletic department and have you declared ineligible to play football until you bring up your grades. At the end of the year, if you don't deserve to pass, you'll repeat this class next year. Do you all understand?"

"Ms. Chavez," John McNamara said with a hint of a Spanish accent, "I don't think you understand. Our families pay your salary, and the headmaster's and half the other teachers here. Not only that, I'm going to be starting at quarterback this year, and these two are starting linebacker and wide receiver. Between us and this new running back they shipped in from Oakland, we're favored to win the district championship and go to state this year. Do you think the headmaster is going to want to either piss off our dads by screwing up our academic records or piss off the alumni by fucking up the whole football season?"

"Mr. McNamara, your foul language doesn't shock me, and your threats don't scare me, although that is the last time I will allow either of them in my classroom. If you want to try me, go ahead. There are laws in this state to prevent what you are suggesting will happen to me if I actually try to make you learn, or at least stop you from preventing other students from doing so.

You and the other students here have the opportunity of a lifetime, and the three of you are wasting it. My number one priority is to help you learn history. If you fight me on that, fine, but I will absolutely not allow you to disrupt my class. Now, please go on to your next class and come back tomorrow ready to learn."

John McNamara, who was apparently the group's leader and spokesman, was turning nearly purple with rage at this prissy little Mexican bitch's insolent tone. She clearly didn't know who she was dealing with. They would show her. She couldn't push them around or do anything to stop them from doing whatever they wanted to do. But right now, he was too angry and flustered by her fucking nerve to do anything but storm out the door. Like obedient puppies, the other two followed along behind.

As fate would have it, the running back they shipped in from Oakland, entered her classroom immediately after the other three boys left. Upon seeing him, Karen's first thought was that one of the students' fathers had gotten lost on the way to the headmaster's office. He was about six feet two inches tall and looked to weigh about 220 pounds. He wore a thin white polo shirt that was stretched tightly across his heavily muscled chest, shoulders, back and upper arms.

"May I help you?" Karen asked.

"I'm Darius Williams, ma'am. Is this Freshman History?" he replied.

His tone and demeanor were a combination of humility, deference and shyness. Having McNamara, Weinstein and Nakimura as her most recent reference point, Darius's respectful tone made her smile. She liked him immediately.

"Yes it is," she said, "Please take a seat."

"Thank you ma'am," he replied, breaking into a hesitant smile of his own.

The rest of the class filed in, and Karen rolled into another first day of Freshman History. This class seemed to be full of bright, inquisitive students who were ready to learn. For that, she was relieved. She had a

Vengeance

feeling she was going to need an easy class after dealing with the three primadonnas every day.

As the class was filing out, she could see Darius hanging back. When the rest of the students were gone, he approached her desk. She was standing behind it, but his eyes were generally aimed at the floor.

"May I help you, Darius?" she asked.

"Yes ma'am. I wanted to tell you I liked your class. Also, I never took history before. They didn't have it in my school," he said, in a tone just above a whisper.

"Thank you, Darius," she said.

"I, uh, I didn't really know none of what you was talkin' about today, ma'am. It seems like I'm s'posed to know this stuff already. I had English and Math this morning already, and it was the same."

"Would you like me to help you find a tutor, Darius?"

"Do you think that'd help? I know they brought me over here to play football, but I really wanna learn too. They told me I didn't have to worry about my grades, but that just don't seem right."

"They were wrong to tell you that, Darius," Karen said, feeling a hot flush in her checks and ears, "Your studies should come first."

She was angry enough that the school would let the rich kids get out of here without learning anything, but the fact that they would bring this young man in to win the district title for them and then suggest to him that he didn't need to worry about studying made her blood boil. It was insulting to the other students, it was insulting to the teachers, and most of all it was insulting to Darius. The days of the black man existing to further the white man's desires were supposed to be over. Apparently that was not the case at the Edison Academy.

Her indignation led her to make a decision that seemed a minor one at the time. It was the right thing to do, she had no doubt about it. There are those who speculate that a butterfly flapping its wings in the middle of the

87

ocean could cause a massive tidal wave to strike the coast many days later and hundreds of miles away. Karen, unwittingly, flapped her wings.

"Darius, I would like to tutor you myself, if you don't mind. I think I can help you in all of your subjects if you want," she said.

"I couldn't ask you to do that, Ms. Chavez," he replied.

At this, he actually looked up from the floor with a gleam of hope in his eyes. That sealed the deal. "Darius, you didn't ask, I offered. And now I'm insisting. When does your football practice end?"

"Around five, usually."

"OK, can you get here by 5:30?"

"Sure. Are you sure you wanna stay around here and wait for me?"

"I'm usually here that long anyway," she said, "I tend to give essay assignments, not multiple choice. It takes me awhile to grade them. My fiancée has been working really late anyway recently, so I don't have anywhere to go. We can spend an hour a night, or longer if you need to. We're going to make sure that Edison Academy and its alumni aren't the only winners in this deal, OK?"

There was a pause as Darius seemed to search for words that would properly reflect his gratitude. In the end, all he managed was a soft, "Thank you."

His humility brought tears to her eyes. "Don't mention it, Darius. Just do your best and get an education, that will be thanks enough for me."

The next class was beginning to file in. "Thanks, Ms. Chavez, I'll be here as soon as I can," Darius said, beginning to back toward the door.

"OK. Good luck at practice," she replied, giving him a little wink as he went.

As Darius left, both he and Karen felt that their hearts were about to burst with joy. Karen's because she was going to help someone who really seemed to deserve it, and because she was going to take a pretty good shot at the old boy network while she did it.

Darius's heart felt that way because he was already falling in love.

24

John McNamara tested her resolve the very next day by arriving about one minute late for class and then knocking the books off of the desks of the first three students he passed on the way to his own.

Before he could even sit down, Karen said, "John, don't even sit down. We're going to see the headmaster."

John smirked at his two buddies, turned around, and said, "No, I don't think I want to go to the headmaster's office today."

What happened next shocked everyone. Karen took several quick steps forward and grabbed John's bulky left bicep with her right hand, and then turned and pulled him toward the door. John was six inches taller than she was and outweighed her by 80 pounds, but he was so surprised that she would lay a hand on him that she was able to jerk him off balance. He certainly wasn't going to let her pull him off his feet, but she pulled hard enough on his arm that he couldn't get his feet under him to dig in. As a result she was able to pull him all the way out the door before he was able to resist. On the way, she said in a tone that was really meant for his friends and the rest of the class, "I told you yesterday that I would not allow you to disrupt this class, and I meant it."

When they were in the hall, he finally got his feet under him and was able to spin his arm out of her grip. She stopped and said, "Come on, John, we're going to the headmaster's office. You don't want me to have to manhandle you again, do you?"

John was furious. This little bitch had made him look like a pussy in front of the whole class. She was definitely going to be sorry. He no longer needed to be told to go to the headmaster's office. He marched off in that direction voluntarily. When he got there, he intended to have a word with the headmaster. If he needed to, he would call his dad and put him on speaker to tell him what kind of school the headmaster was running. He wasn't sure, but he was pretty sure she couldn't touch him, and he was going to make sure it cost her her job.

"By the way, John," Karen said quietly, "I know you think I had no right to touch you that way. You know what, it would be an interesting case if it came before the school's board of directors. In fact, I bet it would make the papers. I tell you what, if I lost my job over it, I'd sue and then I know it would make the papers, considering who your father is. So, unless you want to have the whole Bay Area know that a 110 pound woman was able to push you around like that, and that you ran to your daddy to protect you from the big, mean teacher, I'd recommend you don't say anything about this. If you don't, I won't."

John stopped dead in his tracks. Then, without turning around, he continued his march to the office. Karen kept up with him pretty well. When they got there, she informed Mr. Hollingsworth's secretary that John McNamara would need to stay there for the remainder of the period. If Mr. Hollingsworth wished to speak with him, that was fine. She would come by at lunch to tell him what happened. Now, she had to get back to class.

When she reentered the classroom, all but two of the students began to clap and cheer for her. The three students in the front row who had to scoop their books off the floor five minutes earlier clapped the loudest. Finally, someone had stood up for them. Of course the two exceptions were Weinstein and Nakimura, who glared at her coldly from the back row.

"Yeah Ms. Chavez," called a young lady in the middle of the third row.

"OK, OK," Karen said, "OK, that's enough. Everyone please stop right now."

The clapping died down quickly, but the grins on the students' faces remained.

"Listen everyone. I didn't do that to embarrass John or to entertain all of you. My job is to teach you history, and I intend to do that. Today, it was apparent that he was going to stand in the way of your learning. I couldn't allow that. I really hope I don't have to do that again, to him or anyone else."

She paused and glanced back at John's cohorts. Then she continued, "Now, I know none of you owe me a favor, but I would like to ask one anyway. Please don't tease John about what happened, and please, let's keep what happened between us, OK?"

She might as well have asked a 20 foot tall wave to turn around and go back out to sea. The students nodded in assent, and Karen went back to teaching history. When they left class that day, however, each one told everyone they saw what had happened, with the customary teenage embellishment, of course.

By lunch time, the whole school knew that Ms. Chavez had dragged John McNamara kicking and screaming out of his seat, out of her classroom and all the way down the hall to the headmaster's office. As soon as the lunch bell rang, Mr. Hollingsworth stepped into her classroom and moved aside to avoid the charging students. He stepped over to her desk and stood facing her. When all the students left, he said, "Karen, everyone is saying you dragged John McNamara out of class today. Is that true?"

"Did you speak to him? I took him to your office."

"I asked him what happened, but he refused to say. He only said that you had singled him out to set an example."

"Well, if you must know the whole story, it started yesterday. While I was writing on the blackboard, one of them made an extremely vulgar reference to my backside. I'm 90% sure it was McNamara, but I let it go until the end of the class since I couldn't say for sure. After class, I informed him, Weinstein and Nakimura that I would not allow profanity or any other disruptions in my class. I also told them that if they didn't deserve to pass, they wouldn't, and that if their grades drop low enough, I'll report them to the AD to have them declared ineligible for football.

"Today, McNamara walked in late and knocked the books off of three students' desks. I asked him to come with me to your office. He wouldn't, so I took him by the arm into the hall. He then pulled away from me and walked on his own to your office. That's all that happened."

"Karen, I will have a talk with John about what happened, and I'm sure we can keep this from becoming an issue. I'll also tell him that he needs to watch himself in your class and buckle down on his studies. If he gives me any trouble, I'll get his dad involved."

"Thank you sir," she said.

"Now, about the football and the grades. I think you really need to give him and the other two some space on that. You're a great teacher, and I hate to see you get caught up in something like that."

"Something like what? Are you suggesting I should allow them to pass without meeting the class requirements? And please don't tell me you are saying my job could be affected if I don't," she fumed.

"Karen, calm down please. I'm not threatening you or your job. I just want you to know the parents of our students and the alumni are some of the most powerful people in the world. They expect a football championship this year. If that doesn't happen, they're going to want to know why. You and I would both have a headache we don't need."

"Mr. Hollingsworth, I understand what you're saying, but I'm afraid I can't comply with your wishes or the wishes of the alumni in this case. It's not fair to the other students and it's really not fair to John, Doug and Truman for them to get through here without an education. They're going to go to college and embarrass themselves, their families, and Edison for that matter."

"OK Karen. Let's hope it just doesn't come to that. I don't like it any more than you do, but at Edison, people are used to winning at all costs. They do it in business, and they expect their children and their children's school to follow suit."

"I hope it doesn't come to that either, because you'll have to fire me before I'll look the other way and apply a double standard to those three."

"OK. I'll talk to John. I'm sure everything will be fine."

"Me too. Thank you sir."

"Thank you, Karen. You're doing a great job here. Keep up the good work."

Mr. Hollingsworth's last comment was as empty as the hall outside her room. She knew she was pushing her luck, but she didn't care. David had about $5 million in the bank, and he would be more than happy to support her while she found another job if it came to that. Her mind was made up— she wasn't going to budge.

That evening, she had her second tutoring session with Darius. He was really a bright kid, but his elementary and middle school background had him miles behind the other students, who had all gone to the most expensive private primary schools available. They had been there two hours the night before, and even longer that evening.

Darius worked very hard. Karen got an immediate sense that he was trying to impress her with his level of concentration and dedication. She was flattered. She also thought she caught him a few times looking at her for a little longer than he needed to, but she told herself that she must be imagining that. He was clearly trying to make the best of the opportunity that had been placed in front of him.

Karen's days and nights fell into a pattern as they did every year. This year, the two wrinkles in her pattern occurred during second period and after school. Even though John, Doug and Truman were behaving themselves, she had an unmistakable feeling that something was eventually going to happen. The three of them sat in the back row and glared at her for the entire period, and then stomped out in formation like stormtroopers. John and Doug put forth a minimal amount of effort, and their grades showed it. They both had an average well below 70%. According to the school's "official" policy, any student below 70% in any class would be ineligible for extra-curricular activities until they brought their average up. Of course both students were counting on the unwritten old-boy policy to pull their bacon out of the fire. Truman, however, had a feeling that Ms. Chavez was going to stick to her guns. Fearing what his father would do to him if he were to be put on probation, he buckled down and was actually carrying a 92% average, a fact that he did his best to conceal from John and Doug.

She had the opposite feeling after school. She looked forward to her sessions with Darius as much as she dreaded her interaction with the other three. He was making remarkable progress, although he was in such a hole from the beginning that he maintained averages in the high 70's in most classes. That put him in the C- range, which was passing, and that was better than the alternative. Karen felt if she could make sure he passed his classes this quarter, he could continue to improve and maybe get up to a C+ or B- next quarter. Beyond that, she thought he had a real chance of eventually having a vowel or two on his report card.

Midterms came in the second week of October. When they did, and thanks to John, Doug, Truman and especially Darius, the Edison football team was 6-0 and leading the district. Traditionally, students were given a grace period until midterms to get their ship upright and have their grades above 70%. After midterms, those below 70% were declared ineligible for extracurricular activities. Darius and Truman were both in position in all of their classes to remain on the field. Conversely, John and Doug were failing all of their classes except U.S. Government, which was taught by Mr. Schroll, the football coach. The other teachers, however, were conditioned to look the other way for certain members of the football team and children of influential donors. John and Doug fell into both categories. Both of them knew that all but one of their teachers would fall in line. Ms Chavez, however, was going to need some convincing.

They also knew that Darius had a one on one tutoring thing going with Ms. Chavez. Being a creature of opportunity, much like his father, John McNamara had seen this and befriended Darius several weeks ago. Normally he wouldn't have given the ghetto kid the time of day except for what was required for them to work well together on the football field. Considering that Darius may prove useful to him, however, John and the others, by all outward appearances, took Darius under their wing. He was a

Freshman and they were Sophomores, and they took care to show him the ropes in the school, on the football field and beyond. They bought him clothes, took him to dinner, and even offered him drugs. All three of them nursed a recreational cocaine habit. Darius, however, politely declined. His mother had warned him about drugs, and he wasn't going to dishonor her, himself, or Ms. Chavez by getting involved.

Darius couldn't help but be flattered by the attention given him by the Princes of the Universe. Darius was a good boy. He was a bright boy. He was not, however, adept at dealing with people. He was, after all, a child. Other than his mother, he had never dealt with anyone but other children, and the most complicated issue he ever ran across was whether a pass caught to the left of Mr. Hightower's broken down Falcon was in or out of bounds. His mother was a wonderful woman and raised him the best she knew how. By all accounts, she had done very well for him. She did not, however, prepare him for the type of people he was now exposed to. In all fairness, she had never been exposed to such people herself and probably would have done no better. Darius was not prepared to deal with flattery, jealousy, popularity, status and the other political machinations that now swirled about him.

He was even less prepared to deal with the feelings he had for Ms. Chavez. Darius had never had a girlfriend. He was a shy boy and, although plenty of girls in his previous schools would have loved to be on his arm, he was never able to negotiate the territory between himself and the opposite sex. Now, he was spending most evenings in the company of the most beautiful, kind and generous woman he could have ever imagined. As far as he was concerned, there was no more desirable woman in the world. There are those that would call what he had a case of "puppy love," but "puppy love" is still love and there are few emotions more powerful than that.

The only person Darius could have talked to about his feelings was the object of the most confusing and urgent one. If he had told Karen about what was going on with the other three boys, she probably could have given him some good advice. He was afraid, however, that if he opened up to her on a personal level, his feelings would only become stronger and harder to control. Worse, she may be able to determine the true nature of his feelings for her. With those thoughts in mind, Darius did his best to keep their interactions focused on his studies, and resisted the urge to talk to her about anything else.

The week of midterms brought some clarity to John and Doug. After class on Wednesday, Ms. Chavez asked both of them to stay for a moment. When the other students had left, she reminded them that their eligibility for football hinged on their ability to get above 92% and 94%, respectively, on the midterm examination this Friday. Both boys nodded without replying, and then sullenly left the room. They hadn't studied for the test, nor had they read any of the material all quarter. Their odds of passing were only slightly better than the odds that the bitch was going to get with the program and let them play even if they didn't.

John decided that he needed to play the card he had been holding up his sleeve all quarter. That night after football practice, he, Doug and Truman caught up with Darius as he walked back toward the school building.

"Yo D. You goin' to see Ms. Chavez?" John asked. His voice was tinged with the African-American inner-city roll he affected when speaking with Darius.

"Yeah," Darius replied.

"Hey man, you know she's gonna put us on the ineligible list, right?" John said.

"Naw, is she?" Darius said.

"Yeah. Can you believe that? I mean, that's gonna really fuck up the team, you know," John said.

"Yeah," Darius said.

"You think you can talk to her? See if she'll give us another shot? I don't wanna leave you alone out there. Without me and Truman on offense with you, you'll be the only threat. They'll key on you and you'll get smoked," John said.

"All right, I'll talk to her," Darius promised.

"Good man," John said, clapping Darius on the back, "Come by my room after and let me know what happened."

"OK John," Darius said.

Darius waited for the opportunity to bring up the subject that night, but he couldn't find the words. As their session neared the end, he began to worry that he was going to have to just blurt them out, which wasn't what he was hoping for.

As he was working up the courage, Karen said, "Darius, you're doing great. How do you feel about midterms?"

"OK, I guess."

"Listen, you know what I used to do? Right after the tests, I would always go back and review the material to see if I got the answers right or wrong. It would make me feel better usually, and it's also anther good way to get the material to sink in for the final."

"That sounds like a pretty good idea. I have a game that night, though."

"Well, do it Saturday then. It's not too late. In fact, why don't you come up to my house and we can do it there? My fiancée will be out of town on business, so I'm just going to be sitting around anyway."

"OK," Darius said.

He was unable to fathom this turn of events. How could he be so lucky? She was inviting him over when her fiancée was out of town. His mind raced with the possibilities. Thoughts swirled around his mind that had no business being there. Only he didn't know any better. He found that he was already picturing them ending up in each other's arms, or in her bed.

"Darius?" Karen asked.

Darius gave his head a slight shake and then looked at her. She saw something in his eyes that made her feel uneasy, as if she might have just made a mistake. Then it was gone and she decided again that it was just her imagination.

"Yes ma'am. I was just thinking how I'd get there."

"I'll come pick you up. It's not far...about 15 minutes."

"OK. What time should I be ready?"

"Well, his flight's at noon. He'll probably leave around 10:30, so I'll come get you right after he leaves. I'll probably get here at 11:00. Is that OK?"

"Yes ma'am. I'll wait outside the main building by the fountain."

"That sounds great. I have to skip tomorrow's session if that's OK, Darius. I have to prepare my midterms."

"OK. I'll be fine on my own."

"Great. I'll see you in class tomorrow, but if I don't get to talk to you, good luck on your tests and the game. I know you'll do great on both," Karen said, laying one cool, soft hand on top of his.

Darius's face felt hot as blood rushed to his cheeks. Another part of him somewhat lower also began to fill with blood, causing him to shift in his seat. "Thanks Ms. Chavez. Thanks for everything," he managed.

Darius got up quickly, sliding his books off the desk and in front of his crotch, hiding what was a quickly growing bulge. He moved quickly to the door, said good night, and slipped out into the hall, taking care to conceal his rather large secret.

"So," John said, "What did she say?"

"She invited me to her house this weekend," Darius replied, "I thought I'd talk to her then."

This wasn't exactly true. When she invited him to her house, he had completely forgotten his assignment. He had fabricated this story out of necessity on the way to John's room.

"Damn, son. You really getting along with Ms. Chavez. You think she wanna give you some special lessons?"

"Naw, her fiancee's goin' out of town, so she said she didn't have anything else to do." Darius replied, smiling. He found that he was quite happy that John came so easily to this assumption. In Darius's mind, it validated the similar thoughts he had been having.

"Fiancee out of town! Damn, she might as well have told you she was having you over to fuck," John said, sensing that Darius was hoping that was really the case.

"Don't talk like that man," Darius said, doing a very poor job of feigning anger.

"Sorry man, I was just kidding," said John, "You talk to her for us, OK? We'll win the title if she lets us keep playing. If not, I don't think so. You gotta do this for us, the team and the school. Hell, it's even for her…she just don't know it."

"OK John. I will. See ya," Darius said, pushing out into the hall.

John watched him go, smiling at how easy it was to manipulate the stupid son of a bich.

25

That Friday, everything turned out as expected. Darius and Truman passed their midterms, and John and Doug did not. As it turned out, however, that night's football game, which they won 47-10, was the last for all four of them.

Karen picked up Darius as promised on Saturday morning. They arrived back at Karen and David's house at about 11:30. Just as they were sitting down at the kitchen table to review Darius's midterms, the door that connected the kitchen to the garage burst open, and David rushed in.

"Forgot my notebook," David muttered.

He blew right through the kitchen into the adjoining room. He was back in less than 20 seconds, carrying a black portfolio. When he returned, he looked at Karen and Darius for the first time.

"Oh, sorry," David said, "you must be Darius."

David detoured to the left, and walked toward the kitchen table with his right hand extended.

Darius stood up and accepted David's hand. "It's a pleasure to meet you," David said, "Karen tells me you're doing pretty well."

"Thanks to her," Darius said shyly, "It's nice to meet you too, sir."

"Please, call me David. I also hear you're quite a football player. You guys win last night?"

"Yeah, 47-10," Darius replied.

"Geez. You score any touchdowns, Darius?"

"Yeah, three."

"Wow! How many yards?"

"Hundred and seventy-seven."

"Rushing or both?"

"Just rushing. Forty-nine more receiving."

"Not bad. Maybe next game you'll get 300 combined?"

Darius smiled. He liked Ms. Chavez's fiancée in spite of himself.

"You know, Darius, David used to play football too," Karen said.

"Yeah," Darius replied, "what'd you play?"

"Linebacker and o-line. Linebacker because I loved it, and line because most of us had to go both ways to field a team."

"Wow, iron man football. Nobody does that in California."

"I know. You guys are spoiled out here."

Both of them laughed. Then Darius said, "You must have been good, I bet. In good shape anyway."

"I was OK."

"He was All-State," Karen boasted on David's behalf.

Darius's breath caught in his chest. Hearing Karen brag about her fiancée made him feel sick. It was the equivalent of her throwing the cold water of reality on his fantasy that she might actually have feelings for him.

"Oh," Darius said, buying some time. He knew the conversational ball was in his court, but he couldn't think of what to say. Finally he managed, "You play in college?"

"Nope. Blew my knee out my senior year and never played again. I've always wondered "what if' though. You be careful out there, Darius. We'll be rooting for you to do what I couldn't, OK?"

"OK sir," Darius said. The fact that David seemed to be a really good guy was making it worse for him. Not only did it mean he had less of a chance with Ms. Chavez than the faint chance he felt he had this morning, he also had to deal with the fact that David had treated him quite well. Half of him hated David because he got to come home to Ms. Chavez every night, half of him was happy that Ms. Chavez had such a nice guy to come home to.

"David," David corrected. Then, looking at his watch, he said, "Darius, it was a pleasure meeting you. I have to get back over to the airport. Good luck with your studies and football. I'm sure I'll see you again soon—maybe at your next game."

"OK. It was nice meeting you too," Darius said.

Karen got up and followed David to the door. The door opened in, and she and David stood behind it as they said their goodbyes again. Darius noted the unmistakable sounds of deep kissing, and then heard them exchange "I love you's" and "I'll miss you's." His heart was beating hard. He could feel it not only in his chest, but also in his head. His face burned as blood pounded into it. He wished he could disappear. He didn't feel that he could face Ms. Chavez now that he had seen the truth. Until now, her fiancée was a faceless person that she rarely talked about. Now, he was real, and she was clearly in love with him.

"Sorry," Karen said as she returned to the table, "I just hate to see him go."

"That's OK," Darius lied.

Darius did his best to concentrate for the next hour and a half. Karen was also distracted with worry over David's flight (she was not a big fan of air travel) and so didn't notice that anything was wrong.

Around 1:00, they decided that they had gotten as far as they could on a Saturday, and Karen asked Darius if he would like to get a bite to eat before she took him back to his dorm. He said he would like that, so they packed up his books and headed to a small Mexican restaurant just off El Camino Real in Redwood City.

This was the first time they had been together without books open in front of them, and both of them found that the conversation was surprisingly easy. Karen kept it going mainly by asking about Darius's home, his family, and his childhood.

When they were back in Karen's car, Darius thanked her for her time and for lunch. As they were pulling into the Edison Campus, he said, "Your fiancée seems like a nice guy."

"He is. He has a bit of a temper sometimes, but he seems to have it under control now. All in all, I'm pretty lucky to have him, I guess."

"Well, I hope he knows how lucky he is to have you, Ms. Chavez," Darius said.

They had stopped in front of Darius's dorm. Karen put the car in park, and made a small, almost insignificant movement that would push the tidal wave past the point of no return. She reached over with her right hand and took Darius's left. Surprised, he looked at her. Their eyes met, and Karen said, "Thank you, Darius, that's very sweet for you to say."

Karen meant to convey kindness to the boy of whom she had grown very fond in the past several weeks. In her mind, the look in her eyes could be best described as "warm." At least that is what she was going for. Darius, however, felt her cool skin, looked up and saw much more heat in her eyes than she intended, and gave in to instinct. He tightened his grip on her hand, pulled it past himself in order to draw her closer, and then leaned forward himself to kiss her.

Karen saw what was happening and panicked. She yanked her hand loose and pulled her head back far enough to bang it into the driver's window. Darius was left in no-man's land with his lips half-puckered. He quickly pulled back and began to fumble for the door handle.

"Darius, I'm sorry if I gave you the wrong idea about..." she began.

"No I'm sorry," Darius stammered as he jerked the door handle open. He was out of the car and on his feet before Karen could get out another word.

"Darius..." she said finally, but whatever she meant to say next was cut off when Darius roughly slammed the car door.

He turned his back on her and ran up the steps into his dormitory. He did not look back.

Karen cursed her stupidity all the way home. How could she be so stupid? Thinking back now, she could see the signs of what was happening. The furtive glances; his willingness to do whatever he could to please her; it was all perfectly obvious now. And she had invited him to her home! Even worse, she had initiated physical contact. How many times? At least twice she could think of.

If word of this got out, combined with the earlier McNamara fiasco, she was going to end up in Hollingsworth's office for sure. This time, maybe suspension would result. Maybe worse.

She would have to catch Darius after class Monday for sure. She would make it right with him somehow. He was a bright boy, but at 15 he was certainly not worldly. Nor did he have a chance with a 27 year-old teacher. Surely he would see that. Wouldn't he?

By Monday morning, Karen's nerves were frayed like a severed rope. David wasn't going to get home until Tuesday afternoon, and, not knowing what his reaction would be and not wanting to distract him from his presentation to the military, she didn't bring it up when he called Sunday night. He was the only one she trusted to tell, though, so she was forced to live with the guilt and worry herself for the entire weekend.

Before she could talk to Darius, she was faced with the only slightly less appealing task of handing John McNamara and Doug Weinstein their failing midterms. She handed them out with all the others, and neither she nor they said a word.

After class, however, John, Doug and Truman (who hadn't yet revealed the shame of his passing grade to his compatriots) approached her desk.

"Does this mean you're going to get us kicked out of football?" John asked.

"Until your grades come up, yes," Karen replied, "You and Doug at least. Truman got the highest grade in the class. Good for you, Truman."

John and Doug shot looks of outrage at the traitor, who was scowling at Ms. Chavez for blowing his cover. Their attention quickly turned back to the real enemy.

"You really think you can get away with it, don't you?" John growled.

"Yes, I do. In fact, I have a meeting scheduled Wednesday morning with Mr. Hollingsworth, your coach, and the athletic director. After that, it will be official."

"You fucking bitch! You're going to pay for this. Nobody fucks with us...you'll see," John hissed.

On any other day, Karen would probably have taken him and his buddies on right then in one manner or another. Today, however, she couldn't risk missing her next class. So, she let them slither out of the room without another word.

Darius should have been in her next class, but he wasn't. Karen checked, and not only did he skip her class, he skipped all of his classes. She tried to find out where he was, but he left no word with the office.

Nor did he show up Tuesday. By the time Karen and David met at home Tuesday evening, Karen was in quite a state of panic.

She related the whole story to David, and David was clearly not impressed that she had let her guard down with a student. Even worse, she had invited that student to their home.

"Karen, you let this kid from Oakland into our lives and into our home. What were you thinking?" David said, trying to keep from yelling.

"What does him being from Oakland have to do with anything?" Karen asked, trying to deflect the question for the moment.

"Karen, I know he seemed like a good kid. Maybe he is. But what if he has friends, or even brothers, that are in a gang or something. Do you know where is father is, for that matter?"

"David, that's a horrible racial stereotype. What if he were Mexican? Would you be saying the same thing?"

"If he grew up in Oakland, yeah, I would. It's not because he's black, Karen. That's just a bad place, and even a white kid over there would be dangerous."

"What do you mean 'even a white kid'?"

"Jesus, Karen, stop trying to shift the blame. You know I'm not a racist. But I am a realist, and I'm worried about you. About both of us, in fact."

Karen finally broke down. "I know, David. I'm sorry. I don't know what I was thinking," she said through her tears, "I was just trying to do some good. He was such a nice kid and I felt for him being all alone there. Plus they are using him to win at football and that just made me mad. I'm so stupid!"

David closed the few steps between them and took her in his arms. "Karen, you're not stupid. You're just a good person…the best person I've ever known. I'm sorry I snapped at you. You're right. He seemed like a good kid. I'm sure he's just embarrassed. Fifteen is a tough age for a kid, but they're resilient and I'm sure it'll be fine. Try not to worry."

"I don't know, David. The look on his face…and I thought I knew him but how could he think I…I just…I'm so sorry."

"It'll all be fine," David whispered as he pulled her close to him and stroked her hair tenderly.

"Promise?" she whispered.

"I promise. You know I'd never let anything happen to you," David replied with absolute conviction.

"I love you, David."

"I love you too."

David had made the quick switch to reassuring mode for Karen's benefit, but in his mind he was not at all sure that everything would be fine. The situation with Darius weighed heavily on his mind. Perhaps that's why after they made love later that night he had not been able to sleep. Perhaps it was the frailty of their relationship…the frailty of life itself in fact, that had opened up the floodgates in his mind and poured the memories of their life together into his consciousness. One slip, one lapse in judgment on the part of his lover, of his best friend, and now their lives, which seemed so perfect just last week, seemed on a razor's edge.

David looked up at the TV. Conan O'Brien was on his third guest. In this ignominious position tonight was a third-rate supporting actor from ABC's Thursday night sacrifice to the Seinfeld God this year. Neither this actor nor the show would be back next season…that was a fact as unavoidable as the tide. Something about that gave David a chill. He flipped off the TV and rolled toward Karen.

Before he dropped off to sleep, he looked at her perfect, peaceful face. She had certainly made a mistake, but he couldn't be mad at her. He was lucky to have ever found her, and was lucky she had stuck with him through everything he had put her through. He rarely prayed…maybe not at all since his parents had been killed, but tonight, he uttered a short word of thanks to whomever might be listening for sending this angel from heaven to watch over him.

Part II—Vengeance

26

A noise woke David. He didn't know how long he had been asleep, but it didn't seem like it had been more than a few minutes.

As he sat up in bed, a flash of light burst in front of his eyes followed by a crushing pain on the left side of his head just above the temple.

Instinctively, David threw his hands up to protect his head, but a pair of hands locked on each arm and drug him out of bed. He tried to get his legs under him, but they thumped uselessly on the floor. The pain in his head was blinding, and it seemed to radiate to his limbs. He attempted to fight— to thrash his arms and legs against the two men dragging him across the floor—but his normal strength was not in him.

Still, as they approached the bathroom adjacent to his and Karen's bedroom, he began to gain strength. He was able to pull himself up with both arms and get his legs nearly under his center of mass.

"That's it, drop him!" David heard from above him and to the left.

Suddenly, all four hands let go of his arms and he fell to the floor. He tried to get his hands under him to break his fall, but he was unsuccessful. His forehead thudded hard into the carpet. Ignoring that pain and the pain around his head to the left, David pulled his arms and legs under his body and attempted a pushup. Just as he got to his hands and knees, there was another flash of light and a crunch at the base of his skull. Before he felt any pain, the flash of light bloomed into a purple flower and then faded to black.

David woke up to two sounds. The first was some sort of tribal, profane rap music blaring from the stereo in his bedroom. The second was Karen screaming. His vision was returning slowly. His field of vision was bordered by a fuzzy haze, and the middle was filled with various colored specs of light that chased each other like fireflies.

He was kneeling on the bathroom floor, he knew that much because his head was resting on the toilet seat. He tried to bring his hands up to push himself off of the toilet to a standing position, but he was only able to move them a few inches before they came to an abrupt stop. Metal clinked on porcelain. He became aware of a dim pain around both of his wrists. Another pull provided confirmation that he was handcuffed to the toilet.

Another scream from Karen tore his focus from the handcuffs to the door leading from the bathroom back into his bedroom. What he saw drove all of his pain far into the back of his mind.

Karen was also handcuffed. She was lying on her back with her arms stretched high over her head. The steel bracelets were slipped around each wrist and connected by a chain that was passed through the wrought-iron headboard. He followed her slim arms down to her face. Her eyes were wild with fear. As she eyed her attackers, she continued to scream for help. Blood trickled from her nose, and her left cheek was split open across her cheekbone. The right side of her mouth was beginning to swell. Further down, he could see that she still wore the tank top she had worn to bed. He craned his neck to see the lower half of her body, but his angle was too low and the bed linens were pushed back to the edge of the bed, obscuring his view.

To the right of the bed stood four men, locked in an animated conversation he couldn't hear over the booming rap music. A closer look revealed that they were not men at all. They were big, but they were certainly boys. Three white kids and one black. He didn't recognize the white kids, and the black one had his back to David. An undeniable intuition told David that he knew who that was, though.

The three white boys appeared to be squared off against the other. They kept pointing at Karen as they spoke to him. He seemed to be disagreeing with whatever they were trying to tell him. Finally, however, he put his hand up to stop them and stepped over toward the bed. As he did, his hands dropped to the front of his pants, working at the button fly of his jeans.

David and Karen looked at each other. Both saw fear in the other's eyes, but they both saw strength there as well. Drawing strength from each other, they yelled out simultaneously at the top of their voices.

"GET THE FUCK AWAY FROM HER!" David screamed.

"DARIUS NO!" Karen pleaded.

Darius! He knew it. David had his legs under him as quickly as a snake coiling to strike. He pushed with his legs and pulled with his back and strained with all of his being against the handcuffs. He felt the skin on his wrists tear away under the inflexible steel. The cuffs bottomed out on the tendons of his inner wrists and the bone at the base of his thumbs. Still he pulled. He put every fiber of muscle and strength he had into the effort. He also held his breath. Combined with his quite extensive head injuries, the lack of oxygen in his brain and muscles led him to black out again.

He woke up and immediately looked at the bed. Darius was just stepping to the floor and buttoning his jeans back up. David didn't know how long he was unconscious, but it didn't take a rocket scientist to figure out what that monster had done to Karen while he was out. Cursing, he resumed his efforts to free himself. This time, however, he kept his eyes on the bedroom.

The three white boys were again at odds with Darius. One of them pushed him aside and stepped to the bed—apparently ready to take his turn. Darius attempted to restrain him. David was consumed with hatred for this bastard. He claimed to be in love with Karen. Apparently that did not preclude him from raping her, but when it came to his buddies taking their turn, now he had a problem. How noble. David vowed at that moment to kill him. Neither Karen nor the law nor all the legions of angels in heaven or demons in hell could stop him from taking the life of this detestable scum. Darius's attempts to restrain the other boy were only half-hearted, though. The kid pulled his sweat pants down around his knees and got up on the bed, first with one knee and then the other. David looked at Karen again. The strength remaining in her eyes was astounding. She fixed her eyes on his and shook her head slightly from side to side. The meaning of her this motion escaped him, but the strength in her eyes flowed into his muscles again.

"IF YOU TOUCH HER I'LL KILL YOU, YOU SON OF A BITCH!" David screamed.

All four boys turned around momentarily, and then returned their focus to the bed. Again, Darius stepped forward and grabbed the boy on the bed by the upper arm. The boy swung his arm up and around in a circle to free Darius's grip, and then pointed a finger in his face as he spoke at him harshly.

With his attention focused on Darius, the boy on the bed, who was on his knees with his legs spread apart to balance himself, left himself wide open. Karen saw the opportunity and took her shot. She pulled her right knee up to her chest, and then pistoned it forward. She struck the boy squarely in the balls. The force of her kick was enough to knock him off the foot of the bed.

He hit the floor and immediately curled into a fetal position. The other three boys were too stunned to act, and they all just stared stupidly at their accomplice as he writhed on the floor.

David again put all of his weight against the handcuffs. He felt a sticky wetness in his fists as he pulled. When he relaxed his fingers, he felt the blood dripping in individual droplets off of each finger. Again, David's vision faded to black.

This time, he came back around to see Darius and the boy whom Karen had just kicked struggling beside the bed. He looked at Karen and, for the first time, saw only fear in her eyes. He craned his neck to try to see what about the wrestling match was scaring her so. Their backs were to him, and from his position on the floor in the next room it was difficult to determine what exactly was going on. He couldn't be sure, but it almost looked like they weren't exactly wrestling with each other, but that they were fighting for possession of something. All four of their hands and arms were hidden from David's view as their large bodies bumped and crashed against each other.

David pulled against the handcuffs again, this time trying to get his head as close to the door as possible. He turned his back to the door, rolled his shoulders forward and pulled his head back, turning it as far as he could to the left at the same time. This seemed to be the position that gave him the best angle. As he strained his neck, however, he received a jolt of pain from the back of his head. His vision began to swim out of focus again.

This time he remained conscious, but he couldn't get his eyes to focus. He could smell blood and sweat and fear but he couldn't see anything. He heard the sounds of struggle when the music went low enough. He could feel the pain in his head and wrists, but his eyes betrayed him. He struggled physically to make himself see, but he could not. He felt like a man with weights tied to his feet trying desperately to swim to the surface and catch a breath.

What all of his will could not do, a single sound could. A tremendous bang echoed out of the bedroom at him. It was so loud that it made his ears feel like they were full of cotton, but it did shock his eyes out of their respite.

He looked through the portal that led from his sterile, tile prison into his chaotic bedroom, and he might as well have been looking into the gates of hell. The first sight he took in was Darius, standing perfectly still, with a gun held loosely in his left hand. He was staring at the bed where Karen lay.

David followed the path of Darius's gaze, and what he saw there made the lights go out again. One final scream died in his throat, and then there was nothing but blackness.

27

About an hour later, the phone on the table next to Seamus Molloy's bed came to life. He picked it up in the middle of the second ring.

"Molloy," he said hoarsely, trying to disguise the sleep in his voice.

He listened for a moment, and then said, "What's the address?" He scribbled something on a pad of paper next to the phone. "OK. I'll be there in 20 minutes."

He hung up the phone and looked at the digital clock on the nightstand. It read 3:47 a.m. He reached over and flipped off the alarm. He wouldn't need that this morning.

"You almost made it," said a sleepy voice from behind him.

"Almost," he agreed, rolling over to face his wife.

"Where is it?" she asked.

"Millbrae."

"Be careful," she said.

"I will. I love you."

"I love you too," she replied.

Seamus gave his wife, Molly, a kiss on the cheek and then slid out of bed. If they hadn't started out as great friends, the potential of Molly Cunningham becoming Molly Molloy would probably have precluded a romantic relationship between the two. As it was, they were friends for several years before they became involved in that way. By the time they realized that they were in love, they were too far down the road to go back because of something as trivial as a name that sounded like that of a 1950's cartoon character.

Seamus walked through the bathroom and into the closet. He pulled on some khaki slacks and a light blue shirt. He pulled a tie off the rack and draped it and his jacket over his arm. He debated momentarily whether or not to brush his teeth. The victim probably wouldn't care either way, but he decided he should out of respect for her and for his fellow officers.

That done, he headed downstairs to his office. He didn't need anything from the room, but he had an appointment with two former cops that he had to keep before he headed out the door.

Seamus flipped on the light in his office and walked across the room. On the far wall was a picture of three policemen. The one in the middle was a younger version of himself on the occasion of his graduation from the police academy. To his right and left were his father and grandfather, resplendent in their dress blues. Both men had a white-gloved hand on the shoulder of their progeny.

Seamus grasped a gold chain that hung around his neck and fished it out from beneath his shirt. At the end of the chain was a gold crucifix and a small gold medal depicting the head and shoulders of St. Jude. Seamus held both charms in his right hand as he looked at the likenesses of the men who had worn it before him.

His Grandfather, also named Seamus Molloy, emigrated with his grandmother and their seven-year-old son, Seamus Jr., from Dublin to New York City in 1948. The senior Molloy was able to join the police force, where he remained a uniformed officer for 35 years. His father was also a New York City cop, and he also spent most of his career as a uniformed patrol officer. He was not fortunate enough to retire, however. In fact, both his father and grandfather had died of lung cancer in the early 1990's. His father was just 51 years old. His grandfather, who actually died after his father, was 74.

Seamus Patrick Molloy III was born in 1962 in the Bronx. Both his parents and grandparents moved to Long Island in 1971 in order to provide a better life for Seamus and his sister, Mary Katherine. Seamus entered the police academy right out of high school, fairly rapidly worked his way up to Sergeant, and then transferred across the country to the San Francisco Bay Area, after having been offered a position as a detective.

The South San Francisco Police Department had recruited in New York and Chicago for the position, and Seamus had been lucky enough learn about it, apply and be accepted. He and Molly had moved to South San Francisco in 1992. At age 30, he was one of the youngest detectives in the Bay Area.

He quickly gained a reputation as an excellent investigator, and was assigned to the homicide division in 1994. His success continued, and his reputation spread to neighboring departments. By 1998, he had caught the attention of the brass with the San Francisco Police Department.

"This is it, guys," he said softly to the men in the picture, "next time I see you I'll be in the big leagues." He made a sign of the cross, kissed the thumb of the hand holding the crucifix, and slid it back under his shirt.

This was his last week in the SSFPD. He had been recruited by the SFPD to join their homicide division, and he had accepted. It was amazing the amount of money and opportunity that came with dropping that first 'S'. San Francisco was one of the most prestigious municipalities in the country for a cop. He had hoped since moving to the Bay Area that this would be how it worked out. Not only did he receive a substantial pay increase, but he would also receive the best training and tools available.

Seventeen minutes later, Seamus arrived at the scene of his last case with his current department. He stepped out of his sedan, greeted the uniformed officers standing in the street, and thanked one of them as he lifted up the police tape for Seamus to duck under.

He was greeted at the front door by Lieutenant William Benson. The fact that he was here suggested that this was not a normal case. The last time he left the station house on duty was probably when Seamus was in the academy 3,000 miles away.

"Seamus" Lt. Benson said.

"Hey Bill. What brings you out at this late hour," Seamus replied.

"You're not going to believe this one," the Lieutenant said, leading Seamus through the front door and up the stairs.

"Try me."

"Allright. One of the neighbors called 911 reporting screaming and loud rap music coming from the house. Apparently that was out of character for the couple living here. We had a car stop by to check it out. As the officers were getting out of the car, they heard a single gunshot. They broke down the front door and followed the music up here."

Lt. Benson had paused in the hall in front of the bedroom door. Seamus got the impression that it was for dramatic effect. They should have kept this guy locked up in the precinct.

Now he stepped past another officer into the bedroom. As he did, he said, "When they got up here, they found four kids who had apparently broken in. The young woman you see here on the bed was apparently their teacher down at Edison Academy."

Seamus followed the Lieutenant's gesture toward the bed. Lying there was what he thought must have been a beautiful young woman. Her face was swollen and the left half was covered with blood that had come from a wound the size of a quarter just above her left ear. Her hands were cuffed together to the bed just above her head. Despite her ignominious death, there was a beauty and dignity that Seamus somehow sensed in her. This was his job and by no means the first dead body he had seen. Out of necessity, he had grown a shell around him that kept him from feeling sorrow or grief for the victims of the crimes he investigated. This time was different, though. Perhaps it was because it was his last case or because of the hour, but he didn't think so. He had an undeniable feeling that this woman was someone he would have admired had he known her in life, and that her death was truly a tragic loss.

"What was her name?" Seamus asked.

Lt. Benson consulted a small pad of paper he held in his left hand. "Karen Chavez was her name," he replied, "She apparently lived with her boyfriend here. His name is David McGuire. He's the owner of the house."

"Where is he now?" Seamus asked.

"Mercy. Get this. They hit him twice in the head with a baseball bat and then handcuffed him to the toilet. When the officers got here, he was out. But we think he was awake for some if it, because he really did a number on his wrists trying to pull out of the cuffs. He lost a lot of blood from his wrists and his head."

"Did he wake up at all?"

"Not after the officers arrived."

"OK. So the kids from Edison. I'm guessing that's why you're here, right Bill?"

"I guess that's why you got called up to the show, detective, you don't miss a thing," Lt. Benson said, "Do you know who Walter McNamara is?"

"The Congressman?"

"Millionaire Congressman, I think he prefers. But wait, it gets better. I know you know Barry Weinstein."

"President of Peninsula Systems."

"Yep. How about Ishiro Nakimura?"

"This one I'm not 100% sure on, but given the context, I'm guessing he's the owner of Nakimura Savings," Seamus guessed.

"Not bad. I hear they're up to 45 branches," answered the Lieutenant.

"All right, please don't tell me their kids are the ones that did this."

"Sorry, buddy. John McNamara, Doug Weinstein and Truman Nakimura are all in custody. They're waiting to talk to you when you get done here."

"Great. This is going to be a fucking zoo when the press gets wind of it. You said four, right?"

"Yep. The fourth is in custody too. His name is Darius Williams. He went to Edison too, but apparently he's from Oakland. Not from a wealthy family, but they brought him in for football."

"How did he get in with the other three?"

"I don't know that yet. I guess that's up to you and the DA to sort out. The Williams kid did the shooting, though. He was still holding the gun."

"Did they resist?"

"Nope. Apparently they seemed to think it was pretty funny. They were wisecracking about how their dads would have them out by morning. All except the black kid, who didn't say a thing. They said he looked stunned. Must not have really been ready to be a murderer."

"I guess not. OK, thanks, Bill. I'm going to look around a little and then head down to talk to them. Keep them separate, OK?"

"Already taken care of."

"Great. And let me know as soon as the boyfriend wakes up."

"Of course. This one seems pretty cut and dried, though, don't you think? You're right, the press is going to be crawling all over us. I don't want there to be any complications, you know?"

"I hear you, but I gotta do my job," Seamus replied.

"Of course. Just keep me posted. I think we're both going to end up on TV before the end of the day."

"You're probably right, Bill. Don't worry, we'll do everything by the book and make sure we're covered. If this goes to trial and we don't have our ducks in a row, the lawyers these kids can afford will have them home for dinner."

"Yep, and we'll look like the idiots."

"Say no more, Bill. Let me get going."

"You got it. I'm going to head down to the station. I think I better wake up the Chief."

"OK. I'll talk to you later."

Lieutenant Benson left Seamus alone with two uniformed cops, one taking pictures and one guarding the door.

Seamus walked around the room, not looking at anything in particular yet. He was performing a ritual he referred to as "communing." He tried to open his mind and let the scene talk to him. The victim, the room, the weapon, the blood, whoever had something to say, he wanted to listen.

In spite of his best efforts, his attention continued to be drawn to the sacrilege on the bed. The dead woman, Karen, held his attention. She spoke silently to him, yet louder than anything else in the room. She told him that this was not as cut and dried as it looked. She told him that this was a beginning and not an end. She told him that if he didn't open his mind wider than it ever had been, there would be injustice, and worse, there would be more blood. She told him that the real tragedy had just begun.

"Detective, you OK?" said the officer with the camera.

"Sure, why?"

"You've…been staring at the body for almost 5 minutes. I just thought I'd ask."

"No, I'm OK, thanks. You get everything?"

"I think so."

"Good. Get the ME in here to get her out of here. She doesn't deserve to stay like this any more."

"You got it, Detective Molloy."

Seamus tore his eyes away from the woman on the bed. He couldn't explain what he was feeling, or how it had come to him. He just knew that this was more than it appeared to be, and that there was more sorrow in this room than any he had ever been in. As he left, he vowed to the woman on the bed that he would honor her by finding the truth, no matter how deep it lay.

28

David opened his eyes. At first there was nothing. Even his open eyes only saw blackness. Gradually, his senses began to return. He first became aware of a deep, throbbing pain in his head. With every beat of his heart, the pain in his head grew. As he began to remember what had happened, though, the pain in his heart grew far beyond that in his head.

Soon, he became aware that the blackness was lightening slowly, like the horizon at dawn. First everything was black, then gray, then a pale green.

While his vision was taking its time joining the party, his other senses sprung to life more quickly. He became aware that he was thirsty to the point he had what his father used to call "cottonmouth." He could hear clacking footsteps on a tile floor. He could smell rubbing alcohol. His spatial senses told him he was lying down in a narrow bed with his upper body slightly elevated. They also told him that something was wrapped tightly around his head.

About 90 seconds after he took his first bleary step toward consciousness, he became fully aware. And in his awareness, only three facts came to him, flashing like hideous pink and blue neon signs: he was alone in a hospital room; he was alone because Karen was dead; and Karen was dead because Darius Williams had killed her.

Rage and sorrow clamored for positions in his head and heart. The image of Karen lying in their bed with her head drooping forward and her blood splattered on the bone-white wall flashed over and over in his mind as if lit by a strobe light. He wanted to push that image away, but at the same time he couldn't let it go.

David lifted his hand to touch his head. His wrist was wrapped with gauze and tape. His head was wrapped in bandages. He tapped the wrap just above his left temple, and a bolt of pain shot down the left side of his body. He hissed in a breath as he tried to will the pain back down to a dull roar.

He heard the screech of a chair sliding in the hall. He looked toward the door, and got a brief glimpse of a black cop looking at him. He was only there for a second, and then he rolled back around the corner and out of sight. David could hear him key some sort of radio, but couldn't hear what he was saying. He then caught a brief, staticky response that was also incomprehensible.

"Hey," he called, wincing as his head flared up with the effort of not just speaking, but of yelling.

There was no answer. He called again, and still got no answer. He felt around for some kind of button to call a nurse. He found it lying on a rolling table that was parked beside the bed. He reached for it slowly, and then keyed the button. He didn't know if he was supposed to speak or not. He chose not to.

About 20 seconds later, a middle-aged nurse bustled into the room. She was a large woman, and parts of her moved under her toothpaste-colored clothing where most people didn't have parts. She stopped on a dime at the edge of David's bed like the roadrunner stopping to nibble at a plate of food left by Wile E. Coyote.

The thought of Mr. Coyote struck a chord with David. Perhaps it was the concussion, perhaps it was the sorrow. Probably a little bit of both. Like most people, David had always rooted for the hapless Coyote. By definition, he could never win, or that would be the end of the cartoon. All the same, he never gave up. Until this moment, David had admired that. Now, lying in this bed, with no family left in the world and feeling like the fucking Roadrunner had tricked him into running off a cliff, David felt a kinship to the Coyote. For the first time, though, he saw the truth: The Coyote was a fool. If you can't win, quit. It's as simple as that.

David had a promise to keep. It was a promise he had made to himself while he was kneeling on his bathroom floor, handcuffed to the toilet. He would stay alive long enough to keep that promise. He would fulfill it at the soonest possible opportunity, and then he would quit. He couldn't win, he saw that as clearly as he saw the expansive nurse heaving in breaths in front of him. And if you couldn't win, then why continue to play the game?

With this thought, David's rage died out like a match that had burned all the way to the end. All that was left was a thin, black hole in his heart.

"Mr. McGuire, I'm Nurse Sampson. How are you feeling?" said the large woman.

David thought this was probably the stupidest question he had ever heard. He had no energy to do anything but answer the most basic part of the question, though. "My head hurts," he said absently.

"I'll get you something for the pain. Can I get you anything else?"

"Water."

"OK. I'll be right back," she said.

David watched her go indifferently. His eyes stayed on the door while she was gone, and absolutely nothing crossed his mind until she returned. When she did, she gave him a small paper cup with two mocha-colored horse pills in it, and a glass of water.

"Don't drink too quickly, Mr. McGuire. You've got a fairly serious concussion, and you'll be prone to vomit if you swallow too much."

"OK."

As if she didn't trust him to follow her orders, Nurse Sampson stayed to watch as David swallowed first one pill and then the other, each with only one swallow of water.

Satisfied, she said, "I'm going to go get the doctor. It'll be just a moment."

David didn't answer. He turned his head toward the window and looked out. He must have been fairly high up in the building, because from his angle all he could see was the gray October sky.

The doctor came in a few minutes later. He walked to David's bedside and stood over him. David didn't turn to look at him.

"Um, Mr. McGuire," said the doctor.

"David," David mumbled.

"OK, David. I'm Dr. Zomchek. Do you remember what happened?"

"Unfortunately," David replied in a flat, emotionless whisper.

"First, let me say I'm very sorry for your loss. It's a terrible tragedy."

David turned to look at the doctor, but didn't answer.

"Uh, the police will be here any minute to discuss the, uh, events of last night. I would like to explain your medical condition if that's OK."

"Sure."

"You were struck twice in the head with a blunt object. Once above your left temple and once at the base of your skull above your neck. Your skull is fractured in both places, but not seriously. Both injuries will heal on their own. Of course you have a concussion as well. You will likely experience headaches for the next week or so, as well as dizziness and possibly vomiting. I will write you a prescription to keep the pain down. Be careful not to get addicted to the pills. If you can avoid taking them, please do so, and try to completely stop as soon as you can."

"OK."

"Um, that's about it. You're going to be just fine. In fact, I'm guessing we'll be able to release you tomorrow."

There was an awkward silence. The doctor was happy to hear another voice behind him break it.

"Doctor, is he awake?" asked Detective Seamus Molloy.

"Yes, please come in detective. David, I'll excuse myself now, but if you need anything at all, just ring."

"Thank you," he said quietly.

The doctor and detective gave each other a look as they passed that basically said, "poor bastard." Seamus then stepped to the place beside the bed most recently occupied by Dr. Zomcheck.

"Hello Mr. McGuire. My name is Seamus Molloy. I'm a detective with the South San Francisco Police Department. How are you feeling?"

"Wonderful," David replied.

"I'm sorry, that was a stupid question. Mr. McGuire, may I ask you a few questions about what happened last night?"

"Sure, and call me David."

"OK, David. First of all, are you able to remember anything about what happened?"

"Yes. I remember that son of a bitch Darius shooting my fiancée in the head. She's dead, by the way, right? No one has come out and said it."

"Yes, David, I'm sorry to say that she is."

"So what's going to happen to him?"

"You're referring to Darius Williams?"

"Yeah, him."

"Well, David, let me tell you what has transpired so far this morning. The four boys were brought in to the police station and held separately for questioning. The other three had identical stories and have admitted to everything. That is, that they broke into your house and assaulted both you and your fiancée. They admit restraining you and her. Then they all say that Mr. Williams took a gun that Mr. McNamara had and, after a struggle, shot and killed her."

"What does he say?" David asked.

"Mr. Williams is, at least on the surface, in a state of shock. He hasn't spoken a word. However, he has been able to nod assent or shake his head 'no.' When asked if he is responsible for your fiancee's death, he has nodded 'yes.' He also seems to indicate through the same means that the story the other boys tell is true."

"OK, so it sounds like everyone agrees. Does that mean they'll all plead guilty?"

"More than likely. The other three boys are from extremely wealthy families, and they will have the best lawyers available. They will be charged with murder, but my guess is they'll be able to plea out of that since they didn't pull the trigger. Mr. Williams, however, has a court-appointed attorney and seems to be admitting to the murder. It's hard to say what he'll do."

"So why do you need to talk to me?"

"Procedure, for one. You're an eye-witness and I certainly need to interview you. Beyond that, though, I have a feeling that there is more to this than meets the eye. I'm hoping you can either corroborate the current evidence or give me a clue as to what I might be missing."

"OK, what do you want to know, Detective Molloy?" David sighed.

"Please, call me Seamus. Now, why don't you start by telling me what you remember?"

"I heard a noise and went to sit up when they hit me here," he said, pointing to his left temple, "I think it was with a baseball bat."

"It was," Seamus confirmed.

"They drug me to the bathroom and hit me again back here on the way," he said, now indicating his other wound, "I guess then they cuffed me to the toilet. I tried to get out and help her, but I couldn't..." David's eyes filled with tears as he said this. There was a flicker of anger in his voice, but it quickly retreated and was replaced by anguish.

"I was in and out of consciousness. I remember Darius getting up on the bed to...to rape her. Then one of the others tried to but Darius didn't want him to. Darius had a crush on Karen, you see. I don't know if anyone told you that yet, but it came to light this past weekend and when she told him nothing could happen, he freaked out and didn't come to school for a few days. She hadn't seen him since."

"The other boys had mentioned that, yes," Seamus said, "At least the part about the crush. They didn't know or didn't mention that it had just come out."

"Anyway, Karen kicked this other guy in the..." again, harsh tears came to David's eyes. One escaped from each eye and cut two slick lines down David's pale face. "...in the, you know, groin area. Next thing I knew that one and Darius were fighting for something, which I can now assume was the gun. I kind of blacked out for a second, but I came out of it when the gun went off. Then when I saw Karen…that was it. I woke up here."

"Do you have any idea why the other three would be there?" Seamus asked.

"I guess because Karen was going to get them suspended from football. She took a lot of shit from them and also the headmaster. Something about how the "Old Boys," the donors and alumni, wouldn't take too kindly to her screwing up the football season."

"Hmmm. That is the reason they give me as well. Is there anything else you can remember or that you can think of that might help?"

David thought for awhile, turning to look out the window as he did so. After a moment, he turned and said, "I can't think of anything."

"OK, well, that pretty much jives with what the boys say. If you think of anything else, please give me a call," Seamus said, producing a business card with his home and cellular telephone numbers hand-written on the back. "Any time of the day or night is OK. I hope that I won't have to bother you again, but it's possible that I might. Do you mind if I contact you if I have any other questions?"

"That's fine," David said.

"And, David, I'm truly sorry for your loss," Seamus said.

David turned his head toward Seamus, managed a feeble smile, and then turned his head back to the window.

Without another word, Seamus left the room.

29

"Hello, Jack," said Congressman Walter McNamara, standing up and holding out a hand.

"Walter," said John A. "Jack" Strauss, the District Attorney.

"Let me do the introductions," Walter said, and then proceeded to introduce the DA to Barry Weinstein, Ishiro Nakimura, Walter's son, his son's attorney, and the other men's sons and attorneys. The ten of them shook hands all around and then sat down at a large conference table.

"Jack, I'll be frank," Walter said, "The boys have put us all in a real pickle. Believe me, they will all be sorry in more ways than one. However, I can assure you that none of them had any intention of having that young woman die. It was admittedly stupid of John to bring the gun at all, but it was clearly the other boy who used it. Is he talking yet, by the way?"

"Not yet," said Jack.

"Well, that says guilt if I ever heard it. At any rate, you are obviously in as tough a position as we are. None of us want to see our boys' lives ruined by this, but each of us has our own careers and reputations to think of as well. Yourself included. We realize that it would be politically and potentially financially hazardous for each of us if the public isn't satisfied with the outcome. You and I both have the upcoming elections to think of, and Barry and Ishiro have their businesses and shareholders. Clearly we have to play this properly."

Jack Strauss was very aware of everything just said. He was aware that his job was on the line in more ways than one. The judge couldn't give them any slack, so clearly the pressure was going to come down on him to determine what was going to happen with the rich pukes. And he could feel that said pressure was about to be brought to bear.

When Jack said nothing, Walter continued, "Well, Jack, we have all discussed this with our attorneys, and we feel that the following scenario would fly. The boys will plead guilty to all of the crimes on the table other than the murder, of course. They will also testify if necessary in the other boy's trial that the murder was truly a crime of passion and that John actually tried to stop the crime. That done, you should have no problem keeping the trial in the juvenile system, would you agree?"

Jack nodded.

"Good. Now, the boys will need to do some time to avoid the appearance of impropriety by anyone. My feeling is that one to three year sentences in the juvenile system with probation and community service to follow should satisfy the public. Of course it's very likely that they could be out in six months or so, but that won't be your concern, will it? As long as the public sees them going away, they won't care too much about when they get out."

"What about the other boy? This can't happen in a vacuum, you know," said Jack.

"Very astute. Now, I think the key is that he can't be tried as an adult and end up with the death penalty or 25 to life. Jesse Jackson would be out here in a heartbeat claiming racial injustice. If he is tried as an adult, then the African-American community would want to see our boys in the same boat. So, we need to make sure that the transfer hearing sees him stay in juvenile court. As part of the deal to stay in juvenile court, he could plead guilty to murder two and you could give him the maximum. I think Judge Connors will be happy to have this whole case plead out so he doesn't end up under the microscope as well."

"I'm sure you're right. However, I don't think keeping Mr. Williams in juvenile court will be as easy as you may think," said Jack.

"Jack, I'm as aware of the factors they look at as you. Our attorneys have been over them and would be glad to talk to you about it in a moment. I honestly think that if you decide not to push too hard for adult court, that he can stay in juvy," said Walter.

"If he had one of your attorneys, I would agree with you. But this court-appointed guy isn't going to be able to pull it off," Jack said.

"You let me worry about his attorney," Walter said.

"What do you mean?" asked Jack.

"Better if you don't know. Listen. The only thing that could derail us is some sort of impassioned appeal from her family. Do you think you can keep that to a minimum?"

Jack thought for a moment. "Listen, all of you. First of all, the way this conversation went doesn't leave the room. I'm supposed to be the one making the offers here. Second, I'm not making any guarantees about anything. However, I can see how what you are suggesting would be best for all parties concerned, and I will work toward that end."

"Jack, we understand that nothing is a slam dunk, but if you can pull this off as I've suggested, you can be certain you will have the gratitude of all three families," Walter said.

Jack stood up and was followed half a beat later by the others in the room. Hands were again shaken all around, and then he turned and left the room to set the wheels of justice in motion.

30

Congressman Walter McNamara was no fool. He was a political genius and was widely thought to be a likely candidate for Senator the next time one of the seats in California was up. Beyond that, who knew? The plan he and the others had cooked up was falling into place perfectly. As predicted, the only possible obstacle was the transfer hearing for Darius Williams.

Only a few weeks after Karen's murder, David sat next to Karen's family at that very hearing.

Darius sat stoically about ten feet away from them, staring at his hands. Darius was flanked by Jillian Stern, one of the state's premier defense attorneys. She was well known for riding in to the rescue of the less fortunate members of society, but only when they found themselves embroiled in high-profile cases. While on the surface she had taken the case pro-bono, she was, in fact, being handsomely compensated under the table by some very wealthy but unnamed benefactors.

Ms. Stern had an iron-clad argument against each of the factors which would determine whether Darius would be transferred to adult court. This, she argued, was not pre-meditated in any way. Darius was a boy who had been in love with an older woman, and he was under the influence of cocaine given him by the other boys prior to entering the home. He didn't know what he was doing, and in fact the gun went off accidentally. There wasn't even demonstrable intent. And, according to two psychologists she produced, the accident had caused him so much anguish that he hadn't been able to speak since that night. Clearly, this crime did not merit the transfer of this young boy, who had no previous criminal record, to adult court.

By the time the court was ready to hear from the victim's family, it seemed a foregone conclusion that Darius would stay in juvenile court.

District Attorney Strauss had discussed all aspects of the case at length with David as well as Karen's family. Karen's parents and three brothers had come up from Los Angeles as soon as they were notified. All of them had taken the necessary leave from their jobs and school in order to stay in the Bay Area for the duration of the court proceedings. While on the surface all of them except Michael seemed to be supportive of him and truly concerned for his health and mental state, David felt that only Nicky's actions toward him were completely genuine. Her parents and older brother clearly held David responsible for Karen's death. Lurking beneath their smiles and embraces was blame. Blame that she lived up here with him. Blame that he couldn't stop the kids who had done it. Blame that she had ever met him. Michael, on the other hand, didn't seem to care either way. He wore a look that said he hated everyone, and that he hated David no worse now than he had before. At least he was honest.

Only Nicky, who had just begun his Senior year in high school, seemed to honestly care about David. David and Nicky had always gotten along well. Unlike anyone else in his family, Nicky had played football in high school. In fact, it looked very likely that he would be able to choose his college on a football scholarship. He attributed most of his success to years of lessons from David. Every time David and Karen had visited, David took time with Nicky in the back yard going over both the basics and the subtleties of the game they both loved. Like David, Nicky was a linebacker. Also like David, when he brought the lumber, opposing running backs felt it.

David appreciated Nicky's efforts, but he would be just as glad to see him go along with the rest of Karen's family. He had ice cream and pizza to eat, a beard to grow, TV to watch, and a couch to hold down. Nothing else in the world appealed to him right now, least of all worrying about his almost in-laws.

When the DA was explaining the transfer hearing to all of them the day before, David saw that he may have an opportunity to influence events in the ways he wished, both with regard to the Chavez's and Darius Williams.

"Now, if Mr. Williams is transferred to adult court, he'll very likely end up going to trial, but either way it's likely he'll do pretty serious time," said Jack Strauss after explaining the details of the transfer hearing to Karen's loved ones, "If he stays in juvenile court, he'll more than likely plead out and be out by the time he's 21."

"How do we make sure he goes to be tried as an adult?" asked Francisco Chavez, Karen's father.

"Well, I must be honest with you all. He has a very good chance of staying in juvenile court. There are a number of criteria that the judge will look at, and most if not all of them fall on his side. He is young, this is his first offense, it appears there was no premeditation, and so on. Now if any of you wishes to speak in the proceeding, you may, and that may sway the judge toward moving this to adult court," said the DA.

"Of course we will," said Francisco, "Should we all speak?"

"Well, I would say that David should certainly speak. For the family, it's often best if one member of the family, usually either the mother or father, reads a prepared statement followed by some impassioned remarks. However, you certainly can all speak if you prefer. It's really up to you."

Francisco and Kathryn Chavez looked at each other. Francisco saw the pain in his wife's eyes. He knew she was barely holding together, and decided on the spot that he would speak for all of them. "I think I'll just represent her family. David, you can speak too if you feel like you're up to it."

"I will," said David, resenting the implication that he was too weak to testify against his lover's killer, especially coming from her father. Wait until Mr. Chavez heard what David had to say in court.

"The court will now hear from the victim's family," said the judge.

Mr. Strauss turned toward Karen's loved ones and gave David a nod. He stood up, gave a tight-lipped smile to Karen's parents, and approached the podium in the middle of the courtroom.

"Your honor, I was there when Darius Williams killed Karen Chavez. I was in and out of consciousness while everything was going on, so I can't honestly say that I saw him do it, but in the end he was holding the gun. I know it wasn't his gun and he's just a kid who was confused by drugs and his crush on Karen, but that doesn't mean he should get away without being punished."

No one in the courtroom heard the end of that last sentence. When David referred to Darius as a confused kid, each person was visited by a visceral reaction. Francisco Chavez sucked in a breath and then scowled as if he had been struck. Kathryn's mouth dropped open. Michael actually sat up and took interest, allowing a hint of a smirk to creep into his countenance. Karen's other brothers stared at David with wide eyed astonishment. Ms. Stern fought to suppress a grin. District Attorney Strauss winced outwardly, while inside he breathed a secret sigh of relief. The judge sat back in his chair and raised an eyebrow. Only David and Darius remained as they were. Darius didn't lift his eyes from his hands. David continued with his statement as if nothing was out of the ordinary.

"Karen was the love of my life, your honor, and she was my best friend," David continued, showing very little emotion, "Even if he didn't mean to do it, I really think he deserves to be tried as an adult and be punished like he and those other kids punished me. Thank you."

David turned to sit down. He saw in Francisco's fuming glare that he had accomplished one of his goals, which was to get Karen's family out of his life. He already knew from the reaction of the judge and the attorneys that he had accomplished his real goal. He wanted Darius Williams to stay in juvenile court so he could get out sooner. David wanted to kill Darius himself. He could wait five or six years to do it, but he didn't think he could wait 25 to life. He could probably figure out a way to have him killed in prison, but then he wouldn't get the pleasure of seeing the look in his eyes as the light in them went out forever.

Francisco got up and gave an angry, distracted statement that included the inadvertent phrase, "murdering little bastard." David had called him a kid, and now he was "little" also. The result of this hearing was settled before the judge even spoke, and everyone knew it.

After the judge had confirmed that Darius would stay in the juvenile system and adjourned the hearing, David endured his final few moments as part of Karen's family.

"What the hell was that?" Francisco hissed at him through clenched teeth.

"I'm sorry, I...I didn't mean to say it that way," David said, trying to sound as much like a victim as possible. Doing so brought the bitter taste of bile into his throat, but this was the way to get it over with the quickest.

"Well, you just ensured Karen's killer a very happy 21st birthday," Francisco snapped.

"I'm really sorry," David repeated, this time looking at Karen's mother with his best sad-puppy eyes.

"You're sorry..." Francisco began again, but he was cut off in mid sentence by his youngest son.

"He said he was sorry dad, can you let it go?" Nicky said. He was only seventeen, but there was iron in his voice that made his father stop cold.

Karen's father turned toward her youngest brother slowly, like the turret of a tank turning toward its next target.

Before he could unload, however, Kathryn put her hand on his arm and said quietly, "That's enough, Francisco. What's done is done. Let's go."

Francisco looked first at her hand and then her face. Finally, with tears of pain and anger standing in his eyes, he shook off her hand and headed for the door, but not without a final look for David that said he had better not see him again.

Kathryn and Francisco Jr. turned solemnly to follow him. Michael did as well, smiling openly at the pain everyone else seemed to be feeling. Nicky was last. He looked at David, managed a smile, and lifted his hand just above his waist in a surreptitious gesture of farewell. David smiled back, and then watched him go.

With this hearing out of the way, everything else was just a formality. Within two weeks, the Chavez family returned to their homes in Southern

California and tried to resume their lives without their daughter and sister. Since Karen and David were never married, Karen went with them to be buried near their home. John McNamara, Doug Weinstein and Truman Nakimura went to a brand-new juvenile facility in Marin County to serve what would eventually be five-month sentences. Darius Williams went to a much older facility in the East Bay where he would stay until his 21st birthday, a day that would prove to be infinitely less happy than Francisco Chavez had predicted. And David McGuire, or at least the shell of the man who used to be David McGuire, went home to wait.

31

Two months later, Bartholomew "John" St. John, David's college roommate and best friend, walked up the umbilicus that connected a United Airlines plane to the main terminal of San Francisco International Airport. He had come to Karen's funeral, and when he left he was extremely worried about David's mental state. He had decided that David needed him here for Christmas much more than his family needed him to fly with them to England, so he caught a flight from LaGuardia to San Francisco on December 23, taking a half day off from his father's advertising firm to do so. David didn't know he was coming. He hoped that the surprise visit would cheer his old friend during what must be a brutally painful time for him.

John took a cab to David's place. He had the driver stop around the corner so he wouldn't be seen, and then he walked as quickly as he could to David's front door. Once there, he rang the bell. When David didn't answer after a few minutes, he rang the bell again. At his feet, he noticed four rolled up newspapers. Perhaps David was gone. He cupped his hands around his eyes and pressed his face to the glass to the right of the door. It was late, and there were no lights on outside or in. With his face against the window, however, he could see the blue flicker of a television against the walls of the living room, which he knew from past visits to be through the door to the right of the foyer. He looked at his watch. 10:30…maybe David had fallen asleep watching TV.

John debated whether to walk down the hill and find a hotel or to persist and possibly wake David. He looked at the floor of the front porch again, and the four newspapers there combined with the house lit only by the TV gave him an uneasy feeling. He had an image of David lying dead on the couch with an empty bottle of sleeping pills lying on the floor next to him. He decided to persist with the doorbell.

On the fourth ring, he saw a shadowy figure stumble from the door of the living room. He turned toward the door, and John backed away from the window and stood in front of the door.

"It's late! What do you want?" said a husky, muffled voice from behind the door.

"David, it's John! Open the door!" John called back.

There was a pregnant pause, and then the porch light popped to life. After another pause of almost thirty seconds, John heard the clack of the deadbolt and then the rusty squeak of the latch. Finally, the door opened inward.

John barely recognized the figure standing in the darkness in front of him. The man was wearing a terry cloth bathrobe that was probably a light blue but appeared to be gray in the darkness of the inner hall. It was wide open, exposing a loose pair of boxer shorts and a substantial belly. John wanted to stare at that belly, but he didn't allow himself to do so. Instead, he looked up to his old friend's face. What he saw there was just as unnerving. David apparently hadn't shaven or had a haircut since the funeral. Both his hair and his beard were unkempt. The hair on his face grew up very high on his cheeks, and grew all the way down his neck to his collar. The most disturbing aspect of his friend's appearance, however, lay between the rumpled hair and heavy beard. There, a pair of glassy, lifeless eyes regarded John without emotion or even recognition. John found that he couldn't look at those eyes for more than a moment without glancing away.

David had always taken care of his appearance. John had never seen him with more than a few extra pounds around his middle, nor had he ever seen him with facial hair. The decline of his friend over the last two months was astounding, and frightening. John wondered how far David really was from ending his life, and realized that had he come any later he may have been too late.

"Hey John," David finally said, "What're you doing here?"

"I came to spend Christmas with my old buddy. I hope that's OK...I thought you might want a little company."

"Oh, OK. Uh, did you want to stay here?"

"If that's not a problem. Hey, it's getting cold out here, can I come in?"

"Oh...yeah...sorry," David said, stepping back to let John in. His words seemed to come with great effort, as if he hadn't spoken to anyone in weeks.

John stepped in, and David shut the door behind him. He turned back toward John without bothering to lock the deadbolt.

"You got a hug for me?" John asked.

Without speaking, David took a step forward and leaned into John, accepting his embrace. The smell of body odor and alcohol hung around David like a cloak. John broke the embrace and stepped back, although he kept a hand on David for an extra moment to make sure he wasn't going to fall.

"Uh, the place...it's kind of a mess. You should have called and I would have cleaned up a little," David said, almost as if speaking to himself.

"That's alright, my place isn't that hot eith..."

John's reply was cut off when David flipped on the light in the living room. It looked like six fraternities had joined together and spent a month in David's living room. There were pizza boxes, Chinese food takeout boxes, candy bar wrappers, empty potato chip bags, and half-gallon ice cream containers spread throughout the room. There were also two liter bottles of soda, and a tremendous number of beer cans and empty bottles of Jack Daniels. There were empty and half-empty cups on and under the coffee table at the center of the room. The coffee table, in fact, appeared to be the epicenter of a junk food explosion. There was only about two square inches of wood visible on the table itself. The floor under the table was similarly cluttered. Beyond that, the formerly tan carpet was littered with garbage in increasingly thinner amounts all the way to the walls.

"I told you," said David with just a hint of his old sarcasm. John heard it, and it simultaneously gave him hope and made him intensely sad for what had happened to his friend.

"Jesus man. Did the maid take the week off?" John said, trying to draw the old David out of the protective shell he had apparently built for himself.

David just smiled a little, and then shuffled through the garbage to the couch. There, he picked up the TV remote control and clicked it off. He then stood up and looked around as if he hadn't previously noticed how disgusting his living room had become.

"Listen John, I appreciate that you came, but I'm sure you're tired. It's later for you, right?"

Unfortunately, John thought David really wasn't sure whether it was later or earlier for John after having traveled from New York. To the old David, adding three hours to the time in California to get to New York time would be as natural as tying his shoes. Again, John felt a pang of sorrow in his stomach.

When John didn't say anything, David answered his own question. "Right…it's like 2 a.m. for you. Why don't you go in the guest room and crash and I'll clean up? I think Karen…," he paused, appearing to gather himself to finish, "…kept sheets in the closet. The sofa in there pulls out. It's through the kitchen."

John looked in the direction of David's outstretched arm. Through the foyer was the kitchen, and John saw that it looked much as the living room did. He also saw that David wasn't far enough gone that he wasn't embarrassed, and that the best thing would be for him to comply and not offer to help.

"I am pretty shot," John winced internally at his choice of words, and then continued quickly in the hope David didn't notice, "I'll just go in there and crash. Tomorrow we can catch up and figure out what we're going to do while I'm here."

"OK," David said, still staring stupidly at the cataclysm that was his living room.

"It's good to see you, David," John said.

"You too. I'll see you in the morning," David replied, clearly wanting John to move along.

John did. He moved carefully through the kitchen, not pausing to look around. He opened the door to the guest room, flipped on the light switch, and dropped his bags in the corner. This room had been untouched by David's hurricane of self-destruction. The neat sanity of the room seemed almost surreal after what John had just seen. Only a dead plant on the windowsill provided a reminder of the extraordinary pall of sorrow that hung over this house.

John heard David open the door to the garage. A few minutes later, he heard the sound of a garbage bag being shaken open. Then he heard the sounds of David's cleanup effort. John flipped off the light and lay down on the couch, wondering how he was going to sleep with all that racket. After a few moments, however, he began to notice the startling regularity of the noises from the other room. David was picking up bags, bottles, cans and containers and then dropping them in the bag with an eerie cadence. It was as if a robot were cleaning up the room. John began to count the seconds in between deposits to the garbage bag. One Mississippi, Two Mississippi, One Mississippi, Two Mississippi, One Mississippi, Two Mississippi. After only about a minute, a physically and emotionally exhausted John drifted off to sleep to the rhythm of his best friend's madness.

32

John woke up at 6:00 the next morning, which was 9:00 his time. He took a piss in the adjoining guest bathroom, brushed his teeth, and then slowly opened the door that led into the kitchen.

The garbage on the floors and counter was gone. Both were still covered with various colored stains, but at least the room looked sane. John ventured into the living room and found the same situation. He looked around the carpet and wondered if it could ever be fully clean. Some of the stains were so dark that they looked like they were still fresh. John suspected that when they occurred, David didn't even bother to try to soak up the excess liquid and therefore minimize the damage.

David was splayed on the couch. His mouth was wide open and great, sickly snoring poured from it. He had the look of a man who was profoundly and fundamentally exhausted. In his hand he still held the remote control. He had apparently fallen asleep before using it to turn off the TV, because it was still on across the room.

John was reminded of the Billy Joel song "Sleeping With the Television On," a song that was, by Mr. Joel's own account, about loneliness. That David was in pain was obvious, but people can get over pain. Loneliness, however, is insidious. It's like cancer, and before you know you've got it, it's too late. John was again struck by how completely David had fallen, and by how difficult it would be for him to recover. Not only had he tragically lost everyone he loved, he really had no one here to help him through it.

John tiptoed across the room and pressed the power button on the TV. He then reversed his steps and returned to the kitchen, leaving David to sleep. He checked the refrigerator for something to eat, and found only alcohol and condiments. In one of the cabinets he found four boxes of cereal. He checked each, and finally decided that the Golden Grahams were the least stale. Not trusting the bowls in David's cabinets, he ate a few dry handfuls straight from the box.

John considered going to pick up what should be the fifth paper on David's front porch, but sometime last night David had armed the alarm. Not knowing the code, John was under house arrest until David woke up. He decided that the best use of his time would be to work on the kitchen.

He found plenty of Comet, Windex, Lysol, and other cleaning products under the sink. What he didn't find was any sort of towel, sponge or rag. The paper towel dispenser held only a blank cardboard tube. None of the cabinets seemed to hold a replacement roll.

He remembered from a previous visit that there was a linen closet upstairs, so he headed up the stairs to see if it contained anything he could use.

John made a U-turn at the top of the stairs and walked down the hall to the linen closet. As he approached, he saw that the door to David and Karen's bedroom stood open. He slowed his gait, suddenly unsure whether David would approve of his being up here. The linen closet was on the opposite side of the hall and slightly before the bedroom door. He decided he would go quickly to the closet and take care not to look in the bedroom. For all he knew, the mess in there would be the same as downstairs...or worse. He imagined the same conglomeration of food and beverage containers as downstairs, with two months of clothing mixed in for good measure. David had worked very hard cleaning up downstairs, and he didn't want him to know John had seen the mess up here as well.

John did as he planned, turning toward the closet door before he really needed to in order to keep his back to the open bedroom door. John turned the knob and swung the door wide. He looked straight ahead into the closet, but something from the corner of his eye pulled his head to the right. On the inside of the door was a full-length mirror, and the reflection in that mirror almost stopped his heart.

He was looking directly into the open bedroom door. What he saw there wasn't a litter of pizza boxes and flannel shirts. In fact, the room was fairly tidy. Tidy, that is, except for the rusty brown splatter on the wall behind the bed.

John spun around, unable to breathe. His heart had started up again, and was beating a mile a minute. He knew he was looking at the bed Karen lay in when she was shot in the head, and he was looking at it as it had been left when someone took the body away. David had never cleaned it up. Jesus, no wonder he was so fucked up. Had he been in and out of this room with that on the wall, or had he avoided it all together?

John dragged his eyes away from the room...forced himself to turn around, grab a handful of white towels off the shelf of the linen closet, and quietly close the door. Without looking back, John crept back down the stairs, looking (and feeling) like he had committed a crime.

Dazed, John set about cleaning the kitchen. He moved about slowly and deliberately, trying to concentrate on what he was doing and not the carnage upstairs. At times he was able to put it out of his mind. At others, he found himself staring straight ahead, swirling a towel around the same spot on the counter or floor for several minutes without much vigor.

By 10:00, John pretty much had the kitchen spick and span, in spite of his distraction. As he was wiping down the inside of the sink, he felt a hand on his shoulder. He jumped and let out a little yelp like a puppy that has had his tail stepped on.

"Sorry man," said David, "I didn't mean to scare you."

"That's OK," said John. It was all he could manage for the moment, as his heart was again up in the 200 beats per minute range. The way David had been able to sneak up on him combined with the vacant yet somehow predatory look in his eyes made John uneasy. OK, uneasy was an understatement. He was downright scared.

"You didn't have to do this, I was going to get to it today," said David.

"I...didn't know the code or I would've gone to get breakfast," said John, "I didn't have much else to do, so I thought I'd...earn my keep."

"Breakfast sounds pretty good," said David, "You wanna go down to Denny's and get some pancakes?"

David's face had seemed to brighten a little bit as he said this. John had no idea why, but he was greatly relieved to see a bit of normalcy return to David's eyes. They were still tired...exhausted, actually. But thirty seconds earlier they had also looked like the eyes of a madman. He would take exhausted over mad any day, especially if he was going to be sleeping in the same house as David.

David went in the other room and came back wearing a Stanford sweatshirt and cap. He was still wearing the same gray sweatshorts he had on when John arrived, and he had pulled on some ratty old tennis shoes with no socks. He punched in the code on the alarm system and opened the door to the garage. John was careful to note the code in case he might need it at a later date.

"You wanna drive?" David asked, holding the keys out to John.

"Sure," John said with carefully guarded relief. Getting in a car with David behind the wheel didn't seem like a health choice his doctor would approve of.

The only conversation in the car was David's direction to the restaurant. When they arrived, they were likewise silent, each staring intently at the pictures of pancakes, ham, bacon, eggs, and hashbrowns in various combinations around the edges of the Denny's menu.

After they had ordered, John decided he had to fire an attempt at conversation across David's bow and see where it took them.

"So how's work?" John said.

"I haven't been back yet," David said. He said this rather matter of factly, which John took as a good sign. He hadn't been offended by the question at least, and he seemed open to further conversation.

"Are you going to?" John asked.

"I don't know," David replied, "I liked it there, but I don't know if I can concentrate right now. I don't really need the money either. You know I

144

was doing OK before because of my…inheritance. Well, Karen's family sued the families of the rich kids who…you know. Wrongful death, like OJ. Their lawyer said they would have a better case if I was involved, but I think it was just a bullshit ploy to drive up the settlement so he could get a bigger payday. It worked, anyway. They paid me $2 million and her family $10 million to make it go away."

"Wow," John said.

"Yeah," David agreed.

"So how was it talking to the Chavez's?" John asked. David had mentioned to him when he was out for the funeral what had happened at the transfer hearing.

"I didn't. Everything went through the lawyer. Now that it's settled, I don't think I'll be hearing from them again. I'm responsible for their daughter's death, you know."

John didn't reply to this. They sat in uncomfortable silence for a few moments, and then they were saved by the bell when the waitress arrived with their food. They alternated salting and peppering their omelettes, and then David began to shake an impossible amount of Tabasco on his. John watched uncomfortably as his Denver omelette slowly changed from yellow to orange-red.

"Hey, you remember the time we put Tabasco in Derek's tuna sandwich?" David asked. There was a flicker in his eye as he said it, one that remotely reminded John of the old David. The friend he knew before lightning struck…twice.

John did remember, and they were soon reminiscing in a manner very much akin to two old friends who hadn't seen each other in some time. By the end of breakfast, David had actually cracked a smile several times, and even chuckled under his breath once or twice.

Sensing that he had a chance to really get David turned around, John suggested that they go to San Francisco for the day and hang out like when they were in college. He felt that the worst thing they could do was go back to the cave that David had locked himself in for the past two months. A cave, as it turned out, that still held not only Karen's ghost, but also her blood.

The two friends spent the entire day in San Francisco. They had lunch at a burrito place in the Mission where they used to eat once or twice a month. Maria was still behind the counter, and she recognized John. She asked about David, and then did a fairly bad job at hiding her surprise that the fat, bearded man in front of her was actually David himself. John looked at David, who seemed to make a mental note and then shake off her reaction. John wasn't sure, but he thought that was good.

They knocked around Chinatown and the wharf, finally ending up on Columbus Street for an Italian dinner. At times David was quiet, staring into space and seeming to be thinking...or remembering...intensely. At other times, he was right with John, talking, asking questions and, more and more frequently, laughing.

As they drove back toward David's house in the dark, David said, "So you went upstairs, huh?"

John, who was driving, almost drove into the concrete median. He corrected the car and concentrated on driving straight while he figured out how to answer.

"It's OK," David said, saving his friend the trouble, "I know I seem pretty out of it, but I knew there were no towels downstairs. I may look like a bum, but I still have a few marbles rolling around in the old noggin."

John was silent, still unsure of what to say.

David went on, this time asking a question in a cold, quiet voice, almost inaudible over the road noise. "Did you look in the bedroom?"

John hesitated, and then decided only the truth would work. "Yeah," he said, even more quietly than David's question had been, "I'm sorry...the mirror...I...had no idea."

They were both silent for some time. Then David spoke again, "I haven't been up there since it happened. Couldn't face it. I know I have to eventually, but…"

"I could take care of it for you," John said.

David was silent for a long time. Out of the corner of his eye, John saw tears on David's face glistening in the glow of the oncoming headlights. John put his right hand on David's shoulder. David emitted a single sob, and then brought himself immediately back under control. He wiped his nose and eyes with his sweatshirt, and then reached across his body to pat John's hand with his own right hand.

"Thanks for coming, John, I really owe you," David whispered.

"No problem. That's what friends are for."

"If you start singing, I'll kick your ass," David said.

John smiled, and they drove the rest of the way to David's house in silence.

33

The next day was Christmas, and neither of them had a present for the other. Nor did either intend to go to church or cook a grand Christmas feast. It was decided in a very vague and general conversation that David was going to drive to the coast while John stayed at the house. Both men understood what John would be doing while David was gone, although neither wanted to mention the task by name.

As soon as David was gone, John set about the grim task for which he had volunteered. He scrubbed every surface in both the master bedroom and bath that had even a hint of dried blood. What he couldn't remove with the extensive array of cleaning products Karen had stocked under the sink, he either threw away or painted over with a can of interior latex paint he found in the garage.

He also found both a vacuum and a carpet steam cleaner when he was looking for sheets to remake David's bed. While there was no blood on the carpet, he still gave it the full treatment out of a sense of duty.

When he was finished upstairs, he moved down to the living room. While not as grisly, the living room was much more difficult to clean than the bedroom. The stains on the carpet and furniture upholstery were dark and deep-set. Still, he first scrubbed each of them by hand with 409 Carpet and then followed up with the steam cleaner.

As he was backing out of the living room into the hall, he was again startled by David's hand on his shoulder. He jumped and sucked in his breath, then flipped off the steam cleaner and turned to face David. He was pleased to see that, while he certainly wasn't exhibiting the joy of the season, David at least looked to have his emotions and sanity under control.

"It looks great, John. Thanks a lot for doing this," David said.

"No problem. How was the coast?"

"Good," David said. He paused and seemed to picture it again in his head while he gathered his next thought. "It's...well...the waves just keep coming. They never stop, never pause. They're relentless. All the people in the world could nuke each other and the waves would keep coming. It's kind of hard to get your head around it."

"Yeah, I guess so," John agreed.

David stared into space for awhile, and then seemed to shake off whatever held his attention. "Anyway, you ever been to Pacifica?" he asked.

"No, but I've heard of it. That's where those houses fell off the cliff into the ocean, right?"

"That's it. I hadn't been there either. Everyone goes to Half Moon Bay and Santa Cruz, but no one ever goes to Pacifica. There's not much of a beach there, but the town's sort of interesting. It reminds me a little of South Dakota. It's kind of like the whole Bay Area is jamming ahead toward the twenty-first century and Pacifica is content just to stay right where it is. It's kind of like the town the rest of the Bay Area forgot."

"I guess so. I've never heard of anyone going there. Everyone I know went to Ocean Beach in The City or to Santa Cruz. No one ever went to Pacifica." John said.

"That's the point. Unless you live there, there's no reason to go. I kind of like that idea. I saw some houses for sale on the hillside overlooking the ocean. I think I might go check them out. I don't think it's too good for my health to stay here much longer."

"I'll go with you tomorrow if you want," John said.

"They'll think you're my lover," David said, smiling.

"Wouldn't be the first time," John said with a chuckle.

"Should we wear matching clothes?" David asked.

"Now you're pushing it," John said.

The next day, David contacted a realtor based in Pacifica. By that afternoon, they were looking at houses. The following day, they found one that David thought was perfect. It was on a cliff, but across the shallow bay from the main part of town. The house was about 50 feet from the edge of the cliff. At the bottom of the precipice was a beach that provided a 100-

foot buffer between the surf and the base of the cliff. A past owner had built a set of narrow wooden steps that crisscrossed their way from the back of the house down to the beach.

On the opposite side of the house was a wooded hillside. The road leading to the house wound for about a mile from Highway 1 and Pacifica proper. It only passed two other houses on the way and then terminated in his driveway. There were other houses above this one, but they were concealed by the trees and the undulations of the hillside. No house on this hillside was visible from anywhere on the half acre of property that surrounded the house. In the same vein, none of the neighbors could see this house.

The house itself was good sized but certainly not a mansion. It was 2800 square feet and a single story. The interior was nice, but not spectacular. There were three bedrooms, three bathrooms, a kitchen, a den and a three-car garage. The entire rear of the house, however, was occupied by a living room that was beyond spectacular…it was breathtaking.

The living room was about 40 feet wide and 20 feet deep. There were vaulted ceilings that were 8 feet high on each side and 12 feet in the middle. There was a large brick fireplace on the south wall. The floors were a honey-colored hardwood. All of this was nice, but it was the back wall of the room, the back wall of the house, the wall that faced west, faced the ocean, faced the sunset, that took one's breath away. The wall was actually glass from floor to ceiling. The view, therefore, was a sweeping panorama of the Pacific Ocean.

French Doors in the middle of the wall opened onto a raised wooden patio. Standing on the north end of the patio, one could see back across the shallow bay to the town of Pacifica, and then up the coast to the Marin Headlands. From the south end, one could look along the rocky coastline stretching away toward Half Moon Bay. One could hear the relentless waves and the call of seagulls, and smell the salty sea air.

Standing on the patio, looking raptly out over the gray ocean at the point where it met the gray, winter sky, David said to the realtor, "Offer them what they're asking. Get on the phone and do it right now, please."

"David, it's one-point-one million dollars. Can you get financing for that amount?"

"Don't worry, I'll pay cash. Just do it, and get the fastest escrow you can."

The realtor smiled and stepped back inside to use the phone.

"You sure you don't want to think about it or see some more houses? It is a lot of money." John said.

"Nope. This is the one. Besides, the way real-estate on the peninsula has run up over the past few years, I'll get almost that for my house," David replied, never taking his eyes off the ocean.

While John agreed that this was a beautiful house in a beautiful location, he was worried about David's motivation for buying it. He had a flash in his mind of David sleeping with the television on. He heard Billy Joel in his head again, singing the chorus over and over. John was worried that David was isolating himself, and that he was doing it on purpose. David had made a good deal of progress while John had been here, but he was leaving on redeye back to New York the next night, and he was very afraid that his friend would backslide into the alcohol-soaked and junk-food-choked existence he had led before John arrived.

"OK, we're in business," the realtor said as he stepped back out on the porch, "If you would like, we can go back to my office right now and put together the formal offer. If everything goes as planned, we can get you in here in 30 days or so."

"Great," David said, "Let's go."

34

The next evening, David and John backed out of the driveway and headed for the airport. They had spent the day in the city again, very much the same as the first day of John's visit. John had meant to talk to David about his concerns for his well-being, but the time hadn't seemed right at any time that day. Now he had only 15 minutes before they would arrive at the airport. He cursed himself for procrastinating so long. He didn't know how long it would take, but he didn't think this was a conversation that should be short-changed.

John had thought about how he was going to bring it up, and he couldn't think of a good way to do it. At this moment, something popped into his head and he went with it...he didn't have time to think about it any more.

"David, do you know the poem "Do Not Go Gently Into That Good Night?" John asked.

"Of course. Dylan Thomas, why?"

"Do you know why he wrote it?"

"He wrote it when his dad was dying," David said, becoming suspicious of his friend's intentions.

"I think it...kind of applies to you," John said.

"In case you forgot, JOHN, my DAD is already DEAD!" David snapped.

"I didn't say it applies to your dad, David," John said quietly, "I'm worried about you. Before I got here, you seemed to be just wasting away...letting your life slip through your fingers. You're a lot better now, but I'm really worried you're going to go back to the way you were now that I'm leaving."

"Oh, so I'm supposed to 'Rage, rage against the dying of the light?' First of all, I'm embarrassed that you had to bring up that poem. Everyone knows that one. An educated man like you could have come up with something from Keats or Burns or Browning and then I might listen. Second...fuck you! First my parents were murdered and then my girlfriend was murdered and I couldn't do anything to stop either one of them. Now I've got no one I love, and you're going to sit there and tell me to be cheery? I goddamn deserve to sit around in my underwear and watch TV and drink myself to death if I want to."

John let him vent and waited for the pause that said he was done. Then he said, "David, that's what I'm talking about. Hate me for saying it if you want, but you are going to slowly kill yourself if you don't get your shit together pretty soon. The new house is a start, but you picked the most remote goddamn house in the Bay Area. You can't isolate yourself from the world. You need to go back to work and make some friends or get some hobbies or something. If you just sit there watching TV and drinking for the next six months, the loneliness is going to get to you, and you're going to end up drowning in a pool of your own vomit. The only difference is that, if you do it in that house, no one is going to find you for a hell of a long time. Is that what you want?"

David just sat in the driver's seat, fuming. He was fuming both at his friend's audacity in giving him advice on a subject he knew nothing about, and at the fact that John was more than likely 100% correct. He wasn't going to give him the satisfaction, though. David McGuire didn't need anyone to tell him what to do or how to live his life. As far as David was concerned, John could go fuck himself.

"Go fuck yourself," David said in a much quieter voice.

"Look, David. I guess you're mad that I brought this up, but I know you know I'm right. You can choose to live or die, and it's really none of my business, except that you're my best friend and I love you, believe it or not. And whether you love me or hate me, you need to know that if you ever need anything, you can just call me and I'll be there to talk to you or if you really need me to, I'll get on the first plane and come out here. But I can't live your life for you or force you to get better. Trite as it may be, you really do have to either choose to die, or choose to Rage against the death that's waiting for you."

David was silent as he took the exit off the 101 freeway that would take them to the San Francisco International Airport. He was silent as he negotiated the snarl of traffic leading to the white zone, which was for immediate loading and unloading of passengers only. He swung into an open spot against the curve, applied the brake, and sat looking straight ahead. His body language clearly indicated that John should exit immediately. John took his cue and did so.

John got out of the passenger door and opened the door to the back seat. He pulled out one suitcase and his carry-on. He shut the door, paused a moment, and then started for the terminal.

As John turned his back, David felt a tremendous wave of loneliness sweep over him. Tears stung his eyes as he watched the only friend he had in the world turn his back on him. David opened his door, got out, and called to John over the top of the Honda.

"John!" he said sharply in order to be heard over the din of the traffic.

John turned around and looked at him. David didn't know what he wanted to say, but he knew whatever it was, it wasn't something to yell across the top of his car. He slammed his door and stepped quickly around to the curb. John took a few steps forward to meet him.

"Thanks a lot for coming," David said, "I'm sorry if I've been an asshole…just now or before. It's just…hard."

"Don't sweat it. You just take care of yourself," John said.

"You gonna move this?" a large man in a blue uniform and orange vest boomed in their direction as he stood by David's car.

"Yeah, one minute," David called over his shoulder.

"That's all you got," the man replied.

"Thanks for everything," David repeated.

"No problem. Any time, really," John replied.

David stepped forward and embraced his friend. Tears dropped from his eyes onto John's coat. To both of their surprise, John returned the favor.

They separated, wiped their eyes as unobtrusively as they could, and then started to back away from each other—John toward the terminal and David toward his car.

"Have a good flight," David said.

"I will. I'll call you when I get in," John replied.

"OK. See ya," David said.

"See ya," John agreed.

David got into his empty car and drove back to his empty house. It had been good having John here, but now that he was gone, he felt lonelier than ever. Before he had been here, David had drunk himself into a bittersweet oblivion. Now that he was sober, in a clean and empty house that had been so recently occupied by another living soul, he finally began to have a true appreciation for how alone he really was. It wasn't just that he didn't have Karen...he didn't have anyone.

David looked around. What was there to do? He went to the refrigerator. He looked around for something to eat. Nothing appealed to him. He grabbed a Corona from the top shelf and walked to the drawer to find the bottle opener. He flipped off the cap and let it fall to the floor. As he took his first swig, he walked across the room and picked up his cordless phone. He touched speed dial number 4. After two rings, a man on the other end picked up and said, "Giovanni's."

"Hey Tony, it's David McGuire," David said, his voice low and flat.

"David! You been on vacation? We were getting worried," replied Tony.

"No, just had company. Can you send over the usual?" David asked.

"Sure thing. Be there in 20 minutes. Put it on your card?"

"Yep. Thanks Tony."

"No problem buddy. Good to have you back."

"Bye," David said, and clicked off the phone.

David walked into the living room, flopped on the newly cleaned couch, and picked up the remote control. He clicked on the TV, and flipped to the channels that usually have movies. All three of them were playing commercials. He looked down and saw that he had finished his beer. He set it on the coffee table and got up to go to the kitchen. He returned with two more Coronas and the bottle opener.

Channel 44 was back from commercial. It was a Charles Bronson flick...one of the Death Wishes. Probably not even Charlie Bronson himself could identify which it was, David thought. It didn't really matter; the plot would be the same. Someone messed with Mr. Bronson's family or one of his friends, and now he was going to go kill them all.

David flipped to channel 45. It was one of the Batman movies. David let his remote hand drop on his knee and took another drink of his beer. The Batman series had so much potential, big stars, big budget, and they were based on one of the coolest comic book characters ever. The coolest thing about Batman, David thought, is that he's just a man. He's rich and big, but he doesn't have any super powers. In theory, anyone could be Batman. Anyway, it was too bad the scripts to the Batman movies all sucked.

The doorbell rang. David shuffled to the door and opened it.

"Hey Freddy," David said.

"Hey Mr. McGuire. Here's your pizza," replied the scrawny, pimply-faced young man on his doorstep.

"That was fast. Make sure Tony puts ten bucks on my card for you, OK Freddy? And for the last time, call me David."

"Thanks a lot...David," replied Freddy, throwing in a Butthead-like laugh for good measure.

"Have a good night, Freddy," David said as he shut the door.

He walked the pizza into the living room. He sat down and opened his third beer, downed about half, and flipped open the pizza box. Batman had lulled into some lovey-dovey crap, so he flipped back to Bronson. Not much action there either.

He finished his third beer, and went back to the kitchen for numbers four and five. He got back just in time to see Bronson rack a bullet into the chamber of his Magnum. "They're all going to pay for what they did...all of them," he said stonily.

"That's right, all of them," David said as he raised Corona number four to his lips.

Before it got to its destination, though, David's beer hand stopped. He stared directly at the TV, but he was no longer seeing what was going on therein. "All of them," he repeated, almost robotically, as he lowered his beer and set it on the table.

With the same hand, he picked up the remote control and flipped back to Channel 45. There, Batman was kicking the crap out of some scumbags on a rooftop in Gotham. David watched for a minute and then said, in the same deliberate voice, "Batman was just a man."

Somewhere, deep in his mind, something began to stir. In his eyes, where just a moment before only the reflection of his television was visible, a dangerous red light flickered to life.

"All of them," he repeated, and smiled.

35

A little over four years later, in January of 2003, Ed Schindler was holding court at a table in a shitty little bar in Sacramento called "The Red Rooster." Ed had been a bully in elementary, middle and high school, and he was a bully now. He was a union lathe operator in a factory that made wood moulding. He wasn't the union steward, but he was the one they called on to terrorize the members that had the nerve to speak against union leadership or to vandalize the scabs' cars during various strikes and lockouts.

"Well if he fuckin' shows up here, he'll be sorry, I'll tell you that much," Ed said between swallows of beer.

"What do you mean? No one's been able to stand up to him yet," said Larry Fellows, one of the people who Ed drug along in his wake.

Ed was the kind of person who didn't have any real friends. He collected weaker souls and then used his bulky frame and boorish personality to dominate them and force his opinions upon them. None of the four men who sat at his table really wanted to be there...at least not with him. He had mandated that they meet him for a drink after work, however, and none of them had the balls to say 'no.' To say 'no' to Ed was to be classified a pussy. Such a classification would lead to exile from Ed's immediate circle, which could then lead to harassment on the job and beyond. The last person to refuse to play Ed's game ended up cutting off the tip of his finger on the bandsaw. No one could really blame Ed, because he didn't directly cause the accident. It was strange, however, that every board that went through the soon to be nine fingered man's station that day had a sizeable knot in it. It was only a matter of time before one caught and pulled the board forward along with the unfortunate operator's hand.

"I'll show you what I mean," Ed said, sliding his chair away from the table. He pulled aside his denim jacket to show the butt of a 9mm Beretta sticking out of his pants. "If that motherfucker shows his face around here, or whatever it is he has that passes for a face, I'm going to put a bullet in him and call it self-defense."

"Damn, Ed, where'd you get that?" asked Larry.

"Had it for awhile. Been itching to use it too. Tell you the truth, I hope he's outside waitin' for us right now." Ed said.

"I don't know if we're drunk enough. He only takes on drunks, they say," Larry said.

"Well, we better get on it, then. Hey Nancy, get your pretty little ass over here with another pitcher!" Ed shouted at the harried barmaid. When she arrived with the new pitcher, he said, "You better not let us get dry again, sweetheart, unless you want us to take our business elsewhere."

She did, more than anything in the world, want Ed Schindler to take his business elsewhere. Her boss, the owner, would think differently, however, so she just smiled and turned to head back to the bar. Ed was a scumbag, but he and his buddies spent almost $500 a week in here between them. He knew his place was safe. As such, she wasn't remotely surprised when Ed swatted her hard on her left ass cheek.

"You better move that thing, honey. It's payday and everyone in here is thirsty," Ed called after her as she scurried away.

Three hours later, at 12:45 a.m., Nancy turned down the shit-kicking jukebox and yelled "Last Call!"

"You guys want another?" Ed asked.

"Naw, I had enough," Larry said, "Gotta keep my legs under me if we're gonna take on the Reaper tonight."

"I heard that," Ed said, "I'm gonna take a piss, then we'll all head over to Denny's. I'm fuckin' hungry."

They all stifled their moans and strained to keep from rolling their eyes. Three of them had bitches for wives that would already be fuming at the hour. The other still lived with his parents, and he was going to get another lecture about responsibility from his old man because of this. Still, the kind of trouble they were all in for at home was better than what would await them if they refused Ed's invitation for a very early breakfast.

"We'll wait for you in the parking lot," Larry said.

Ed banged through the door into the Rooster's filthy men's john. He pushed past a few of the other patrons and commandeered a urinal. It was clogged with cigarette butts and pubic hair. The urine stood right at the rim of the porcelain. Ed didn't want to risk splashing the piss of a hundred other assholes on his boots, so he turned about 20 degrees to the left and pissed on the wall. When he was done, he zipped up and left the room without a glance toward the vomit-covered sink.

Ed pushed out into the damp January night. He pulled his coat around him and turned to head around the back of the building where he and the others were parked. He could hear the four assholes singing something that sounded like Margaritaville, only it sounded like it was being sung on a bus to the Retard Olympics.

Ed smiled at the thought of a bunch of retards singing Jimmy Buffett, and quickened his pace so that he could poke fun at the morons before they stopped singing. Before he reached the back edge of the building, however, the song ended abruptly. It was replaced by yells of surprise and a scream like that of a little girl.

Ed broke into a run and rounded the back corner of the building in time to see a big son of a bitch in a black overcoat and black hood land a crushing overhand right to Larry's jaw. Larry's head snapped to the left, and the rest of his body followed it around as he slumped forward onto the hood of Ed's Valiant. Larry's limp body then slid to the ground like an empty laundry sack.

Bill Wilson and Jake Alexander were statues, staring at the big bastard like they'd seen a ghost. His back was to Ed, but he knew from the accounts in the papers over the last year or so what Bill and Jake were looking at. It was the Reaper, goddammit, his wish had come true.

Ed reached for his gun as Jim Swenson, apparently the only one of the three who still possessed a pair of balls, stepped forward and looped a roundhouse toward the guy's head. The man who Ed had decided must be the one the papers called the Grim Reaper spun his left arm around Jim's right, bringing Jim's into his armpit like it belonged to a rag doll. He then grabbed the front of Jim's jacket and lifted him briefly in the air. When Jim's feet were about a foot off the ground, the Reaper pushed forward and down with such force that Jim's feet flew up in the air as his upper body was propelled savagely into the asphalt of the parking lot. Even from halfway across the Rooster's back lot, Ed could hear the sickening crunch.

Bill and Jake were apparently galvanized by what had happened to Jim. But instead of attacking, they both turned to run. Before either of them could take a step in the opposite direction, the Reaper was on them. He grabbed them both by the back of their jackets, paused a moment for their forward momentum to cease, and then slammed the two of them together like a naughty child pounding erasers on the playground after school. Both sets of legs buckled, and the Reaper pulled back on both of their jackets in a ferocious rowing motion. The two men flew backwards, landing square on their backs between Jim and Larry.

Ed was now upon the scene. He had the gun out and had it pointed squarely at the back of the marauder who had apparently knocked his four companions out cold in the time it took Ed to run fifty feet across the parking lot.

"You picked the wrong bar tonight, motherfucker!" Ed yelled in the most menacing voice he could muster. The four men lying motionless on the ground next to him took away a lot of his steam, however. This guy had taken care of four beefy guys who handled hundreds of pounds of wood every day without even breaking a sweat. In fact, Ed couldn't even see the guy breathing. Shouldn't he at least be out of breath? What the fuck was this guy?

The man in the black overcoat spun around and strode toward Ed. When Ed got his first look at the Reaper's face, even though he knew what to expect, he froze. Peering out at him from inside the black hood was the face of death. The papers said he painted his face to look like a skull. They were right, but they never mentioned the teeth, or the eyes. His mouth was open wide, and he had three-quarter inch long fangs hanging down on both sides of his mouth like icicles, except instead of water dripping from the end of these, there was blood. His (It's?) entire mouth was full of blood. A small amount had escaped from the right corner, and it was now making its way toward his chin.

The mouth was bad enough, but the eyes were the worst. They were blood red, and they glowed with flat murder.

Ed couldn't breathe. His heart was pounding so hard it felt like it was going to blow a hole in his chest. His knees felt like water, and the beer that had made it to his bladder since he pissed five minutes ago began to escape into his faded jeans.

The Reaper was 20 feet away when Ed had called out his threat, a threat that now seemed as serious as one a little girl might make. He hadn't run toward Ed, he just walked quickly, but his walk was menacing. By the time Ed gained control of himself, the monster was only five feet away and coming fast.

Ed still had the gun out in front of him. He raised it slightly and squeezed the trigger. He had fired it at the range a thousand times, but right now his control was weak. The gun jerked up and to the right as it fired point blank into the Reaper's chest.

Ed had a momentary feeling of triumph as the bullet slammed into the Reaper, causing him to pivot his trunk violently to the left. His left foot stepped back to brace him, and then the triumph drained out of Ed as the Reaper brought his body back to square, opened his mouth with a hiss of pain and anger, and closed the last five feet between him and Ed.

Ed, who had dropped his gun hand to his side after firing, tried to bring it up to fire again, but the monster in front of him swept his left hand down and away from his body, grasping Ed's right wrist and twisting it quickly so that his palm was facing the sky. He then brought his right palm upward like a rocket into Ed's exposed elbow, first hyperextending it and then shattering it so that Ed's arm was bent 45 degrees opposite of how God had intended for it to move. The gun fell harmlessly from Ed's hand and clattered to the pavement.

Ed uttered the first true scream of his life, both from the pain of his mangled arm and from the certainty that this devil would kill him. "Please...no..." he screamed as his bowels emptied into his filthy jockey shorts.

The Reaper brought his right hand back across, smashing the back of his fist into Ed's temple. Something on the back of his wrist opened up a wide gash from Ed's temple to his mouth. Ed's scream ended abruptly, and he joined his four friends in the land of Nod.

The man in the black overcoat, who was still holding Ed's right wrist, used it to drag him over by his four companions. He stooped over the fallen men, moving quickly from one to the other, pausing for just a moment at each and appearing to rustle in their back pockets. Finally, he stepped back over to where Ed's gun had fallen. He picked it up, looked around, and disappeared into the bushes on the hillside behind the Red Rooster.

36

David McGuire ran up the hill behind the Red Rooster. He moved more slowly than usual, as the drunk's bullet had knocked the wind out of him. When the battle rage was still upon him, he hadn't noticed. Now that it was residing, his breathing came hard, as if an icy knife were stabbing at his lungs each time he sucked in the cold air.

His right hand alternated between pumping the air in the runner's motion and pressing against the left side of his chest where the bullet struck. The area was numb right now, but he had a feeling that the pain would come soon. He wasn't sure if the bullet had broken the skin in spite of the protection he wore, but he wasn't going to check now and risk leaving any blood that may or may not be there for the cops to find.

David heard shouts from behind him as other patrons of the piece of shit bar happened upon his latest victims. They were undoubtedly summoned by the gunshot.

David looked down momentarily at the gun in his left hand. How the fuck had he gotten into this? He had just about gotten himself killed by some drunken vigilante who had probably been carrying the gun just for him. Well, not really for David, it would actually have been meant for the Reaper. *It takes a vigilante to stop a vigilante,* he thought, without much humor.

David saftied the weapon and dropped it into one of the big pockets in his overcoat. He then placed both thumbs under his chin and rolled them upward, catching the edge of the thin, rubbery mask he wore. He peeled it upward, wadded it up, and stuffed it into the same pocket as the gun.

Before he crested the hill, David reached into another pocket to pull out a small, plastic case with a lid and four slots. He dislodged the false fangs he wore on his upper canine teeth and dropped them in one of the slots. He then popped out first one red contact and then the other, placing them carefully in the slots already filled with Saline Solution. He replaced the lid and returned the container to its place in his overcoat.

This done, he paused at the crest of the hill and looked for either people or vehicles on the road. He saw neither, so he walked out normally with the disguise he had worn on his face just minutes before all but gone. The only evidence remaining was some residual redness in his mouth from the fake blood capsule he had bitten before attacking the drunks. He lowered his head, hunched up his shoulders, and walked across the street at the top of the hill and then down a dark residential street. Halfway down the block, he turned into an alley overgrown with weeds and barren blackberry bushes.

His good old Honda was there waiting for him. He opened the rear door on the passenger side. It remained dark, as he had switched off the dome light long ago. He grasped the seatbelt clasp that stuck out from the middle of the back seat. When he pulled, the entire bench pulled up on several hinges attached on the front of the seat. Beneath the seat was a fairly large open compartment. He had put his mechanical engineering degree to good use when he designed this hiding place. It was big enough for his body if necessary, but for now it would just hold his gear.

David slid off his overcoat, hooded sweatshirt and several other items that had been attached to his person in various places. These were the things that would, if they were spotted by some nosy cop, get him in serious shit. All of the items went under the back seat. Once unloaded, he pushed the seat back to its normal position and leaned down on it until he heard the confirming clank of the lock engaging.

David picked up a light jacket from the seat and slipped it on over his white T-shirt. He then carefully closed the rear door and opened the driver's door. Once in, he picked up a bottle of water. He took a slug, swished it around in his mouth violently to clear out any remaining trace of fake blood, and then swallowed the resulting sweet, pink concoction.

David keyed the car into life and crept out of the alley onto the main road. Once there, he flipped on his headlights and picked up speed. When he was a few miles away, he reached under his seat and flipped a switch he had installed at the same time he modified the back seat. He could hear the mechanical whir as the motors attached to his front and rear license plate holders began to turn. When he was parked, the license plates on his car had been those of another blue Honda Accord he had found in the parking lot of an apartment complex in Menlo Park. He had quietly removed those plates, and then installed them on a rotating contraption he had built some time ago. Now that he had flipped the switch, his real license plates would be displayed. If he should be stopped for any reason now, his plates would match his driver's license and registration, but they would definitely not match the plates of the similar car that had been parked near the scene of the Reaper's latest attack, just in case anyone had noticed the unfamiliar car and taken down the numbers.

David sped up the onramp to Interstate 5 and merged into traffic. He kept up with the other cars…no faster, no slower. When he had reached his cruising speed, he reached down and pushed in the tape that stuck out of his cassette player. "Black Celebration" by Depeche Mode had been his album of choice since he began his mini-crusade. He had never been a big fan, but Karen loved Depeche Mode, and he thought both the title and lyrics of this particular selection were quite appropriate. He thought of it as a tribute to Karen, although he was not yet lost enough to really believe that it was a tribute she would appreciate. He let David Gahan's melancholy vocals wash over him as the broken lines on the freeway sped by on either side.

After about fifteen minutes, the pain in his chest began to flare up. He slid his right hand under his shirt, feeling for the sticky liquid that would indicate the skin was broken. He didn't feel any, but he was able to discern a harsh, raised welt on the lower part of his left pectoral muscle. He pressed on the spot, first gently and then a little harder. When he did, he felt a sharp pain beneath the surface. Broken rib, he surmised. Shit.

"What the fuck are you doing?" he said. He was speaking to himself, to the car, to the road, to the night.

When the car, road and night were silent, he answered himself, "I don't think you even know what you're doing, do you, you stupid fuck? You almost got yourself killed by a couple of drunks. What for? It's time to quit all this bullshit. These fucks are arming themselves, and that's not what you wanted, was it?"

David watched the road go by for a few moments, and then he mumbled, "Talking to yourself again, great."

He switched to a mental conversation with himself, no longer saying the words out loud but thinking them. *What good is this doing? Is it helping Karen? Is it helping you? I don't think so. What was the point of all this? It was to prepare yourself to kill five people before you could be caught. Now what? You think you're some kind of superhero? You think you're Batman? Well guess what, you were wrong all those years ago. He's not just a man...he's just a cartoon. Cartoons don't get killed by bullets...they get killed by the writers sometimes, but not by bullets. You, however, are going to run out of luck and get yourself killed. "Batman is just a man!" Ha...what a naïve jackass you were.*

37

"Batman is just a man," David said aloud as he watched the caped crusader deal with more of Gotham's scum. "Just a man," he repeated over and over again, staring at a place just above and to the left of the TV.

He looked at the coffee table where the beers and pizza sat. Suddenly he wasn't hungry for either. He flipped back to Bronson for a moment, smiled, and flipped off the TV. He kicked his feet up on the couch, put his hands behind his head, and stared up into the darkness. The purple afterglow of the television swam around on the ceiling, drifting to the left and the right as David's eyes chased after it. For the first time since Karen was killed, he was fully awake. Long dormant parts of his mind were waking up…doors closed since just after his parents were killed were opening and letting red light pour in. David basked in his newfound awareness, letting it wash over him; letting it carry him out to sea.

David woke up the next morning, shaved off his horrible beard, showered, ate a piece of toast, got in his car and headed to work.

After clearing security, he walked directly into Mr. Greer's office, shutting the door behind him. "Hey boss," he said softly.

"David?" Mr. Greer said, standing up so quickly that his straightening knees pushed his chair back all the way to the wall.

"Do I still have a job?" David asked.

"Well, yes, of course. I told you that you would. How are you doing?" Mr. Greer stammered.

"Please don't ask. In fact, if you could somehow get the word out that I'd rather nobody ask about what happened, or how I am, I'd appreciate it. Answering the question 'How are you doing?' fifteen times isn't something I really feel like doing. I'll be alright, and I'm ready to come back. That's all I can say," David said.

"No problem, David," Mr. Greer said, clearly uncomfortable and unsure of what to say next.

"So do you want to bring me up to speed?" David asked.

"Sure," Mr. Greer said. Then, shedding some of his uncertainty over how to treat David, he said, "Sure. Let's walk down to the lab while we talk. Do you need to stop by your desk?"

"Yeah. Why don't I do that and meet you in the lab in five minutes?" David said. That would give Mr. Greer time to prep the rest of the team, and they both knew that was the purpose of David's detour to his desk.

Five minutes later, David slid his mag card through the reader to the right of the lab door. There was a mechanical clank, and he pushed his way in. Mr. Greer was waiting there for him.

They walked through a bank of cubicles. As they did, David nodded to several of his co-workers, all of them clearly as unsure of what to say as Mr. Greer was. On the other side, they stopped at another security door. This time Mr. Greer slid his card and held the door for David to walk into the lab.

The lab was long and narrow, like a railroad car. It was dimly lit by overhead fluorescent lighting. The wall to their left was lined with various types of workstations: some dark, some harshly lit by incandescent lamps, some empty, some cluttered with fabrics and plastics, and several with bottles and vials of various colored liquids.

Along the wall to their right, it appeared there had been a mass execution. Ten humanoid figures hung stiffly in the shadows. Upon closer examination, one could see that these were actually what appeared to be crash test dummies. About half wore what appeared to be bulky, black nylon jumpsuits. The other half were clad only in their birthday suits.

Mr. Greer led David silently through the gloomy tunnel into the test facility, which was affectionately referred to by the team as "the range." Before sliding his mag card, he pushed the talk button on an intercom mounted to the left of the door.

"We're coming in, Carl," he said.

"OK boss," squawked a high-pitched voice from the box.

Mr. Greer slid his card and again held the door for David. David walked into what appeared to be a compact gun range. There were four stalls, each with a weapon mounted on a frame and aiming down the range toward four more of the crash test dummies. Each of these wore one of the black jumpsuits.

David and Mr. Greer walked past the .45 caliber pistol, the 357 Magnum, the M-16 and finally the AK-47 assault rifle. Past these was another small room.

"Take a break, Carl," said Mr. Greer.

"Sure thing, boss. Hey David, welcome back," said Carl. Carl was one of those geeky genius types who was too unaware of social norms to feel self-conscious around David. Unfortunately for the project team, Carl was more geek than genius, and they were still coming up short on some of their key objectives.

"Hey Carl," David said with a nod.

Carl picked up a black thermos and some sort of science magazine and headed for the door that led back into the main lab.

When he was gone, Mr. Greer said, "OK, David. I brought you back here because I wanted some privacy and I think better here. This is where the rubber meets the road, I guess. Anyway, I know you're intimately familiar with our objectives, but it will help me to explain where we stand if I repeat them."

"OK."

"I only say that because I don't…that is…I didn't want you to…"

"I got it. Go ahead, boss."

"OK. Well, as you know, the military wants body armor that is more lightweight and flexible than the standard Kevlar vests, and is inexpensive enough that they can buy the suits in massive quantities. While they haven't given us specifics on the weight, thickness or flexibility, they have said generally that soldiers should be able to perform all of their standard duties with such armor underneath their fatigues. Also, they specify that the armor should stop bullets fired from various common weapons at a distance of 20 yards. Now, by 'stop bullets,' they say that they just want to preserve life. Therefore, welts, contusions or broken bones are acceptable, but they don't want to see any damage to internal organs. Finally, if possible, they want coverage of the extremities and head in addition to the torso, although they don't want that to delay the delivery of the torso-only model if it comes to that."

"Right," David said impatiently, indicating that he hadn't needed the refresher course.

Sensing David's frustration, Mr. Greer said, "I know you know this. Just bear with me, David. Now, your idea to sandwich a gel between two thin layers of Kevlar is still the direction we're pursuing. Our testing has continued to show that that configuration can easily put us in range as far as weight and flexibility. So that leaves protection and cost, and I'm afraid those two are going to be at odds. At any rate, right now we're using two layers of three-sixteenths inch Kevlar. Any more than that and it seems to get unwieldy, not to mention the added cost. Any less and we start to lose integrity. So, that leaves the gel, and that's where we're running into trouble. Carl, god love him, is trying but he's just not you. I'm afraid we haven't really made much progress since you were last here. Carl's had a few formulas he's tried, but he can't get the reaction time down as low as we need it. Not only that, he's using agents that will drive the cost out of range. In other words, David, your return couldn't have come at a better time."

"Thanks," David said, "Now tell me this. Is Carl using heat or compression to cause the gel to harden?"

"Heat, like we were when you left, why?"

"Well, I've had some time to think, as you know. Now we still want the gel to harden within 10 milliseconds of impact, right?"

"Right."

"And we're still going for a protective radius of one-half inch from the point where the projectile strikes the armor, right?"

"Yep."

"OK. I've got an idea. We still have to use the heat from the bullet as a catalyst for the reaction, but I think we can use a fibrous material in the gel to get it to harden faster at the point of impact. Not only that, I think it will be stronger at that point and thus provide more protection. The only problem is I think the spot will stay solid after it is struck, whereas with the heat strategy it would liquefy again when it cools down."

"Why is that?" Mr. Greer asked.

"Well, you know what happens when you bend a coat hanger, right? When you bend it in one place you can never get it straight again? That's because the fibers in that spot are broken and bound up and it becomes very difficult to get them to bend in the opposite direction."

"Of course. Sorry, I should've known that right away. Once the fibers in the gel are bound up, they won't go back to normal. Well, if it's a circle with a half-inch radius, I don't think it'll be a deal-breaker. Having one or two or several of those hardened circles won't make it any less protective, just a little less flexible, depending on the point of impact."

"Right. Hey, knowing the military, they'll issue a new one every time a suit takes even one hit. That'll increase sales, you know?"

"I missed you, David," Mr. Greer said, favoring David with a warm smile.

"Thanks," David said shortly, trying to get Mr. Greer to drop any sort of emotional moment he may want to foist on David. "Now, if it's OK with you, I'd like to pursue this idea."

"Absolutely…at this point it certainly can't hurt," said Mr. Greer, getting back to business.

"Good. Now, as far as the cost versus protection element, here's what I want to do. Let me go balls out on five or six prototypes. Make them as strong and fast-acting as I possibly can. Then we'll see both how expensive it is and how much protection it will provide. If it's too expensive, we can back off and make some sacrifices in its strength, or we can try another route.

But if the cost looks good, then we'll know we've got the best protection we can provide and we can go forward with a prototype to the military."

"That sounds good. Keep me in the loop as far as your development costs, of course, but consider this the go ahead to do just as you've said," said Mr. Greer, clearly starting to get excited about what David was saying.

"OK. I'll get started right now. Thanks, Mr. Greer."

"Thank you, David. It really is good to have you back."

David smiled and picked up a notebook that had been sitting on the desk. Taking his cue, Mr. Greer also smiled, and then turned and headed back out to the lab.

38

By the time David moved into his new home in Pacifica a month later, he had dropped 20 pounds, bringing him in at a still rather portly 270. He had joined a gym in Daly City that was equidistant from his house and work. He had begun hitting it twice a day, before and after work and also on weekends, on January 2, 1999, the same day as all of the other folks who had made a New Year's resolution to get into shape before summer. By the end of January, David was one of about 10% of those people still attending regularly. By the end of February, he may have been the only one who had started at the beginning of the year and was still going twice a day.

It wasn't really a fair contest for the others, though. There are many motivating factors in the world. Different people are motivated by different things, but, on the whole, those motivating factors fall into a fairly predictable scale. On the weak side of the scale are health, well-being, and charity. In the middle are appearance, money, power and love. The strongest motivators, however, are hate, spite, and, the strongest motivator of all, revenge.

In David's mind, everything that had ever mattered to him had been stolen by two men: Darius Williams and LaShon Jackson. He found that, although his hatred for those two could have filled Stanford Stadium, he had enough hate left over for the other three kids that brought the gun and gave Darius the drugs to have plans for them as well.

When he reached 250 pounds in mid-March, he joined a martial arts studio he found in Colma, a city aptly known as the "City of the Dead" because of its many cemeteries. The studio was near the top of the coastal mountains that separated the peninsula from the ocean, and it was buried in a deep layer of fog most of the time. It was in the back corner of a mini-mall attached to a Safeway. It was almost completely hidden, as if it didn't want to be seen. David had found the name in the phone book and it had sounded so strange he just had to stop by before he chose another dojo. If the name hadn't been so unique, David would have taken one look at the humble exterior and kept right on going to the next one on his list.

The name of the dojo was Chen-Cervantes Martial Arts. Martial arts studios with Asian names were common, especially on the northern part of the peninsula. Martial arts studios with an Asian name hyphenated with a Spanish name were not.

David parked his car in an open slot and walked up to the studio door, hands in pockets and shoulders hunched up to keep the fog from slipping its chilly fingers around his neck. He pushed a shoulder against the glass door and stepped into the austere entryway. There was another door directly across from the one he had just entered. This one was wooden with a small window in the center. Just under the window was a cardboard sign on a piece of string, hanging from a single hook. The sign said, "CLASS IN SESSION. YOU MAY OBSERVE BUT DO NOT ENTER."

David looked around. There were a few 8 ½" x 11" colored pieces of paper tacked to the wood paneled walls advertising various upcoming martial arts events. Otherwise, there was nothing in the entryway; not even a bench or chair in which to sit. This was the least inviting room David had ever been in. It was almost as if they were trying to drive people away instead of inviting them to join.

Undeterred, David stepped across the milky gray tile and stooped a little bit to peer into the window. On the other side was a square room. The walls were a completely unblemished white, save another wooden door directly across from him. There were no posters, no slogans, no mirrors, no distractions. The floor was covered by black mats, except for a two-foot ring around the outside walls of exposed hardwood.

In the center of the room, a half-dozen men knelt in a semi-circle facing two other men. All of them wore identical black pants and thick, white martial arts gis. Their attention was fixed on the older of the two, who was kneeling behind the younger. He had his hands on the younger man's shoulders as he spoke to the rest of the group. After about five minutes, he brought his left knee up so that he could lean forward against the younger man. He wrapped his right arm around the young man's neck and brought his left hand up against his right fist. He said something else, and the younger man raised his right hand to the side so that it was parallel to the floor. Then the older man bore down. The actual amount of movement was very slight, but his body language and the look on his face, as well as the face of the young man and those of the others, had changed from rapt attention to something much more primal.

David saw that the others were counting out loud, and he began counting too. When he hit six, the young man's arm dropped to the mat. His eyes rolled back and his legs began to spasm. The older man released the hold (David had watched enough pro-wrestling as a kid to already be thinking of it as a "sleeper") and held the young man's shivering body upright. He then struck the young man on the right shoulder blade with an open palm and uttered a short kiyei in his ear. The young man's eyes opened and his legs slowly stopped quivering. The older man massaged the young man's shoulders and arms vigorously, but with a gentleness that suggested deep caring for the younger man's well-being. As he did so, he continued speaking to the others, obviously finishing the lesson.

David would visit no other studios. He wanted to know what that man was saying. He saw that everyone in the room was wearing a black belt, so he wasn't sure how long it would be before he earned the right to witness the same lesson. He did know, however, that it didn't matter how long it took, this was where he was going to learn martial arts.

After class, he waited in the lobby for someone to emerge. The students did first, passing him without so much as a glance or a word. Some time later, the young man who had been the subject of the day's lesson opened the wooden door. He looked at David and asked, "Can I help you?"

"Yes. I would like to join," David said.

"You sure about that?" asked the young man.

"Yes, I am. I watched the class and I want to learn what you were doing."

"Do you even know what class that was?"

"No."

"Jesus. Listen big boy, this studio isn't some boutique you can join and take a shit on like all the others. If you join, you are making a commitment to Master Cervantes and Master Chen, as well as your classmates. We aren't here to get in shape, and I think that's what you're really looking for, isn't it?"

The young man looked at David's still-expansive gut, and blew air out of his nose in disgust. David's cheeks flushed, and his eyes blazed. When the young man looked back at David's face, he realized he had made one of the more serious misjudgments of his life. The molten, murderous gleam in David's eyes fixed upon his own, and, in spite of the extensive martial arts knowledge he possessed, he found that he was afraid of the big man in front of him.

He dropped his bag and stepped back, holding his hands up in front of him. "Hey, I'm sorry, I didn't mean anything by that. Let me go get Master Cervantes."

The young man disappeared back into the studio. David felt his rage begin to subside, but he didn't allow it all to go. Something in his eyes had gotten the attention of the young man. He got the sense that getting into this group might be harder than just signing some waivers and writing a check. He thought he better keep some of the edge about him, enough, anyway, to get the attention of Master Cervantes, whoever he was.

The young man returned in a few minutes and said, "Come on back."

David followed him across the studio floor and through the door in the rear. They were in a narrow hallway that smelled of sweat and Icy Hot and discipline. They walked between two doors, one displaying a stick figure with legs, the other a stick figure wearing a dress. Beyond that were two more doors, one to the left and one to the right. At the end of the hall was a fire door that must have led outside.

The young man stopped outside of the door on the right and knocked. "Yes," came mildly through the door.

The young man turned the knob and pushed the door open. Inside was an office nearly as austere as the entryway. Sitting in a metal folding chair was the older man who had recently applied the sleeper better than Rowdy Roddy Piper or Chief Jay Strongbow ever had.

"Thank you Preston," the older man said.

The young man, Preston apparently, nodded and backed out the door, pulling it shut behind him and leaving David alone with the older man.

"My name is Master Diego Cervantes," he said with a slight Spanish accent, holding out his hand.

"David McGuire," David said, taking it.

"May I call you David?"

"Sure."

"It is tradition to address me as Master Cervantes and my colleague as Master Chen, in case you are wondering. It may sound a bit pretentious, it does to me, in fact, but respect is of utmost importance here. I hope you don't mind."

"Not at all."

"You may have gotten the impression from Preston that we don't welcome outsiders here. That is not far from the truth. Most of our students are recommended by other students. I don't remember the last time we accepted someone who walked in off the street, but something about you clearly struck a chord in Preston. It wasn't all positive either. Preston is one of our most senior students, and I've never seen him afraid of anything. He would never admit it to me, but I know he was afraid of you. I must admit, Preston's fear arose my curiosity. Otherwise, both of us would have asked you to keep looking."

"You see, David, Master Chen and I think of this as our family. Neither of us has any blood relatives, not in this country anyway. We are very careful of who we choose to join us. They say you can't choose your family.

Well, we are happily in the situation that we can, and we take the choice very, very seriously. If we accept you, and that is a big 'if', you will be joining that family, and you will be expected to act as such. Master Chen and I teach not only how to block and throw punches, but how martial arts can provide balance in your life. That may sound like something from the Karate Kid, but again, we take our lessons very seriously. We are as committed to improving the lives of our students as we would be to our own children."

"Now, David, I am going to ask you some questions. Depending on your answers, I may ask Master Chen to meet you. More than likely, though, I will thank you for your time and ask you to leave in the next few minutes. I hope you will understand."

"OK," David said, never taking his eyes off of Master Cervantes' own. He knew the older man would be looking for him to falter, to shrink away and head for the door. Whether or not he had the right answers, he wasn't going to give him the satisfaction of breaking him.

"Have you ever studied martial arts before," Master Cervantes asked.

"No."

"Why do you want to now?"

"I normally wouldn't tell this story to someone I just met. It's not my way. However, I can see that I have one chance with you to tell the truth. If I don't tell the truth, you'll know, and that will be it. And I don't want this to be it. I watched you put Preston out. That was something, but the way you woke him up was what impressed me. I could see how much you cared about him in your body language. Not only that, clearly he has a lot of trust in you to let you do that. I don't have a family either, and I what I saw in those few minutes showed me that you can provide that. I'm guessing your next question was going to be 'why here' or something like that. The reason I answered that first is to explain why I'm going to tell you what I'm about to tell you.

"Several years ago, my parents were killed by a drunk driver. They were the only family I had. My girlfriend, Karen, who was literally the best person who ever lived, helped me get over that. She and I were going to get married this spring. Last October, some of her students broke into our house and one of them shot her in the head while I was watching. She died on our bed while I was handcuffed to the toilet, helpless to do anything.

"Master Cervantes, I don't have anyone. Since she was killed, I've had all this rage inside me. The kids that did it are all locked up, and I've been consumed with the need for revenge. I have no family, and I have no outlet for my rage. I got up to almost 300 pounds anesthetizing myself with alcohol and food. Around Christmastime, I decided that I didn't want to die. I want to live, and I've lost a little over 40 pounds since the first of the year. But my rage and thoughts of revenge aren't going away. I hoped joining a gym and lifting weights would help, but it hasn't. I've heard martial arts can help you channel your aggression, as well as be an outlet. That's why I was interested in martial arts. I've been to some other places, but after what I saw and what you said, this is the only place for me."

So far, David had told the absolute truth, and he could see by the expression on Master Cervantes' face that he had a real shot with him. David thought that Master Cervantes was a man who was rarely caught by surprise. David's story and candor had done just that, and now that he had him reeling, it was time for David to go in for the kill. This would require David to tell his first lie, but now that he had Master Cervantes sucked in, he didn't think the older man would be able to tell.

"Master Cervantes, to be honest, right now I want to kill the kid who shot Karen. He gets out in a few years, and if I don't find a way to control what I'm feeling, I really feel I might try to do just that. I don't want to feel this way anymore, and I definitely don't want to feel this way for the next three years. I want to get on with my life...I want to get past all this. Most of all, I want to get this rage out of my system and stop obsessing about him. When he gets out, I want to be past it enough that I can just go on with my life and not think about the fact that he's getting on with his too, even though he took Karen's life."

Master Cervantes' expression hadn't changed, so David knew he had carried off the untruth at the end successfully. He sat quietly looking at David, cogitating over everything he had just heard.

Finally he spoke. "David, I must admit that your story isn't what I was expecting. I am normally a man in complete control of my emotions. Your story, and the openness and candor with which you have told it has moved me in a way I find both touching and intriguing. First of all, let me say that I am sorry for your loss. That one man can sustain so much and still want to go on is a testament to the human spirit. The fact that you are willing to admit the feelings you are having about those who have hurt you, I feel is a good first step. While I am moved to help you control these feelings and, as you say, get on with your life, I must tell you that I have a selfish motivation as well. That is, I am very curious as to whether I can help you or not, and as to whether you truly can shed this rage you are currently harboring. Right now, I sense, and I believe Preston sensed, you are a loaded weapon that could go off at any time. With all of Preston's training, I don't think he felt he could stop you if you attacked him. I'm not sure if he could have either. There is little in this world more dangerous than a man with nothing left to lose. Maybe it's my ego, or just morbid curiosity, but I don't think I could stand not knowing how you deal with this. I can tell you're a good person at heart, David. I don't know how, but I have learned to trust my own judgment and perception. So I want to help you. I think I can help you, I really do. But it wouldn't be honest of me to tell you I didn't have my own curiosity in mind as well. That is your first lesson and the most critical one I can give you. We do not keep secrets from each other in this family, David. I hope I have demonstrated that. If you can live with that, then I will welcome you to our family."

"Didn't you have other questions?" David asked.

"They are no longer important," Master Cervantes said flatly, "Now, let me tell you about us. I was born in Spain, but my family moved to Brazil when I was a boy. There, I learned Jiu-Jitsu, and became a master of that art. That is the primary focus of my teachings here, although I am also considered a master of Krav Maga and Judo. I bring elements of those and similar arts such as wrestling into my personal art. Since I will be your sponsor, you will be required to take my course first. Should you become a black-belt, you will be allowed to either continue with me, or begin taking Master Chen's course, or, if you have time to devote to both, you can do so.

"Master Chen was born in China and emigrated to America almost 15 years ago. While my art focuses on self-defense, holds, counters, grappling and throwing, Master Chen focuses on striking. His primary art is Kung-Fu, and he holds what is commonly known as a tenth-degree blackbelt. He is also a master of Karate and Tae Kwon Do. As in my teachings, Master Chen introduces elements of those as well as boxing and other arts in his course. If you become a blackbelt in both of our courses, you can be assured that you will be familiar with almost every known martial art. You will be able to defend yourself in any situation, and you will also be very dangerous. If we do right, you will also have achieved a balance in your life."

"I'm sorry, Master Cervantes, but does this mean I can join?" David asked, trying not to sound as overwhelmed as he felt.

"Oh, yes, if you wish. I thought I made that clear."

"Didn't you say I had to meet Master Chen?"

"He will trust my judgment. With your permission, I will tell him your story, and that will be enough. I wouldn't dream of making you tell it again."

"I'll tell him if you want," David said, with a touch of defiance.

"David, if you join us and stick, a day will come when you and Master Chen will talk at some length about your story. I have no doubt. Now, would you like to get started?"

David said he would, and they did.

39

The day Master Cervantes spoke of came two and a half years later, on the night of the third anniversary of Karen's murder.

David had earned his black belt in Master Chen's version of Kung Fu three weeks earlier. He had been the fastest student to achieve a black belt in either master's course. When he had received his black belt under Master Cervantes, he had continued in that course and added Master Chen's as well. He was attending eight classes a week, including back to back classes on Saturday. Both masters and the other students were astounded by his focus and dedication. He had not missed one class since he first told his story to Master Cervantes.

Both masters had grown to love David as a son. There was something about him that drew them to him. He was a child of tragedy, yet his apparent drive to escape that tragedy and not allow it to define him was inspirational to both of them. Neither had ever had a student as thirsty for knowledge or as devoted to them and to their craft. He inspired them to be better teachers and to be better men so that they, in turn, could help him to put his demons behind him.

Although Master Cervantes was his original sponsor, David and Master Chen were actually closer. Master Chen knew the date of Karen's murder, and he had asked David to stay after class that night to spar with him. Of course that was just an excuse to delay David's return to his empty house in Pacifica, and David knew it. He appreciated the gesture all the same, and he agreed to stay.

The two men stood in the center of the mat now, Master Chen taking and offensive stance against David's defense. Master Chen was flicking punches and kicks at David's head and torso. David blocked all of them easily. Master Chen increased the rapidity of his blows, and David continued to deflect each one. Master Chen's hands and feet flew faster and faster, and David's matched their every movement.

Master Cervantes had been in back, preparing to leave. He planned to exit through the back door, as he knew Master Chen's plan for the evening and did not wish to interrupt. Hearing the sounds of the sparring match, he could not resist taking a peak at his partner and their favorite pupil in combat.

He walked silently to the door leading from the back hall to the studio. He stood to the side of the window so as not to be seen, and then slowly brought his head around so he could look through the small window. What he saw caused his heart to speed up and his jaw to drop.

Master Chen was moving faster than he had ever seen, and David was keeping up. Not only that, something in David's posture said he had another gear that he could kick in at any time. Master Chen, meanwhile, was beginning to get winded, and was clearly at the very peak of his ability.

Their hands and feet were moving so fast that Master Cervantes could barely follow what was going on. With all of his martial arts knowledge and experience, he wasn't able follow the techniques that Master Chen was employing and David was countering. They were just moving too fast.

Suddenly, David broke his defensive stance and came at Master Chen, moving faster than ever. Master Chen retreated, whipping his eyes back and forth frantically like a cornered tiger looking for an escape route. There was none. In the end, David was moving so fast that his hands were a blur. Master Chen blocked a left and then right-handed punch from David and then David came back with another right that he couldn't get to. David's fist slammed into Master Chen's chest, knocking him abruptly off his feet.

"Madre de Dios," Master Cervantes said under his breath reverently as he watched David move quickly to help Master Chen to his feet. "He pulled that punch. If he hadn't..." Master Cervantes couldn't finish the thought. He saw the look on David's face as Master Chen hit the mat, and he knew it was over. He turned toward the back door to leave them alone.

"I'm sorry, Master, are you OK?" David said sincerely.

"Yes, David, I'll be fine. I saw you tried to hold back. As fast as we were moving," he paused and took several deep breaths, "it's hard to stop something like that once it is set in motion."

David stepped back and faced Master Chen. At 6' 2" tall and 225 pounds, David had eight inches and almost 80 pounds on Master Chen. Not only that, under David's gi was a physique that was as sculpted and solid as a marble statue. His body fat was 6%, and he was currently bench-pressing 450 pounds. Still, Master Chen was stunned that he could be bested physically by any of his students.

What he couldn't fathom was the speed the bigger man had demonstrated. He had never seen anyone move faster than he could himself. He had never been pressed to the limit like this before. What's more, he had always known that if he did have to go to top speed, he could best anyone. Maybe not anyone in the world, but he thought the odds of meeting one of the few who were as fast as he were very, very slim. Now he knew he was wrong. He had thought if he would ever meet his equal in speed it would be a small, Asian man like himself. Not a big, bulky American like David.

But there was more, wasn't there? There was something in David's eyes that had set him back on his heels. David's eyes were moving, they had to be, but Master Chen could have sworn that they had been staring straight ahead like some sort of robot. Not quite like a robot, though. There was a fire of uncanny intelligence in them. Intelligence and something else. What that something was he couldn't put his finger on. What he could say, however, was that something made him feel incredibly uneasy.

As Master Chen struggled to catch his breath, he said, "David, please sit with me a moment."

Without a word, David dropped into a cross-legged sitting position. With some effort, Master Chen duplicated the pose opposite David.

After several minutes, Master Chen hitched in one last great breath through his nose, let it out slowly through his mouth, and then began to breathe normally, as if nothing had happened. "David," he said, "that was a very impressive display. I had no idea you could move that fast."

"Thank you, master, neither did I," David replied.

"Your progress here has been uncanny, David. At least in your physical ability. What I'm wondering tonight is, how have you progressed mentally and spiritually over these three years?"

Master Chen had a much deeper voice than one would expect from such a small man. He spoke with very little accent with almost a singsong rhythm. David normally loved to listen to him speak. This question, however, was not one David wished to answer or discuss tonight. "Fine, I guess," he answered, trying to make it clear that that was all he intended to say on the subject.

"I see. David, I don't believe I ever told you the story of how I came to America, did I?"

"No master," David replied, feeling a mixture of relief and suspicion at Master Chen's apparent change of subject.

"Almost 20 years ago now, I was living in a farming village about 100 miles from Beijing. I had a wife and a three-year-old son. My parents as well as my wife's had passed some time before, so we lived alone in a small hut.

"I had a small parcel of land that I tended to. One day, a man you would call a gangster sent his men to buy my land and that of my neighbors. The price they offered was unfair, and my neighbors and I refused to sell. Several nights later, his men returned and burned down our huts. I was away at the market, and I returned to find my home burned to the ground with my wife and child inside. I don't know if the men knew they were there, but they had murdered my family all the same.

"I was enraged. All I could see was red. I took a sword and stormed off to the gangster's stronghold. I crept in at night and killed seven people, including the gangster himself. I murdered him as he slept, not even allowing him to wake up and face me. I was able to escape, but not before taking all the money I could find in his bedchamber.

Knowing the gangster's people would find me and kill me, and since I had no family or home to return to, I went immediately to Beijing, and paid most of the money to a merchant to help me stow away on a barge headed to America.

"They got what they deserved," David said bluntly.

"That is what I thought, David, but at what cost?" Master Chen replied. "My honor? My soul? Certainly it cost me my homeland. Taking a life is not a small thing, David. It is impossible to know what consequences there are for doing so."

"Why are you telling me this, Master Chen?"

"I want to believe that you have achieved balance with your life and with the boys who have taken from you. I want to believe that very much. But I don't know that I do."

"Why not?"

"Because, David, you are still training like you are preparing for something. You are not training for balance or fitness or spiritual fulfillment. You have the demeanor of an athlete training for the Olympics."

"What's wrong with that?"

"Because you're not. And if you're not, then what are you running toward?"

"Master Chen, I appreciate your concern, but I can assure you I am not preparing for battle."

"I didn't say you were, David."

David felt a dull heat in his face, but he tried to hide it as he continued. "That's what you were implying, I think. Master, I don't have much else. Just work and this. I work just as hard. I'll give you my boss's phone number if you don't believe me. If I don't keep moving, my past will catch up with me. If you're concerned that I'm not all the way past what happened, well, you're right. I don't think you're over what happened to your family either. But I have it under control, just as I believe you do."

Master Chen was silent for some time. Then he said, "David, please consider whether you really do have it under control. If you don't, Master Cervantes and I are here for you."

David considered this, and then said, "Thank you, master. I appreciate your concern. I really do. I'll think about it. By the way, I'm sorry about what happened to your family."

"Thank you David. I am here for you any time you need to talk. Will you be OK tonight?"

"Yes. Goodnight master."

"Goodnight, David."

The two men stood and bowed to each other, then walked toward the locker room. They bowed back to the room one more time and then turned to leave the site of Master Chen's first defeat.

40

Ten minutes later, David was motoring through the fog at a speed that was far beyond what was safe. He was pushing his reliable old Honda to the limit. He knew the way like the back of his hand, so he wasn't likely to go off the road. If a car, person or animal got in his way, however, it was unlikely that he would be able to stop.

He thought he had played Master Chen and Master Cervantes well enough to escape their suspicion of his true motives. Apparently Master Chen, at least, was more perceptive than he had thought. He shouldn't have been surprised. He had never met a man who was wiser in the ways of the human mind than Master Chen.

Now David was faced with a dilemma. He desperately wished to continue training, but he clearly was no longer able to hide his true intentions from Master Chen. He had gotten so keyed up over the past three years that he felt like he would explode before he had a chance to execute his plan. That was what Master Chen was sensing now, he thought. Unfortunately, Darius Williams wouldn't be out for another two and a half years. He felt he was almost ready to begin his revenge, but he had to wait. If he went after LaShon Jackson or one of the others, he risked getting caught. If he got caught, Darius, his primary target, would go unpunished.

So it came to this. If he wanted to continue training with Master Chen and Master Cervantes, somehow he would have to convince them that he had "achieved balance" and was no longer looking for revenge. As perceptive as they both were, that wouldn't be easy unless it were true, and it was never going to be true. The trick, it seemed, would be to somehow put his true feelings on hold for now. Get them to go underground, and bring them back to the surface when the time was right. He was afraid that would be easier said than done.

Suddenly, a black Ford pickup swerved out in front of him from a side street. David slammed on his brakes and then flashed his high beams on the asshole. He stepped on the gas to catch up to him. He had just enough time to notice the Confederate flag sticker on the truck's rear bumper before he had to brake again. The driver, who was weaving back and forth violently, took at least one hand off the wheel long enough to stick his arm out the window and show David his middle finger. Out of the passenger window, another arm emerged and hurled a beer can up in the air, clearly meaning for it to hit David.

These fuckers were clearly drunk. His body pulsed with rage and adrenaline, but he slowed his car and let them go ahead. If he tried anything, they would probably just run him off the road, either purposely or accidentally in their drunken stupor. The irony of another McGuire dying at the hands of an intoxicated driver was more than he wanted to think about.

They turned north at Highway 1 and David went south. His heart was still racing from the encounter. As he chased his headlights into the darkness, he began to curse himself as a coward for not doing something to those bastards. It would have felt good, in fact, to beat a measure of his revenge into those two assholes. He thought about turning around to go find them, but at this point the odds of that happening were very slim. Instead, he continued toward his house, his mind clouded with a smoky haze of hate and rage.

After exiting the freeway and forging a careening, dizzying path along the road that led around the mountain to his home, David rolled his car into his garage and killed it. He banged open the driver's door and then through the door that led from the garage to the house, leaving both wide open. His car called after him persistently reminding him that he had the keys in the ignition with the door ajar.

David stalked down the hall to one of the spare bedrooms. He pushed that door open and flipped on the light switch. Laid out in front of him was the bedroom furniture he had shared with Karen before she was murdered. It was arranged in exactly the same pattern it had been in their old house. There were times when his focus waned, when he lost the furious edge that kept him moving toward his final purpose. He kept the furniture this way to help him find his way back to the path of vengeance.

Once in this room, the anger he felt when the drunks cut him off was magnified into a ferocity that he could barely control. He had come here to focus so that he could think of a way to get past his dilemma with Master Chen, but the opposite was happening. He was spinning toward the edge.

He went to the long closet and opened the double, slatted white doors. They opened in opposite directions like an accordion, leaving the closet wide open to him. He lifted the wooden dowel on which some of his cast-off clothes hung and dumped it unceremoniously on the floor behind him. When the dowel was gone, a small indentation in the wall above its support was revealed. Inside that indentation was a small, brass key. David grasped the key and walked the length of the closet to where the other end of the dowel had been. Similarly, the removal of the dowel had revealed a keyhole on that side. David inserted the key there, turned it 180 degrees, and then removed it and put it in his pocket.

He stepped over the pile of clothes on the floor and flopped heavily on the bed. The bed no longer squeaked, but the absence of the squeak and the reason it was gone made hot blood rush into his face and burn the backs of his eyes with guilty tears. He denied them, though, as he had all the others that had attempted to escape his eyes since the day John left him almost three years ago. Instead, he leaned forward and tipped up the lamp on the end table. Its base was recessed, and high up in it was a tiny switch. He flipped it with the fingernail of his left index finger.

Servo-motors immediately sprung to life and whirred behind the back wall of the closet. Had he not disabled his security mechanism with the key, the noise of the motors would have disguised the sound of carbon monoxide gas seeping into the room from the heating vents.

The room was decorated with the wood paneling that had been installed in 1972 when the house was originally built. David had updated some of the other rooms' décor to his taste, but the paneling in this room, and, more specifically, the paneling in the closet, suited his needs just perfectly as it was.

As the unseen motors spun, three breaks appeared from floor to ceiling in the paneling that lined the back wall of the closet. The golden light that glowed through each of the breaks divided the wall into four equal sections. Before the lights had come on behind the paneling, the breaks had been completely disguised as seams in the paneling. The center two sections slid mechanically out of the wall and then split in the center, moving smoothly left and right toward the closet walls. When they stopped moving, they left exposed a two-foot deep, lighted compartment. He could have done the same thing with manual-opening doors and without the recessed lighting in the ceiling, but David had romanticized what he was doing to the point that this dramatic touch seemed appropriate. In addition, he had both cash and time to burn, and building such a frivolous storeroom took care of both.

David sat on the bed looking at his personal armory. In the center of the opening were two department-store mannequins he had purchased for cash at a second-hand store in Fremont. The bodies of the mannequins were covered with what appeared to be black spandex. They were placed directly under the center two recessed lights. A closer look showed that the black spandex outfits were split into sections: torso; upper legs; lower legs; upper arms and lower arms. The heads were covered by a tight-fitting hood like the ones speed-skaters wear.

These were the very best suits of armor that David could build. They were constructed of the strongest and densest Kevlar available and had the optimum and most expensive gel formula he could concoct hidden inside. These suits were well beyond what the military wanted to spend per suit, and they were much, much better than what the military was going to end up with.

He had convinced his boss and co-workers that going to the top of the line and then backing down to meet the military's budget was the best way to go. These were two of the ten most expensive prototypes they built.

Ballistics tests showed that they could stop a .357 Magnum round from close range with minimal injury to the wearer. Only a direct hit in the head would likely cause serious injury or death. They weren't able to create enough separation between the hood and the wearer's head without going to something closer to a riot helmet. Still, the hood would deflect shots that did not strike directly, and did seem to be able to save the life of the wearer on long-range testing.

David had smuggled them piece by piece out of his office in his duffel bag with his sweaty gym clothes. Every few months, he would curse and then cast a piece in the trash next to his desk. In his log, he would make an entry such as "Leak" or "Bad Reaction." His co-workers had never regained a comfort level with him, so none of them ever questioned why the piece had to be scrapped. In fact, when David was angry, they were happy to stay as far away from him as possible. They would usually try to clear out early, while he would work late those nights. Technically, any bags carried in and out were to be searched by security, but David had developed a better rapport with the low-paid security guards than with his brainy co-workers. They were so used to his David's easy smile and bulging gym bag that they just let him pass, making a joke about the smell that would emanate from it if opened.

The mannequins didn't have hands, but pinned to the wall where they should be were black leather gloves. David had modified these on his own to increase the damage his punches would cause. He added small pouches of granular lead to the knuckles, the outside ridge of his hand and the base of the palm. These had the essential effect of brass knuckles, yet did not restrict David's movements or the use of his hands. He practiced breaking boards and cinder blocks in his garage two or three days a week. Using these gloves almost doubled his breaking ability and protected his hands at the same time.

To the left of the world's best protected mannequins were three busts made directly from David's own head. David had taught himself how to make casts of his face and head using books and some information from the internet. He had several false starts, but he finally came up with these three that were very good likenesses.

At first glance, it would appear that the busts were painted to look like skulls. In reality, they were covered by a thin, flexible plastic coating. David had helped himself to a great many bottles and vials of chemicals from work and had developed a tough, thin, flexible material that could be molded to fit his face. In addition, it was porous enough to hold an adhesive on one side and paint on the other.

David had known from the beginning that he would need a disguise. Everything he could think of, ski-masks, panty-hose, Halloween masks, even bandannas caused a problem by either restricting vision or breathing, and just generally were too bulky to be effective. He also knew that intimidation was one of his goals. If he could gain an extra half-second by startling or even scaring his victim, he would have a better chance of defeating him quickly and silently.

It occurred to him while watching professional wrestling on cable one afternoon that face paint was just as effective as a mask in hiding a person's identity. Even a partially painted face was enough to completely disguise a person, as long as it covered his eyes. What's more, it would leave both vision and breathing completely unaffected, even peripheral vision. The only problem was that it could not easily be removed if he needed to quickly abandon his costume. It didn't take him long to decide that he could solve that problem by creating a "second-skin" that could be painted in advance, put on at the right moment, and then removed quickly and easily when it was no longer needed.

After developing the casts and the masks, David bought boxes of black, gray and white face paint. As always, he used only cash and bought the paint at dozens of different stores around the Bay Area. He had never used his name or anything but cash in any of his purchases connected with his mission of revenge. With the paint, he practiced for months painting the masks. He had decided after watching a news report on "Dia De Los Meurtos" celebrations in Mexico that a skull would be his disguise of choice. Combined with a black hood, a well-painted skull face would call up images in his victims' minds of the Grim Reaper or Charon, the boatman on the River Styx. After some time, he was able to create a face that met the standard he was looking for. He used solid black to create cavernous eyes, a nose, and teeth. He used black fading to gray to create the illusion of depth under the cheekbones and the lower jaw. With a few cracks thrown in for good measure, David's painted skulls would appear, in the dark and with the element of surprise at least, to be the real thing.

Later, he would add false fangs and fake blood along with opaque, red contacts to complete the look. He bought the contacts partly to hide the color of his eyes, and partly because they looked evil as shit. The fangs and blood, well, those just looked evil as shit. The false fangs that slipped directly over his canine teeth and blood capsules were readily available where he bought his face paint. The contacts, however, took some finding. Eventually he got a greasy-haired Trekkie clerk at the "Master of Disguise," a shitty costume store in San Jose, to hook him up with a guy who could get special contacts. Using the name John Bartholomew, the alias he used whenever a name was required, he purchased two pairs each of red, white and black contacts for $200 each, plus a $250 finder's fee to the Trekkie. It was money well spent.

Mounted on the wall to the right of his suits of armor were three .45 Caliber handguns. The top one was of standard, dark-gray gunmetal. One of the handgrips was missing, and David hadn't replaced it. David had a strong sense of family history, and replacing the handgrip would be like replacing the nose of the Sphinx or the arms of "Winged Victory."

This was his Grandpa Red's sidearm from World War II. His Grandpa had been a Colonel in France for most of the war. He didn't have many memories of Grandpa Red, but one of them was watching him disassemble, clean, and reassemble this weapon. The memory stuck with him, and he had later asked his dad about his Grandpa's guns.

"We sold a lot of them when he died, buddy," Bill McGuire said to his seventeen year-old son. "We did keep a few of them, though. Do you want to see them?"

"Sure, dad," David replied.

Bill had taken David to the attic and opened the gun safe that stood in the far corner. Standing upright were a .270 and a 30/30 rifle, both with scopes and both well maintained. Bill and David had hunted with them on occasion, bringing home three deer in David's youth.

In the top of the cabinet were three pistols, each oiled and wrapped in soft leather. The first one that Bill opened was his Grandpa's service sidearm. "This was Grandpa's pistol in the war. He was an officer so he got to carry it. He said he didn't remember how the handgrip came off, but I'm not sure if I believed him."

Bill handed David the gun, demonstrating wordlessly that he should point it away from both of them as he held it. While he did so, Bill took down one of the other pistols. "These," he said, "Grandpa wasn't supposed to have. The military doesn't know he got them, and of course they aren't registered. So we'll just keep this between us, OK?"

"OK, dad."

Bill unwrapped the weapon, and its spotless beauty stood in stark contrast to the beaten and worn look of the one in David's hands. It was nickel-plated and polished to a mirror-shine. The handgrips were ivory, and were also polished so they gleamed. It looked like it had never been fired, and that was very close to the truth.

"The other one's just like this," Bill said. "Grandpa said he found these in an abandoned officer's tent at the Battle of the Bulge. My guess is 'found' is not exactly accurate. I'm pretty sure he stole them. At any rate, he was never much to talk about the war, but I think these belonged to a General that he wasn't particularly fond of. Somehow he smuggled them back here and has had them locked away since he got home."

These two weapons, also .45 Caliber, were the ones mounted below his Grandfather's sidearm in David's cache. They gleamed at him, reflecting the light from above. He had registered his Grandpa's gun when he brought it to California, but these two were still a secret. The only people other than he who knew his Grandpa had them were dead.

Only the armor, guns and masks were mounted on the wall. At either end of the secret compartment were chests of drawers. In these were various other accoutrements that David had purchased, stolen or built, including the deadliest item in the entire arsenal which was tucked away ominously in the bottom drawer.

David sat on the bed and looked at all of it, hoping for inspiration. His eyes scanned back and forth, then closed futilely. He couldn't focus. Wherever he looked, he saw that goddamn pickup with its leering Confederate flag and flying fingers and beer cans. He'd heard in other countries that cops shot drunk drivers on site. Here we give them a slap on the hand and maybe take their license for a few months. Someone should really...

There it was. David was suddenly aglow with the utter perfection of the solution that had literally hit him from out of the blue...or maybe from out of the black.

He could really start at any time, but as he rolled it over in his mind, he felt there was one more piece to complete his masterpiece, and he was pretty sure he knew where he could find it.

David stood up and reversed the process he went through upon entering the room, leaving only an innocent-looking guest bedroom behind him as he walked back to his car.

41

Twenty minutes later, David pulled his Honda to a stop, bringing with him a cloud of dust from the access road he had just traversed to get to the Bay Tavern. His was one of three cars in the large patch of dirt that served as a parking lot. There were also half a dozen motorcycles and eight or nine pickup trucks, most of which rolled off the assembly line in Detroit during Ronald Reagan's first term.

The Bay Tavern was near Half Moon Bay, but it was removed from town by a considerable distance of winding, gravel road. The road seemed designed to ward off unwelcome guests. It was unmarked, narrow, unlit. There was no sign advertising the Tavern. The road wound treacherously around stands of trees and over blind undulations in the land. Anyone who didn't know the way would assume they had made a wrong turn and head back to the highway. That was exactly how the owners and patrons of the Bay Tavern wanted it.

The building itself was low and boxy. It was made of wood, and the formerly white paint was flaking away in large chunks. The exposed wood was black from the sea air. Large, rotten patches of wood showed through like sores. The building looked sick…like it was dying of some pestilential infection.

There were no windows visible from the front. There was a narrow, unpainted wooden porch, which was covered by an extension of the building. From the extension hung a blue light that was intended to zap bugs in the summer. In the cold October night, it was silent and served only to cast an eerie blue glow over the face of the building.

David mounted the steps and pulled open the flimsy, wooden screen door, taking care not to tear it loose from the top hinge, which was hanging on by only one screw. He then threw his shoulder against the heavy wooden door, which was swollen with moisture and stuck in the jamb. It burst open with a harsh squeal, and he half-stepped, half-fell into the Bay Tavern.

When he did, all of the patrons turned toward the door, many of them reaching for their hips or inside their jackets. When they saw that it was David, they all relaxed. Most of them grunted at him to acknowledge his presence, this being the most pleasant gesture of which they were capable.

David's boots clunked across the uneven, wooden floor as he wound his way through round tables full of rough-looking men. Most of them wore jackets of either faded denim or military green. At least three-quarters wore beards, and several had on dark glasses. Their heads were covered with caps and bandanas. Nearly all of them had bottles or mugs of beer in front of them. They leaned in and spoke quietly across the table to their compatriots. The ancient juke in the corner was currently silent. The air was thick with the smells of tobacco, beer and sea-rot. If a stranger had made it up the road, one look in the front door would have them quickly on their way.

David crossed the room, nodding hello to most of the patrons as he passed. They nodded back, some of them adding a short word of welcome to the youngest member of the Bay Tavern's regular crowd.

He reached the bar and sat on one of the open stools. The stools were made of rough wood and were detached from the bar. They were of several different heights. David happened to get one of the high ones. He turned to the man next to him and asked, "Richard here tonight?"

"Yep," the man said without turning his head. He was watching the thirteen-inch TV that was sitting on the counter behind the bar. It was currently broadcasting some sort of show about duck hunting.

"Well I'll be! If it isn't John Bartholomew!"

David's head snapped to the left as the name of his alter-ego boomed forth from the back room. The owner of the strong, deep voice that had spoken it was holding aside the red curtain that separated the storeroom from the main room of the bar. He was a short, stocky man, with broad shoulders and thick arms that were too short for his body. Both forearms were tattooed. One appeared to be a woman and the other some sort of animal, but time and thick gray hair made it difficult to tell their exact nature. His face was dark and weathered. His deeply lined skin had the appearance of a man who has spent a great portion of his life at sea. He had a thick, gray beard with no mustache and a thatch of unruly, gray hair on top of his head.

"How ya doin', Richard?" David asked, smiling.

"I'm OK now, buddy. I was gettin' worried. What's it been, two months?" bellowed the ancient mariner as he walked around the bar.

Richard Barnes wasn't actually an ancient mariner, although that was David's thought when he first saw him. That was over two years' prior, when David brought his grandpa's .45 to the Half Moon Bay Gun Club. He had taken the day off work and showed up a little before noon on a Tuesday.

He walked in and at first thought the place was closed. There was no one there. No gunshots, no people, no attendant, nothing. "Hello?" he called into the stillness.

"Hello back," said a voice from behind him, almost making him jump out of his shoes.

"Sorry about that, son, had to use the head," said the stocky man behind him. He was still cinching his belt while he walked toward David.

David's heart was pounding, but he did his best to sound calm. "I'm sorry, are you open?" he asked.

"Sure are, mate, although you wouldn't know it. Don't get much business this early on a weekday. Most of my clients are working or still asleep," the man said. His tone was pleasant, although David noticed that he was looking at him with a wary eye.

"I...I don't really know how this works. I've never shot a pistol before or been to a gun range," David began.

"What makes you want to come to one now?" asked the man.

"I don't know for sure. I've got my grandpa's gun and I figured I should know how to use it, I guess."

"You thinkin' I'm gonna show you?" he asked, raising one bushy eyebrow.

"I don't know. Would you? I'll pay you if you will. I don't have any friends…who have guns."

"Let me see what you got there," said the old man, holding out one snarled hand as he did.

David just looked at the hand at first, then held out the leather wrapped bundle he had brought in with him.

The old man took it and walked over to the counter that separated the entryway from the door that led to the gun range. He unwrapped it as carefully as a mother would her newborn baby. He laid the leather strip out and let the gun rest in the middle of it.

"This your grandpa's, you say?"

"Yeah. It was anyway."

"He was in the war. An officer," said the old man. This was not a question.

"Yep."

"Where at?"

"Europe, mostly. He was a Colonel."

"I was in the Pacific. Philippines. I was a Sergeant Major. Met McArthur. You know who that is?"

"Yeah. Were you in the Navy?"

"I should kick you out of here for that. There's no Sergeant Major in the Navy. The sailors have Master Chiefs. Didn't your grandpa tell you that?"

"I was five when he died. He didn't tell me much that I remember. But I do remember watching him take apart this gun, clean it and put it back together. I used to love watching him do it. Maybe because it was the only time he stopped cursing."

"Too bad. I bet you could've learned a lot from him. Probably had some pretty good stories about the war."

"My dad said he would never tell him about it. Didn't like to talk about it."

"When'd your dad tell you that?"

201

"When I was in high school."

"Maybe you should ask him again. He mighta thought you were too young then."

"My dad's dead too. So's my mom and grandma. Look, maybe I should just go."

"Don't get your panties in a knot, I didn't know," said the old man scornfully.

"All the same, maybe this was a bad idea," said David quietly.

"Look, go if you want, I ain't gonna stop you or feel bad about what I said. There's enough regret in this world and I don't need any more'n I already got, believe me. But I think there's a reason you came here that you're not tellin' me. Probably a good reason...I can see it in your face. I'm thinkin' you wanna stay in touch with your family, that it?"

"Sure, that's it," David said, looking down from the man's eyes to the gun as he did.

"No it ain't, but I can tell you ain't gonna tell me the real reason, so I ain't gonna push it. Around here we don't ask questions that don't wanna be answered. That's my first rule, and if you're gonna come around here more'n this once you'll need to keep that in mind."

"That's fine with me," said David.

"Alright then," said the man, "name's Richard."

David took his outstretched hand, trying not to wince at the clicking in the knot of bony knuckles that gripped his own.

"Ain't you got a name?"

"Oh, sorry...yeah...it's...uh...John," David said, blurting out the first name that popped into his head.

"That would be uh...John Smith I suppose," Richard replied.

"No," David said, laughing a little nervously, "It's Bartholomew."

"Well, whatever it is and why you don't want to tell me the real one is your own business, not mine. Like I said, I don't wanna know what you don't want me to know. Folks that come here feel the same way…uh…John."

David's face flushed slightly at being so easy to read, but he did feel an odd comfort here all the same. Richard reminded him of the old-timers back home that used to come around his dad's store. All vets of the Big One, all bitter about something or other, all spoiling for a fight, and all in love with America.

"Alright, let's see if she still fires," said Richard, taking the gun from the counter.

David stepped closer, and so began the relationship that would eventually become the antithesis of the one he had with Master Chen. While Master Chen knew David's real name and the truth about his life and his past, he had only an inkling of his motivations and desires. Conversely, Richard Barnes, while not knowing David's name or story, understood completely the nature of David's intent. That is, Richard Barnes knew the thirst for revenge. He knew it from personal experience, and he knew how it looked in others. He saw it every day in his gun range and in his bar. And he knew the first day he met David that he was hell-bent on avenging some kind of wrong that was done to him. To Richard Barnes, that made David an interesting person to have around. To Richard Barnes, there was nothing more fascinating than a person motivated enough to kill another man…or men.

While Richard's natural penchant for encouraging and helping those with the need for revenge would have been enough for him to invite David into his fold, it turned out that Richard actually liked the younger man. Despite their nearly 50-year age difference, they hit it off immediately. Richard did a lot of talking, and David began to enjoy listening to the stories. They were stories of heroism, of tragedy, of bravery, and of great loss. Although he didn't know it, David's need for a father figure opened the door to his soul wide enough to allow Richard to slip in and become just that, just as it had Master Chen. Richard, for his part, enjoyed David's company.

David didn't talk much, but he was as interesting a person as Richard had ever met that hadn't been to war or at least lived through one of the big ones. Richard was fascinated by his intelligence and his sense of dark purpose, although David never spoke about his past or what that purpose might be.

Over the next several months, Richard taught David everything he needed to know about his grandpa's gun, and about many others that he had stored in a huge gun-safe in the small office behind the counter. David attacked shooting with as much focused dedication as he had martial arts, and within six months he could put every bullet in the target. By the time he showed up in the Bay Tavern on the third anniversary of Karen's murder, he was the best shot Richard Barnes had ever seen.

Now, as they embraced in the Bay Tavern on that pivotal night, David would ask Richard for one last favor…the one that would complete the quest of the person David had become. That person's name was John Bartholomew, and his mission was to gather everything needed to execute David's revenge. But the acquisition of this last piece of knowledge would give birth to a third, more primal being, one whose sole purpose was to carry out the plan that David had conceived and John had prepared. On this night, the Reaper would be born.

42

"What brings you in, kid?" Richard asked.

"Just came down to say 'hi' to my old buddies," David replied with a sly wink.

"Bullshit! You're here for something. Spit it out so we can get it out of the way and get down to the serious business of getting you drunk off your ass!"

"Alright, Sergeant, I do need something."

"That's Sergeant-Major, you little maggot. Now what is it?"

David put his arm around Richard and turned them both so that their backs were to the rest of the bar. "I need to learn how to fix myself if I get hurt. Field dressing wounds, setting broken bones, all that kind of shit."

Richard pulled out from underneath David's arm and looked up at him, concern driving the frivolity from his face. "You finally goin' to war, Johnny?" he asked gravely.

David looked blankly back at him. "What makes you think I'm going to war?"

"Come on, Johnny. I've told you before I know you got an axe to grind. Loner like you, don't wanna talk about nothing to do with your life, and all the shit you been wanting to learn. Now you wanna be able to heal yourself? You're expecting to get hurt, and don't wanna go to the hospital when you do. Mosta the guys figure you wanna be a thief, and they all like you so it ain't nothin' to them as long as you ain't takin' from them, but I don't see it that way. You got a score to settle...maybe a big one. Don't worry, I ain't told no one what I suspect, and I'll sure as shit take it to the grave." As he spoke the last word, he held up his right hand, displaying the tangled web of scars that represented the brotherhood of many men, including David.

David looked at his own right hand, letting his eyes traverse the length of the thick scar that ran diagonally across his palm. Even though he was quite intoxicated at the time, he remembered the night he got that scar like it was yesterday.

In the spring of 2000, when he had been coming to the shooting range regularly for about six months, Richard called David into the range's small back room. "I got in another shipment, you wanna see it?" Richard asked.

"Sure," David replied.

As David had discovered over the past six months, Richard was running a minor survivalist group in Half Moon Bay. Most of the people who frequented his shooting range were veterans of various wars. Most of them held down jobs during the day, but none of them had ever really been able to shake the war that still raged inside their own minds and hearts. Very few of them were married, or at least not any more. Their children, if they had any, lived far away and visited rarely.

These men were first skeptical of their spiritual leader's choice to allow David to continue coming to the gun club, but they trusted his judgment enough to let it go and see what would happen. Although few of them could articulate the reason why, the roughly hewn men all took a liking him. Richard knew why, though. David gave off the air of a man whose war was still ahead of him, and he was running toward it with stunning temerity. These old warriors were long past their times of battle on the fields of honor. The battles that remained for them would be against alcoholism, old age, and, death. Being around this young man preparing for war made them feel young again, and that was good.

While they knew in their hearts that they would never have a call for action, these men had long attempted to hang on to their virility by forming this loose militia under Richard's benevolent watch. They kept their past alive by gathering at the range to shoot their guns and trade stories about shots they had made and bullets they had taken. Then they would tromp over to the Bay Tavern to drown their past in a sea of beer and broken dreams.

Richard was ever aware of the mood of the group, and how precarious it could be. If not for him, the group would have splintered and left behind dozens of used up loners with nothing to live for but the next social security check and the beer that it would buy them. Richard took steps to keep their minds active and their thoughts away from the loneliness that otherwise consumed their lives. He organized "retreats," which usually consisted of wilderness adventures such as white water rafting, hiking or camping. He often included games of a military nature in these trips. He also encouraged what he called "skill-sharing." Most of the men had specific skills that they had either learned in the military or their lives since. Richard would identify interests in the group and then pair the men so that everyone could learn something new when they wished. The nature of the group being what it was, most of the skills being transferred were the type that could be used most readily in illegal pursuits. In Richard's estimation, however, a mind that was learning anything was healthier than one that was stagnant.

Richard also encouraged the men to take up hobbies and collections. Many of the men did so, and, as Richard had suspected, those that did responded positively. They had something to save their money for other than drugs and alcohol, and they also had something to research and think about in their spare time. Most of the men had collections of some sort of military memorabilia, either weapons such as guns or swords, or other items like uniforms, flags or documents. Some of the others collected and painted small, die-cast military figures. Still others had non-military collections like model planes or cars, sports cards, or even comic books (Tony Gianelli took a lot of ribbing for his extensive collection of Superman comics, but he stuck with it all the same).

Not many of the men were wealthy, but Richard was. He often purchased items in bulk that he thought might interest some of the guys, and then he would let the guys take them and pay him when and what they could.

On the day David was officially invited to join Richard and the others in what they referred to as "The Brotherhood," Richard had received a shipment of World War II memorabilia. David had shown an interest in World War II, and Richard had encouraged him to begin a collection.

"Here you go, Johnny," said Richard as he began to pull items out of a large wooden crate that sat in the middle of the floor. Each of them was wrapped in a khaki-colored cloth. Richard handed them to David, who carefully undid the cloth and placed each item on the desk. Soon, the desktop was full of canteens, compasses, spectacles, boxes of medals, and various other accessories that a World War II soldier might have carried on his person. There were no weapons, though, and David didn't find any of what was here of interest.

"Hey Richard," David began as they unloaded the crate, "I, uh, I've heard some of the guys talking about teaching each other different things."

"Yep, we sometimes share our unique skills around here."

"Well...I don't know how to put this exactly..."

"Just goddamn say it," Richard grunted as he hauled another treasure out of the crate.

"OK. I was wondering if anyone can teach me to hotwire a car," David said tentatively, watching Richard closely for his reaction.

"Why do you want to know that?" Richard asked, stopping to look at him intently.

"You know, in case King Kong is coming up behind me and I need to boost a car. I'd hate to have to explain to the girl I'm with she's gonna go for a ride with a big, hairy ape because I don't know how to hotwire a car."

Richard kept staring at him. The look on his face was that of a man trying to compute differential equations in his head. Finally he said, "I don't know what the fuck you're talking about Johnny."

"It's a movie. You see..."

"Nevermind," Richard said, cutting David off in mid-sentence, "we'll talk about this later. There's one last thing in the bottom here that I want you to see." As he spoke, Richard turned back to the crate and lifted out the final item. Richard pulled the cloth away from this one himself, revealing a slick, flat mahogany box about 18 inches long and six inches wide. He stood up and walked toward the desk. As he did, David cleared a spot for him to set it down.

Richard set it on the desk and then flipped the small, gold latch on the front. He then placed one index finger on each side of the lid and lifted it as if it would break if he did it too fast or with too much pressure.

Inside the box, seated in indentations cut exactly to their size in the golden velvet, was a matched set of bayonets. They were a little over a foot long and fashioned of solid, polished steel. Unlike other bayonets he had seen, the point and edges of these were filed to a bright, dangerously sharp edge. The sight of them took David's breath away. The moment he saw them, he knew exactly what he wanted to do with them. Or, more specifically, what he wanted to make with them.

"These belonged to a General in…"

"I want them," David said, cutting Richard off, "How much do you want for them?"

Richard looked at him, unable to suppress a grin at David's enthusiasm. The younger man had shown very little emotion since he'd known him, and the shock of seeing it pour forth like this made his heart leap. He liked David a lot, probably more than he should, and seeing him break through the gloom, even for a moment, was wonderful.

"I tell you, Johnny, if you want 'em that much, they're yours."

"I've got money, Richard, just tell me how much."

"They were part of the lot. I got it in an estate auction in Santa Rosa. The old gal didn't know what she had. Probably didn't even look. I'm sure her old man would have killed her, but I got all of this for fifty bucks. So, really, you just take 'em."

David ran his finger lovingly down the length of one of the gleaming weapons. When he reached the loop that was intended to affix it to the user's rifle, he popped one finger under it and flipped the bayonet up on one side. He brought his other hand under it lifted it out of the box, holding it in both hands, feeling its satisfying weight. He gazed at it, turning it so that the light reflected back off the blade into his eyes. As he turned it, he watched the light skate around the sharpened edge. The reflection there was not mirror-like, as it was on the haft, but harder, and more deadly.

David shook his head slightly as if to clear it and then placed his new toy back in the indentation in the box next to its sister. David picked up the box with both hands, gazed at its contents for another minute, and then closed and latched the lid. He put the box under one arm and then held out his right hand to Richard. As Richard took it, David said, "Thanks, Richard. Really. And not just for this. I really appreciate everything you've done for me. It…it means a lot to have someone…"

"I know, kid. You don't have to say it, you're gonna make me cry and my mascara will run. Anyway, me and the boys like havin' you around. Makes us all feel a little bit younger that a buck like you would want to hang around with us. In fact, I think it's time you knew about our other clubhouse. I got a little bar up the hill a ways. Most of the guys come up at night, especially on the weekends. It ain't much to look at, but it suits us just fine. I'd like it if you'd come down tonight and join us."

"OK," David said absently, still giddy from his recent acquisition.

Richard bent over the desk and squeaked open a heavy drawer. He pulled a stump of a pencil and a tattered notebook from it. He opened the notebook and scrawled on one of the pages. Then he tore it out and handed it to David.

"This is the highway, this is the bar," he said, pointing at the page. "You'll think you took a wrong turn, but keep going, it's pretty far back in the woods. When you come to a little building with all our trucks parked around it, you're there. Think you can be there by eight or so?"

"Sure," said David, "I'm gonna take these home and then I'll come back in a little while."

"Good. We'll see you there," Richard said, smiling.

"Thanks again, Richard," David said, his dry mouth clicking out the words.

"No problem, kid. Now you calm down a little, OK? I don't wanna hear about you drivin' into the ocean on the way home."

"I'll be OK. See ya," David said, turning to leave with his newfound treasure.

43

Four hours later, David piloted his Honda cautiously along an overgrown gravel road. Richard had been right…David did think he had taken a wrong turn, but he persisted and eventually came to the shack indicated with an 'X' on Richard's rudimentary map.

He got out and closed the door. He stood for a moment leaning against the car, looking hesitantly at the building in front of him. He asked himself if he was really going to go in there. He had never seen a place that filled him with such a sense of foreboding. Yet around the edges of his fear were both curiosity and excitement. He leaned forward to propel his body off of the car, climbed the rotten steps of the porch, and pushed through the door and into the belly of the beast.

As they did every time it opened, all of the bar's patrons turned abruptly toward the door. David would eventually get used to this, but this time it caused him to freeze in the doorway. Most of the men turned back to their drinks when they saw it was him, but some of them kept their eyes on him, if for no other reason than to see how he was going to react to his new surroundings.

Richard was behind the bar when David entered, and he quickly rounded the bar and headed toward David to reel him in before he could slip off the hook and get away. Richard moved well for a septuagenarian, and he caught David's arm before he was able to adequately formulate his thoughts and decide whether to stay or head for the hills.

"Johnny Bartholomew, come on up to the bar and sit down. I'm buying tonight, but don't get used to it, OK buddy!" Richard exclaimed, leading David with a persistent tug on his left arm.

David asked for a beer, and got one along with a shot of Mescal. Before an hour was up, he had had three of each and was cruising. He was dimly aware that his guard was coming down, and he made a concerted effort to build a mental wall around his true name and true self. In spite of America's

212

finest brew and Mexico's worst poison, the wall held and he was still known as John Bartholomew when he left early the next morning.

As David was finishing his fourth beer, the conversation between him, Richard, and two other men who could be thought of as Richard's captains began to lull. Chuck Walker and Harry Dent were also World War II vets and had been some of the first to join Richard in forming The Brotherhood. They had been consulted and agreed to participate in what was about to happen, representing the rest of the group by proxy.

"Johnny," Richard began as he poured David another shot, "I heard your question earlier about boosting cars. What you were asking ain't no small thing. We ain't comf'table havin' just anyone even come to the range or the bar here, let alone havin' 'em know what we talk about. I call what you're asking for "Skill Sharing" and I guess you picked up on some talk of it at the range. Not that it's any big secret once you been coming there as long as you have, but you mentioning it forced me an' the boys to make a decision on you anyway."

"I don't know if you heard of this or not, but we call ourselves The Brotherhood. We ain't no motorcycle gang or militia, but we do stick together and try to make more for ourselves than we would have alone. You're a hell of a lot younger than the rest of us and there are those that don't see that you fit, especially since you never been in the service. But me, Chuck and Harry all agree, along with most 'a the others that you fit good enough to let in. No one can really say why. Even I wonder why I didn't send you packin' that first day. Anyway, you seem to stick OK and we're willin' to have you join us officially if you want to."

David stared blankly at Richard for some time, not quite getting what was just said. "So you want me in your club?" David slurred. "Do I get a uniform?"

"You'll get your ass whupped if you make fun of it," Richard barked back.

"Sorry...I..." David stammered.

"That's OK," Richard said, "I know you're on your way under the table. Doesn't look like you drink that much, eh? Anyway, if you join, you're in for life, and you will be treated as a brother. You still don't have to tell no one anything about your life if you don't wanna, but in matters that affect the group, you need to be straight. And we'll be straight with you. Anything you need, we'll help if we can. First thing is we'll get Luis over there to show you how to hotwire any vehicle on the road if that's what you want. I heard you say you know a little karate. Maybe you can show Luis some of that in exchange, or maybe some of the other boys. Point is we all share what we can, and we all stick together. There's no dues, no meetings except whatever happens here, no bullshit, just a bunch 'a guys lookin' out for each other. But we gotta know we can trust you to keep our secrets."

"OK," David said dully, "How do I do that. You want me to say a pledge or something?"

"Nope. None of that bullshit. No chanting or candles or swatting you on the ass with a paddle. If you want in, you come in the back with us for a minute and I'll show you."

The sober part of David, which was now deeply buried in his drunken counterpart, tried to set off the alarm bells that it wasn't a good idea to follow them into the back room. But Johnny was in charge now, and he slid off the stool and walked around the bar and through the stained curtain into the back room.

Richard had gone ahead, and Harry and Chuck were behind him. They were both fairly big men, standing about six feet each and weighing in at a sloppy 250 pounds or so. Standing side by side, they blocked any retreat.

Richard pulled a string that hung down from a bare light bulb. The bulb popped on, and then swung drunkenly about on the cord that attached it to the low ceiling. The ceiling and walls were constructed of dark, unfinished pine. The floor was smooth concrete. The room was furnished only by a small desk and ancient wooden chair on great, brass casters. Crates of alcohol and kegs of beer dominated the room. There was barely room for the four of them to stand.

David had had enough training from Master Cervantes at the time to know he was in a pinch. The beer and Mescal were wearing off quickly, and he began looking for a point of egress should it become necessary. His senses were beginning to gear up as the adrenaline challenged the alcohol as the dominant chemical in his body.

Richard turned around and looked at David's face. He saw the look of a trapped animal in David's eyes, and for the first time he questioned whether this was a good idea. All the other men he had initiated into the club this way had been old and slow and had been in a lot worse places than this room. He got them drunk to loosen them up, but most of them really had nothing to lose anyway, and therefore it didn't occur to them that they had anything to be nervous about.

David, however, was young, and had grown up soft. He had demons, no doubt about that, and there was a storm coming that he was getting ready for. All the same, this situation was unfamiliar to him, and where the others would lay down and let it happen, David was getting ready to fight.

Richard saw all of this in one glance, and thanked whatever god there was that he had not yet pulled the knife from behind the crate of Bushmill's. "Boys, why don't you let me do this one on my own, OK?"

Harry and Chuck looked at each other, then back at him. He nodded to them as if to assure them he knew what he was doing. They shrugged and, without a word, pulled aside the curtain and headed back out to the bar.

"I'm sorry Johnny," Richard said in his most soothing voice, "I should have told you better what was going on. You see, we don't make you sign no paper or say no pledge. All we ask is that you take a blood oath with me. When we do that and I look in your eyes, I'll know if you're true or not. That's all there is to it."

"By blood oath, you mean…" David began.

Richard didn't speak. Instead, he held out his right hand for David to see. It was crisscrossed with old scars. David gathered that each of those scars bore the name of one of the men on the other side of the curtain.

"So we become blood brothers, then?" David asked.

"That's the plan. You OK with that?"

David was OK with that. Underneath it all, David was a romantic, and this seemed to fit perfectly with the journey he was on.

"Yep," David said calmly, "You got a knife or are we supposed to break a bottle over our heads and use that?"

Richard chuckled, relieved to see that things were going to be fine after all. "Got one right here."

Richard pulled out a sheathed knife. It was long and thick, the kind David thought of as a "Rambo-knife." He slid it out of the sheath and held it up between them. "Ready?" he asked.

"Yep," David said.

Richard pressed the point of the blade into his right palm, then cupped his palm slightly and pulled the blade down and out. As he did, he winced slightly and made a fist. He then flipped the knife around and held it out to David, hilt-first.

David took it and looked at it for a moment. The single light bulb was still swinging back and forth. When it swung forward, David could see his reflection in the blade. Behind him, he could see the glow from the bar filtering through the red curtain. His face, the red curtain, the swinging light, all of it together with the alcohol and the hammering music from the bar swam together in the blade of the knife. The light swung away and the blade went black. It swung forward, and he saw his own face, but this time it appeared to be ringed with fire. It swung back and forth again, and now the fire was coming from his eyes as well. It swung back and forth again, and now his face was a ghostly white. As he watched, his reflection opened its mouth to reveal a demonic grin full of razor sharp teeth. Fire poured forth from its eyes and it began to laugh. And in that laugh there was pure insanity.

David screamed and plunged the knife into his right hand, opening up a deep wound that would later require eight stitches. Richard leapt forward and took the knife, which David now held loosely in his left hand. "Jesus, Johnny, you didn't have to go so deep. You OK?"

"I'm fine," David said mildly, almost robotically. He looked up at Richard, and for a moment the older man thought he was looking directly into the gates of hell. Then David blinked and his expression returned to one of a man who had just stabbed himself and was in mild shock. "Are we supposed to shake hands now or something?" he asked.

Richard stepped forward, in spite of the fact that every instinct he had told him to get the hell out of there. He held his right hand up, and David took it.

The two men locked their eyes upon each other, and for a moment, Richard knew everything. What's more, David wanted him to. The demons that had passed through David were gone now, and the man that was left was the one Richard had come to...what was it...love? Yes, he supposed that was not too strong a word. The young man had more sorrow, more loneliness, and yet more nobility and strength of purpose than all the men in the other room combined. Richard wanted to know him. Richard wanted to help him. And David wanted those things too.

Yet again the moment passed. They released their grasp, each man retaining only a shadow of what had passed between them. That shadow, however, was enough to bind the two men more closely together than the blood oath had ever done before.

44

Now, more than two years later, as Richard held up his scarred hand to remind David of their oath, that shadow did come back to him. As always, it brought with it the memory of that night, and of the feelings that passed between them. In a way, he had loved and lost more in that one moment than in his entire life before. In that brief moment he saw in Richard that he could still love and be loved, yet he knew in the same moment that he could not allow it to happen. His nature was no longer one of love, but of revenge. He could not betray his past loves for new ones. If he did, his thirst for revenge would wane. He would grow soft, complacent, and he would forget what he must do in their names. For his purpose to remain true, he must remain true to them, and not allow himself to love again.

David looked up from his scarred hand and met Richard's eyes. "I'd rather not say whether or not I'm going to war, for your protection and mine. I will tell you this, though. After this, I'm not sure if I'll be around much. It's probably best that way, for everyone's sake."

"I'm sorry to hear that, Johnny, but I've always known this day would come. Do me a favor. When the time comes, don't say goodbye. Just stop coming in. I'll know, and you'll know that my thoughts will go with you."

Tears stung the backs of David's eyes. He nodded and said nothing.

"All right then," Richard said, clearing his throat. Then he raised his voice so that he could be heard over the juke. "BONES! Get over here."

Edwin "Bones" McIlroy had been a medic in Korea and had his own medical practice until he retired a few years ago. He was also a huge Star Trek fan. The fact that his last name was close to Dr. McKoy's made it inevitable that he would pick up the same moniker.

David knew Bones well, and had assumed he would be the one to teach him what he wanted to know. Bones, in fact, was the one that had stitched his hand after his over zealous cut in the blood oath.

When Bones, a short, fat man with a bushy gray mustache, approached, Richard stepped forward and put an arm around him. He spoke in his ear for a moment, loud enough for Bones to hear but not loud enough for anyone else. Then Bones nodded and they turned to David. Richard nodded toward the back room and they all filed through the red curtain.

"So, John, Richard tells me you want to learn to treat yourself should you ever be injured," Bones began.

"That's right. Can you teach me?"

"Of course. Do you have anyone else that could serve as a…nurse?"

"Nope. Is that a problem?"

"Not really. Just don't get stabbed in the back."

"OK. I try to avoid that anyway."

"Of course," Bones chuckled. "I understand that you have taught some of the other boys some self-defense. Could you teach an old codger like me anything?"

It was a well-known fact in The Brotherhood that David was a martial arts expert. Over the past two years, he had bartered lessons in self-defense for training in car theft, breaking and entering, burglary, surveillance, explosives, and anything else the boys had to offer that he felt he might be able to use in his future endeavors. He didn't know what the circumstances would be when it came time for him to take his revenge, so he followed the Boy Scout motto and absorbed all the preparation he could get.

"I sure can, Dr. McIlroy."

"Please, John, call me Bones like everyone else. What say we meet tomorrow at the range and then I'll take you to my place and we can get started? I have plenty of spare equipment I'd be glad to give you in case you need it, and I've also got a big room we can clear out for my lessons."

"Sounds great, Bones. How's noon sound?"

"Perfect. I look forward to it, John."

"Me too. Thanks a lot."

"My pleasure."

The three of them filed back out to the bar, and Bones rejoined his table. David and Richard hung back by the bar and faced each other.

"Thanks a lot, buddy," David said.

"Any time. You gonna stay around for awhile?"

"No, I'm gonna head out. I'll see you tomorrow, though."

"OK. It was good to see you again, Johnny."

"You too."

And with that, David walked out of the Bay Tavern, never to return.

45

David and Bones had taught each other everything they could by the middle of December. The week before Christmas, Bones shook David's hand and sent him on his way with a brand-new black medical bag he had purchased for David. The bag was stuffed with antibiotics, local anesthetics, pain-killers, syringes, needles, and a hundred other things that David now knew how to use if the occasion arose.

While David had been in training, his restlessness, the urgent need to get on with his revenge that Master Chen had sensed almost three months earlier on the anniversary of Karen's murder, had been on hiatus. It occurred to David that as long as he was working toward his revenge, or preparing himself in some way that would make the success of his plan more likely, he could keep his emotions under control...at least outwardly. As soon as his medical lessons were done, the urgency began to creep back into his life like fog creeping in from the ocean. He could think of nothing else he needed to do to prepare, other than to continue to train with Master Chen and to keep the other skills he had obtained over the last three years as sharp as possible.

He had over two years to kill until Darius got out. If he didn't do something to lift the lid off of his rage and let the steam out, he was very likely to explode long before then. The idea that had occurred to him after the drunken rednecks almost ran him off the road addressed all of his problems. He needed to keep his rage under control for two more years, partly so he could continue to train with Master Chen and partly so he didn't do something stupid like go after LaShon too early and get caught before he could take out Darius. He also needed to practice the other skills he had learned from Richard and his other friends in Half Moon Bay. It would be a shame to think he had spent so much time learning these things, only to forget them in the two years before he could actually put them to use.

Most of all, he needed to do something…something that had an outcome. An athlete can't train forever and never actually compete, and neither could he. His solution, his outlet, would address all of this. And, in his mind, he might even do something that would have made Karen and his parents proud. He wouldn't be specifically avenging their deaths, but the idea was in the same ballpark, and that would have to do for now.

David really wanted to begin on New Years' Eve. It would be so appropriate in so many ways, but he couldn't chance it. The police presence on the roads and around every bar in the area would be just too heavy to risk. Instead, he used that night and the weeks to follow to scout his first location. He knew from what he had read and seen on TV that he shouldn't hit a place near his home. Once he had several hits, the law would try to triangulate his place of residence by the places he struck. He decided from the very beginning that he would only hit cities above the Golden Gate Bridge as far north as Santa Rosa, or East of the Bay Bridge as far to the northeast as Sacramento and as far to the southeast as Modesto. Based on what he could glean from crime investigation, if he didn't ever strike in San Francisco or the peninsula, they would be very unlikely to come looking for him there. Living in Pacifica, a city almost forgotten by the rest of the Bay Area anyway, he felt confident that if he stuck to that plan and very carefully scouted every location before he struck, he would be able to pull off approximately one hit per month until Darius' release became imminent. And that, he thought, should really be enough.

And so it was, that on Thursday, January 10, 2002, David crouched in the bushes on the edge of the parking lot of The Gull's Nest, an out-of-the-way tavern in Petaluma, a town about 50 miles north of the Golden Gate Bridge along Highway 101. He hadn't taken the Golden Gate, however. He had driven all the way around the south end of the Bay and up the east side. The trip took four hours instead of about one and a half if he had taken the direct route over the bridge. In a similar vein to his strike pattern, he had also resolved to never cross a bridge on the way to or from a hit. Bridges had toll booths, toll booths had cameras, and those would record his passage. Caution, caution. Caution above all else. Whenever he felt like he should take a shortcut in this area, he remembered that, if he got caught, Darius and the others might go unpunished. His planning was flawless, his research painstaking. He would not…could not…be caught.

He waited. He wore a black overcoat and a black, hooded sweatshirt. The hood of the sweatshirt was very roomy, and he could pull it forward far enough to hide his face almost completely. His dark attire allowed him to blend completely into the shadows. He waited almost two hours before a candidate emerged from the bar. He was a fairly large man wearing faded jeans, a flannel shirt and a green baseball cap with the bill curled almost into a half-circle. He was so drunk he couldn't hold a straight line. Instead, he was banging from one parked car to the next, stopping at one point with one hand on the hood of an old Buick, bending over as if he might vomit. He didn't, though, and continued, muttering to himself as he went.

It was his first night…first of many, he hoped…and fate was with David. The drunk made his way through the entire lot to a brown and tan pickup that was at least fifteen years old. It was parked no more than 20 feet from the bushes where David was concealed, and the driver's side was facing toward him. The truck would block what was happening from anyone else who may exit the bar in the next few minutes. For now, however, it was only the two of them in the parking lot.

With some effort, the drunk fished a full key ring out of the front pocket of his tight Wranglers. As he fumbled with the lock, David stepped from his hiding place and crept silently up behind the man. His heart was pounding. His mind was telling him to turn around and go back in the bushes and wait for another person…or another night. He couldn't believe he was actually going through with this. At this moment, he realized that all the time he had planned this, and his actual murderous revenge for that matter, that there had always been a part of him…a significant part, in fact…that never believed it would happen. Well, here he really was, and his nerves were buzzing like high-tension wires. For all of his physical preparation, for all of his careful planning, he was not fully prepared mentally, and he cursed himself for it.

He paused, one foot in front of the other, as if he were listening to something. He was, in fact, listening to two sides of an argument in his own mind. After a moment, he decided that it was better that he should experience this hesitation, this case of the nerves, now as opposed to when it really mattered. If there was ever going to be an easy one, this was it, and he had better take the chance while he had it or he might never get up the nerve again.

He took another few steps, finally entering the beam of the floodlight that shone off the back of the bar toward the lot. He was five feet from his target. He stopped, readied himself, and spoke. "Give me your keys," he whispered.

David had purchased a state-of-the-art voice-altering unit. The microphone was so small he could run it under his thin mask, which provided enough tension to hold it close to his mouth. The wire ran down to the unit, which altered his voice to sound slightly higher pitched and quite a bit more harsh. When he whispered, he found, the alteration made his voice sound satisfyingly evil.

"Wha..." said the drunk, turning to face what he expected to be some sort of scumbag car-jacker. What he saw was not what he expected.

As the man turned, David raised his face into the light to allow the man to see his skeletal disguise. He bared his teeth to show the fangs and the blood dripping from them. He drew himself up to his full size, and he stepped aggressively toward his prey.

"Jesus Christ," gasped the drunk in what sounded like a thin scream, "What the fuck..."

"I said give me your keys," David whispered again, continuing to advance.

The drunk had been in his share of tight spots, and the initial shock he felt now had his adrenaline pumping. "I ain't givin' you my keys, you freak," he said, pulling the keys into his right fist.

His nervousness was gone now, replaced with a steely focus. David closed the remaining few feet between them so quickly that the man didn't even have a chance to assume a defensive posture. David grasped the man's right hand with his left, curling his fingers around the man's thumb and finding the back of the man's hand with his own thumb. With a violent twist, he turned the man's wrist outward, curling it forward at the same time. The man dropped to his knees with a squeal, reaching across with his other hand in attempt to relieve the pressure on the one David held in a death-grip.

The man now realized that he was truly in trouble, and he began to plead with David not to hurt him. David clapped his right hand over the man's mouth to shut him up, and then whispered, "You're too drunk to drive. I don't intend to hurt you, but I will take your keys. If you follow my instructions, you'll be fine. If you don't, or if you cry out, I will give you pain that makes this feel like nothing. Are we clear?"

"Yeah," blubbered the drunk. He didn't have to release his hold on the keys, because his hand was so twisted that closing his fist was impossible. Still, he relaxed it enough to demonstrate that he had relinquished his right to them.

David took his right hand from the man's mouth, reached under the man's curled hand, and plucked the keys from it like low-hanging fruit. Without hesitation, he cast them over the truck and into the bushes. In the darkness, it was impossible to tell exactly where they went.

Without letting go, David twisted the man's hand back the other way, causing him to turn away from David. David produced a pair of handcuffs from one of the many inside pockets of his trench coat. He had purchased a gross of handcuffs from a sex-shop in San Francisco just before Christmas, telling the owner that they were for a special Christmas party he was throwing. The owner wanted to know if he could come, and David took his name and number in case a spot were to open up. How would the handsome gentleman be paying for 144 pairs of handcuffs? Cash, of course.

David slapped one bracelet around the man's right wrist. Keeping his arm twisted so that he couldn't escape or even turn to face David, he stood the man up and led him firmly but without undue infliction of pain over to the door of his truck. The door handle was flat against the door, so no handcuff could fit there. David wouldn't have used that anyway, because it would be simple for the man to break it off and go back inside to call the cops. Or, even worse, go looking for his keys, find them, and drive off anyway. Having already tossed away the keys, David was faced with one option. He made a fist with his right hand, and then swung his right arm in a tight, rapid arc so that the back of his fist and his forearm smashed through the driver's side window. As he did, the man let out a surprised little scream and then stared at David's arm, waiting for the blood to start dripping on the pavement. It didn't, though, and David pulled the man forward and looped the cuffs through the steering wheel.

"Now give me your other hand," David whispered, and the trembling man obeyed. David repeated the process so that the man stood facing the driver's door of his truck, both arms handcuffed to the steering wheel.

"I'm going to place a note in your back, left pocket. It is for the cops…not you. Point it out to them when they get here. If they don't get it, I'll know, and I'll find you. Do you understand?" David rasped.

The man just nodded, looking like he might throw up in the driver's seat of his beat-up truck.

"Drinking and driving kills. Don't let me catch you doing it again," David said. There was no question, and no threat other than that which was implied. It was enough…the big man never again attempted to get behind the wheel when he'd been drinking.

The man waited for the next command, or the next threat, but none came. After a few moments, he risked a glance over his shoulder where his attacker had been. There was no one there. He gave it about five minutes to make sure that fucking freak show was gone, and then he began to scream for help.

46

The next morning, David scanned the San Francisco Chronicle for news of his excursion to Petaluma. There was nothing. He went on the Internet and checked the Santa Rosa paper. There, he found a short article about the previous night's events. It only stated that Jacob Rock, 36, of Petaluma, claimed to have been attacked in the parking lot of the Gull's Nest by "a guy dressed like the Grim Reaper." The assailant took his keys and handcuffed him to the steering wheel of his truck. Rock suffered minor injuries and nothing was stolen. Rock said that his attacker left a note for police, but police are not commenting on the existence or contents of such a note, or on the nature of the crime in general.

It would take two more of what David thought of as "hits" before he would actually make the Chronicle. That article came on March 14, and was actually in a box on the lower right hand corner of the front page, continuing onto the back page. The title was typical of its author, a little-known, smarmy police beat writer named Douglas Fairchild. It read:

Police: "Fear the Reaper"

FAIRFIELD—The man that has become known as the "Grim Reaper" or simply "The Reaper" has struck again, this time in Fairfield. Police in Fairfield say that, based on information received from investigators in Petaluma and Dublin, the sites of his first two attacks earlier this year, it appears "very likely that this is the work of the same person."

Two men were attacked and subdued by "The Reaper" outside of JB's Tavern as they left the bar. In previous incidents, there was only one victim, but the results were the same. "The Reaper" took both men's car keys and handcuffed them to one car, leaving them with only minor injuries and nothing taken other than their keys, which were found later in the bushes near the bar.

As in the previous two cases, both men were well above the legal blood alcohol level allowable to drive. However, since none of the victims had actually been able to drive their cars, none has been charged with a crime.

To date, "The Reaper" has only been seen by his four victims. However, all describe him in much the same manner. He dresses in a black overcoat with a black hood, and he either wears a mask or face paint to look like a skull, thus the nickname of "Grim Reaper." Reports of his build put him at above average size, but the victims' estimates vary widely enough that actual height and weight estimates would not be much more than a guess. All of the victims do agree in saying that he is very adept at hand to hand combat, each saying that they have never seen anyone move so quickly or with such strength.

In a joint statement, Chiefs from the three local police departments as well as the state police, who have now joined the investigation, have said the following: "Indications are that this man is attempting to stop bar patrons around the area from driving while intoxicated. To date, he has not shown a motivation to hurt or rob anyone. However, we are still considering him to be dangerous and we are working jointly to investigate each crime and apprehend the offender as quickly as possible. We are asking the public to be on their guard. If anyone sees this man or has any information about these crimes, they should call their local police department. Under no circumstances should anyone approach or try to confront him."

Police declined to speculate whether "The Reaper" would strike again.

After this article, every one of his hits was front-page news in the Chronicle, as well as many other local papers. It wasn't until July, however, that he made the front page headline. The July 9th edition of the Chronicle, in fact, had three articles on the front page that David cut out and added to his rapidly growing collection.

On that date, the front-page headline read simply:

REAPER STRIKES AGAIN!

DAVIS—The vigilante known as "The Reaper" made his sixth appearance on the Northern California bar scene last night, this time in Davis.

In what is now becoming a familiar pattern, "The Reaper" surprised four bar patrons of the Roadside Pub as they attempted to get in their cars. As in past cases, all four men were found to be legally intoxicated.

Previous attacks had been on only one or two victims, and none of the previous victims was seriously injured. The victims of last night's attack, however, did not get off as easily. One of the victims suffered a broken jaw, another a concussion, and a third a broken arm.

According to Lawrence Turner, the State Police Detective who is in charge of "The Reaper" investigation, "The four victims were somewhat prepared for the attack, and fought back. However, it appears that the perpetrator of these crimes is extremely well trained in martial arts and is physically overpowering. The men are very shaken by what they saw, and how easy it was for him to subdue them. They do say, however, that as soon as they surrendered he stopped his attacks and went about his normal routine of taking their keys and restraining them with handcuffs."

As in the past, Detective Turner warned the public to steer clear of "The Reaper." "This man is extremely dangerous and has been escalating the boldness of his attacks. While it appears his motive continues to be stopping people from driving while intoxicated, it is only a matter of time before he seriously injures or kills someone. Bar patrons should take extreme care when returning to their cars. Again, if anyone has any information on this case, please contact the police."

The byline of the headline gave credit to Douglas Fairchild, his first headline credit ever. In fact, being assigned to report on "The Reaper" case was the best thing that had ever happened to him. He had even begun to gain a little notoriety of his own, appearing on a few local news shows to share his insight. As "The Reaper" began to capture the attention of the Bay Area, Douglas Fairchild also began to capture a little slice of fame.

To the right of the top story was another article on the subject, also by Mr. Fairchild. It read with lurid alliteration:

Drunk Driving Dropping—Is Reaper Responsible?

According to statistics released yesterday by state and county law enforcement officials, injuries and fatalities attributable to drunk drivers over the recent July 4th weekend were down 20% in the Bay Area as compared to the same weekend last year. This comes on the heels of a 15% drop over Memorial Day weekend, also versus last year.

While these measurements had been dropping throughout the 1990's, they had risen each year since 1999. The amount of the drop from 2001 to this year is unprecedented, which begs the question: Why are injuries and fatalities due to drunk driving falling so dramatically?

Opinions vary, but more and more people are speculating that The Reaper deserves much of the credit. It is unclear whether bar patrons are choosing not to get behind the wheel because they fear The Reaper or because they are wary of the admittedly increased police presence around Bay Area watering holes. Either way, the advent of The Reaper seems to be the most logical reason for the change in habit.

Diana Wells, Bay Area Director of Mothers Against Drunk Driving, commented, "I can't say that I approve of his methods, but if this person has something to do with the trend we're seeing, then it would be hypocritical of me to denounce him. It saddens me that it takes something like this to make people act responsibly. I can only hope that people are actually making this choice because it's the right thing to do, and that they continue with this behavior for the long term and not just until this man is caught."

According to a Bay Area police officer, speaking on the condition of anonymity, "This is a real pain in the neck for us in a lot of ways, but you can't argue with success. If he has gotten people to think when everything the government and law enforcement tried to do couldn't...I mean, if losing your driver's license and spending $5,000 in court costs isn't enough but getting slapped around a little is...it doesn't make much sense to me but *maybe what he's doing isn't all bad. Believe me, we'll catch him, and we want to catch him, but there are those of us who think this has been a good wakeup call for some folks."*

Of course the official statements from law enforcement do not credit The Reaper as being a factor in the sudden drop in drunk driving. According to State Police Detective Lawrence Turner, "I suppose you could speculate that the increased patrols we have had to enact around bars and taverns could have something to do with this drop, but that does not make what is happening OK. The officers performing these patrols have been pulled from their normal duties, and, while drunk driving may be dropping, the fact that the officers are away from their normal positions leaves opportunities for other crimes to increase elsewhere. Make no mistake, we want to catch this man and are making every effort to do so."

For the first time since Karen's murder, David felt an emotion that was in the neighborhood of joy. This is exactly what he had hoped for. He was kicking ass and taking names, and people were noticing. He was actually bordering on being a super-hero. Like Batman, he was just a man, but he was prepared for battle and he was doing something to stop crime. If he had been around before LaShon Jackson sent up whatever rocket he took before smashing into his parents…well, so much would have changed that it's conceivable even Karen would still be alive.

As quickly as they had come, his good feelings were gone. He slipped back into his morose, brooding self and thought about his lost loved ones. As he did so, his gaze moved slightly to the left, stopping on a picture in the middle of the front page. Normally his vision would have blurred at this point, as he stared straight through the page and cast his mind back to happier times. Something in this picture, however, caught his eye.

There were two men shaking hands behind a podium, mugging for the cameras. The one on the right was the mayor of San Francisco. He was a whore for the press and was on the front page once or twice a week. It was the other man that got David's attention. He looked familiar, but David couldn't immediately place him. He glanced down at the caption, which read, "Agent Seamus Molloy, left, accepts key to city from Mayor Green."

The name brought it all back to David. This was the detective who came to his hospital room after Karen was killed. He was the guy who did the little bit of investigation that was necessary on the case. Intrigued, David read the article that was positioned directly under the picture.

Molloy Receives Key to City

SAN FRANCISCO—FBI Agent Seamus Molloy, pictured above, accepted the key to the city from a grateful Mayor Robert Green for his role in foiling the bombing attempt at the Moscone Center last month.

Molloy led a team of agents that broke up a plot by "The New Dawn," a white supremacist group that has been called "The KKK on Steroids," to detonate a bomb in the Moscone Center during a job fair geared toward minorities.

An estimated 3,000 people were in the building when Molloy and his agents apprehended Luther Haines, the alleged leader of the Northern California "New Dawn," and four of what he calls his disciples. They were in possession of an explosive device said to be large enough to level at least half of the Moscone Center. Police and FBI spokespeople declined to comment on the exact nature of the bomb.

"Thanks to Agent Molloy and his team," commented the Mayor in front of a gathering of city leaders, "there are 3,000 families who still have their mother, father, sister, brother, son or daughter coming home to them. All of those families and the entire city of San Francisco owe Agent Molloy and the FBI a tremendous debt of gratitude."

Molloy accepted the key on behalf of his team, thanking the mayor and the city for the honor.

Haines and the rest of the "New Dawn" members are being held pending trial for Federal Weapons charges. If convicted, they could face up to life in prison in a Federal Penitentiary.

Small world, David thought as he clipped out all three articles and folded them into the scrapbook he kept hidden in his spare bedroom with the rest of his secrets. Their names had appeared on the front page of the Chronicle together almost four years ago. What were the odds they would be on the front page together again? Well, Molloy and David's alter-ego, anyway. Who would have guessed back then that this would be happening now? Molloy was a hot-shot FBI agent and David was *(a superhero)* something quite different.

David chuckled a little at the absurdity of the coincidence. They were both public figures now, but he was sure this would be the last time they would share the front page.

If David only knew.

47

The next morning, David finally quit his job. He had only been to work about half of the time since he began his night job. His boss hadn't said much. David had gotten the team to where they were today, almost single-handedly. When David called and said he wouldn't be coming in anymore, Mr. Greer was relieved. He was going to have to fire David soon anyway, in spite of his contributions over the years, and he wasn't looking forward to it, partly because he had always liked David, and partly because David sometimes scared the shit out of him. He couldn't really pinpoint why, but he knew the others on the team felt the same way. All in all, David quitting was the best thing for everyone at BioMech.

It was the best thing for David too. Even though he struck only once a month, researching his next hit was taking more and more of his time. The cops were definitely stepping up their presence around bars, and David had to spend several nights monitoring their patterns before he would pull the trigger. What's more, he had to drive two to four hours each way to the bars he was targeting, as he would not compromise his "no bridge" rule.

Time wasn't the only thing working against his ability to continue with BioMech, though. David was finding it more and more difficult to concentrate on anything but planning his hits. What's more, now that he had his hits to plan and look forward to, his feelings of rage and urgency to get to LaShon, Darius and the others were much easier for him to control. He was able to continue his training with Master Chen, who now had the feeling that David was finally achieving balance in his life and putting his thoughts of revenge behind him.

And, in fact, Master Chen was not far off. David was so focused on his current activities that there were times he nearly forgot that this was just a tune-up for the real thing. There were certainly times when his rage would bubble to the surface, but those were really few and far between. When it did, he would put it out of his mind by getting in the car and driving to scout locations. He found that as long as he was actively planning his next appearance, he could keep his mind from wandering back to the rage and hate that always simmered beneath the surface.

David struck five more times before the night at the Red Rooster, where he finally encountered a bar patron with a gun. Each attack was more difficult to plan than the last, and each group he attacked was more ready for him than the last. Still, he found that he couldn't resist taking on larger and larger groups of people. A little over a month before he hit the Red Rooster, he took out six big guys, college football players from Cal, he thought, at a bar in Clayton. He had to strike them hard and fast, and he had rendered four of them unconscious before the other two flopped on their stomachs with their fingers laced behind their heads like they were under arrest. Fucking Cal pussies.

He hurt his victims more each time. He told himself that it was because there were more of them and he had to strike harder to subdue them all. What he knew deep down, though, was that he didn't have to choose such large groups to accomplish what he wanted. The papers said drunk driving was still falling, and that had nothing to do with the size of the groups. He passed on singles and doubles on every hit, opting for the larger groups. Deep in his heart, in the dark place where the hate and anger lived when it wasn't dominating his mind, he knew the truth. He was enjoying this. Not because he was doing good, but because he was doing bad.

His conscious mind wasn't taking messages from the dark places inside him, though. He told himself that he was choosing larger groups to prove to the patrons that there wasn't even safety in numbers. He also told himself he was doing it to keep himself sharp and to prepare himself in case he needed to take out a lot of people when he went after Darius and the rest of Karen's killers. Who knew what kind of protection those rich little bastards might have, especially after he took out one or two of the others?

These reasons dominated the day, but at night, his dreams were always the same. His fists smashed into nameless faces, his feet shattered bones, and his guns…even his guns sometimes came out to join in the fun. To date he hadn't had to employ any weapon other than his own body, but that day was coming, and the primal side of him couldn't wait.

Even during the day, David's more carnal instincts would put in a guest appearance. David would sometimes realize with a start that his mind was filled with acts of unspeakable violence…snapped necks, voice boxes torn out, bullets to the temple from his grandfather's guns. He would have to physically shake off the tingling sensation he felt in his limbs when he did. His heart would be pounding; he would be sweating from every pore. And what's worse, he would often look at the clock and realize he couldn't remember the last fifteen or twenty minutes, or he would look at the TV and see the sports on the news when he didn't even remember what the headlines were, let alone the weather.

Most of the time, though, David was in control. He was moving forward. He was doing something. He was performing a community service. He was a superhero, after all, and superheroes didn't hurt people unless they had to, now did they?

Did they?

48

David woke up the day after he crippled Ed Schindler at the Red Rooster and walked out on the front porch to get the paper. There were four there. Had he not picked them up for four days? Weird. He picked up the one least yellowed by the sun and left the rest. He would come get them later.

He walked slowly back into the house, massaging the welt on his chest where that fucker had shot him. He had really given himself the business last night on the way home. Told himself he was going to quit and everything. In the light of day, though, it didn't seem so bad. His armor had done its job, and he handled the five of them pretty easily. Still, bar patrons were getting pretty wary of him. He wasn't going to quit, no matter what the pussy side of him thought. He might have to consider changing tactics, though.

David rolled the green rubber band off the paper and let it shoot away into the living room. He sat at the kitchen table and unfolded the paper. As he expected, his exploits of the previous night were front-page news. It would be on the local news too…maybe the top story. The big question would be whether it would be on CNN again. They had been slow on the uptake, but when he beat up those football players from Cal, they had finally sent someone out to interview that prick reporter Fairchild that was getting famous off of him.

Speaking of the Devil, David had gotten him the front-page headline again. David did have to hand it to him, though; that little weasel sure did come up with some clever headlines.

Reaper Shot in Sac

SACRAMENTO—Five men are in the hospital this morning after being attacked by the Grim Reaper behind the Red Rooster, a Sacramento tavern.

This was The Reaper's twelfth attack, and by far the most brutal. As of this writing, one of the victims was still in surgery to repair his shattered right elbow. All five were rendered unconscious in the attack. All five also suffered moderate concussions. Among the other injuries were a broken jaw, a cracked vertebrae, and several broken and separated ribs.

As has been the case in his recent attacks, the victims were prepared. One of them had carried a gun last night and, according to bar patrons, had bragged that he would use it if The Reaper were to attack. As it turned out, he got his chance. The gun, however, did no more to stop The Reaper than anyone else has been able to do.

I spoke to Russell Terry, who had been leaving the bar with his girlfriend, Edna Samms, at the time of the attack. "We heard screams from behind the bar, so we ran around the back," Terry said. "Just as we got around the corner, Ed [Schindler, the victim that is still in surgery] shot him. I'd say The Reaper was no more than five feet from Ed and the bullet hit him right in the chest. I know because it stopped him and spun him toward us so we could see his face. Scariest [expletive deleted] thing I ever saw. His face looked like a skull, but he had red eyes. Like blood. Anyway, after about a second, he straightened out and came after Ed like nothing had happened. The guy's [expletive deleted] bulletproof. That's when he broke Ed's arm like it was a toothpick. Then he drug Ed over by the rest of them and I guess that's when he cuffed them and took their keys. Then he just ran up the hill and me and Edna ran back inside to call the cops."

Preliminary reports from police indicate that no blood has been found between the site of the attack and the hill behind the Red Rooster, or on the hill itself. Police speculate that The Reaper must have been wearing some sort of body armor to deflect the bullet. They have confirmed that the weapon was fired, and they have apparently located the slug, although they have declined to comment further on the subject of the bullet or on any other details of the attack

Reading about the attack was surreal for David. Could he really have hurt those people that badly? He tried to remember what it felt like, but it was like trying to remember a dream. When he concentrated, he could remember the details, but it was almost like he had watched someone else beat up those guys as opposed to doing it himself.

Still, a wave of satisfied pride washed over him. The armor had had its first field test, and it passed. Maybe not with flying colors, but if he could take a bullet from five feet and keep fighting, that was good enough. What's more, he had easily taken out five big men, men who had been ready for him, without even breaking a sweat. He had smashed all of their heads before they could get in their cars and hurt anyone else. And they were bad singers anyway…he had never heard a worse rendition of "Margaritaville" in his life, and he had heard many.

He chuckled at this, but the smile quickly faded. Thinking of those guys, the four that seemed like regular guys, anyway, singing together and having a good time brought about a feeling of guilt that was almost crushing. Not long ago, that was him and his college buddies. What they were about to do was wrong, no doubt, but they weren't out to hurt anyone on purpose. It wasn't like they were thieves or drug dealers or rapists or wife-beaters or something. Well, one or two of them were probably one or two of those things, he guessed, but he still didn't feel right about beating them so badly. Maybe he needed to rethink his methods. Not only had he nearly been killed, but he had sent five guys to the hospital. This hadn't been what he had intended, had it?

Glancing down, a familiar name caught his attention and drove the arguing pride and guilt to the back of his mind again. The name was Molloy, the man whose face was apparently on the other side of his coin.

Molloy/FBI to Join Reaper Investigation

SACRAMENTO—State Police Detective Lawrence Turner announced this morning that the FBI would be joining the State Police and the many municipal police departments already involved as active participants in the "Grim Reaper" investigation.

He went on to say that the FBI task force would be led by Agent Seamus Molloy. Agent Molloy gained notoriety last summer when he stopped a bombing attempt at the Moscone Center by the white supremacist group "New Dawn." The five perpetrators of the foiled attack are currently awaiting trial.

"We are very pleased to have Agent Molloy and the FBI join our investigation," Turner said. "He brings a great deal of investigative experience to the table, as well as the extensive resources of the FBI."

When asked what prompted the FBI to join the investigation, Turner said, "They recognize as we do that we cannot allow this type of vigilantism to continue in our society. Our system of laws and law enforcement certainly has its flaws, but we cannot allow citizens to take the law into their own hands."

Molloy and his team are expected to meet with State Police today.

David read the article three times, trying to digest it. Call it fate, call it destiny, call it whatever you want, apparently he and Seamus Molloy were meant to play out their roles on the same stage. Did this change things? He thought it did. He hadn't known Molloy for more than a few minutes, but he seemed like a pretty sharp guy. A pretty nice guy too, for that matter. He must have something on the ball, anyway, if he busted those New Dawn assholes. Not only that, how'd he get from a police detective to FBI agent in four years? He must be pretty goddamn good.

Yes, David thought, this was going to force some rethinking...perhaps even a change of scenery for him and The Reaper. Hanging out at bars was getting old anyway...it was time for him to graduate and move into the real world.

As for Mr. Molloy...what was that old saying? Oh yes...keep your friends close and your enemies closer.

"See you soon," David whispered to the newspaper as a sly grin spread across his face.

49

The following morning, Seamus Molloy walked into the State Police Department Headquarters in San Francisco. He showed his badge and then waited a few minutes for Detective Turner to come to meet him in the lobby.

"Agent Molloy?" Turner asked, holding out his hand as he walked toward him across the heavily polished floor.

"Yes," Seamus said, holding out his own hand.

"Detective Larry Turner. Great to have you here."

Detective Turner gave Seamus's hand a few quick pumps and then said, "Please, come with me."

They crossed the lobby and stopped at the elevators. Detective Turner tapped the up button and stood back. "We're on seven," he said nervously, looking at the elevator position indicators above each car. The one on the left was quickly ticking toward the "L."

The doors split open, and the passengers spilled out like insects from rotten fruit. No one made eye contact with anyone else. Gloom ruled the roost at the State Police Headquarters.

The two men stepped wordlessly into the elevator. Detective Turner pressed the button with the "7" on it, and the elevator bumped to life, ascending quickly to the seventh floor.

The doors opened, revealing a stark corridor that extended to the left and right. Detective Turner stepped out of the elevator and turned left, commenting, "We're down here," with a brief glance back at Seamus.

The hallway dead-ended into a wooden door. Detective Turner slid a magnetic badge into the slot above the door handle. It clanked, and he turned the knob to let them in.

Inside was the Grim Reaper war room. The room was almost stark white, save the off-white institutional looking tile on the floor. There were three desks to the right, all of them empty at the moment. The left side of the room was dominated by an industrial-sized bulletin board that covered the entire wall. On it was a map of the Bay Area. A dozen thumbtacks were scattered around the north and east bay. Pinned up all around the map were various typed sheets of paper. They were loosely grouped under pink cards with the names of a dozen cities printed on them. A few more odds and ends were sprinkled around the edges of the board, like garnishes on a salad.

"Well, this is it," Detective Turner commented. "We really are very glad to have you, Agent Molloy. I'm sorry if I seem a little nervous, but this case is really getting to me, you know. I used to think I was a good investigator, but this one has me baffled. I'm sure you know from your cop days that having the higher powers called in isn't great for one's career, right?"

"Detective Turner, I'm here to work with you, not to upstage you. I've had my moment in the sun. When we get this guy, and it's only a matter of time before we do, we'll share the credit. Now, let's get to work."

"I appreciate that," Detective Turner said, with only a hint of mistrust in his voice. "OK, I guess we can just go right to the wall of fame."

Detective Turner walked over and stood next to Seamus in front of the map. "Of course you know this is the map of his attacks. To the left and right here are the names of each city and the various information we have associated with each. The local police report, names and vital stats of the victims, and of course our report from each."

"What's that," Seamus asked, pointing to a piece of paper on the right side of the board, adjacent to the window.

"That's the note from the first attack."

"Do you mind if I read it?"

"No, of course not."

Seamus walked across the length of the board to where the letter hung. It was tacked on all four corners, but the lines where it was originally folded were still plainly visible. It appeared to have been printed on an inkjet printer.

"Anything on the printer?"

"HP. Only about a million of them in the Bay Area."

"I figured," Seamus said, as he began to read the note.

Dear Police,

I want you to know that I do not intend to hurt anyone. Drunk driving is on the rise again and someone has to do something about it. I know you're trying, but the law is not on your side. I am.

I may decide to do this again. If I have any future messages for you, I will leave a note such as this in the back left pocket of the person whom I have just stopped from driving while intoxicated.

It wasn't signed. Seamus read it four times silently, trying to glean something of the perpetrator.

"Anything jump out at you?" Detective Turner asked.

"*Whom,*" Seamus replied.

"What?"

"He used 'whom' correctly. In fact this last sentence is pretty complex, and he's right on the money grammatically. He's definitely educated."

"That's what the profilers say also," Detective Turner said.

"They always say that, though. Probably say he's a white male in his late twenties or early thirties too. Middle class, neighbors say he's an angel?"

"You got it."

"Well, so far I tend to agree. That's the one they use for all serial criminals. There must've been a whole chapter how all serial criminals fit that profile in Psych 101."

Detective Turner chuckled at this. Seamus kept looking at the letter for a little while longer, and then moved back to the map.

"Any appreciable pattern?"

"Nope, not that we can figure out anyway. They're all North and East Bay. Profilers say he lives between Concord and Fairfield. They think he uses the 680 as his main thoroughfare going one way or the other."

"They would think that. Did you check the cameras at the toll plazas on the nights in question?"

"We had a computer run scenarios if he lived in the City, on the Peninsula, in the East Bay or North Bay. There were only a few interesting ones from the City and Peninsula, and they all had rock-solid alibis. From the North, like around Fairfield, most of his hits would not have required use of a bridge coming or going. From below the Benicia Bridge, well, he would've had to cross that, but so do thousands of other people every day."

"Could you look for cars that crossed those specific days and no others?"

"We did, also came up empty there."

"Seems like this guy's pretty careful," Seamus said.

"Yep. I'd like to think that's why we haven't even been able to even catch a whiff of him," Detective Turner replied grimly.

"Well, I guess you better begin walking me through your reports and evidence from each crime scene."

"I guess so. You wanna start with Petaluma...the first one?"

"Chronological is probably best. From what I understand, he's escalating. I'm hoping that will make him more careless. Maybe there'll be something a fresh set of eyes will spot."

"OK, here we go," said Detective Turner, placing a foot-high stack of files on the table in the middle of the room.

The two men pulled chairs up to the table, and Detective Turner opened the file marked 'Reaper—Petaluma—January 10, 2002.

Almost five hours later, Seamus Molloy emerged from the State Police Headquarters. His head was swimming with information, or, more specifically, a lack of information. The victims' names, injuries and stories were a jumble in his mind. Despite all of the information on the crime scenes and the victims, it seemed the combined efforts of the State and local Police Departments had come up with a shutout on useful clues and evidence that might help him find the perpetrator. He came close to mentally using his target's popular moniker, but he was trying to refrain from dignifying what the man was doing by acknowledging his pop-culture-darling nickname.

Seamus got into his black Yukon and pulled away from the sidewalk. He was so focused on his new albatross (and, he feared, that may be what this would turn out to be) that he didn't notice the dark blue Honda Accord pull out behind him and follow him toward the freeway.

50

A few weeks later, Seamus was no further along than he had been when he left the State Police Building on his first day on the case. He had visited every one of the crime scenes, trying to commune with each one. He was attempting to get a feel for what made The Reaper tick (he had given up on his denial of the nickname his second day on the case). So far, he had about as much as the previous stewards of the case had come up with.

The good news was that The Reaper hadn't struck again. Of course if he did, then Seamus would have a fresh crime scene to work with instead of these others, which had been spoiled by time and bumbling investigative practices.

It was Friday night, and Seamus was leaving the State Police Building after his briefing with Detective Turner. They had decided to close each day with a meeting here at 3:30 p.m., sharing any new leads, theories or evidence they may have gathered that day.

They were usually done by 4:30, which meant if he hustled he could get to the gym by 5:00 for a quick workout before heading home to see Molly. He swung the big Yukon out into traffic and stepped on it. Unlike most of the previous nights since beginning the investigation, there was no blue Honda trailing behind him. Having been so wrapped up in the case, he hadn't noticed it on previous nights, so he certainly didn't notice its absence now.

As fate would have it, about 20 minutes later he pulled into the parking lot of the Gorilla Gym in Daly City, and parked right next to that very same Honda Accord.

Seamus went inside and changed into sweats and a black T-shirt that had faded to dark gray after numerous washings. He then grabbed his towel and headed out to the gym floor.

The Gorilla Gym was in a fairly small building in a strip mall. Seamus liked it because it felt like a real gym, like the one Apollo Creed took Rocky to in the third movie of the series. Seamus was a bit romantic in his own right, and this just made him feel more like working out than did some of the Yuppie Gyms closer to his house. What's more, the people here generally kept to themselves. No talk meant faster workouts, and that meant he could get home sooner to see Molly and continue working on making that baby she had been bugging him for.

It was Friday, so it was chest and back night. One of the three flat benches was open, so he hurried toward it quickly. Out of the corner of his eye, he saw another guy heading the same direction. He quickened his pace, but the guy was coming from a closer position and had fewer obstacles in his path than Seamus did. It was going to be close.

Seamus saw that the guy realized what was happening. He could have beaten Seamus, but instead he slowed his pace and began to mill around in the area as if he weren't sure what he was going to do next.

Seamus felt a little guilty that he had been in such a hurry. Even though this guy looked (under his baggy sweatpants and sweatshirt) like he was pretty well put together, he was apparently shy and non-confrontational. Seamus, in his haste, had seemed to have scared him away.

As Seamus began to slide a 45-pound weight onto the end of the bar, the big guy turned and looked at him briefly, trying to pretend he hadn't noticed Seamus was there. The guy nodded and gave a quick smile, and then sidled away.

In spite of himself, Seamus's heart went out to the man. When he looked in his eyes, there was something sad and lonely there. Something that said he would rather pretend he hadn't been heading for the flat bench than risk confronting another person who had the same destination.

Seamus watched as the man chose an open chest press machine. He bent down deeply to place the pin in the rack. At first, Seamus thought the guy dropped the pin. Then he realized that the guy had just chosen the whole rack (Seamus believed that the bottom block on that machine read 400 pounds). Seamus had seen guys go up almost that far, but they had all warmed up first. As he watched, Mr. Big and Lonely sat down and began to hammer out reps with the full rack sliding up and down behind him. Seamus counted 12 reps before the guy eased the weight back down.

"Jesus," Seamus breathed. Then he went back to loading the bar for his own warm-up set.

Seamus saw the shy guy several times over the next week or so. He must have been either new or he had just kept a low profile before now. Seamus thought it was the former, because he overheard comments from time to time about the big, new guy who could put up so much weight but never said a word.

Seamus decided that night that he would attempt to make the acquaintance of the newcomer. He still felt guilty over the race to the bench, and he was also charmed by the quiet manner in which the man carried himself. What's more, Seamus couldn't shake the feeling that he knew the guy from somewhere. For the life of him, he couldn't place where.

Seamus exited the locker room and looked for his mark. He spotted him quickly. Conveniently, he was loading what looked like a warm-up weight on the flat bench again.

Seamus sauntered over to the flat bench area. The other two were occupied by groups of two and three people working out together. This also played into Seamus's favor, because it gave him an excuse to ask only the shy man if he could work in.

"I see you're just starting," he said to the shy man, "do you mind if I work in?"

The man thought for a moment, staring rather stupidly at Seamus. Then he replied. "Sure. This OK for warm-ups?"

"It is," Seamus replied, glancing at the bar with one 45 pound plate on each side.

"Shall I go first or would you like to?" the man asked.

"You go ahead," Seamus added, again feeling both guilt and sympathy for the man's polite manner in spite of his obvious shyness.

The big guy laid back and banged out 20 reps with 135 pounds. Then Seamus took his turn and did eight, and then turned and held out his hand. "I'm Seamus," he said.

"David," replied the shy guy, and then, "How much for your next set?"

"Twenty-fives are good," Seamus replied.

They worked out pretty much in silence, communicating only to indicate how much weight to add to the bar.

As David finished his third set of ten reps with 365 pounds on the bar, Seamus felt he could no longer contain himself. As he watched David's face strain into a concentrated grimace, he felt the feeling grow even stronger that he had seen this man, and more specifically that look, before.

"David, do I know you from somewhere?"

"Well, I wasn't going to say anything because I'm sure you get recognized a lot and you probably don't want to be bothered," David replied, almost apologetically.

"So we have met? Where?"

David paused, seeming to compose himself, and then said, "You investigated my girlfriend's murder a little over four years ago."

It all came rushing back to Seamus then, and he felt he knew why this poor guy was so shy. The tragic memory of the formerly beautiful woman with her brains blown all over the white wall of her (and his) bedroom swam into his mind's eye. Close behind was the memory of his conversation with David in the hospital afterward. His grim and pained look of determination when he was working out matched the look he wore in the hospital room that day.

"David…McGuire is it? I'm sorry I didn't remember you before. You've either lost or gained weight since then, am I right?"

"I don't know, but I'm in a little better shape, I guess, than the last time you saw me."

Seamus smiled benevolently and asked, "How are you doing?"

The look on David's face answered the question, and the answer almost broke Seamus's heart. "I'm OK," David replied, managing a brave smile.

"I'm sorry, that's probably a stupid question," Seamus said, feeling like the world's biggest asshole.

"That's OK. Hey, I saw you in the paper a few times. Congratulations on that New Dawn thing. That's one of the greatest things I've ever heard of anybody doing. I wish once in my life I could do something that heroic."

"Thank you. That's very kind of you to say. Just doing my job, you know."

"Sure. I saw the article the other day also. You're on the case of this Grim Reaper now, right?"

"Yes, I am. Can't really comment much, you know."

"I understand. I bet your family is really proud of you, though," David said, dropping his eyes as he spoke the word family.

"I suppose," Seamus said. The details of Karen Chavez's murder were clear in his mind now, as if it had happened yesterday. The look on David's face when he spoke of family reminded Seamus that he had lost his parents in a drunk-driving accident before Karen was murdered. If he remembered correctly, David didn't have any other family, at least not in California.

"How did you get from police detective to FBI agent so fast?" David asked.

"Right place at the right time, and a little bit of luck."

"I doubt that's the case," David said, producing a smile that lit up his face momentarily, giving Seamus a hint of the man he must have been before tragedy found him.

"What about you," Seamus asked, "What do you do for a living?"

"Well, I'm kind of between jobs now. Between gyms too. I just happened by this place and started coming in about a week ago. I think I like it better than the foo-foo place I used to go to. Have you been coming here long?"

"A few years now. I like it too. Like you say, it's not so foo-foo here. People are here to work out and not to chat, you know."

David's eyes dropped when Seamus said this. Seamus realized that what he had just said might have implied that he didn't want to be stuck in this conversation with David. The truth was actually quite the opposite. Seamus found David both intriguing and charming. He was shy, intelligent, polite and respectful. What's more, Seamus got the feeling that he was still very much alone, but was bravely moving forward with his life anyway. How else could you explain his phenomenal strength?

Seamus didn't want David to go on thinking that he hadn't wanted to converse with him. Hadn't he, in fact, come over specifically to meet David? Well, here he was, and he was considering breaking one of his own cardinal rules: Never make friends at the gym. He had seen it before...once you have a friend at the gym, you need to plan an extra half hour to bullshit every night. Somehow, though, he didn't think that would be the case with David. In the interest of removing the abashed look he had helped put on David's face a moment ago, and also because he was beginning to genuinely like David, Seamus decided to break his rule.

"David, I hope you don't think I meant you when I said that. In fact, I have been looking for someone to work out with. I come every weeknight at about 4:30 or 5:00. I need someone to push me a little, and it sure looks like you could do that."

David's face turned a dull pink, and he grinned sheepishly. The look on his face was that of a geek who had just been asked to prom by the most popular girl in school. "Really? I've been kind of hoping to find someone to work out with too. It gets a little lonely being by yourself all the time, you know."

"OK then," Seamus said, "enough talk...let's get going, partner."

The two men resumed their workout. As Seamus turned to return one of the 45 pound weights to the rack, the sheepish smile on David's face morphed momentarily into something completely different. A look of malicious triumph flashed across David's face, retreating immediately back into the shadow of the painfully shy, lonely persona he had brought out for the occasion.

"I usually do incline next...is that OK?" David asked.

"That's great, David," Seamus said, smiling at his new friend.

51

Ever since Karen's death, David had somehow projected an aura that caused older men to want to help him out of his lonely and troubled existence. Mr. Greer, Master Chen and Richard Barnes had all taken up the father-figure mantle at one time or another. David, in his own right, had liked each of them, but he never lost sight of the fact that he was using each one to prepare in various ways for his revenge. It suited his purposes for the men to take him on as a project...as someone who needed saving, or as someone who needed a father. It occurred to him as he was sitting in his car across the street from Seamus Molloy's house one night before they actually met in the gym that none of his other three benefactors had sons (or daughters) of their own. Perhaps these men needed David to fill a void in their own lives left by sons who had never been born, or, in Master Chen's case, had been killed before he had a chance to live.

David knew from observing his house, his wife, and their comings and goings that Seamus didn't have children, and that made him confident he would be able to work the same charm or magic or whatever it was on Seamus that had worked on the others. When he thought about it, he couldn't really say what he had done to draw the others to him, but for some reason he was sure that when the time came, he could produce the same effect on Seamus without much effort at all.

As it turned out, he was absolutely right. Seamus and David worked out together almost every night of the week. As often happened in such situations, they formed a loose dependence on each other for motivation in their workouts. At least that was what Seamus thought. David didn't need any more motivation to work out than he already had. All he had to do was close his eyes and picture his parents in their caskets or Karen's bloody hair splayed across her face, and he could pump out two or three extra reps after he thought he was finished. Still, he played his part well, giving Seamus the impression that his friendship was helping David come out of his shell.

About six weeks after they began meeting at the gym regularly, Molly Molloy left for a week to visit her mother in New York. Seamus would not be able to join her, of course. The Reaper had been quiet since he joined the investigation, but it was like the calm before the storm. He and Detective Turner were sure that he would strike again soon. Serial criminals like this very rarely just stopped. He might be regrouping or scouting a new location, but they were sure he would be back. If Seamus was in New York when it happened, he might as well just mail his badge back to the FBI field office in San Francisco with his resignation letter.

"Hey, I'm batching it this week," Seamus said as they were finishing their last set of the day, "Do you wanna go get a beer and something to eat? I don't feel like going home and cooking for myself tonight."

"I know what you mean, believe me," David said, with just a slight hint of dejection…just enough to bring Seamus just a bit further into his web.

"Sorry, I guess you do," Seamus said, a little ashamed of his selfishness and for saying such a thing without realizing that David had probably gone home and cooked for himself every night for the last four and a half years.

"Oh, don't worry about it," David said, perking up noticeably. "Sure, a beer sounds great. I think there's a basketball game on tonight, maybe we can go watch it at McSorley's down the street?"

"McSorley's, is that a good place? I've never been," Seamus said.

"It's a wanna-be Irish pub. It's not bad. The owner seems to be trying really hard, but I don't think he has the budget to really go all out. He's got a few maps of Ireland up and has Guiness, Bass, and Harp on tap. No shepherd's pie or anything, but they do make a pretty good burger if your stomach isn't averse to a little grease."

Seamus was very proud of his Irish roots. He hadn't found much in the Bay Area to remind him of some of the places in New York he used to go to. It had occurred to him that David was of Irish descent, but he had assumed he was one of the Irish whose roots had become so tangled with all of the others in America that he could no longer see their origin. The kind of Irish-American who would pronounce his name "See-Muss." Although the place David was suggesting didn't sound like it would help much, the fact that David knew what a real Irish pub should look like and the fact that they should serve shepherd's pie made Seamus like David even more. Maybe he had finally found someone with just a little green still running in his veins along with the red, white and blue.

"That sounds perfect. I'll follow you there?" Seamus said, grinning.

"Cool. Let's go."

That was one of three meals they shared that week. When Seamus thought about it, he could barely believe it. Four years ago he had investigated the murder of this guy's fiancée. Now, for better or for worse, David was quickly becoming one of Seamus's best friends.

David was the most intelligent person Seamus had met in the Bay Area. Seamus was a very smart person in his own right, but he could barely hold a candle to David in most conversational areas. Seamus found their conversations challenging, enlightening, educational, and extremely enjoyable. They spoke often of Ireland, of its geography, its mythology, and its political history. David also knew much of the Irish experience in America. Seamus was thrilled to have found someone with an interest in this area, and it allowed him to exercise mental muscles he hadn't used in years.

It occurred to Seamus more than once during their conversations that David might be able to provide some help on the Reaper case. It was a long shot, but David was so intelligent and knew so much about so many things that he might just see something that Seamus wasn't seeing. Of course this was seriously against protocol, so he resisted the urge, at least for now.

What's more, he appreciated that David never brought it up after he said the first night that he couldn't discuss it. He guessed David would probably be very interested in hearing about the case, especially from an insider. But if David could keep from asking about it, then Seamus damn well couldn't bring it up either. Now that he thought about it, David was the only friend or acquaintance he had (including Molly) that never asked about the Reaper. All of them knew the subject was off limits, but apparently it was still too much for any of the rest of them to resist. He was now spending more time with David than any of them but Molly, and he never said a word. The level of respect that David showed him by leaving this subject alone was almost staggering to Seamus.

He found himself looking forward more and more to spending time with David. He and Molly weren't having any luck in conceiving a child, and that was quite a source of tension in the Molloy household. David asked so little of Seamus that it was just refreshing to be around him. Seamus had a feeling that if he told David he wouldn't be around for a few weeks or a few months, David would just say "OK," and not give him any kind of hassle or ask why or what for.

Even so, Seamus felt a growing interdependency with David. He began to think of David as the little brother he never had…maybe even the son he couldn't have. They were close in age, but David's pain and vulnerability gave Seamus the feeling that David was much younger than he. Although they didn't talk about it directly, Seamus was almost sure that spending time with him had brought David out of his shell, at least a little. He compared the man he knew now with the one he met just a short time ago, and it made him feel good to think he had something to do with the transformation.

David was soon a regular for dinner at the Molloy household. Molly found him sweet and charming in much the same way Seamus did, and she didn't mind having him over at all. In fact, having him there precluded the possibility of conversation about the baby-making difficulties, or the lack of conversation about Seamus's job and current case. In fact, both Molly and Seamus had the distinct feeling that they got along better when David was around.

For David's part, he began the process of getting close to Seamus by putting on an act, although the character he was playing was not far from reality. As the relationship began to grow, it became more and more difficult for him to maintain a true separation of his feelings for Seamus and Molly from his original intention. The fact was that he liked them both very much. They were two of the nicest people he had ever met, and he was touched that they truly seemed to care about him.

For the first two months after they officially met, David spent almost no time scouting locations for his next hit. He wanted to gauge what he was up against, and what he discovered was no surprise—Seamus was one sharp guy.

As he was leaving the Molloy's house one evening, however, he came to a realization that he was no longer just delaying his next hit because he was learning about his opponent. He realized that there were times when his monthly appearances as The Reaper, as well as his eventual revenge, left his mind entirely. When he was with Seamus and Molly, he actually had feelings that approached contentment. When that happened, his desire to continue with his other activities waned, and sometimes almost disappeared.

Until now, there hadn't been a moment since Karen was killed that he wasn't consumed by his need to avenge her. Whether it was the initial descent into depression, or the subsequent training and preparation, or finally his life as The Reaper, all of his thoughts, all of his time, all of his energy was focused on preparing to kill Darius, LaShon and the others. The fact that something had finally caused his desire and determination to fade filled him immediately with emotion. Guilt was the first, that he could so easily forget the faces of his loved ones. Anger was next, that he would let himself be deterred from his course for any reason. Underneath those, however, was a degree of confusion as to how he would handle the Molloys from here on. He would need to rededicate himself to his life's work and do so immediately, there was no question about that. With regard to the Molloys, though, he was having trouble making himself believe that he didn't want to continue his friendship with them. It was good to keep Seamus close in hopes that he may eventually share information about the case and give David clues as to how to avoid capture. For that reason, David felt he should continue to see them. He would have to be very careful, though, lest his true feelings begin to slip out. If Seamus began to suspect the truth…well, who knew what would happen? If he did, David may be forced to take actions that he would prefer not to, or that he would prefer to take at a later time.

That night, he thought long and hard about the patterns he had established as The Reaper, and he tried to put himself in Seamus's shoes with regard to the investigation. After much deliberation, he decided that he should take his hits in a slightly different direction. He needed to keep Seamus off balance, or Seamus would catch him.

52

The next morning, David woke up early and got ready to spend the day driving around the North and East Bay scouting locations for his next appearance. Due to the change in strategy he was planning, he expected to be gone most of the day.

Before he left, he opened the front door and picked up the newspaper. He thought he would check the local sections and see if he could get any ideas as to where to start. He spun the rubber band off and shook it open as he walked back to the kitchen. When he saw the headline, he stopped and stood like a statue in the kitchen door, not believing what he saw.

REAPER CAUGHT!!

SAN FRANCISCO—Police in San Francisco last night apprehended a suspect fitting the general description of the vigilante known as the Grim Reaper, or just The Reaper. He was seen hiding near the parking lot of The Applewood Inn in San Francisco. Those who saw him immediately used their cell phone to call 9-1-1, and police responded quickly and apprehended the suspect.

Neither the FBI nor the State Police have offered comment as of yet on whether or not the man they have in custody is actually The Reaper...

David didn't turn the paper over to read the rest. He was sick with rage that someone would copy him and bring doubt to the people of the Bay Area as to his effectiveness and ability to avoid capture. All of the mixed feelings from the previous night were gone. David the Reaper was all the way back, and he wanted to make a hit soon to send a statement. In fact, he thought it might be time to leave Seamus and the other cops another note.

Three days later, David was ready to go. He was somewhat afraid that he was rushing it, but the risk was one he was willing to take. Even though the papers said that police had confirmed that this was just a copycat to the real Grim Reaper, David felt they would still be off guard and focusing on processing this guy as well as the media frenzy right outside their front door. And he had a message for the cops that couldn't wait.

Seamus hadn't shown up at the gym the first two days after the supposed capture, so David skipped the third in favor of further planning. Neither had called the other. If it came up, David would tell them that he read the news and knew Seamus would be too busy to get together.

David headed out that evening at dusk and drove around the south end of the Bay and came back up the East Side. He passed three bridges that could have made his trip much quicker, and finally arrived at his destination. It was a town called Richmond, and he suspected that it would provide him as good a chance as any town in the Bay Area for some action.

He parked his car on a very dark commercial street that was well removed from the main part of town. He parked next to a hedge that divided a tiny market and an auto parts store. Both businesses had bars on the windows and doors, and both looked like they had seen their better and more profitable days. The streetlights were few and far between here, and he didn't see a soul walking, riding or driving on this street.

A few blocks over was a residential neighborhood consisting of a few streets of run-down homes and then a great many low-income apartment complexes. He had located this place on one of his scouting trips. It reminded him of the area LaShon Jackson and his mother still lived, and that was why he chose it. He thought the odds of a crime happening here were very good, and that was what he was hoping would happen while he watched and waited. Moreover, he thought if he established this as his new *modus operandi,* he could take out LaShon and remove much of the likelihood that Seamus would link LaShon to him. If that worked, he would have the breathing room he needed to go after Darius and the others.

David pulled his black hood down as far as it would go. He felt for his weapons, checked the operation of his vocal equipment and his mask, pulled his gloves on tight, and began to walk toward the residential neighborhood. He put his hands in his pockets and hunched over as much as he could, trying to appear to be either a vagrant or a wanderer who was not worth a second look by anyone who might pass.

David walked quickly down the streets with houses, and then began to criss-cross the grounds of the apartment complexes. Most of them contained five or six buildings with eight units each, four upstairs and four down. The buildings were constructed of cheap wood with various colors of paint flaking from the walls. Most of them had bars on the windows and deadbolts on the doors. The pavement of the driveways and walkways was buckled and crumbling. The common areas, which had once been planted with grass and shrubs, were barren of vegetation. In one, a lonely swingset stood in the middle of a dusty circle. Only one swing remained where there had once been three, and this one emitted a rusty squeal every time the wind gusted.

As he walked, he watched carefully both for people who might have taken notice of him and for people who might present an opportunity for him. At the same time, he listened. After about an hour, he heard what he was listening for coming from Building 4, Apartment 1 in the Richmond Arms Apartments.

The sound he was listening for was the sound of fighting. When he came here, he figured the chance was pretty good that he might go all night without hearing or seeing an opportunity to stop a crime in progress. As had always been the case in his time combating drunk driving, luck was with him tonight.

As he walked between the yellow-green buildings of the Richmond Arms, he heard a deep-voiced bellow come from Building 4. He stopped, faced the building, and waited for the next sound to determine the source. He faintly heard a woman respond, and then there was another bellow from the man. "YOU BEST GET BACK OVUH HERE, BITCH!"

This was it, he walked quickly toward the door of Apartment 1 and paused right in front of it. He heard a grumble from the woman again through the paper thin wall. He couldn't hear what she said exactly, but he thought he heard both defiance and fear in her voice. Good for her.

He felt a steely calm fall over him. His heart was beating hard, but unlike his first attack as the Reaper in Petaluma, he was neither nervous nor frightened. His heart was beating because he was excited. It had been almost three months since he had been to battle, and he realized now that he had missed it like a weary traveler misses his home. Now that he had finally come home, his familiar battle rage fell over him like a misty, red curtain. His muscles tensed like steel cables, his eyes narrowed, and his ears strained to hear the one last thing he was waiting for.

"WHEN I TELL YOU TO GET OVUH HERE, YOU BEST GET THE FUCK OVUH HERE!!" The angry roar from the other side of the door was punctuated by a slap and a high-pitch scream of pain. He had been invited in.

David delivered a rapid and devastating kick to the door just to the left of the deadbolt. It crashed open, splinters of wood flying everywhere as the locked deadbolt pulverized the doorjamb. David blew through the door like a hurricane and stormed without hesitation into the room and toward the couple in the middle of the room.

The man was huge—probably 6' 7" and maybe 300 pounds. He was grasping the upper arm of the slender young woman, presumably to keep her from falling so that he could hit her again with his raised right hand. Her right cheek and eye were already swelling, and she looked like she was close to losing consciousness. When David crashed through the door, they both froze like statues and turned to look at the door.

"WHAT THE FUCK!" the man yelled, his voice raising noticeably on the last word.

"Get your hands off of her," David said in a quiet but commanding tone as he strode toward the behemoth in the middle of the room.

The man's eyes were as big as saucers. David had clearly caught him of guard, but his adrenaline was already pumping in preparation for the beating he was about to deliver to the woman. He shoved her aside roughly, causing her to fall over a rotten old recliner onto her back.

The man turned toward David to meet him in battle, but he underestimated how quickly David was moving. When he realized this, he brought his right arm around in a hurried roundhouse. David was already inside his range, and he caught the man's arm and turned his back into the giant, at the same time pulling his arm down and bending over at the waist. The man was off balance and top heavy to begin with, so David flipped him over his back with ease.

The man crashed down hard on his back, the wind leaving his lungs in a rush. He attempted to roll over onto his stomach to push himself up, but David was on him, delivering a crushing elbow to the base of the man's skull. The man thumped to the ground again with a grunt. David jumped on his back and slipped his right arm around the man's neck and under his chin. He reached down with his left and grabbed his right fist, which had circled the man's neck in a perfect imitation of the hold Master Cervantes had applied to Preston years ago. He pushed with his left hand against his right fist so that his forearm applied the maximum pressure to the man's left carotid artery. His bicep was doing the same on the right side.

Unlike the unreal world of professional wrestling, "The Sleeper," when properly applied, takes less than 10 seconds to render a victim unconscious. David counted, and he estimated that the man beneath him made it to 12. Pretty good for someone who had the wind knocked out of him and had sustained a blow to the back of the head that would have smashed a cinder block.

When the man stopped moving, David became aware that the woman was on her feet again, screaming incoherently. He ignored her for the moment, quickly producing a pair of handcuffs from his coat. He yanked the man's hands around behind his back, and realized that one pair wasn't going to do. The tremendous girth of the man's back and the thickness of his arms wouldn't allow his wrists to get within the proper range. Luckily, David had a backup pair, and he snapped the two pairs together to cuff the man's meaty arms behind his back. He then slipped a folded white envelope into the back left pocket of the man's jeans.

He used the man's broad back to push himself up. He began to walk toward the hysterical woman. She put her hands up and backed away toward the kitchen. He put his own hands up in the air to indicate that he didn't wish to harm her, and asked her softly, "Where is your phone?"

She stopped screaming for a moment, clearly puzzled enough by the question to give it some consideration. She started to point toward the kitchen when her eyes left his face for a moment and looked past him. David spun around to his right and away from where he had been standing just in time to avoid being shot for the second time in his life.

The young man holding the gun had crept out of the hall behind David. The bullet he had fired narrowly missed the woman, slamming into the wall where David had been standing. The man tried to bring the gun around to point it at David, but David was a blur as he grasped his wrist, pushing the gun away from his body. The man was holding the gun with both hands, and he threw his body against David's in attempt to separate himself from the skeletal figure that had so easily subdued his older brother.

David was slightly off balance, and when the young man surged against him David was almost sent reeling. He swung his right hand around behind him looking for support. When he did, the back of his wrist struck hard against the wall. There was a metallic click and then two long, gleaming blades shot forth from beneath the sleeve of David's coat, emerging above his right hand like talons. Both the young man and the woman's attention switched to the blades, and the woman screamed again. The man pulled back, now trying desperately to free his gun hand. When he did, he pulled David back into a balanced position.

David had never used this weapon in battle, and the feeling of the blades snapping out of their housing just as he had designed them filled him with adrenaline. He thought of the weapon as his "claws." The blades, of course, were the two bayonets that Richard had given him some time ago. The idea came to him the moment he saw them. He constructed the housing using leather straps and the flat, iron bars from the bedspring of the bed Karen had been lying on when she was murdered. He felt that using a part of their bed would bring her spirit along with him, and would thus bring him luck.

He had welded the bars together so that they circled his forearm, and then used leather straps to hold them in place. He built a housing for the blades that rested on top of his forearm. The blades themselves were welded to two short support bars that ran perpendicular to their length. The support bars were then welded to what he called the sled. The sled was a flat, metal plate that slid along the top of his forearm. It was held near his wrist with two industrial, high-tension springs. When he pushed the sled all the way back to his elbow, it clicked into place with a catch lever he built. This lever held the sled from sliding forward, and the tension of the springs pressed against it so that it was quite difficult to release. The catch could be opened using a metal switch that protruded from the top of the assembly. Pressing down on the switch released the catch, and the sled and blades were pulled forth so rapidly that the eye could not follow their progress. They were just there. When they emerged, they had enough momentum and force to puncture a 2 x 4. To increase their potential to inflict damage, David had sharpened the blades to a razor's edge.

Adrenaline coursing through his veins, David swung the claws in a tight arc toward the young man's arms. The young man let out a short scream and tried to pull away, but David held his wrist firmly. At the last moment, David let off the gas and changed the angle of his strike. If he hadn't, he may very well have severed the man's hand and wrist cleanly from his arm. As it was, the blades passed shallowly across his the underside of his wrist, slicing open his artery and severing his tendon in two places.

The young man let out a cry of pain and released the gun, letting it thump to the floor. He clutched his right arm against his body and fell to the floor, curling into the fetal position.

David reached down and picked up the gun. He turned to the woman and said fiercely, "Your phone!"

She was wailing with fear, but she managed to point to the kitchen counter. David backed toward it, keeping his eye on the young man. He picked up the receiver, dialed 9-1-1, and laid the phone on the counter. He picked up a towel that was sitting in a damp wad next to the sink and walked back out of the kitchen. He dropped it on the young man and said, "Press this on the wound hard until the ambulance gets here." Then, without another word or a look back, he walked quickly to the door and out into the night.

He didn't immediately remove his mask. He broke into a dead run in a direction 90 degrees to the left of his car. He stopped only briefly to place the tips of his blades against one of the buildings and lean against them to force them back into their housing. The spring tension required to make the blades snap out to his satisfaction caused the weapon's only drawback—it was goddamn hard to get the blades back in.

He was aware that the gunshot would have people looking out their windows at a minimum, but he didn't think they would have emerged from their apartments yet. Still, he would almost definitely be seen leaving. That was OK with him, as long as they weren't able to follow him. In fact, the more people that saw his ghastly face leaving the scene, the more the legend of The Reaper would grow. They should all know who had done this...who had stopped a monster from beating up a woman...even if she didn't seem to appreciate his help too much. He wanted them to see who had done it so that if they were in a habit of doing the same, they might think twice.

In the end, he hoped that the effect he had had on drunk driving throughout the area could be duplicated if he went after more serious criminals. His strategy was to put himself in places where it was likely for a crime to occur, and then take the first one that came up. Tonight it was domestic violence. Next time, maybe robbery or drug dealing. He would take whatever came his way, and punish the criminals as best he could.

Unlike the drunk driving, however, he hoped that he would be able to leave enough evidence of their crimes so that they would actually be punished by the law as well.

David ran in a wide circle, eventually going back toward his car. Before he touched it, he hid in the bushes for about fifteen minutes, waiting to make sure that all the emergency vehicles had passed, and that no one had followed him. While he waited, he counted three police cars and two ambulances. That was good. He had dialed 9-1-1 himself because he had the distinct feeling that if he didn't, they wouldn't either. The cuffs would eventually be removed with a hacksaw, and the young man would be driven to the hospital saying he had cut himself on broken glass. He wanted the police to go there, and he wanted them to find the note.

When he felt safe, he quickly stowed the incriminating evidence in his car, started it up, and headed for the freeway. He had brought a new tape for the occasion, and he pushed it into the player. It was Metallica's "Black" album. James Hetfield began to growl the lyrics to "Unforgiven" as he drove away, and David thought that was quite appropriate.

53

Seamus awoke to the sound of the phone ringing. The clock by his bed told him it was just after midnight. He picked it up and grunted, "Molloy." Two seconds later, he sat bolt upright and swung his legs to the floor.

"Where," he said. Then, "I'll call you on the way to get directions."

He slammed the phone down and turned to Molly, who was still awake and reading a book. Some shit about relaxation techniques to help one become pregnant. "He's back?" she asked with genuine concern.

"Yep. I don't know how long I'll be. I'll call you in the morning and let you know."

"Be careful."

"I will. I love you."

"Love you too."

Seamus got dressed and pelted down the stairs. He skipped his meeting with the elder Molloys tonight. The Richmond police and whatever state cops that were there were probably already fucking up his crime scene.

He arrived in Richmond about a half hour later. He pulled into the parking lot next to several flashing police cars. He got out and walked toward the crowd that was gathered around one of the buildings. The crowd murmured as one, and the one word that came to his ears again and again was "Reaper."

He ducked under the police tape, flashed his badge to the uniform assigned to crowd control, and stepped into the apartment. Detective Turner was already there, along with a Richmond police Lieutenant and three other cops.

He strode over to Detective Turner and the Lieutenant. "Lieutenant, I'm Agent Molloy, FBI. As you know, this is my crime scene now. Please have your officers exit immediately," Seamus said with polite authority.

"Sure thing. Mind if I stay on?"

"Not at all. This is your city. I'd just appreciate it if you let me take a look around before anyone else touches anything."

"Ok. Out guys," said the lieutenant.

The three other cops cleared out, leaving the three of them alone in the room.

"What do we know so far?" Seamus asked, addressing Detective Turner.

"The story is a little sketchy, but here goes. This apartment is rented to a Tawanda Adair. She apparently lives here with her boyfriend and his little brother. She was pretty shaken up when I got here, but I talked to her for awhile and then had an officer take her to the hospital to see the two men.

"She claims that "The Reaper" broke in out of the blue and attacked her boyfriend. He's a big son of a bitch...probably about 300 pounds. She was sporting a fresh shiner on her left cheek, though, and something tells me it was the boyfriend that did it. If you want my guess, the guy was in the area for some reason and heard the fighting and broke in to stop it."

"What makes you think that?" Seamus asked.

"He left another note...in the guy's back left pocket."

Seamus's heartbeat jumped by about 40 beats per minute upon hearing of the note. The fact that it was in his back left pocket almost certainly meant this was the real Reaper, and not a copycat like the guy they grabbed the other night.

"Where is it?" Seamus asked.

"Right here," Turner said, holding up an evidence bag with the unfolded note inside, "Wanna hear it?"

"Yeah, read it to me," Seamus said, closing his eyes so that he could concentrate fully on the words.

"Dear Agent Molloy and Detective Turner," Turner began, "It kind of gives me the chills that it's addressed to us."

"I know. Go on."

"Dear Agent Molloy and Detective Turner," he repeated, "I'm sure you are aware by now that the man you caught the other day is not the person known as The Reaper. I hope that you believe that I am, as I told you with my note to you in Petaluma that future correspondence would be through the back left pocket.

"Let's start with the name. I don't find "The Grim Reaper," appropriate for what I am trying to accomplish. If we need to base my name on my appearance, then I would much prefer 'Charon.'"

Seamus's eyes flew open. "KAREN?" he questioned, almost yelling. The image of David's murdered girlfriend flashed like a bolt of lightning into this mind's eye.

"Charon, you know, the boatman from Greek mythology. Ferries the dead across the Styx into Hades?" Detective Turner replied.

"Sure, I know who he is, I just thought you said Karen, like the girl's name. I'm not sure, but I think the accent for Charon goes on the second syllable. Sorry to interrupt. Go on."

Detective Turner continued, "...I would much prefer Charon. I know it's splitting hairs, but I'm not here to take peoples' lives, I just want to deliver them to where they're going.

"Where are they going, you ask? Well, they should be going to jail. I don't know if I really had anything to do with the drop in drunk driving, so I figured I would test the theory by moving on to other crimes.

"Let me reiterate that my intent is not to hurt anyone. However, in my line of work, I have to break a few eggs once in awhile to make my point. I know you're after me, and I don't blame you. It's your job. Just know that in the end, we are on the same side.

"Since it appears we may have some brave souls trying to copy me, I will start leaving an item in the back left pocket of one or more of my criminals each time I apprehend one. How does a match sound? It's small and easy to carry, and it's not something people would likely already have in their pocket. When you see a match, you'll know it was I.

"With that, I'll leave you to your investigation. As I have written this in advance, I am not sure of the nature of the crime I stopped. I truly hope that everyone is OK and that you are able to prosecute the offenders properly.

"With my regards, Charon."

Detective Turner lowered the letter and looked at Seamus. "What do you think?" he asked.

"He's a goddamn good writer, for one thing," Seamus said. "This guy is frigging smart. Not everyone knows about Charon either. And his grammar is flawless. He's highly educated...has to be."

"Yep. This is the guy, right?" Turner asked.

"I'm 99% sure it is. The only way it's not is if a copy of the first note got out, and I don't think that's what happened. The grammar is too similar. Anyway, tell me the rest."

"Well, like I said, I think he heard the boyfriend slapping the lady around and kicked in the door to stop him. When we got here, the guy was awake and pretty much unharmed. He said the guy jumped him, otherwise he would have kicked his ass. Yeah, right."

Seamus couldn't be sure, but it seemed to him like Detective Turner was starting to identify with and maybe even admire The Reaper—er—Charon. Turner's eyes were gleaming and it seemed he was proud to tell of his exploits. Now that he thought about it, Seamus had just a hint of the same feeling. For better or for worse, if he stopped a man from beating up a woman, Seamus had to take his hat off to him. He also had to respect his physical prowess and intelligence. As a cop, it was very hard not to condone what Charon was doing. He was going to have to make sure he kept these feelings in check, and he would have to keep his eye on Turner as well.

Turner continued, "He apparently locked up the big guy, and then she says he was coming after her when the little brother came from the hall with a gun. She says he hit her—again, I don't buy that—and then he turned around and caught the little brother by the wrist. A shot went off into the wall over there. Then, she says two long shiny blades popped right out of his fist like that comic book character...Wolverine. He supposedly tried to cut the brother's arm off, but only sliced it in two places. He must've severed an artery, because there's a lot of blood over here by the kitchen. Then she says he picked up the gun and left. She dialed 9-1-1 and then got a towel to press against the brother's cut."

"Lucky she did," Seamus said.

"Yep," Turner said, "Anyway, that's her story. We can go talk to her later after we go through this place."

"Agreed. I'd like to know a little more about these knives that popped out of his fist. That's a new one for our guy. Let's get started," Seamus said.

Later that morning, Seamus and Turner were questioning Tawanda Adair in the interrogation room of the Richmond Police Department. She was badly shaken, but she was sticking with her story. Seamus thought she sensed that Turner was on Charon's side, and she seemed afraid to tell him anything.

"Detective Turner," he said, "Would you mind getting me a cup of coffee?"

"Sure," he said disgustedly, exiting the room.

Seamus put on his most charming smile and spoke gently to Tawanda. "Now Tawanda, I think there are a few things you aren't telling us. I really, really want to catch this guy, and I need your help. Can you do that?"

She didn't say anything, but much of the fear and mistrust seemed to have left her face.

"Now, I promise that nothing you tell me is going to put your boyfriend or his brother in any jeopardy. We are after the man who broke into your house. What you tell me will only help me find him, OK?"

"OK," she whispered.

"Tawanda, were you and your boyfriend fighting?"

"Yes."

"Did he hit you?"

"Not real hard."

"But he did."

"Yes. Then that Reaper broke in and whipped him good. I don't care what Phil says, The Reaper beat his ass good. But you won't tell him I said that, will you?"

"Of course not. Then what happened?"

"He...he asked for the phone. Then Marcus came up behind him with the gun. I thought Marcus had him, but he spun out of the way so fast you could barely see him. I think he dodged the bullet. He got Marcus's wrist and then those knives came out."

"How?"

"I don't know, they just did."

"Think hard, Tawanda."

After a few moments, she said, "I guess he might have smacked his arm on the wall. I can't be sure though."

"Great, then he cut Marcus's wrist?"

"Right. Then Marcus dropped the gun and The Reaper picked it up. Then is the really weird part. I didn't tell the other guy because...because I probably wouldn't have known what to do but I wanted him to think I did, you know?"

"Go on, Tawanda."

"He, he asked for the phone again and went over and called 9-1-1. Then he got a towel from the kitchen and dropped it on Marcus and told him to hold it on his wrist. I couldn't believe it."

"Is there anything else, Tawanda?"

"Well, you promise not to tell Phil or Marcus?"

"Yes."

"I think he came in to save me, and I don't think he wanted to hurt Marcus. As big as Phil is, he handled him like he was nothing. But still, he used that chokehold to put him out instead of beating on him like most guys would do. Then he gave the towel to Marcus. He could've killed him easy, but he didn't even try," Tawanda began to weep softly, and then continued, "I felt safer with him in there than I ever did alone with Phil and Marcus. I was scared, but...but he really saved me a beating. Is it wrong that I feel this way?"

"Not at all," Seamus said, "Thank you so much for your time, Tawanda."

"Are you leaving?" she asked.

"Yes."

"What do I do now?" She asked this question as if she were twelve years old and needed the advice of a parent.

"Leave your boyfriend, Tawanda. You don't deserve to be beaten by anyone."

She straightened up and wiped her eyes. "You're right, sir. I'm gonna try."

"Good," Seamus said, turning toward the door.

"Sir, can you do me one favor?" Tawanda asked.

"If I can," he said, pausing and looking back at her.

"If you catch him, tell him I said 'Thank you.'"

Stunned, Seamus managed to say, "OK," and then walked out the door.

54

David continued to execute bold attacks throughout the spring and early summer. After each one, Seamus would not come to the gym for several days. When he returned, though, David was there waiting for him and they took up their friendship where it had left off.

The urge for Seamus to consult David about The Reaper (he tried to call him Charon, but the image of David's Karen popped into his mind every time, so he reverted to The Reaper) was becoming unbearable. Seamus and Detective Turner were making absolutely no headway in the case, and desperation was setting in.

The Reaper had struck three times since the attack in Richmond. He stopped another domestic abuser at a trailer park in Vacaville, beat up two kids who were apparently in the midst of a drug deal in Hayward, and stopped a hold-up at a liquor store in San Rafael as the robber was leaving. As was the case when his focus was on drunk drivers, the severity of the beatings was escalating. He hadn't used his knife-weapon again, at least not yet, but he had broken several bones with his bare hands. Also similar to the drunk driving cases, The Reaper's victims were not charged with any crimes. While Seamus and the police honestly believed that the men were committing crimes when The Reaper stopped them, there was not sufficient evidence to charge any of them. Neither of the women whom he saved from being beaten would press charges nor bear witness against their boyfriends. The liquor store owner also chose not to press charges, probably out of fear of retaliation from the robber's friends. The drug dealer and buyer claimed that the reaper planted the drugs and cash on them after he beat them up. In each case, without the testimony of The Reaper himself, there were no grounds for criminal charges.

Although The Reaper's activities continued to be unsuccessful in sending criminals to jail, his fame continued to grow. Based on the sensationalism in the paper and on TV, The Reaper was reaching nationwide celebrity status. In the Bay Area, he was already there. To Seamus's dismay, the goddamn guy had become a cult hero. The other day, he even saw a guy wearing a T-Shirt featuring a skull and crossbones featuring the words, "Fear the Reaper!" This was getting bad, and fast. He was getting relentless pressure from above, and talk had started about removing him from the case.

On the morning of July 6, 2003, about a week after The Reaper's last attack, another of Douglas Fairchild's over-dramatic articles graced the front page of The Chronicle.

The Reaper—Does Celebrity Equal a Free Pass?

As the reign of The Reaper continues unchecked by local or state police, or even the FBI, many in the area are questioning whether authorities are doing everything they can to locate and arrest the perpetrator.

Now that he has moved on from his focus on drunk drivers and begun to attack more serious criminals, the celebrity status of The Reaper has grown to new levels. Based on a poll on the streets of San Francisco conducted over the last week, over 65% of Bay Area residents questioned expressed approval for what this mysterious man is doing.

"He's like Batman," said Bob Childers of Emeryville. "He finds the criminals where they live and teaches them a lesson. When it happens in the comic books it's OK. Why not in the real world? More power to him, I say."

"It sounds to me these guys are getting what they deserve," said Janice Blumenthal of Redwood City. "Don't tell me the cops would've stopped any of these crimes. Especially the two woman-beaters he stopped. You know the women weren't going to say anything, so even if the cops knew about it nothing would happen. If this guy's actually punishing wife-beaters where no one else can, then God bless him. I hope they never catch him."

The majority of other comments echoed these sentiments. There were those, however, those who would rather see him stopped. Among those who disagree with The Reaper's actions was Cedric Jones of Oakland. "I don't think the cops are trying that hard to catch him. You notice he's after black folks now, and the cops like anyone who does that. They figure if he's gonna bust down some that they wouldn't have been able to get to, let him keep doing it. He's probably working with them...just a cop in disguise."

It is true, in fact, that four of the five most recent victims have been African-American, whereas the great majority of the victims who were stopped from driving while intoxicated were white. However, Mr. Jones was not the only citizen to question whether the police and FBI are doing everything they can to catch The Reaper.

While 15% of citizens polled did not have an opinion on The Reaper, the remaining 20% who do want to see The Reaper stopped overwhelmingly suggested that the police and FBI are not doing everything they can to stop him.

"Have you ever seen a serial criminal of any type continue to strike regularly for 18 months with impunity?" asked Debra Wilson of Concord, "Don't tell me there's any urgency to this case. Neither the media nor the law wants this guy stopped. You are encouraging him to continue, and the law is only going through the motions. This guy is going to start killing people pretty soon. Is that what you want? The cops better get on the ball or that's what's going to happen."

When asked about opinions such as Ms. Wilson's, Detective Lawrence Turner of the State Police said, "The State and local Police are cooperating fully with the FBI in this case. It is preposterous to say that we are not doing everything we can to apprehend this man. The fact is that we have had very few credible leads from the public. In addition, this man is very well prepared and is acting over a very large geographic area. Make no mistake, we'll catch him."

The question that it seems Bay Area residents must ask themselves, it seems, is whether or not we want them to.

As Seamus read this article over his morning coffee, he began to feel stomach acid begin to creep up his gorge, causing a sick burning just below his breastbone. This feeling was not unfamiliar. He was going through a bottle of Tums per week. If their marketing claims were true, he was going to have the strongest bones in town. It didn't seem to be doing much for his heartburn, though. He was thinking he better go to the doctor and see if he was getting a goddamn ulcer. He'd also read (well, actually Molly had read to him) that stress could interfere with conception. That was just great...stress was keeping him from giving Molly a baby, and that fact and her gentle complaints were giving him more stress. His whole fucking life, so wonderful just a year ago when he was being handed the key to the city, was now in a downward spiral that he didn't know how to pull out of.

He dropped the paper on top of his bowl of cereal and got up from the table. He walked across the kitchen to the cabinet where he kept the Tums. When he was halfway there, his cell phone rang. Just as it did, Molly walked into the kitchen. She only heard Seamus's half of the conversation, but it was pretty obvious what it was about.

"Molloy...Yes, I saw it...I know...Yes...Yes sir...Sir, I'll be there in an hour."

Seamus clicked the phone shut and turned to Molly. Seamus was the most level-headed man she had ever known. He was always in control of his emotions and the situation. The look on his face of panicked frustration scared her.

"Everything OK?" she asked.

"Not really. Did you see the crap in the paper this morning?"

"Yes."

"So did my boss, and he's not too happy. Wants to see me right away."

Seamus looked out the kitchen window. The absent look in his eyes was another that Molly was unfamiliar with. It looked like he was giving up, like he was resigned to failure.

"Seamus, you're going to get this guy, I know it. You got all the others," she said, trying to sound confident in spite of her own doubts.

"He's not like all the others, Mol. I honestly think he's some kind of genius. You should see his writing. I think if I ever meet this guy he's gonna turn out to be the smartest person I've ever met."

"It would be pretty hard for him to be smarter than David," Molly said, hoping the thought of his friend would lighten his mood. It didn't, but it did seem to spark something in Seamus.

"Did you ever think of asking David for help?" she asked gently.

"I can't, Mol, you know that."

"You're not supposed to, but that's a long way from can't. David isn't going to tell anyone. Just let him see the notes and see what he says. What can it hurt?"

"Maybe. I'm gonna try to get to the gym tonight. If I do…we'll see."

"Do what you think is best, honey," Molly said, "but I know you're going to get this guy one way or the other. David and this other guy may be smart, but you're no dummy, and you've got the best instincts of any cop in the world. Isn't that what they said when the asked you into the Bureau?"

Seamus didn't reply. He just kept looking out the window. After a moment, he looked down at Molly and gave her a kiss on the forehead. "Thanks, honey. I better get going."

55

Seamus spent most of the morning being dressed down by various superiors at the bureau. Apparently this was now reaching the attention of the Director of the FBI. One of the toadies on his staff had called Seamus's boss this morning and demanded an update. Apparently there had been talk of putting The Reaper on the ten most wanted list, but they didn't want to bring the added attention to Seamus's ineptitude. By noon, Seamus took his sore ass and headed for the State Police headquarters.

When he arrived, he found that Detective Turner had received the same treatment. They ordered Chinese for lunch and spent the rest of the day pouring over the assembled evidence from the past 18 months. When Detective Turner went to the bathroom in the afternoon, Seamus acted on an impulse and made photocopies of the two notes they had received to date from The Reaper. He had the originals back in place before Turner returned, the copies tucked safely in his briefcase.

They called it quits at 5:00, promising to start early the next morning. They parted company on the street, and Seamus pointed his Yukon toward the Gorilla Gym.

When he got there, he was happy to see David's Accord in the parking lot. He went inside and found that David was halfway through his workout.

"I...uh...didn't expect you today," David said apologetically when Seamus walked up to him.

"You saw the article this morning?"

"Yeah. Sorry man, I try not to bring that up. I'm sure you get that plenty."

"I know. I can't remember a time you've ever brought it up. I've always appreciated that, David."

"Well, I won't make you dwell on it now...unless you want to talk about it, of course. I'd be glad to listen, but only if you want to talk."

Vengeance

"You know, David, I think I would like to talk to you about it a little. Not here, though. You mind getting a bite to eat after this?"

"Sure."

About two hours later, they were seated at the back booth in McSorley's. Over three beers each, Seamus had given David a fairly comprehensive summary of each of The Reaper's attacks, in chronological order, of course. As of yet, he hadn't brought out the copies of the notes he made earlier in the day. Telling him the details of the case was bad enough, so Seamus thought he'd see what David had to offer before he did something that would really get him fired.

"Let me ask you some questions," David said, "and if you can't answer, just tell me."

"OK, shoot."

"I read that drunk driving was falling, and some were speculating that it was because of him. I'm sure he read that in the papers. From what you tell me, you believe that was what he wanted to happen. So why would he switch his approach just when he was having success?"

"Of course all we can do is guess, but we think it's either because there were getting to be too many cops around bars, or because he wanted to broaden his impact. In other words, he was hoping to have the same effect on another facet of crime."

"Did you ever think maybe he was frustrated that the people he attacked weren't getting arrested?"

"Well, I guess that's another thought. But the new victims aren't either. His problem is that he's stopping crimes in progress, and the only way many of the victims could be prosecuted is if he testified himself. The prosecutors don't even want to bother, because any defense attorney worth his salt could find a sympathetic jury that would let the criminals off simply because of the nature of their arrest."

"You think that's why he's escalating the level of violence?" David asked.

"Possibly. When he was doing drunk drivers, we thought he was escalating because people were leaving in groups and he had to hit them harder to subdue them all. So far in 'Phase 2,' he's still been hitting single victims, and he is starting to beat them pretty bad. I guess it's possible he's getting frustrated at our lack of ability to prosecute."

"Do you see any way he could do it so that the people he's attacking did get prosecuted?"

"He needs a witness who will actually testify or press charges. Absent that, he'd need videotape or something. Otherwise, he's going to keep coming up short in that area."

"How long until he kills someone, then?" David asked.

Seamus looked at David and shrugged. "I don't know, but if he does, I'll be out of a job."

They both took a long drink of their fourth beers. This was two more beers than David had had in one sitting in over four years. He was definitely buzzing, and maybe that's why he felt a little sorry for his friend. David's luck, combined with his ability to plan and his incredible patience was clearly more than a match for Seamus, which, he thought, meant he was probably going to be just fine whether Seamus or someone else was looking for him. Still, he would feel bad if he were the reason Seamus lost his job. He had gone after Seamus and his friendship for exactly this conversation, but now that they were having it, he was having a different feeling than he would have ever expected: Guilt.

His vision and his thinking were becoming a little soft around the edges. As they sat there silently, David tried to think of a way to help Seamus just enough to save him politically, but obviously without hurting himself. Nothing was coming to him, but he thought he'd better think of something to ask so that Seamus would keep talking. Now was not the time to celebrate and become complacent. He was where he was because he was relentless and took no chances. As long as Seamus was talking, he wanted to hear all he would say.

"So you say this Charon left notes. Can you tell me what they said?" David asked.

"What did you say?" Seamus replied, looking abruptly up from his beer into David's eyes. He looked as if David had just said The Reaper was his next door neighbor.

FUCK!! SHIT FUCK MOTHERFUCKING SHIT SONOFABITCH FUCKING MOTHERFUCKER!!

David tried to gather his thoughts and did his best to appear calm on the outside despite the storm of profanity flying around his head. After a brief pause, he managed to reply, "I know the media calls him The Reaper, but I've always thought of him as Charon. That's the boatman in Greek mythology that ferries the dead across the river Styx. I'm very familiar with the mythology of Charon, but I really don't know much about the history or mythology of the Grim Reaper. I just know what everyone else knows, and the sensationalism of calling him that just doesn't appeal to me. I guess I'm just not one to follow the crowd and call him what the media tells me to call him."

Seamus kept staring at him at David. Every bell he had was going off like there was a five alarm fire. Like Molly said, he might not be that smart, but he had good instincts. David looked cool on the outside, but there was something in his eyes, if only for a moment, that looked guilty. He had the look of someone who had just made a colossal mistake.

"Huh," Seamus said pensively, "It just struck me because that's what he told us he preferred to be called in his last note."

"Really?" David said, doing his very best to recover. Suddenly, he didn't feel drunk in the least. What he did feel was a combination of panic, rage, and the desire to go out and literally kill someone. "You did say he seemed to be pretty well educated, right?"

"Yeah," said Seamus, "He definitely is. I wish I'd brought copies of the notes. His grammar is flawless."

David relaxed a little. The fact that Seamus wished he had copies of the notes was probably a good sign. Still, he didn't like the way Seamus was looking at him—like he was a criminal.

"You know," Seamus said, "I better get home. Molly's ovulating, and you know what that means."

"Yeah. Good luck. If you want to show me those notes another time I'd be happy to take a look."

"David, I probably better not. Telling you what I did could get me fired, but showing you those could get me in even worse trouble. I appreciate your help though."

"Any time," David replied.

With that, Seamus stood up and shook David's hand. His eyes hadn't left David's since he used The Reaper's preferred name, and they remained locked in as they shook hands. Each was sizing the other up, trying to figure out what the other had taken from the last five minutes of conversation. Neither liked what they saw.

"See ya later," Seamus said.

"OK. My best to Molly," David replied.

Seamus smiled, turned, and walked briskly to the door. He didn't turn around when he reached the door—he just pushed out into the night.

David stood up and dug a $100 bill out of his pocket. He dropped it on the table and strolled toward the door. As soon as he saw Seamus's Yukon pull out of the parking lot, he stepped outside and stalked across the parking lot to his car.

56

David spun out of McSorley's, leaving a cloud of dust behind him. He was so angry he could barely see, or think. While he was no longer aware of the effects of the alcohol, it was still very active in his system. His flawless judgment, normally so perfectly cold and calculating, was challenged both by the alcohol and the overwhelming rage boiling out of his pores.

He had really blown it. Not just tonight, but six months ago when he thought it would be a good idea to become friends with Seamus. Well, maybe that wasn't the stupid part, but letting himself actually become friends with Seamus and begin to care about him and his wife was. He had had other relationships over the past four years that he was able to keep in the proper perspective. That is, he used them for what he needed but never became close enough to affect his overall plan. Now, with zero hour approaching, he finally fucked up, big time.

This called for serious damage control. If Seamus was allowed to maintain whatever suspicions he now had, David's ultimate revenge could be seriously threatened. That was not acceptable. What was the best way to make Seamus abandon his suspicions? The best way David could think of would be for The Reaper (or Charon—wasn't that what he fucking preferred) to strike tonight, and as soon as possible after David and Seamus were together.

David sped down the hill to his house. Once there, he pelted out of his car and inside. He raced down the hall and disarmed his security system in the back bedroom. As he raced to prepare for a strike, he ran through all of the places he had scouted in the past four months for the one that would be the most likely to produce a quick hit. He had rejected all of them thus far, and nothing he could think of made him feel that they would be good candidates now. The last thing he could do was go sit all night and not have an opportunity to strike.

There was one possibility that occurred to him. There was one place that he was very familiar with. It was a place he had been visiting regularly for nearly 10 years. He had always planned to make a hit there, just not yet.

He glanced at his watch. If he hurried, he would time it perfectly. Just as LaShon Jackson took out the trash in the back of the Redwood City Jack in the Box where he still worked weeknights, The Reaper would strike. The police would think he thought Jackson was attempting to rob the place. Or maybe not, but as long as he left a match in LaShon's back left pocket, they would know it was him, and that's what he needed right now.

Yes, this was the only way to guarantee himself an opportunity to make a hit as soon as possible after he and Seamus were together. And, as he had just learned, Seamus and the others would not find it too difficult to believe that The Reaper had escalated to murder. He probably would need to make it look like he murdered him in the heat of battle and not in a premeditated fashion, but he thought this next step would be appropriate at this stage of the game.

About 40 minutes later, David was concealed in the shadowy bushes behind the Jack in the Box where LaShon Jackson worked as a cleaner of tables, mopper of floors and emptier of trash. David had spent hundreds of hours watching him, learning his patterns, and cataloging the exact movements of everyone who worked there.

It was now five minutes to nine. LaShon would be out at 9:00 exactly, and he would be alone. He would open the door, drag out two or three 50 gallon garbage bags, and then use his foot to slide a chunk of cinder block in front of the door to keep it from closing. David had checked, and he knew the door would lock if it closed, so his plan was to quietly slip the block out and let the door close while LaShon hoisted the trash into the dumpster. David would then slip back into the bushes and let LaShon finish. When LaShon turned around and began to fumble with the lock, David would attack. In David's estimation, both the folks inside and the cops would assume The Reaper had happened upon LaShon and thought he was trying to break in. He couldn't decide whether he wanted them to open the door in time to see him finish off LaShon. That would make his escape more difficult, but it would confirm the fact that he was there. If he knew the type that worked inside, that is, young assholes, they would probably leave LaShon hanging and make him walk around the front anyway. More than likely, David would have all the time he needed, including the opportunity for a leisurely escape. All he needed to do to get to his car was go through the bushes into the deserted parking lot on the other side. Thanks to years of planning and perfect circumstances, this had all the makings of the easiest hit he had done to date.

The alcohol was nearly gone from his system, but the rage remained. He was still furious about the situation he had created with Seamus. He considered that Seamus would be here in less than an hour, cleaning up the mess that LaShon was about to become. He wondered if he would connect LaShon to his parents' death. Probably so. David decided he better get home as soon as he could afterward and maybe give him and Molly a call. Maybe he'd even call from his cell phone. He hadn't intended to hit LaShon until Darius was released. The events earlier this evening had forced his hand, but a hit on someone associated with David might confirm Seamus's suspicions if he didn't take further precautionary measures.

The back door knob began to turn. No more time to think now—it was time for action. As usual, all thoughts cleared out of his mind as the cold, red haze of battle dropped over him.

The door swung open, and first one then another large bag of garbage thumped out onto the pavement. Then LaShon emerged. As soon as he came into view, David felt a scalding hot rush of blood burn his face and ears. His heart sped up and his mouth dried up like a sponge left in the sun. His palms began to sweat inside his gloves. All of his extremities tingled. This was it. This was finally it. The man who killed his parents was going to pay. If nothing else, he would have that.

Vengeance

LaShon slid the cinder block in front of the door and let the door bump against it. Then he turned and went to work on the trash. He was humming something. David couldn't be sure, but he thought it was the theme from Sesame Street.

David took two steps out of his hiding space, grasped the cinder block with one hand and the door with the other, and lifted the cinder block out of the way and let the door swing closed, controlling it so that it closed with a soft click. He then retreated to his former position to wait.

David's heart hammered away inside his chest so loudly that, in spite of the clear knowledge that it was impossible, he worried that LaShon would hear it. He watched the man heave the last bag into the dumpster and then turn toward the door. He took three steps and then stopped cold. "Oh man!" he said when he saw that the door was closed. He then stepped forward and tried the knob. As David had known, it was locked.

David drug in a deep breath and stepped out of the bushes behind LaShon. "LaShon," he whispered in his most sinister voice.

LaShon jumped and let out a little scream. He then seemed to relax, and began to turn around. As he did, he said in a simple, smiling voice, "Hey Billy, I told you not to..." His light-hearted admonition of whoever Billy was stopped abruptly when the face of The Reaper came into his field of vision. Whatever he was going to say was replaced by the scream of a child facing the monster that lives under his bed.

The scream lasted only a second, and then David shot both of his hands out like twin vipers. His palms struck LaShon squarely in the chest, knocking the wind out of him and abruptly cutting off his scream. LaShon was propelled violently into the door. He struck it with his back and then crumpled to the ground. The thud of his body against the door reverberated in the air, and David knew at once he would have to make this quick. He passed his left hand over his right wrist, ejecting his claws.

He reached down to grasp the heaving mass on the floor by the throat. Time was short, but he would not miss the opportunity to look in the eyes of his parents' killer as he extracted a revenge Hammurabi would have approved of. His left hand slipped under LaShon's chin, and David forced his back and head up and then back against the door. As he did, he brought his right arm back into a striking position. He pushed his left thumb into the flabby flesh underneath LaShon's chin to force him to look in the face of death before it came to him. When he saw LaShon's face, however, he froze.

The look of terror on LaShon's face was as complete as David could have ever imagined. Tears streamed from his wide, terrified eyes. His mouth worked up and down like a fish out of water, trying to draw in a breath. He was moaning from deep in his throat. When David forced his face up, LaShon closed his eyes and began to shake his head from side to side, trying to negate the image of the demon that held him in its grasp. David had known, of course, that LaShon had the mentality of a nine-year-old, but until now he hadn't grasped the full meaning of that fact. Now it became clear—he was holding up the body of a man in his late thirties, but he was looking into the face of a child.

David stood, frozen in place, watching as LaShon continued to shake his head from side to side. After a moment, LaShon was able to draw in a sip of air. With it, he began to repeat one word over and over. "Mommy mommy mommy mommy mommy," he sobbed, still refusing to open his eyes. A single string of saliva stretched from his lower lip and hung like a spider web. He raised his hands slightly and began to flap them up and down like a penguin that hasn't yet been told that it is unable to fly.

Tears came to David's eyes. His right arm, still cocked to strike began to fall slowly to his side. Images flashed through his mind like a slide show on turbo speed. His parents, Karen, Darius, Mr. Greer, Master Chen, Richard, Seamus, along with pictures of his own solitude. The last image was his own mother leaning down to kiss him on the forehead as he passed through his own ninth year.

"LaShon, you OK?" came from behind the door, shocking David back into motion. He shook his head to clear it, and looked at the blubbering mass that had killed his parents over ten years ago.

"LaShon, open your eyes NOW," he commanded in a harsh whisper.

LaShon, continued to shake his head and repeat the word mommy over and over.

"LaShon, open your eyes or I will kill your Mommy next."

Finally, LaShon stopped moving his head and opened one eye just a crack. When the face of The Reaper was again visible, he let out a sob of despair and began to cry even more desperately.

David raised his arm again, and brought it around toward LaShon's exposed throat. LaShon saw the shining blades through his squinting eye, and tried to pull back, opening both eyes wide as he did. His back was to the door, though, and he had nowhere to go.

The blades arced toward his throat, and they would surely have separated the boy's head from the man's body, but David put on the brakes and stopped them an inch from his throat. LaShon's knees buckled and he evacuated both his bladder and bowels. David released his grip on LaShon's throat and let him collapse to the ground. He let out a primal scream of rage and frustration, and crashed through the bushes just before the back door opened, banging into the crumpled mass that lay sobbing but unharmed on the pavement.

57

David ran directly to his car, stopping only to push his blades back home. He hopped in the driver's seat and spun out of the parking lot. He was fairly sure that he was gone before LaShon's co-workers could see him, but that was the only coherent thought in his mind, and it didn't stay long.

Rage boiled in his brain. Pure, white-hot malice obscured all rational thought. He was driving with his mask on, his contacts in, his fangs in place. His hood was pulled forward and it was dark, but if he stopped at a stoplight and turned his head to the car next to him, the driver of the other car would get the shock of his life. He didn't turn his head, though. He drove as fast as traffic would allow, heading straight for the freeway. When he reached it, he barreled around the pigtail and headed north.

Intellect had checked out. David had been able to stop himself from killing LaShon, but the rage of The Reaper was in control now. It sorted through David's mind like a card catalog, picking out the information it needed. It knew where it wanted to go, and it went, with the singular focus of a lightning bolt.

The tires of the old Honda squealed as he merged from Highway 101 to Highway 92, which led to the San Mateo Bridge. He pointed the car straight ahead and pushed the pedal all the way to the floor. The speedometer climbed up to 100, and then past. At some point he had turned the stereo all the way up, and Metallica's drums and guitars pounded away in his head, urging him to go faster and faster.

Now the speedometer was at 110, and he was passing the cars in the right-hand lane as if they were standing still. It was still climbing, but more slowly now. The Honda was doing admirably, but it had its limits.

No matter, he was almost across the bridge. Before he reached the toll plaza, he flipped his license plate switch to make sure the cameras wouldn't catch David's plates. He then checked David's card catalog and found that he would get to where he was going in about 20 more minutes. His rage roiled and seethed under his skin, exciting every pore to full awareness.

Images flashed in front of his eyes, but he couldn't slow them down enough to see what they were. They only registered as carnal emotion: fear, pain, anguish, sorrow, rage, hate. He was a creature of instinct now, and his instincts were those of a hunter.

He exited the freeway in Oakland and stopped at a red light. He peeled off his right glove with his left hand and reached inside his overcoat. His hand found the cold steel of the nickel-plated .45 that rested in the holster under his armpit. He pulled it out, set it on the passenger seat, and repeated the process with his left hand, extracting the weapon from under his right arm.

The light turned green. He ignored it. He was in a desolate part of the slums of Oakland, and there were no other cars in sight. He dropped the safety on one pistol, pulled back the hammer, and reset the safety. He did the same with the other weapon. Now that he was "cocked and locked," he could move on.

The light was now red, but The Reaper rolled forward anyway. No one noticed. He pulled into an alley he had marked on an earlier scouting trip and parked. He retrieved both guns from the passenger seat and exited the car, closing the door quietly.

The dark red battle haze was back again, suppressing the reckless violence that brought him hurtling across the Bay from Redwood City. Every nerve in his body hummed with perfect awareness. The danger he was walking into only increased his focus. He had driven by this place several times, but he had always decided that the risk was too high to justify a strike.

Every time he had passed the broken down house on Malton Street, he had observed a crime in progress. While he could guess there were many others going on in and around the house, the one he had observed was abhorrent to him. Malton Street ran through a predominantly African-

American section of Oakland. The majority of the buildings in the area were tenements maintained by the city housing authority for very-low income or welfare families. During the day, when David had made all of his visits, there were children everywhere, playing or just hanging out in the street.

The house at 622 Malton Street was one of four houses in a row that were sandwiched between brick project buildings. It had a porch, and on that porch were usually at least three or four older kids, in their teens or early twenties, dressed in their Sunday best: baggy pants, bandanas, white wife-beaters, and myriad Oakland Raiders coats and baseball caps. Diamond earrings twinkled in their ears, and fat gold chains hung around their necks. David wasn't interested in what they were wearing, though, he was interested in what they were handing to the younger children that passed by. Kids as young as seven or eight made regular trips across the dirt that used to pass for a front lawn, stopping at the bottom of the porch steps and waiting to be invited up. When they were, they would accept small packages palmed across by the gatekeepers of what was almost certainly a crack-house.

David had driven by many times, knowing that pausing would cause trouble. As such, it was difficult to follow most transactions fully, but he had been able to observe some of the small children taking their secret packages back to their tenement, hopefully to deliver to their parents and not to put into their own bodies. Some older children could be seen reselling down the street. The drug trade was thriving on Malton Street, and it was being carried out and supported by the sweat and tears of small children. David guessed that this was one of those places where the police seldom rolled through, and never stopped.

Across the street from the den of iniquity were more of the brick tenements, and The Reaper now stood in the shadows between two of them. He was looking at the house, and what he saw gave him pause for the first time since he left LaShon lying on the pavement. He had expected three or four of its denizens in front of the house, and that was going to be plenty. He had never planned to go in, as he was sure that would be the end for him.

It would be like going into the lair of a snake. The snake knows its own den better than any of its enemies, and in it they don't stand a chance. The street, however, was where The Reaper ruled, and his plan was to take out those who were posted outside and then retreat before reinforcements could pour out of the house.

Tonight, however, it seemed there was a meeting of the Scumbag Sewing Circle on the front lawn. The Reaper counted eleven of them, standing on the lawn and yelling at each other with unintelligible bursts of profanity. Most of them were holding 40 ounce bottles of malt liquor or hand-rolled joints. True businessmen, it didn't look as if any of them had partaken of their true cash crop. The crack was for the kids, after all.

The Reaper held one of his guns in each hand. Each had seven rounds in the mag and one in the chamber. Sixteen shots to hit eleven targets. He hadn't been to the range in some time, and he wondered if he should just call it off and head for home.

But that wouldn't work, would it? If he didn't strike right now and leave the prescribed matches to prove it was he, he could be in trouble. He hadn't left a match with LaShon, and if he struck now this soon afterward across the Bay, the attack on LaShon would hopefully be thought to be another copycat. If he didn't strike now, LaShon's story of The Reaper's attack combined with Seamus's suspicions could be all she wrote.

More importantly than that, his animal side told him, was that The Reaper had dressed to kill tonight, and he would have that kill. There were eleven of them, and no doubt they were all armed. His chances of complete victory were admittedly slim, but if he died now, so what? It would be over then, wouldn't it? Would that be bad? He had already pussed out on LaShon...who could say he wouldn't do the same when it came time for Darius and the others? No...he wasn't going anywhere without spilling blood into Malton Street and letting it run like a crimson river toward the tenements, delivering his message to those who may think growing up to become a drug-dealer was a noble ambition.

His targets milled around in a tangled knot on the lawn. He had trouble picking out individual targets, and that would be a problem. He was reminded of a program he saw on TV about zebras. Their stripes are not actually to hide them in the high grass as most people think. The stripes serve to confuse the lions that chase them so that they cannot lock in on one individual zebra to chase and kill. The Reaper thought about this, and decided that, to be successful, he would have to draw them out into the street and create some separation in the group. He would have to do it without raising their suspicion enough for them to draw their guns, however, or he would have very little chance of getting out of this one. His armor would stop bullets, but he had a feeling that if he was hit by more than one or two he could be knocked down or out, and that would be all they needed to gain the advantage. And, of course, a face or neck shot would do him in immediately.

He watched as the monsters across the street continually picked on the one who appeared to be the youngest and weakest. This gave him an idea. If there was one thing he thought he could count on, it was that the only way for that weak kid to get a break would be for a weaker target to present itself.

The Reaper released the safeties on both of his guns, and then crossed his arms in front of him, concealing the weapons under his arms but outside of his coat. He bent his head low and stepped out of the alley. He turned to the right, and began to limp slowly up Malton Street, staying on the opposite side from the eleven predators who were about to become his prey.

One of them noticed him almost immediately, and he yelled something across the street. When The Reaper didn't stop, more yells erupted. Most of them were yelling at him now, and the best he could understand was that they wanted him to stop and come over to their side.

The Reaper hobbled forward, pretending not to notice. As he had suspected, the clot across the street began to break apart and spread across the street toward him. *Not until you see the whites of their eyes,* he thought.

The one who must be the leader was within ten feet of him now. "Yo, are you deaf motha-fucka?" he yelled as he stalked toward him.

One in the head for him, and then center mass for the rest, The Reaper thought coldly, flexing his hands one last time.

Three feet away now, and as the leader opened his mouth to spew forth more of his putrescence, The Reaper went to work. He spun with catlike speed toward the oncoming crowd, unfolding his hands and their lethal secrets as he did. The speed of his turn cast his hood halfway back on his head, revealing his snarling, evil countenance. A bullet from the right hand tore a hole through the right side of the leader's head, sending him spinning and sprawling out of the way. A bullet from the left struck the next one in the middle of the chest, flipping him onto his back and neck. Then all was fire and blood and noise and fury as his guns blazed away at the mob.

As soon as their leader fell and they saw the demon that slew him, the ten others tried to flee. They were all armed, as The Reaper had guessed, but despite their hard disguises, they were still children underneath. Only two of them had ever fired a gun, and those two were both dead with the first two shots. The others hit the brakes and tried to turn and run back to the safety of 622 Malton.

Six of the eleven were dead or fatally wounded in less than five seconds, before they could even stop their forward progress. Four of the other five fell in the process of turning around. If they had dropped to their stomachs instead of attempting to turn and run, they would have had a chance. Instead, they presented perfect, almost stationary targets for The Reaper. The only thing worse than standing still is stopping and turning around. It is a slow process that provides no change in the essential position of the vital organs of the target, a lesson learned well by those that fell with bullets in the center of their backs.

The last of the eleven was the small one that had been the target of the others' ridicule less than two minutes ago. The Reaper recognized this fact as he watched him begin to run back toward the house. The Reaper lowered his right arm slightly, and fired a perfect shot that struck the boy directly in the upper left hamstring. The boy spun around to the right and fell on his back.

As he watched the boy fall, The Reaper became aware that he was screaming. He also felt a dull pain in his lower lip. He realized that he had bitten through it with his false fangs while he was firing, causing his own blood to mix with the crimson corn syrup that dribbled from his mouth. With some effort, he cut off his scream and began to step over and through the fallen boys in the street.

The young boy saw him coming, and he flipped over onto his stomach and tried to military crawl away from the oncoming beast. Only seconds later, The Reaper was upon him. He grabbed his jacket and violently spun the boy onto his back. He then grasped the boy by the front of the jacket and pulled him up close to his leering face.

The boy's expression was not unlike the one LaShon wore less than an hour ago. The Reaper released his right hand and slapped him hard on the face. "Listen to me," he commanded, "When they ask you, tell them The Reaper did this, and tell them it's not over."

He released the boy's jacket abruptly, letting him drop to the ground. Like a cat, the boy half turned in the air and finished on the ground, continuing his crawl toward the house. The Reaper turned and stepped back across the field of death he had wrought. As he did, he glanced down, catching the eye of one that was still alive. The boy coughed and ejected a cupful of blood onto his chin and neck. His mouth worked to say something, and he reached a trembling hand up toward The Reaper. The Reaper paused only a moment, and then reached a hand into his pocket. He pulled out a handful of matches, and dropped them indifferently into the face of the fallen boy. He then stepped over him and plunged into the alley. Once concealed by its blackness, The Reaper broke into a run.

58

Twelve hours later, an exhausted, nearly broken Seamus Molloy walked into the office Lionel Babcock, his boss. Three letters shorter, and his last name would have said it all. Babcock was about 5'5" tall and had every bit of the Napoleonic complex one would expect.

Seamus had the look of a man who had just gone 30 rounds with John Sullivan. His bloodshot eyes looked like they were going to be swallowed by the dark circles around them. The right side of his hair was still sporting the cowlick he had woken up with when the phone rang the night before to alert him to The Reaper's latest transgression. He hadn't shaven since the previous morning, and he had enough stubble to show that his beard had begun to gray. His red-blonde hair would certainly not be far behind. His shirt was rumpled, his tie askew, and the cuffs of his pants had traces of blood as high as three inches up.

Babcock looked him up and down as Seamus stood silently in front of his desk. "Sit down, you look like shit," he said.

Without a word, Seamus stepped between the chairs on his side of Babcock's desk and flopped into the one to his right. His back, legs and feet began to throb as the pressure was taken off of them.

Babcock continued to look at him like a lion might regard a cornered antelope. Although he knew he was about to take at least a severe tongue lashing, Seamus looked right back at Babcock, refusing to let the little bastard intimidate him. Had he shown a little bit more contrition, perhaps by avoiding direct eye contact, he might have been given another chance to continue his pursuit of The Reaper, and things might have ended much, much differently.

"So you wanna tell me what the fuck is going on?" Babcock began, already boiling under his smarmy calmness.

"As you know, he shot and killed ten kids in their teens and early twenties in Oakland in the street in front of a known crack house. Most of them had records and all were known to have gang ties."

"We're sure it was him?" Babcock asked.

"He shot the last kid in the leg, then told him to tell us it was The Reaper and that it wasn't over. He also dropped a handful of matches on one of the victims. He's never used guns before, but this follows his pattern and as far as we know, no one outside the Bureau or the State Police knows about the matches."

"What about this kid in Redwood City?"

"We're not sure, but the timeframe makes it pretty unlikely it was the same guy. There's only twenty-five minutes between the kid's coworkers calling 9-1-1 and the 9-1-1 call in Oakland reporting the shots. In all previous attacks, we believe The Reaper was at the site for some time waiting for a crime to occur so that he could step in. Even if he did happen upon the kids at this crack house right away, it's still almost impossible he could've gotten from Redwood City to Oakland that fast. Not only that, he has never struck on the Peninsula before. And The Reaper's recent strikes have all been on either domestic abusers or criminals. This kid was taking out the garbage and he's had some kind of brain injury that makes him pretty slow. We're still running down the details on him, but he's not exactly a hardened criminal. We've already apprehended at least one copycat, and we think that's what this was."

"Well God knows you've been right about everything else," Babcock said derisively, "What do we have on the guns?"

"They're .45 Caliber. U.S. Military issue. Running down the specifics beyond that will take some time. If we're lucky we'll be able to find out the name of the man they were issued to."

"They?"

"He used two. Shot with both hands…like a cowboy. Most accurate shooting I've ever seen at a crime scene. Couldn't even tell the difference between the shots from the left and right. The kid and a few other witnesses we've scared up say it happened in less than 20 seconds. Fucking amazing."

"Well, before you get on your knees and give him a blow job we're going to have to find him. Did you get anything that's going to help with that, Agent Molloy?"

Babcock's insinuation that he had grown to admire The Reaper was not lost on Seamus. Nor was the fact that he used 'we' when referring to finding him. He had been debating all night whether or not to mention his suspicions about David. On the one hand, any lead was worth chasing at this point. Not only that, he had lied about not knowing the details of LaShon's injury. He had recognized the name and symptom immediately and knew he was the man who had killed David's parents. On the other, both attacks had happened less than an hour after he had left David. David lived in Pacifica, and it would have been difficult for him to get home, get ready, and get back to either location in time. And there was the nature of these two attacks. Seamus had harbored some suspicion of David throughout the evening until he received the calls reporting the two attacks, not only because he referred to The Reaper as Charon, but also because he could almost see David doing it…because The Reaper's cause was, although misguided, almost noble. He couldn't, however, fathom David attacking a mentally challenged man, even if he did kill his parents. He thought it even less likely that David could kill anyone, let alone ten people. And there was now the military link. David had not been in the military, Seamus knew, and he had never mentioned guns as a hobby of his. As the night had gone on, Seamus had begun to feel more and more that his suspicions of David had been groundless fabrications based on a coincidental piece of knowledge from the most knowledgeable person he knew, and also from the several beers he had drunk.

Still, he might have mentioned David, but the bullshit that Babcock was spewing closed the door on that thought. He would keep his own mind open to David as a suspect, but he wasn't going to subject his friend, who had just been trying to help him last night, to the world of shit that would come down on him if Seamus mentioned his name to Babcock.

"We think the guns are a good break. They point to ex-military. The way he shot, he's gotta be some sort of special forces or marksmanship expert. We're already in touch with the military to see what we can come up with there."

"That's it? You've been on this case for what, seven months, and the best you have is that he might be ex-military? Jesus, Molloy, what am I supposed to tell the press? We think we've narrowed it down to about 100,000 people?"

"We've got a lot more than that…" Seamus tried to interject.

"Shut the fuck up, Molloy! Do you have any idea the kind of press this is getting? Washington wants to know if they need to send someone else out here to manage this case, and I'll be fucking damned if I'm going to let that happen."

Babcock paused to catch his breath. He looked at Seamus, and perhaps the glaring hate pouring out from beneath Seamus's furrowed brow made him rethink his approach. "Look, I'm sorry to come down on you like this Seamus, you're a talented agent, but you are pretty new. You did a hell of a job on that New Dawn thing, and we thought you were ready for this. In fact, we didn't realize what a bastard this fucking Reaper was going to turn out to be. I hope you understand, but I've gotta take you off the case. The New Dawn has been heating up again anyway since you've been on this one. They have some new guy up there that's supposed to be a hell of a lot smarter and more organized than your old buddy Luther. I need you to debrief Johnson on The Reaper and then get up to six and get back into the New Dawn thing. We won't make any announcement to the press, OK?"

Seamus was seething. "Would that be Agent Johnson or Special Agent Johnson," he asked sarcastically.

Babcock caught the reference to Die Hard, and, like most of the agents in the Bureau, didn't find it that amusing, especially coming from within.

"Don't be a fucking smartass, Molloy. I'm trying to cut you a break here but if you wanna be an asshole, then you'll find out that I can be a bigger one. Now get out of my fucking sight before I change my mind!"

Seamus opened his mouth to say something else, thought better of it, and got up without a word and left the room.

He left at about 4:00 that afternoon and, after a short debate, decided to go to the gym and see if David was there. After eight hours of non-stop contact with pricks like Babcock, Johnson and Rich Rodham, who was now his partner in the New Dawn babysitting gig, he could scarcely imagine that he had ever thought that David might be The Reaper. David was truly a good person, not like these other assholes. Until today, Seamus would have even said that The Reaper had these assholes beat. Of course that was before he became a murderer.

Seamus hoped that David would be there. He wasn't going to apologize, because that would require that he admit what he had been thinking. Still, he wanted to see if he could tell if David had caught his suspicion, and then try to remedy that by acting like nothing had changed.

He arrived a little earlier than usual, and David wasn't there yet. He did arrive about ten minutes later, and came right over to Seamus.

"Hey man," David said, "Didn't expect you here today."

"You saw what happened, then?"

"Hard to miss. It's everywhere."

"I figured. It's not my problem anymore anyway. I'm off the case."

"That's bullshit. Why'd they do that?"

"Like you say, it's everywhere. Bad publicity for the Bureau. They put their big gun on it. We'll see if he has any better luck."

"I doubt it, man. Did they tell you what you're going to be working on now?"

"Back on the New Dawn. They say that's heating up again."

"Is it?"

"Well, for once it seems like they aren't lying. But I can't talk about it, you know."

"I know. At least it's something you're familiar with."

"Yeah," Seamus agreed.

As they began their workout, something occurred to Seamus. He hadn't mentioned LaShon, and neither had David. In fact David seemed completely normal, which was good, but it also meant he probably didn't know that LaShon was back in the news. His name had probably not been released as of the last time David read the paper or watched TV or listened to the radio. If David had heard LaShon's name, at a minimum he would see preoccupied, Seamus thought. More likely, he would have asked Seamus about the details of the attack. Seamus decided that he should mention it to David, instead of David hearing about it later and wondering why Seamus hadn't told him.

"So did you hear about the attack in Redwood City also?"

"They mentioned it on the radio on the way up here, but they were spending a lot more time on the...uh...what happened in Oakland."

Seamus smiled at David's attempt to downplay the bloodbath across the Bay. "Listen, you're going to hear this eventually, so you might as well hear it from me. The guy who got attacked in Redwood City was LaShon Jackson."

David froze and looked at Seamus. "You mean..." he began, and then ran out of words.

"Yes, him. He apparently has never recovered from the...accident. He works at a Jack-In-The-Box and was taking out the trash when it happened."

David was silent. He kept opening his mouth to speak, and then would shut it and look away. He eventually made his way around and sat heavily down on the weight bench.

Seamus came around beside him. "You OK?" he asked.

"I...I don't know. I hadn't thought about him in so long. I keep wanting to ask what happened...exactly, but I know you probably can't tell me. And that's OK, because…because I can't help but hope that he got his ass kicked good. I feel like crap thinking that, but I do."

Seamus tried to think of something to say that would help, but came up empty. He laid his hand on David's shoulder, hoping that would be better than nothing.

David looked at it, and then up at Seamus's face. Seamus gave him a tight-lipped, humorless smile. David returned it, took a deep breath, let it out, and stood up. "I suddenly don't think I'm going to finish my workout. I hope you don't mind."

"I don't blame you. I hope it's OK I told you," Seamus replied.

"Sure. I appreciate it. You didn't have to, but it's probably easier that it came from you. Still, I may not be back for a few days, OK? I don't really feel very social."

"That's OK…I don't feel all that social myself. Maybe I'll take this opportunity to try to get things back on track with Molly. Between the case and trying to get her pregnant…"

"Yeah…you're getting it from both sides. I guess I don't have much to complain about."

"No, David, I didn't mean that. You've been through more than I could imagine…it's me who shouldn't complain. You take care, OK? Give me a call if you need anything at all."

"Thanks," David said. He held out his hand and Seamus took it. Then he turned and headed to the locker room without looking back.

59

Snapshots. It was the spring of 2004, and all David's memory could supply him between his encounter with LaShon and now was snapshots.

Sitting on his sofa, watching Conan the Barbarian, as he relentlessly sharpened his claws. Life, death, none of it mattered…only Steel.

Running up and down the steps that led from his house down to the beach. Realizing he had lost count at 126 trips. Feeling he should stop for a break at the bottom. Falling on his back in the sand, listening to his breath heaving in and out as his chest rose and fell like the tide. Looking up, watching the seagulls. *They swim. Their wings don't go up and down, they look more like they are swimming. Fascinating.*

Watching a black kid in a plate glass window across the street as he crept up to the alley David was hiding in. Raising his claws to eye level. Pressing down on the release lever as the kid came around the corner—sending his claws into the kid's skull. He kicked the dead kid in the face afterward—why was that?

Back on the sofa. Looking down to see two piles of unwrapped Starburst candies on the coffee table—one by his left hand, one by his right. He is practicing his dexterity by unwrapping Starburst two at a time—one in each hand. He sees the left pile is larger. Is that the first time that has happened?

Driving home from…where? Listening to Black Sabbath screaming out of the tape deck. Apparently Metallica had become too pristine at some point. Ozzy in his prime, thundering away, unknowingly singing The Song of The Reaper:

> *Now in darkness world stops turning,*
> *ashes where the bodies burning.*
> *No more War Pigs have the power,*
> *Hand of God has struck the hour.*
> *Day of judgement, God is calling,*
> *on their knees the war pigs crawling.*
> *Begging mercies for their sins,*
> *Satan, laughing, spreads his wings.*

Reading a newspaper article speculating that he was racist since most of his victims were minorities. Hammering out a note saying simply, "I'm helping most of the people in the communities I visit. I only hurt the evil ones. I'm the opposite of a racist. I've done more for them than Jesse Jackson ever did. If this note is not released to the press, I'll double my activity."

Sitting in a club in San Francisco. Minding his own business at a back booth. Kids yelling at him...not backing down. He couldn't do anything in public...had to remain calm. Leaving the club. Did he kill those kids?

It took every bit of David's will to stop The Reaper from killing LaShon. When he did, he lost the will to stop The Reaper from killing anyone else, and the ability to control it. The Reaper was in charge now, and David made fewer and fewer appearances at the controls.

David had stopped going to the gym the day after he spared LaShon's life. He had spoken to Seamus on the phone a few times since and had been over for dinner once, but that was only to make sure that their parting of company did not directly coincide with The Reaper's escalation to murder and Seaumus's removal from the case. He hadn't spoken to him at all since Christmas, when he called to thank him and Molly for the Christmas card.

David had stopped cutting out newspaper articles a few months ago. He had stopped paying the bill for The Chronicle so they had stopped delivering it. He couldn't remember how many people he had killed or the exact circumstances of the killings. He did know, however, that The Reaper had stuck with his essential roadmap. He was still very, very careful whenever he struck, and he still struck only bad people. The biggest difference...the crucial difference, was that The Reaper didn't use handcuffs. Dead people, after all, didn't require restraint.

It was now April 16, 2004, and Darius Williams was enjoying the last day of his twentieth year, the last day of his incarceration, and, if The Reaper had his way, the last day of his life. Even when David was himself, he had not changed his plans for Darius at all. He and The Reaper agreed in principle on most points, although David didn't fully condone the murders The Reaper so craved. On the subject of Darius and the others involved with Karen's murder, however, they were in full agreement. There would be no interference from David as there had been with LaShon. Darius knew what he was doing. Darius did not sustain any injury as a result of his murder of Karen. Darius had lived six years longer than he had deserved to. This time David would not step in and stop The Reaper from exacting the revenge that they both had lived for.

And now, the wait was finally over.

60

Darius Williams was finally going to get out of the shithole in which he had spent the last six years of his life. He had tried to spend that time well, God knew, but the place was still a shithole. He had gotten his GED and had taken several college courses via the internet. He had also sustained a broken nose and several broken ribs. He had given better than he got, though. He had stayed in pretty good physical condition, and he had been able to fight off most attacks. No one would come after him one-on-one— at least not after he sent that neo-Nazi punk to the infirmary his first year in. Then they came in twos and threes, and then four and five at a time. Eventually he made enough friends and cracked enough of their skulls that they stopped messing with him. That was good. He just wanted to get to his twenty-first birthday and get out of here and get on with his life. He knew he would never play pro football like he had hoped as a child, but he still thought he might be able to make something of himself. More importantly, he thought he would be able to help his mom and little brothers.

His mom had sacrificed everything for Darius, and she was heartbroken when he was arrested and convicted of Ms. Chavez's murder. He knew she believed he did it. He didn't give her any reason not to for over a year afterward, so he couldn't blame her.

As he packed his belongings into a large, gray laundry sack, he thought about the day he had finally told his mother the truth. He remembered that he had begged his Aunt Helen to bring his mom to see him for his seventeenth birthday. His mom had previously refused to see him in the detention facility. She said it would break her heart to see her boy locked up like his father and grandfather had been. They had written each other a few letters, but that was it.

Darius had been too consumed with guilt to tell anyone the real story of what happened the night Ms. Chavez died. He knew in his heart that he hadn't actually been the one to pull the trigger, but he also knew that he had killed her all the same. His heart, his foolish heart, had told him that telling the real story would be like seeking to abdicate responsibility for what had happened, and he refused to do that. It was his fault that she died, whether or not he actually pulled the trigger. He couldn't dishonor her memory by trying to lay the blame elsewhere. In his mind, what he got was nowhere near what he deserved.

As time passed, though, he began to see that denying the truth was only hurting his loved ones and helping the three bastards who had gotten him into this mess. It was too late to do anything about the fact that they had gotten off with basically a slap on the wrist, but he thought that the truth was the first step in rebuilding his relationship with his mother. With a solid foundation there, he could begin to re-enter the lives of his brothers, and hopefully be a positive influence on them, even from behind these thick, gray walls.

His mother had bent to her sister's persistence, and had come to see Darius on his seventeenth birthday. They met in the room known as the Visitor's Lounge, a room whose name was clearly chosen in the *"What name least describes this room?"* contest. It consisted of a water cooler and several low, round tables ringed with black chairs fabricated of molded plastic. Hardly a place one would come to lounge in.

She and his Aunt Helen were already seated at the far table when he was escorted into the room. He made his way through the other tables toward them. When he got there, his Aunt Helen stood to give him a brief hug. His mother stayed seated, gazing at the center of the table. The look of discomfort on her face was enough to break his heart.

"Aunt Helen, thanks so much for coming," Darius said. "If you wouldn't mind, may I have a moment alone with my mom?"

Aunt Helen smiled and said, "Of course child. You take all the time you need now." With that, she got up and moved to one of the empty tables across the room.

"Mama?" Darius said, hoping for some sort of reaction. "Mama, I got a lot to say to you and time is gonna go fast. Can you listen to me please?"

His mother finally brought her heartsick eyes up to meet his. They had the look of someone who was accustomed to being hurt by those she loved. She had grown to expect it, but it had only become slightly easier over the years. "Sho', boy. You go on," she managed before she had to look away again.

"Mama, I know you think I killed Ms. Chavez. Everyone does, and I haven't done anything to tell anyone otherwise. I don't wanna make a big issue out of this with the courts because nothing's gonna change, not with all the rich lawyers the other guys got. I didn't confess in so many words, but they got enough to say I did. I guess I'm just ready to tell the truth now…to get it off my chest so it can stop burning me up inside. And I wanna tell you first, Mama. I want you to know what really happened so we can get back to being a family. I got pretty lucky I'll be out when I'm 21, and I wanna get back to helping you and the boys when I do…if you'll have me, that is."

His mother looked at him and gave him a wordless grimace that said, *Go on then, but I ain't promisin' nothin'.*

Darius took in a deep breath and let it out. His mother wasn't going to make it easy, that was clear. He had to do it, though, and so he told her the story of what had happened to Karen Chavez. And every word of what he told her was the absolute truth.

"OK mama. I did fall in love with Ms. Chavez, you know. I know now it was puppy love, but it sure felt real at the time. I was just fifteen and she was really helping me out with my studies and she invited me to her house and all. I mean, I'm only seventeen now, but I've been through a hell of a lot since then. She was just so nice to me that I guess I figured she must like me too. So when she was taking me home one day, I…I tried to kiss her. She pulled back and I got so embarrassed I ran away.

"I couldn't go back to school and face her, I was so embarrassed. One of the guys, John McNamara, must've seen what happened because he came after me. I thought he was helping me out because he got me a place to crash for a few days while I worked things out. Then he and the other two, Doug and Truman, brought some booze and we all got drunk. They came back the next night and the next. I don't know what I was thinking, mama, but I guess it felt good to have friends and forget about what an idiot I had been with Ms. Chavez.

"I knew it wasn't her fault, but those guys kept talking and talking and filling my head with all kinds of nonsense like she was just helping me so she could embarrass me and such. It got so I wanted to get back at her...when I was drunk anyway. In between, my head was hurting and I got really sick. I didn't know what was up anymore and I was starting not to care. I figured I would be kicked out anyway, so I hadn't gone back to school.

"On Tuesday night, the three of them came back with more alcohol, and I drank with them again. I'm so ashamed, mama, but by that time they really had me going. I was calling Ms. Chavez...I was even calling her a bitch like they were..." At this point, Darius's eyes filled with tears and he had to pause to get rid of the hitch in his throat. Then he went on, "Anyway, after we drank for awhile, they got out some white powder and we all snorted it. Coke, they said, but sweeter than Coca-Cola. I didn't care, so I did it with them.

"I don't remember how, exactly, but we ended up at Ms. Chavez's house. I guess I must've given them directions. Don't ask me why, but I had looked over her shoulder when she was undoing her alarm before and I remembered the code. Doug could pick locks, and we got in and I did the code and I guess they didn't hear.

"We went upstairs and found their bedroom and me and John stood by Ms. Chavez and the other two took a bat around to where her fiancée was. I met him...he was a real nice guy to me. Truman hit him in the head and then the two of them drug him out of bed to the bathroom. Me and John tried to handcuff Ms. Chavez to the bed, but she was struggling and John hit her in the face two or three times. Between him hitting her and the other guys hitting her boyfriend, I think it started to wake me up. I'm pretty sure they told me we were just going to scare them, but this was sure more than that.

"Before I knew it, Ms. Chavez was cuffed to the bed and her boyfriend was in the bathroom cuffed to the stool. They were both pretty much out of it. Doug turned on their radio, I think, because there was loud music playing. Then John went and pulled off her underpants and that woke her up. John told me to get on the bed and rape her. All three of them were yelling at me to do it, and," again Darius paused to wipe the back of his hand across his eyes, "and I went to do it. I got on the bed and…and I think I had my pants down. But she looked at me and said 'No' and I just couldn't do it. She didn't deserve that after all she had done for me.

"So I got down and pulled my pants back up. John and the others started calling me…you know…bad names and things for not doing it. Then John said he was going to do it if I wasn't. I tried to stop him, but I was so out of it that I guess he got up on the bed. Then I grabbed him again and that's when she…she kicked him…between the legs."

Darius paused for a moment, seeming to remember fondly, for at least a moment, the strength his former teacher and friend had shown even at that terrible time. Then he went on. "John fell off the bed and rolled around for awhile. Then he got up and went over to his backpack. He pulled out a gun and walked right over toward Ms. Chavez. I remember I saw him cock it and I remember the look in his eyes. Rich bastards like that know they can get away with anything, and I could tell by the look in his eyes he was going to kill her and he would let his daddy figure out later how to get him out of it.

"I couldn't let him do it, mama, so I jumped on him and grabbed for the gun. Everyone was yelling and the music was blaring and my head was too, but I wouldn't let go. He fought me for it, and at some point the gun just went off...that or he pulled the trigger, I can't say for sure. As soon as it did, though, he slid his hands out of there and somehow I ended up holding it. I swear I never had my hand on the gun until then, but I guess it was close enough that their test said I fired it. Then we all looked at the bed, and..."

Now Darius was weeping openly. He put his face in his hands and tried to stifle the tears that had finally come after eighteen months. It was no use. They poured like rain from his eyes, through his fingers and down his arms, falling drop by drop from the points of his elbows onto his faded jeans.

As he wept, he felt an arm fall across his shoulders and a hand rest on his arm. Then his mother's hair was pressed into his hands and face as she embraced him. He heard that she was weeping too, and the two of them stayed that way as long as the guards would let them.

Now, as he packed his bags to finally leave this place, Darius could still feel the cascading relief he felt when he told his story to his mother, and the joy he felt that she had accepted him back into her arms.

This was his last night here. Tomorrow he would go to her and begin again. This time, he thought...no, this time he swore, he would stick by her and his brothers forever. They would be a family again, and if anything wanted to get in the way of that it was going to have to kill him and step over his dead body to do it.

61

There had been a welcome home party for Darius the next day. All of his relatives that were in the area came to his mother's house to greet him as he returned to them. It was a wonderful afternoon and evening, and he was giddy with excitement at the possibility of beginning anew.

At the end of the evening, after all of the dishes were done and the garbage taken out, Darius's mother kissed him on the cheek and hugged him tightly to her. "I'm so glad you're home, my son," she said through joyous tears.

"Me too, mama," he replied, choking back tears of his own.

"I'm goin' to bed now. Too much excitement for this old gal."

Darius smiled and said, "Goodnight mama."

"Goodnight son," she said as she turned and creaked back down the hall toward her room.

Darius sat in the living room and watched TV for awhile, feeling almost at a loss of what to do with all of his freedom. Part of him wanted to go out and do something, but more of him just wanted to stay home and go to sleep in his own bed.

He looked at the clock. The right angle of the hands told him it was nine o'clock. He felt silly going to bed this early on his first night home, but at this moment, nothing sounded better.

He stopped by the room his little brothers shared. He looked in, smiling at the contortions their pre-teen bodies had gotten into as they slept off the food and fun they had consumed earlier. "G'night, guys," he whispered.

He stopped next at his mother's door. He opened it a crack, and heard a rumbling coming from beneath the sheets that was either a chainsaw or his mother snoring. Again, he smiled and whispered, "Goodnight, ma," as he pulled her door closed.

He reached the room he had occupied the first fifteen years of his life. He opened the door, and realized his heart was beating. Was he actually nervous to go to sleep in his own room? Weird. He took a deep breath, let it out with a soft laugh, and stepped into his room.

The room was very dark, lit only by the moonlight from the open window across the room. He reached to his left to turn on the lightswitch. He flipped it up, squinting his eyes to protect them from the sudden flash of light from the bare lightbulb in the center of his room. The flash didn't come, though. He flipped the switch up and down a few more times and then gave up, heading across the room to the reading lamp by the bed.

The reading lamp was on an old table that stood under the window. When he reached it, he felt that the table was damp. It was raining outside, and it was coming in the window and wetting both the lamp and table alike. *Wait a minute*, he thought, *what is the window doing open? I didn't open it.*

Suddenly he was aware that someone was behind him. He stiffened to turn and strike, but he was too late. He felt a cold, metallic circle press against the back of his head, and then he heard the click of the hammer of a pistol being pulled into the lethal position.

"Hello Darius," said a silky yet sinfully wicked voice from behind him, "If you make a sound, I will kill you and your mother and brothers. If you follow my instructions to the letter, they will be spared."

"OK," Darius whispered, "I'll do what you say, just leave them alone."

"Very good," hissed the voice. "Now, I am going to step back and allow you to turn around. However, let me warn you that what you see will startle you. If you scream, you and your family will all die tonight. Is that clear?"

"Yes."

"Then turn around."

Darius turned, and the face he saw turned what had been fear into utter despair and terror. He wanted to scream, or at least whimper. Instead, he bit his lip to avoid making a sound that would set this monster off.

"Do you know who I am?"

"You're...The Reaper."

"That is correct. I see they allow you television in juvenile detention. Good, then you know I will kill, correct?"

"Yeah, black folks especially," Darius heard himself say. He winced as soon as the words left his mouth, hoping that he hadn't just sentenced his family to death.

"You are lucky I'm in a forgiving mood tonight, Darius, or that little comment might have caused your brothers great pain. I trust you will keep your editorial comments to yourself from now on?"

"Sure."

"Good. Now, crawl out of the window. When you get out, lay face down in the dirt with your arms and legs spread eagled. If you don't, I'll shoot you and your family."

Without risking another word, Darius did as he was told. After only a moment of lying on his face, he heard the monster land quietly behind him.

The Reaper whispered from behind him, "Now, get up and walk around the corner into the alley. There is a blue Honda Accord parked there. The trunk is popped but still down. When you get there, open the trunk and put both of your hands on the floor inside."

Darius got up slowly and did as he was told. He didn't dare turn his head, but he switched his eyes wildly back and forth to see if anyone was watching. As near as he could tell, there wasn't a soul in sight.

Darius saw the car right away. It was an older model Accord—maybe mid nineties—but a car that well maintained stuck out in this neighborhood like a flower in a field of weeds. He walked to it, placed one hand under the trunk, and pulled it up. Slowly, he placed both hands out in front of him and lowered them to the well-vacuumed carpet that lined the trunk of the Accord. He was not surprised to see that his hands were shaking.

"Darius, I'm going to hold the gun to your head with one hand. With the other, I'm going to reach around and place a cloth over your nose and mouth. It will put you to sleep but it will not cause you pain or permanent

Vengeance

injury…you have my word. If you make any noise or struggle, I'll kill you and go back and kill your family…you have my word on that as well."

"Wait," Darius said desperately. The fact that this guy was actually going to knock him out and shove him in the trunk brought the reality of the situation home to Darius. After six years, he had finally come home to his family. The same night, this asshole forced him out of his own window and down this alley. Until this moment, there was something about it that told Darius it was just a bad dream. The truth now hit him like a sledgehammer— this wasn't just a bad dream, it was a nightmare.

"Wait, why me?"

"I will tell you soon. I promise," The Reaper whispered, sounding almost compassionate.

"But…please…I just came home to my mama," Darius said, now very close to tears.

"Calm down, Darius," The Reaper said, quickly losing his compassion, "This will only take a second."

Darius opened his mouth again, but before he could say anything, he simultaneously felt the barrel of the gun press against his left temple and a cloth cover his mouth and nose. He wanted with all of his being to struggle, but the thought of his mother and brothers sleeping contentedly around the corner forced him to stay still and allow the chloroform to slip into his nose and mouth. He tried to breathe shallowly, and he allowed his body to become slack before he actually passed out, hoping the bastard would let go early. No such luck. When he slumped forward, the cloth stayed pressed hard against his face. Within a few more seconds, the world swam out of focus, then turned a hazy gray, and finally faded to black.

62

"Darius? Darius? Come on, it's time, Darius."

Darius began to stir back toward consciousness. He felt like he was underwater, and the voice was coming from the surface. No, it was more like he was underwater at the bottom of a well, and the voice was coming from 30 feet above him.

He began to swim toward the surface. As he did, he became aware that he was lying face down in something prickly. He was cold, too. This wasn't his cot, that was for sure.

But he shouldn't be on his cot, should he? He had gotten out of detention. He should be in his bed. But wait…

Then it all began to come back to him. It was real, wasn't it? The Reaper had knocked him out and shoved him in the trunk of his car. Now he was…where? Outside somewhere. Were those pine needles pressing against his cheek? He wanted to get up and look around, but his head refused to send the appropriate signals to his head and arms.

"Darius!"

The voice was still almost a whisper, but its owner was losing patience. Darius tried to get his arms under him to push himself up, and he found that he couldn't. They were behind his back, and when he tried to bring them around front, they were held back by thin, cold metal against his wrists. Handcuffs.

"Darius, get up now. I don't want to have to put a bullet in the back of your head."

It wasn't the words that forced him to finally get up, it was the cold conviction with which they were spoken. There was no question in Darius's mind that he would do it, and Darius wasn't ready to give up…not by a long shot.

Darius squirmed around until he could get his knees under him. He heaved his weight backward and was able to bring his torso upright, his rear end resting on his heels. He opened his eyes and, although he knew what to expect, felt his heart skip a beat when he saw the horror that stood in front of him.

"Welcome back," it said, "When you faked passing out back there, I had to leave the cloth on extra long to make sure you were really out."

"Are you gonna tell me what's going on," Darius asked, risking a glance around. They were in the middle of a pine forest. From his angle and in the direction he was facing, he could see no lights other than what the full moon was able to offer through the treetops above.

"Yes, Darius. I'm a man of my word, after all. I'm afraid I'm going to have to make it quick. I'd love to draw this out, you know, really enjoy it, but time has grown short."

"What do you mean enjoy it?"

"Well, Darius, you killed the love of my life, and I've been waiting a long time for my revenge. Quite honestly, I thought I'd have more to say to you. But right now, I think I just want to kill you."

"You mean you're...you're...Ms. Chavez's..."

"That's right, Darius. Please don't tell me you forgot my name."

"It's...it's..."

"It's David you son of a bitch," The Reaper thundered as he leveled the gun at Darius's head, "and now you're going to see what it feels like to have a bullet smash into your head while you're handcuffed and defenseless."

"WAIT!" Darius said as The Reaper pulled back the hammer with his thumb. "Wait, I didn't kill her!"

"I was there, you lying bitch," The Reaper said with chilling calmness.

"No, it was John McNamara. He pulled the gun after she...kicked him...I was trying to stop him. Didn't you see that?"

"Are you questioning what I saw?"

"No...no...I just know Doug hit you pretty hard and you were...in the bathroom. Could you see?"

The Reaper paused, thinking back. There were some blank spots in David's memory, but he wasn't going to let that pussy stop him on a technicality like he had with LaShon.

"No matter," he said, "I saw you rape her and my guess is you showed them to our house and let them in. Whether or not you pulled the trigger, you killed her."

"No...no...I didn't rape her either. I got up on the bed and then I couldn't do it. I swear, David...I was trying to stop John from doing it too when she kicked him."

"Don't you dare call me David, you little shit. And don't think you're going to talk your way out of this!"

Thinking fast, Darius offered, "Just...give me a chance. I'll call John and tell him I'm going to tell the real story now that I'm out. You can listen and you'll see from his reaction that he really was the one that did it."

"Enough talk Darius..." The Reaper started to say, but then he paused. This whining little bastard had given him an idea.

"Wait..." Darius said.

"Shut the fuck up for a minute. I want to think about what you said."

The Reaper stood, a gun he had taken from one of his victims pointing directly between Darius's eyes (The Reaper didn't want credit for this one...not just yet anyway...so his grandfather's guns were still in their holsters), and didn't say anything for at least a minute. Darius didn't know what to think, but he was beginning to think he might have a chance to get out of this after all.

"All right, mother fucker, I'll give you a chance. Any bullshit, and I'll put a bullet in your head and drive straight to your mother's house and finish the job. Do you understand?"

"I'll do whatever you want, just promise you won't hurt my family."

"I'm not promising anything, but if this works out the way I want, I don't see why I would have a reason to hurt them. Now, do you think you can get all three of those fuckers to come meet you tonight?"

"I can try, but I don't know how to reach them."

"Try gets you killed. Do it and you have a chance. And I happen to have all of their addresses and phone numbers."

"How am I going to call them?"

"Shut up and listen…I'm getting to that. We're near Woodside, off the 280. Do you know where that is?"

"Kind of."

"It doesn't matter. You're going to get in the driver's seat and I'm going to get in the back seat and point this gun at your head. You will drive where I tell you until we reach a pay phone. You need to call them and get them to meet you. I'll give you the directions where I want them to go on the way."

"Then what?"

"We'll drive there and wait. I'll hide so they can't see me. When they come, you need to get them to admit to as much as you can. I happen to have a small tape recorder in the car here…I use it to record my thoughts about potential target sites. I think I'll record your conversation so we can discredit them and their fathers as well, depending on what you can get out of them. If you can get this John to admit that he was really the one that killed Karen, I might spare your life."

"What happens if he admits it?"

"You let me worry about that. But if you see me come out at them, I'd suggest you drop to your stomach and wait for the commotion to end. My guess is they'll be armed, and you know I am, so you'd better stay out of the way. And do I have to tell you what I'll do if you try to escape?"

"You'll kill me and my family."

"You're a quick study, Darius. Now let's get going."

63

An hour and a half later, Darius watched as a pair of headlights bumped down the narrow turnout road The Reaper had described for him, and he had in turn described to John over the phone. Getting him, Doug and Truman to come had been easier than he had expected. He told John he was going to the papers to tell the truth about that night and also about what had happened in the courts to assure that they would do the minimum amount of time possible while he took the fall. He only had to hint at what it would mean for all of their promising careers as well as their fathers' political careers and thriving companies, and John was on his way. He didn't even ask what Darius wanted, and to Darius, that meant he probably intended to silence him instead of pay him off. What a pleasant surprise they would have when they arrived.

Over the past hour, Darius had played over all of the potential scenarios in his mind. The one that he thought was most likely to play out was that he would get them to admit what The Reaper wanted, and then he would kill the three of them. If that happened, Darius would have to do some fancy talking to keep The Reaper from doing the same to him. He thought he had a pretty good idea of what he might say to give himself a chance, and the time to try out his line of bullshit was almost here.

The Mercedes coupe lurched to a stop, dust billowing up and around the headlights. Three of the doors opened, and his good old friends from Edison stepped out. They left the lights on, and the three of them walked around the front of the car and then proceeded toward Darius. As they got close, John McNamara reached around behind him and pulled a handgun out of his waistband. He leveled it at Darius and pulled back the hammer for emphasis.

"Yo, my brotha," John said with complete disdain. Truman and Doug chuckled, but looked fairly uncomfortable that the gun was already out.

"Hey, that's not necessary John. I just wanna talk," Darius said, raising his hands and taking a step backward to demonstrate his point.

John didn't stop walking forward. He didn't even break stride until he pressed the gun against Darius's forehead. *I hate to burst your bubble John,* thought Darius, *but this ain't the first time I've had a gun to my head. Not even the first time today…and I'm a helluva lot less scared of you than the other guy.*

John must not have seen the fear he had hoped for in Darius's eyes, because a look of exasperation bloomed on his arrogant face as he said, "You don't think I'll use this, boy? You don't think I'd get away with greasing a fucking murderer like you? I got witnesses here that'll say you came at me."

Darius kept looking John in the eyes, his gaze nonplussed and unwavering.

"Doug, get up here and check him," John said with a hint of whiny brat in his voice.

"For what?" Doug asked.

"For guns or a tape recorder, or even a wire you asshole. Am I the only one here with a brain in his fucking head?"

Maybe not for long, Darius thought, and had to suppress a smile. With that thought, he found that, through the maddening events of the evening, something incredibly unexpected had happened. While he had hated the bastard more than Satan himself only two hours before, he now felt almost as if he and The Reaper were on the same team against these assholes. He had followed The Reaper's career, and, before he kidnapped him from his bedroom anyway, he had something close to admiration for the guy. In spite of some misguided actions, he felt The Reaper's motivation was a thousand times more honorable than what these three had to offer. There was a growing hope inside him that if he could get these three to admit the truth, he could stay low and let The Reaper do his work, and then talk his way out of this mess. There was a chance, maybe even a decent chance, that he may see his mother and brothers again.

"I don't feel anything," Doug said, after patting Darius down.

"All right, I guess you're clean, but that doesn't mean you're out of the woods, so to speak. Now talk, asshole," John beckoned.

"Listen John, we all know I didn't rape her, right? And I didn't kill her either," Darius said in his most rational voice.

"Oh yes you did, my good man. Just ask the courts."

"Come on John. You brought the gun, and you got it out when she kicked you. I was just trying to stop you from doing something stupid."

"Jesus, are you still fifteen fucking years old? I told you we were just going to scare her, and that's what I was doing. I wasn't going to really shoot her. If you hadn't jumped in to stop me, it would never have happened. Don't you know that you numb fuck?"

Darius felt hot fire rush into his face. He didn't know if this was going to be enough to get him off. He had a partial admission, but the way John put it, he was still at least as much to blame as John was.

"You sure looked like you were going to kill her, and the truth of the matter is that it was still your finger on the trigger when it went off. You didn't let go of it until after it went off. You guys saw that, right?" Darius said this last looking at Doug and Truman.

Neither of them said a word, but the looks on their faces told both John and Darius, as well as the observer who was lurking in the bushes, the truth.

"You two don't need to answer this motherfucker. He isn't on the same social plane as either of you. It's hurting my stomach bad enough to stoop to his level, but I'll take one for the team. Now, bitch, what's your point?"

"Listen, I don't need to debate who killed her. The point is I took the rap and didn't say shit. I could have, and it was your gun and you guys could've done a lot more time than you did. I might have given up an NFL career for you. A college football scholarship for sure. I'm just looking for just compensation for my time."

"You ignorant fucking monkey! Do you think it would have made a difference for us if you had said something? My dad and their dads met with the judge and the DA before anything happened. Who do you think paid for your lawyer? You think she did it out of the goodness of her heart? You had nothing to do with what happened to you or us, and nothing you could've done would have changed it. My dad got us off with a slap on the wrist, and the only price was six years of your life and a few favors for the judge and DA. And you know what? He's going to do the same after I kill you."

John raised the gun and pointed it Darius. As he did, Truman said, "John what are you doing?"

"He can really fuck us up and our dads too with what he knows, and I'll be damned if I'll pay him off! Now get the fuck back and let me do this asshole!"

Truman and Doug looked horrified, but didn't move to stop John. He raised the gun again and flashed a sickening smile at Darius. "Say goodnight, nig…"

The end of John's last hate-filled word was cut off by a crash that came from almost directly behind Darius. As he watched, a spray of blood erupted from the right side of John's neck. The drops of blood were back-lit by the headlights of his Mercedes, and for a moment it looked like hundreds of rubies had fallen from the sky. John dropped the gun that he had held in his right hand and slapped it hard against his neck, as if he were swatting a mosquito. A moment later, he pulled it away, held it out in front of his face and looked dumbfoundedly up at Darius. Then his knees buckled and he collapsed to the ground in a heap.

It was only about a second between the report of the gun and John's collapse. Doug and Truman, who were looking at Darius instead of John, hadn't even realized that the report wasn't from John's gun until he fell. By that time, Doug was on the way down also with a tunnel leading through his chest and into his heart. He was dead before he hit the ground.

Truman saw John fall, and then saw Doug clutch his chest. He had just enough time to glance back at Darius to see where he had gotten the gun. Instead of Darius holding a gun, Truman saw him dropping to a prone position. Behind Darius and slightly to one side, he saw the angel of death striding toward him. He screamed, and as he did he saw a flash of fire come from the demon's outstretched hand. Then there was no more.

Darius saw Truman take a bullet right in the forehead and then fall next to the other two. Then he saw the blackness of The Reaper's coat as it passed almost directly over him. "The Reaper to the rescue," he said in a low voice. His ears were still ringing from the shots, and he couldn't even hear the words coming out of his own mouth. He guessed The Reaper hadn't heard either, because he didn't even break stride.

The Reaper bent over each of them in turn, checking the effectiveness of his shooting. He looked coldly for a moment at the writhing, choking, blood-spitting man that had been John McNamara. John was clearly not going to be able to make a play for the gun he had dropped, so The Reaper left it where it lay. Then he reached in his pocket and pulled out the tape recorder. He clicked it off and then turned to Darius and said, "OK, get up."

Darius did as he was told. He stood there, staring at the monster in front of him. He couldn't decide what to feel...hate, fear, gratitude...as it turned out, he felt almost nothing except the urge to say something. Anything to break the awful silence between them.

"Thanks for saving my life," Darius said, hoping that would put forth the concept to The Reaper that they were in this together.

"I didn't do it for you. Now, I'm guessing you think there should be a way out of this, am I right?"

"I...I hope so. I just want to see my mom again."

"OK, there is a way out, but you have to do exactly as I say."

Darius nodded, finding it impossible to say anything. His heart was leaping with joy. He watched as The Reaper popped the clip out of the gun he had used to shoot John, and to kill Doug and Truman. After he did, he looked up at Darius. Despite his relief, Darius could scarcely look at the horror that was now glaring at him. It was the eyes. Those red eyes. They made it impossible to see what the man behind them was really thinking.

"You need to take the blame for their murder. I have it on tape, and you may be able to get off on self-defense. I got this gun off a kid in the street in Oakland, so you need to make up some story as to where you got it. I'm also going to need you to put a bullet in your friend John over there. Put him out of his misery, as they say. More importantly, the cops will test to see if you fired it or not. You can't have credit for shooting three people if you never fired the gun, you know."

"But you pulled out the clip."

"There's one in the chamber. I don't want you to get any bright ideas." As he spoke, he reached inside his coat and pulled out another stolen gun. "Do you understand?" he said as he pointed the new gun at Darius.

"I got it," Darius said.

The Reaper held out the gun so that it was pointed toward John's body. Darius took it and slowly moved in that direction, taking care not to change the position of the weapon.

He stood over John, who was violently struggling for breath. He was emitting sickening gurgling noises and coughing crimson blood out into the night. When Darius appeared above him, John's face, which had worn a look of fading surprise, awoke into a mask of combined fear and hatred. His mouth worked to speak, but nothing came out but a large bubble of blood and saliva. It floated for a moment over his lips, streaks of blood swimming around its periphery, and then it popped as John's body racked with another watery cough.

Darius regarded John with an indifference that surprised him. A few hours ago, he could never have conceived of killing anyone. But now, well, a lot had changed, hadn't it? For one thing, he did literally have a gun to his head, so it wasn't like he was doing this by his own choice. And if there was anyone on earth that deserved killing, it was John. Besides, he was clearly going to die anyway. Darius would actually be doing the Christian thing by speeding up the process. As if he could hear Darius's thoughts, all of the hate melted out of John's face and his eyes grew as wide as the full moon.

Darius glanced down and saw a dark stain growing around John's crotch and down toward his knees. In spite of himself, he smiled.

Darius pointed the gun at John's face, sucked in a deep breath, thought of his family, closed his eyes and squeezed the trigger. The bullet crashed into John's mouth, shattering his teeth and causing fresh blood to spray in a wide arc around his face. Darius felt a few drops hit his own face, and looked down to see that his clothes had also received a fine spray from the impact.

"Nice shot," The Reaper said, with more than a hint of sarcasm.

Darius let the gun go limp in his hand. He held it away from his body as if it might bite him. He began to back away from John's body, never taking his eyes off of the cavernous hole he had created just below his nose. Just seconds ago he had been strangely comfortable with the thought of shooting John McNamara. Now that it was done, he felt like he was going to vomit.

Seeing the sick look on Darius's face, The Reaper offered his best words of comfort. "It's not easy to pull the trigger the first time when you're aiming to kill someone. It gets easier, though. I can vouch for that."

As Darius backed toward him, The Reaper continued in his friendly, almost conversational tone, "Darius, now that we're sharing, let me ask you a question that has always bothered me. How did you guys get in the house without tripping the alarm?"

Darius could barely think. He was holding the gun away from him, wanting desperately for The Reaper to take it away. "Uh...I watched Ms. Chavez enter the code when I came over to your house that weekend," he heard himself say. His voice sounded like it was coming from a speaker phone 100 feet away.

"So, you entered the code so you guys could sneak up on us?" The Reaper asked, as he reached for the gun.

"Yeah, David I'm so sorry about what happ..."

"DON'T CALL ME DAVID!" The Reaper screamed as he snatched the gun away from Darius. In one lightning quick motion, he slammed the clip back into the gun and began to raise it as he jacked the slide to chamber another round. As the barrel passed Darius's shoulder he thumbed the hammer, and when it reached Darius's head, he pulled the trigger. Darius, who had been transfixed by what he had done to John, had just begun to turn his head. The bullet tore into his temple and blew Darius's brains in a grayish pink spray out the other side. Darius fell over stiffly like a tree that had been felled by a woodcutter's axe.

The Reaper bent over and carefully placed the weapon back into Darius's dead hand. He caught Darius's sightless, questioning gaze as he did. "What, were you surprised? I don't think I ever said I had a way out of this for YOU, my friend. But a murder-suicide is a great way for me to get out clean."

The Reaper got up, fished the small tape recorder from his pocket and dropped it on the ground next to Darius. He turned around and surveyed the scene. He couldn't see anything that needed to be changed. At long, long last, his work was done.

He turned and ran into the woods. His car was parked about a mile away on a different access road than the cops would take to get to the scene. He had to hand it to Darius, without him, he never would have come up with such a perfect way to kill them all and get away with it. As he ran, he couldn't help but laugh out loud.

Part III—Reckoning

64

David McGuire was standing on the beach. It was the time of the morning just before the sun peaked over the coastal mountains behind him. Bluish gray light colored the sand, the ocean and the sky. The waves crashed on the break over and over, pushing white foam up toward where he stood.

As he watched, a shape began to grow out of the churning, white water near the shore. It rose out of the waves, narrowed, and became a human figure. It wore a flowing, white dress that blew back away from shore. Its head was looking down into the water, but it had now taken form enough to see that it was a young woman. Her long, chestnut colored hair also blew out behind her.

As David stared at the impossible sight, the sun crested the ridge and sent the first beam of day down upon the figure. Just as it struck her, she raised her head and looked at David. For a moment she was too bright, too angelic for David to recognize. Then, as his eyes adjusted, he saw that it was Karen who walked toward him on top of the water.

"David," she said. Her lips were moving, but the voice came from everywhere. He felt as if he were in a movie theater and she was speaking to him in DTS. Even so, her tone was supremely gentle, and undeniably benign.

"David," she repeated.

"Karen, is that you?" he asked incredulously.

"Yes, David."

"Karen, I miss you so much."

"Then come back to me."

"But…how?"

"David, you are lost. You must return to yourself, and then you can return to me."

"Karen, I can't. The Reaper…is too strong. I know it's me…but I don't even know what's happening most of the time. I don't think I can control him…"

"You can, David. You have to."

"I know, but…I just don't think I can do it alone."

"You won't have to."

"You mean…are you coming back to me?"

"Open your eyes now, David."

"But…but…I don't know what to do…" David cried plaintively. As he did, Karen began to dissolve back into the waves. Even before she was gone, the beach, the ocean, and the sky began to fade to gray. Only the sun remained.

David blinked his eyes. He looked around, unsure for a moment where he was. The sun was shining through the frosted glass of his front door directly into his eyes. As they became accustomed to the light, he realized that he had been sleeping on his living room couch. It must still be early, because the sun had to come at a fairly low angle to shine through his front door and make it this far into the house.

He looked closely at the door, and realized that there was something there that he hadn't noticed at first. Through the frosted glass, he could see the silhouette of a person standing on his front porch. As he watched, the silhouette moved closer to the door and knocked three times. An undeniable feeling of deja-vu told him that this wasn't the first time the shadowy figure had knocked. In fact, he was fairly sure the first knock was what had interrupted his dreamland reunion with Karen.

The weight of his dream still hung heavily upon him. It was close enough that his mind had still not completely accepted the fact that it wasn't real. As his eyes grew more used to the light, the figure on his front porch began to come into focus. As it did, Karen's voice came to him. "You won't have to," she said.

The figure on the front porch was wearing a flowing white garment that flapped in the wind. Just above, the figure's hair also blew out, long and dark. With Karen's image and voice still ringing in his mind, David vaulted from the couch and across his entryway. He didn't know how it was possible, but he was sure that Karen had come back to him.

He reached the door in a flash, flipped the deadbolt to the right, and threw the door open. "Karen!" he cried with unbridled joy as sunlight flooded into his entryway.

"What?" said the tall, young man standing in front of him.

"Oh, I'm sorry, I thought you were someone else," David said, trying to disguise his heartbreak and gather his wits about him at the same time.

"David, it's me, Nick. Did you really think I was Karen?" said the young man.

"Nick? Jesus you've grown. No, I…I just had a dream about her and…I guess I was still a little caught up in it. Sorry about that," David said, still a little bewildered by the events of the last five minutes.

"That's OK, David. How you doing man? You look like you're in good shape."

"You too. What's your dad think of that hair?" David asked, nodding toward the flowing locks that hung down to the middle of Nicky's back. Except Nicky didn't look much like a Nicky now. He was at least as tall as David, and roughly the same size. It was hard to tell in the loose-fitting white shirt he was wearing, but David guessed he was pretty well put together as well.

"He didn't like it much, but I haven't seen him in awhile," Nick said, looking first down and then away toward the horizon.

David felt an awkward silence bloom over them. It was clear that he should either ask why Nick hadn't seen his father or invite Nick in or both. Unfortunately, as it wasn't really him who had come home last night after finally putting a bullet in Darius Williams' head, he couldn't be sure he had

333

properly stowed all of his Reaper gear. Clearly now was not the time for visitors.

"Nick, I'd invite you in but the place is kind of a mess. You wanna go get some breakfast?" David offered.

"Sure, that sounds great," Nick said with a smile so like his sister's that it made David's heart ache.

"Let me get some clothes on and I'll be right out, OK?"

"No problem. I'll just wait out here."

"Great. I'll be right back. It's great to see you, Nick."

"You too, David."

As David closed the door, he listened to see if any of the echoes of his dream were still in his head. He could barely see her anymore, and the only words he could really remember were Karen's last: "Open your eyes now, David."

65

Thirty minutes later, the two men who had almost been brothers-in-law sat across the table from each other in Ma's Country Kitchen. To David's relief, Nick was the first to fill in the gaps since the last time they had seen each other just after Karen's murder. This would give David time to piece together a story from what he had really done that would sound believable and still account for five and a half years of his life.

Nicky, it seemed, had been able to graduate from high school on time despite missing two months of the fall semester due to various events surrounding Karen's death and the subsequent court proceedings. He had not, however, been able to finish the football season, which ran concurrently to the time he was out of school. He had been on track to be named to the all-city team for the second consecutive year, but missing over half of his senior season took him out of contention for that honor. He also lost out on much of the scouting and recruiting that would have certainly guaranteed him a football scholarship to a Division 1 school.

He likely could have still gotten a scholarship, maybe still to a good program, but he found that thinking of playing football was too painful. Football reminded him of David, which reminded him of Karen. Better not to even go there.

So, much like David had 10 years earlier, Nick decided to choose academics over football. Also, like both David and Karen, Nicky chose Stanford. His 4.4 grade point average and 1520 SAT score, combined with football and his participation in student government (he was Student Body President) was enough to get him in.

Nick started in computer science, since that was the wave of the future when he started college. Unfortunately, the future came and went with the dot-com bust, leaving computer science majors out in the cold. As such, he added electrical engineering and finished both degrees in the winter quarter of his fifth year. It was almost unheard of to complete two engineering degrees in five years, let alone four. Nick almost made it, but he needed to come back for one extra quarter to pick up a few required courses he had put off. He accepted both degrees after the winter quarter of 2003.

He went home after finals and found that his family was almost completely disintegrated. None of them had been the same since Karen's murder. His parents weren't able to concentrate on work anymore, and the multi-million dollar wrongful death settlement had allowed them the luxury of quitting their jobs. They bought a house in the hills above Glendale, where they spent most of their time avoiding each other.

They did put aside $1,000,000 in a trust fund for each of the boys, payable only after each one graduated from college. Francisco Jr. had taken a few years off from school after he graduated high school, but had been going regularly to Cal State at Northridge until the time of Karen's death. He only had one semester to go, and when he saw what things would be like around the Chavez household, he went right back to college after they returned from the Bay Area in late 1998, completing his degree in Pharmacology in May of 1999. He was now working in the San Fernando Valley as a pharmacist, and had made only rare appearances at home in the past five years.

Michael was 23 when Karen was killed, and he had never gone to college. While Francisco Jr. had remained in close touch with his family between high school and Karen's murder, Michael left home the day after he graduated high school and got an apartment with his friend Wayne in Pomona. None of the Chavez's were sure how he was paying for it, but they did know he had a job stocking groceries overnight at a Von's Market. He came by for Christmas and birthdays, but that was about it. He had been increasingly introverted and secretive throughout high school, and his early exit from his parents' house was the logical next step.

When his parents' made their offer to basically pay him to go to college, he jumped on it. He was spooky, but far from stupid. He enrolled in Mount San Antonio College and completed his general education requirements in three semesters. Apparently his grades were good, because he was able to transfer to Cal Poly at Pomona for his final two years. He graduated in the spring of 2002 with a Bachelor's degree in Chemistry. With his degree, he accepted the million-dollar payout from his parents and dropped almost completely off the radar. His parents had his address and phone number, and knew he had started some sort of company east of San Bernardino. It was something having to do with chemicals, but they didn't know what.

Michael had come home for Christmas in 2002, but he was distant and left immediately after dinner. That was the last time any of them had seen him. They had spoken on the phone infrequently throughout 2003, but he stopped returning calls in November.

Nick found this out when he returned home after graduating from Stanford in December of 2003. He was appalled at his parents that they could lose track of his brother, but they were only shells of their former selves anyway. Nick drove out to the address they had for Michael, but found a new family in the home he had occupied. They had purchased the house from Michael, and said that all they knew about his present whereabouts was that he had said he was going to live with some friends of his in the San Francisco Bay Area.

Nick was further shocked to find out that Francisco Jr. was not intending to come home for Christmas either. He was going to stay in the valley with his wife and her family.

Nick felt like he was the only sane person in a world that had gone mad around him. He was clearly heartbroken over what had happened to Karen, but he wasn't going to let it keep him from living his life. Apparently his brothers felt the same way, and therefore divorced themselves from their parents, who had refused to give up the ghost of their only daughter.

Christmas dinner was a short one that year, and it ended in Nick screaming at his parents. "You two need to wake up before your whole family is gone!" he said, "We all loved Karen, but we love you too! Don't you love us?"

With that, he had stormed out and driven out to the valley to see Francisco Jr, his wife, and their six-year-old daughter, Jessica. Nick stayed with them for a few days. Nick and Francisco had always been close and had stayed in touch while Nick was in college. They spent a great deal of time together, enjoying the feeling of having a family again. Nicky eventually caught Francisco at a weak moment, and talked him into coming home to see their parents.

They returned on New Year's Day to find their father watching a football game in one end of the house, and their mother reading a book in a dark bedroom at the other end.

Together, Nick and Francisco Jr. performed a sort of intervention. They screamed when they had to and cried when they couldn't hold back. They begged their parents to snap out of their mourning period, telling them five years was long enough. Karen may not be here anymore, they said, but she can see what's happening, and this is not what she would have wanted for her family.

After what seemed like the longest afternoon of their lives, their parents agreed to change, or at least to try. Instead of shaking hands on it, the four of them ended up in a huddled, teary embrace in the middle of the Chavez living room. It was a good start.

Francisco took all of his leave from work and Nick put off looking for a job so that they could spend time as a family. By the end of January, when Francisco Jr. ran out of leave, they had made great strides in rebuilding the family.

By the end of March, the Chavez family was almost whole. Nick's parents and brother credited him with saving them and bringing them back together, and hearing that made him happier than he had been since he was a young child. There was one unavoidable fact, though. His job wouldn't be complete until he brought Michael back home.

And so he had purchased the convertible black mustang that he and David had taken from David's house to Ma's Country Kitchen, and driven from Los Angeles to San Francisco. He told his parents that he would be back when he found Michael, hopefully with him in the passenger seat. What he didn't tell his parents, though, was that Michael wasn't the only person he intended to see in San Francisco.

Nick had always felt very close to David, he said, and he felt sick about how his father and the rest of his family had abandoned him after Karen's death. He knew perfectly well what had happened to David's parents, and he also knew about David's falling out with the rest of his family and that he and Karen didn't really have any close friends in the Bay Area. Nick knew, as they walked out of the courtroom after Darius Williams' transfer hearing, that they had left David all alone in the world. Nick also knew how devoted David was to Karen, and how much he loved her. Nick knew in his heart that what they were doing was wrong...dead wrong.

His father, however, forbade Nick from calling or otherwise contacting David. He reiterated this point when Nick left for Stanford, making Nick promise not to contact David, and also telling him that he would cease paying for Nick to go to Stanford if he found out that he had done so. Nick promised, but was angry that his father made the threat to withhold the money. Nick was not someone who would go back on a promise, especially to his father. And he didn't, but he always felt his father was wrong.

Now that he was finished with college, though, he thought he saw a loophole in the promise he had made. Since his father had said Nick couldn't contact David while at Stanford, and had underlined that point by his threat to stop paying for it, Nick felt that his promise ended when he graduated. Absolved of his promise, Nick decided to stop and see David immediately upon returning to San Francisco.

"How'd you find me? I'm not in the phone book." David asked around a bite of his Denver omelette.

"Internet. You can find anyone on the internet," Nick replied.

"Is that how you're going to find Mike?"

339

Vengeance

"I guess I misspoke. You can find anyone as long as they own property or have a mailing address. I looked for him when I was looking for you, and I came up empty. The people who bought his house down south said he was staying with friends, so maybe that's true."

"How are you going to find him then?"

"I don't know," Nick said, sipping his coffee and looking out through the dusty Venetian blinds into the parking lot. "Anyway, enough about me. What have you been doing?"

David told Nick a story that was almost completely true, although he left out a whole other life he had also led over the past five and a half years. He told Nick that he had worked at BioGen until recently (he felt he stretched the truth a little here with the word 'recently,' but it served his purpose) and now he was taking some time off to re-evaluate what he wanted to do with his life. He had made some friends, but not anyone he spent much time with. He had some hobbies, which included frequent exercise, martial arts, and an occasional trip to the gun range to fire his grandfather's old gun.

"Martial arts, huh? Are you any good?" Nick asked.

"I'm not bad, I guess," David replied.

"I don't think I mentioned it, but I started karate my freshman year at Stanford. I needed something to do that was competitive physically since I didn't have football anymore. I stuck with it until I graduated. I'm a black belt and I've won some competitions. What do you study?"

"I go to a dojo that has two masters, and each has their own style. They both mix in several different disciplines. I suppose I'm best at Kung-Fu," David said, wondering how much he should actually be telling Nick.

"Wow! Can you show me some later?" Nick asked, smiling. His smile was so disarming that David felt himself being swept away in it. He was trying, but it was almost impossible for him not to open up to Nick. He reminded David so much of Karen that it was unnerving and wonderful at the same time.

340

"Sure Nick. We can go down to the beach behind my house later if you want. The sand will break my fall after you whip out your moves on me," David said, for the first time in years feeling honestly happy to be talking to someone. Maybe it was because this was the first time since Karen died that he was talking to someone in friendship without having the true motive of using that person help him toward his revenge. Yes, that was it. He was finally talking to someone without a single thought in his mind as to how he could help David be successful in his plot to avenge Karen's murder.

David had chosen the path of deception years ago to help him toward his destiny. Now, as he sat facing Nick, he felt the weight of his revenge begin to fall away. He had completed his task, and fulfilled the destiny he had made for himself. He now had the opportunity to stop living a life of secrecy and deception, and he intended to start with Nick. He resolved at that moment that he would take his life back, and that The Reaper would never make another appearance. He had reached the end of the path, and it was time to start a new one. No more deception, no more lies, no more killing, no more Reaper.

As he was about to find out, however, once one begins down a path of deception, it is not easy to just step off. Past lies always come home to roost. Likewise, he would soon find that a man cannot decide when his destiny has been fulfilled. Only destiny itself can make that determination. And destiny was not finished with David McGuire. Nor was it finished with The Reaper.

66

"I doubt if you'll be the one falling in the sand…" Nick began, but his thought trailed away as his eyes moved away from David's and focused on a point that was above and behind David's head.

"Jesus David, look," he said in a breathless whisper.

David turned around to see that Nick was looking at the television mounted in the upper corner of the room. The morning news was on, and there was a familiar face on the screen.

Nick got up and walked over in front of the TV. David got up and followed him, feigning the same type of shock Nick was exhibiting. It didn't take much acting. While he clearly remembered what he had done the night before, his time with Nick had driven it far out of his mind. It seemed like it had occurred in another lifetime. In a way, after all, it had.

"Police say this man, Darius Williams, was recently released from a juvenile detention center after serving over five years for the murder of Karen Chavez, who was his teacher at the time," said the voice on the TV. Then the picture of Darius that had filled the screen disappeared and was replaced by a serious-looking reporter standing in a wooded area. Next to the large '2' at the bottom of the screen was the word "Woodside," telling viewers where he stood.

Now on camera, the reporter continued. *"Details are still sketchy, but it appears that Williams lured the three men who had been with him when he committed the previous murder out to this remote section of woods, and then shot and killed all three of them. He then turned the gun on himself.*

"The three victims this morning are sons of very prominent Bay Area families. John McNamara is the son of Senator Walter McNamara, Douglas Weinstein is the son of Barry Weinstein, president of Peninsula Systems, and finally Truman Nakimura is the son of Ishiro Nakimura, founder and CEO of Nakimura Savings. Clearly, this is going to be a very high-profile investigation that we'll be hearing a lot more about.

The screen split, showing the reporter on the right half and the talking head bimbo in the studio on the left. *"Is there anything else you can tell us, Bob?"* she said vapidly.

"Well yes Julie. Apparently Williams made some sort of recording. A neighbor who was first on the scene told me that he saw a small tape recorder on the ground near Williams' body. Of course police are not commenting on the existence or nature of such a recording. If there is anything on that recorder, they would have to take it in to examine it before they make a decision to release anything to the public.

"That's all we know at this moment, but we will keep you posted of any new developments as they happen. Reporting live from Woodside, I'm Bob Lewis. Back to you."

"Thank you, Bob, for that chilling report," said Julie sternly. Then she turned to another camera, brightened up, and informed her viewers that after the break they would be treated to a cooking demonstration by some famous chef.

David and Nick turned from the TV and made their way slowly back to their table. They sat in silence for a few minutes, sipping their coffee and staring at various points in space.

"Jesus, David," Nick said, as if that was all that could be said about the topic.

"I know," David replied.

They sat for another moment, then David pulled his cell phone from his pocket, looked at the display, and said, "I'm going to make a quick call, OK?"

"Sure," Nick replied.

"I have to go outside. No signal in here."

"OK."

David stepped out the swinging door into the parking lot, went around the side of the building, and hit speed dial number 3 on his cell phone. This might not be a very good idea, but he had to get a read on the situation. The phone rang three times, and then a staticky voice came on the line.

"Molloy," it said.

"Seamus, it's David. I just saw the news. Do you know what's going on?"

"David? I haven't heard from you in awhile," Seamus said. The line was too bad to read his voice, but David didn't like the sound of it. Seamus was off The Reaper case, but David knew him well enough to know that, if he ever had suspicions of David, this would bring them back to the surface.

"Yeah, sorry about that," David said, searching for an excuse. Then, the perfect one came to him. "I've had company staying at my house."

"Really, anyone I know?"

"Believe it or not, it's Karen's little brother, Nicky. Except he's all grown up now. Graduated from Stanford in December."

"Oh," Seamus said. David wasn't sure, but he thought there was a bit of apology in that word. He just might have given Seamus enough pause to shake him off of David again.

"Yeah, he's a great kid. We're at a restaurant right now having breakfast and we saw it on the news. I told him I knew you and I'd give you a call to see if you knew anything."

There was a pause on the line as Seamus processed David's request. David wished desperately that he could be standing in front of Seamus so he could read his face as well as his voice, but a bad cell phone connection would have to do.

"I don't know any more than the news is saying, at least not that I can tell you. You understand," Seamus finally replied. His voice was companionable and most of the edge that David had sensed at the beginning of their conversation was gone.

"Do you think the tape is going to be released to the press?"

"Hard to say, David. It depends what's on it."

"Are you going to get to hear it?"

"I would expect to. I was the original detective, of course, so I should have no problem swinging that."

"Seamus, will you tell me if there's anything on it...that...you know?"

"I can't promise anything, buddy," Seamus said. His demeanor had now swung completely around to one of compassion for his one-time good friend. "I'll listen to it and I'll give you a call."

"I'd appreciate it. I don't know what's on there, but if it has to do with Karen, I'd really like to know."

"I understand. I'll do what I can."

"Any message for Karen's family?" David asked in a subtle reminder that he had company and therefore couldn't have gone out last night and committed a quadruple homicide.

"Not right now. I'm not sure how this is going to play out, but more than likely I won't be involved in any official capacity. If they are going to be contacted, as I'm sure they will, it will be by the new investigators."

"OK. I'll let you go, but give me a call if you find anything out," David said.

"I will. We should get together sometime. You can bring Nick down if you want."

"I'd like that," David lied. "I think both of us are in a little shock right now. Maybe in a few weeks when we're both better company?"

"Sure. Take care, David."

"I will, thanks. Bye."

"Bye."

The line went dead. David snapped the phone shut and went back inside. He was pleased with the outcome of the call, but it gave him a task to complete before he could celebrate too much.

"Hey," he said, sitting down across from Nick.

"Hey. Everything OK?" Nick asked.

"Yeah. I didn't tell you, but I ended up running into the detective who investigated Karen's...you know. We actually became friends."

"No shit? Wow, that's kind of weird, isn't it?" Nick asked, clearly not sure what to think of this information.

"It was at first, but he's a pretty cool guy and his wife's a great cook. It was just a coincidence, but he kind of came along when I really needed a friend, you know?"

Nick nodded, and some of his doubt seemed to melt away in favor of guilt at the reminder that he and his family had left David to deal with his loss alone.

"Anyway, he's in the FBI now, but I called him to see if he knew anything."

"Did he?"

"Not that he could tell me. I really wanted to see if he knew what was on the tape. He said he'd probably get to listen to it and then give me a call if he could tell me anything about it."

"I'd like to hear it too," Nick agreed solemnly.

They were silent for some time, and then David took a deep breath and spoke. "So Nick, do you have a place to stay up here?"

"I got a hotel last night down in Palo Alto. I was just going to stay there until I found Mike."

"You can't do that. Why don't you stay with me?" David asked.

"Oh, David, I don't want to impose."

"You wouldn't be. Besides, I don't think either of us should be alone right now, you know? The best thing for both of us is to get busy and do something, not to sit around and watch the news all day. And that's what I'll do if you don't come over. I bet you'd do the same, right?"

"Probably. All right, if you're sure, I'll just go get my stuff and check out and come back."

"That's great. It'll give me a chance to clean up a little."

Some emotion began to bloom on Nick's face for the first time since the news report came on. David wasn't sure, but it appeared to be some sort of sentimental contentment. As for David, it was all he could do to keep from beaming like a fool. He couldn't have planned for this, but even if he had, it couldn't have worked out better.

And just like that, David fell right back into the business of using people. This thought hung in the very back of his mind, but David thought that this time it was more acceptable than before. It was convenient that Nick was here and, as long as neither of them was directly questioned, he would provide enough of an alibi to keep Seamus from sniffing around again. That was only part of it, though. David was excited to have Nick here. He was excited to have a friend, or at least the beginning of a friendship. Most of all, he was excited to get started on his new life.

David dropped a twenty on the table and they stood up to go. "I'm really glad you came, Nick," David said.

"Me too," Nick said, and David could tell by the look on his face that he really meant it.

67

Several hours later, Nick and David stood barefoot in the soft sand at the foot of the cliff behind David's house. They decided that they needed to blow off some steam, and they needed to do it in a place where there was no radio or television to remind them of the hottest news of the day. The earlier suggestion of a match of martial arts skills was the perfect solution.

"Ready?" Nick asked.

"Whenever you are," David said.

They both wore eight-ounce boxing gloves, shorts, and sweatshirts. The ground rules were discussed on the way down the steps, and now they would see what the other had to offer. David fully expected that he would have to hold back to avoid eliciting questions from Nick, as well as to avoid injuring him. Knowing Nick's work ethic and the fact that he had studied for four years, however, David did expect this to at least be a decent workout.

Nick threw a tentative punch in the general vicinity of David's head. David flicked it away like a mosquito, then dropped his hands and said, "Come on, Nick. You're not going to hurt me. Let's see what you got."

Nick smiled and threw a combination of punches with only slightly more verve. David deflected all three punches with only his left hand, leaving his right down at his side. Nick stepped back, and David gave him a wordless look that said, "See?" He then raised both gloves and beckoned Nick to give him his best. This time, Nick did.

David had seen a lot over the last several years. He had been in a lot of fights both in the dojo and on the street. In all that time, even when facing Master Chen, he had never seen someone move with the liquidity and speed that Nick showed when he finally came at David with all he had. When he did, David had to take a step back raise both hands in defense. He worked quickly and efficiently to block all of Nick's punches and kicks, but he couldn't remember the last time he had come so close to the top of his ability in combat. He had more in reserve, but not much. If Nick was holding back now, David wasn't sure he would be able to completely protect himself against Nick's very best.

After about sixty seconds of furious action, Nick danced back out of range. His face was a picture of both shock and exhaustion. He was looking at David as if he were a god. Clearly David was better than Nick had expected. David was relieved to see this in Nick's face. It meant that Nick likely had given everything he had, which also meant that, as good as Nick was, David was still better.

David only gave Nick a second to breathe, and then he launched his own offensive. Nick's hands raced to block the punches and kicks David threw at him from various and unexpected angles. Only Master Chen had had more luck against David than Nick, but it soon became apparent that David could hit him with a knockout blow at almost any time he pleased. Nick was good, but his offense was clearly better than his defense. And neither was quite to the level of David's.

David sensed that Nick was tiring, so he let up and backed away without striking his new friend. When he did, Nick dropped to his knees and put his fists in the sand, struggling for breath. David was only slightly winded, but he walked over and knelt next to Nick. He even breathed harder than he needed to so that Nick wouldn't feel bad about his performance. He had no reason to, after all. Nick's skills were nothing short of world-class. They just weren't honed on the field of battle like David's had been. Nick had the quickness and instincts of a cat, but David's were those of a tiger.

David put a hand on Nick's back. "You OK?" he asked.

Nick took several deep breaths in attempt to gather himself. When he had, he whispered, "That was...*(gasp)*...unbelievable. I've never...*(gasp)*...seen anyone...*(gasp)*...move that fast..."

"You should see my teacher," David said, trying to downplay what had happened. He was suddenly self-conscious about the awed and almost adoring look on Nick's face.

"He must be amazing," Nick said.

"You're pretty damn good yourself. Other than Master Chen, the owner of the dojo I go to, you're best I've ever seen," David said, hoping his praise would bring Nick back to earth.

"I'm not even on the same page as you, David," Nick said, with absolutely no hint of malice or embarrassment. Now that he had his breath back, he was smiling warmly.

"Don't sell yourself short. You must've been pretty good in school."

"I won a quite a few competitions, but I guess I was lucky I never ran into anyone from your dojo. David, can you teach me some of those things you were doing? I couldn't even tell where the next punch was coming from. I know you were holding back, and don't get me wrong, I appreciate it, but I'd really like to learn more and someday see you come at me with all you've got."

"I'd be honored to work with you, Nick. I've never taught before, so I'm not promising anything, but I think we'll have some fun anyway as long as we don't take this to seriously," David replied, and he meant what he said. He was honestly looking forward to training with Nick. He had a feeling that Nick had the potential to be better than David himself. And for some reason, David didn't find that threatening in the least.

"Cool," Nick said, getting to his feet. David noticed that he had his wind completely under control again, which was impressive in itself. Yes, Nick had potential all right.

"I'm going to have to think about how to train you, buddy," David said, "so let's just spar for now and I'll get a better idea of where you're at."

"Sounds good. Just try not to take my head off, OK?" Nick replied, smiling.

"Don't worry. I'd sooner knock off my own head than hurt you, Nick," David said with complete honesty.

Nick got that look on his face again. It had been so long since David had experienced any genuine emotion that he was having trouble reading Nick's face. If he didn't know better, though, he would have sworn that Nick was feeling something akin to love.

They battled back and forth amiably for about a half an hour, and then they sat in the sand, continuing to develop what was a quickly growing friendship. They had always been close, and they had shared a great loss several years ago. What's more, David had been there for Nick when he received the news that brought Karen's murder crashing back into his life. While the word of what had happened the night before clearly wasn't news to David, nor was Karen's murder ever out of mind for him, he did appreciate very much having Nick with him, especially today when he would most likely have had a huge empty place inside him where his thirst for revenge had been. Their shared history and shared experience of the day had the effect of pressing the fast forward button on a VCR. By the time they stood up to climb the stairs to David's house, both men were on the way to filling a void in their souls that had been there since Karen had died.

As they put the setting sun behind them and began to walk up the steps, David put his arm around Nick and let out a soft chuckle.

"What's so funny?" Nick asked.

"I was just thinking you'd make a great Dread Pirate Roberts," David said, trying to contain the first genuine laughter that had bubbled to his lips in years.

"You mean the guy from the Princess' Bride? I don't get it," Nick replied. His lack of understanding didn't prevent him from smiling along with David.

"Yeah, that's the guy. Sorry, just the cliff and…you know…the fighting. It just struck me as funny, that's all."

"You sure it's not because I thought I was going to beat you and you beat me instead?"

"Not at all," David said coyly. That had occurred to him, but that wasn't the real reason. What he was really thinking was that if he were ever going to turn over the reins and train another Reaper, Nick would be the perfect candidate.

As the thought crossed his mind, his smile faded. Who was he kidding? Nick was a good person...not a monster like David. Or could he safely say that Nick was not a monster like he had been? It had been a hell of a day, between his dream in the morning and spending the rest of the day with Nick. He knew it was too soon to tell, but for the first time since Karen died he couldn't feel the presence of The Reaper at all. Maybe he really wasn't a monster any more. Just the thought that he might actually be able to move out from under the shadow of The Reaper filled him with hope.

"You OK, David?" Nick asked.

"Yeah...sorry. I was just thinking."

"You want to tell me what about?"

"Just remembering your sister," David said, "You remind me of her."

"You want to know something funny," Nick replied, "I was just thinking the same thing."

Nick looped his arm under David's and found his shoulder with his hand. They walked up the steps like that, arm in arm, leaving at least a small part of their painful pasts on the beach behind them.

68

Seamus Molloy sat bolt upright in bed. He was sweating buckets, and he was breathing like he had just run a 100-yard dash. He had just had a dream, but it was fading so fast that all that was left was a feeling of panic and confusion.

It had been almost a month since the murder-suicide in Woodside. It had been the same amount of time since he'd had a good night sleep, and he would be damned if he knew why.

Seamus was still assigned to monitor the friendly-neighborhood racists of the New Dawn, and that group deserved his full attention. Even so, he found that he was spending more and more time thinking about two of his former cases at the expense of his current one.

Being removed from The Reaper case didn't sit well with him, and it continued to haunt him. He had never failed in an investigation before, and the fact that he had failed in this one ate away at him like an ulcer. It wasn't so much that he wanted to stop The Reaper, he just wanted to find out about him to stop the cacophony of questions that were ringing in his head. Almost in spite of himself, he found that he couldn't entirely condemn what The Reaper was doing. In fact, he wondered whether or not he would actually even want to apprehend The Reaper if he were lucky enough to learn his identity and thus answer the questions that burned his insides. His cop's rationality of good versus evil said he certainly would, but his heart wasn't so sure. If he could just know the truth, he really didn't know what he would do with it.

Seamus's curiosity had forced him to stay up to speed on the case, although doing so was a tricky business. He was lucky that Special Agent Johnson's office, and thus The Reaper base of operations, was in the old section of the building. Gaining access to the floor required cardkey access in the elevator, but he found that the night cleaning crew was not incredibly strict about people tagging along with them as they did their nightly chores.

About once every three or four weeks, Seamus would work late. He knew the guy that did the sixth floor usually left the fifth around 8:15 p.m., sliding in his key to move the elevator up one level. Seamus would watch surreptitiously from around the corner and then rush around and block the elevator's safety edge while the cleaning guy pulled in his cart. Seamus would then step in, nod and smile, and accept the free ride to the sixth.

Once there, he took a circuitous route through the center of a bank of administrative cubicles and then down a short hallway into The Reaper war room. This section of the building didn't have the extensive camera surveillance of the new part, so his route only required that he pause briefly to wait for the camera in the hall to automatically swing to the other side before entering the hall from the cubicles. Once it moved to the left side of the hallway, he had about 10 seconds to get in and open the door using the key he had lifted from the top drawer of Special Agent Johnson's desk one day when Seamus knew he was in the john. Seamus knew that Johnson was too vainglorious to admit he had misplaced a key, knowing also that he would have a spare and would use that instead of having the lock changed as he should.

Seamus hadn't learned much in his monthly visits that wasn't already printed in the paper. He hadn't done that great of a job, but he was pretty sure that Johnson was doing even less. From what Seamus could tell, Johnson wasn't any farther along than he himself had been when he was booted off the case. One thing about the FBI was that no one wanted to admit he was wrong. Babcock couldn't remove Johnson because he had already put him there when he booted Seamus. Doing so would be tantamount to admitting he had made a poor move. Since he couldn't do that, he supported Johnson's outlandish claims that he was making progress and would have The Reaper 'any day now.' Right.

After Darius Williams' exploits, however, The Reaper wasn't the only one of his former cases that haunted him. The murder case surrounding the death of David's fiancée, Karen, was now fresh in his mind as well. He had visited the crime-scene that day, and was fairly pleased to see that his old mates at the police department were going to handle things just fine. He had been allowed to listen to the tape out of professional courtesy. He listened to it only once, and was surprised to find that he flinched when the gunshots rang out. He had been so floored by the admissions the McNamara kid offered so boldly that the gunshots had caught him off guard. After the first two rang out, his old friend Ted Denholm clicked off the tape and said, "That's it. He shuts it off after the third shot, before he put the clincher in McNamara and then himself."

"You guys going to release this?" Seamus asked.

"Don't know yet," Ted answered truthfully. It wasn't often that a local PD found itself in possession of a tape that would more than likely dethrone a senator.

"Thanks for letting me hear it, Ted," Seamus said, still a little dazed from what he had heard. "Sounds pretty cut and dried. You think there will be much of an investigation?"

"I don't think so. Based on what we have, our doer is dead, so we just need to dot the 'i's and cross the t's and feed the press as much as we can. It's going to be up to the captain what to tell them, and that's fine with me."

"No shit. That's going to be a tough call. I don't envy him."

"Me neither. I better get in there now. We're probably going to listen to this about 100 times and then get the DA in and listen to it 100 more before we figure out what to do."

"Good luck," Seamus said as he got up to go. "Let me know if you need any help."

"Will do. Take care buddy."

"You too."

Seamus had walked out of the police station and then gone for a long, long drive. He replayed the entire case in his mind, trying to figure out how he missed the true facts of the case. He remembered thinking that there was more to this case then met the eye, but Darius's silence and the other three boys' lies and their fathers' manipulation of the system apparently combined to conceal the real truth. Even though he couldn't see where any of it was his fault, he couldn't help but feel that the miscarriage of justice over five years ago, and by extension the murder-suicide that had just occurred, were at least partially his fault.

There was something worse, though. The tape should have provided him closure, but it didn't. As he looked back, he remembered looking at Karen and having the sense that she wanted to tell him the real story. Apparently he wasn't listening closely enough then. But surely now the story was complete, right? Something told him that it wasn't, but he couldn't put his finger on what piece was still missing, or what he should do about it. The case was long closed, and the perpetrators were now dead, as was Karen herself. What more could there be, and why would it matter anyway if all the players were dead?

All of these questions raced around in his head, but he found he had no answers. He attempted to push them all away and return his focus to the New Dawn case, where things were really heating up anyway. He had some luck during the day, but the night was another story. Some sort of recurring dream was playing havoc with his beauty sleep, and it was really fucking up his world.

Now, four weeks later, he stood in front of the bathroom mirror moving his toothbrush aimlessly around his mouth. He stared at the man looking back at him, wondering when he had gotten so old. There were black circles under his eyes, gray hairs peppering his temples, and a two-day beard shadow growing on his pallid face. He moved like a man in a dream.

He had to do something to knock himself off dead center. He couldn't think of anything he could do about the Chavez case, but he could make a trip to Reaper HQ and see what was new there. The Reaper hadn't struck in almost two months, and there was some speculation in the papers that he had finally retired from the vigilante business. Making a visit tonight was a long shot, but it was the best he could think of.

That settled it, and he felt slightly better having a plan. He would work all day on the New Dawn, trying to pin down enough evidence to raid the place they kept in Marin County. He and his team suspected they were planning something big, and suspected heavily that they had somehow been involved in the Berkeley Labs chemical theft. God knew the New Dawn deserved his full attention, and he would do everything he could to give it. At night, however, he'd be back on The Reaper case, if only for a few fleeting moments.

The day dragged by, and they didn't make any appreciable progress on New Dawn. By 5:00, Seamus was exhausted, and considered going home and saving The Reaper for tomorrow. The thought of another sleepless night, however, helped him get his second wind and stay on until late.

At around 8:30 p.m., after executing his usual routine of sneaking in after the cleaning guy, he stood in the darkened room that contained everything the FBI had on The Reaper. He walked first over to the board, and studied it closely. He didn't see anything different. He turned around and carefully looked through the files and stacks of paper on the ancient conference table in the middle of the room.

The pile on the right side of the table bore no fruit, so he stacked it back up just as he found it. As he moved toward the right side of the table, his eye was drawn to some loose papers in the middle of the desk. There was something under them. He pulled the papers aside, revealing an old tape recorder, the boxy kind with one square, silver speaker on top and a regular-sized tape deck on the bottom. In the middle of the speaker was a post-it note with two words: 'Williams-Woodside'.

Seamus felt a rush of heat roll through his body. Perspiration immediately sprung to his forehead and armpits. Was that what he thought it was? If so, what was it doing here?

He stared at the recorder for a full minute. Then he reached out a tentative finger to press the rewind button. At the last moment, he folded the finger forward and used his knuckle to push the button instead. The tape whirled backward for a few seconds, and then stopped hard. Barely able to breathe, Seamus pressed the play button.

The noise of an automobile skidding to a stop sprung from the box. A moment later, a contemptuous voice said, "Yo, my brotha."

Seamus listened intently to the entire exchange between Darius and John McNamara, an exchange that ended in gunfire. After the three shots rang out, he reached out again to press the rewind button so he could listen to the whole thing over, but before he could do so, he heard something. It was faint, but it was there. Someone said something after the last shot.

He tapped the rewind button and then the play button in rapid succession. The shots rang out again, and he moved his head close to the recorder, not wanting to fool with the volume control. What he heard was a simple sentence, spoken presumably by Darius Williams. "The Reaper to the rescue," it said.

Seamus stood up, and for a moment he couldn't register what was going on. That sentence explained why the tape was here, but why did Darius say that, unless...

THE REAPER WAS THERE! The thought hit Seamus like a bolt of lightning. And when it hit, it threw open the floodgates of understanding.

He knew who The Reaper was. He had known deep down in his gut for almost a year now. He had known since a very good friend of his slipped and used The Reaper's preferred name. He had denied the possibility with every fiber of his being, clinging desperately to the plausible evidence that suggested it couldn't be who he knew it was. But now, there was no more denying it. The Reaper had pulled the wool over his eyes and everyone else's long enough to kill the people who had been responsible for his lover's murder. Like it or not, there was no way that Seamus could deny the truth any longer. That truth, so elusive for so long, could be stated in four simple words.

"David is The Reaper," Seamus whispered under his breath. As he did, the strength ran out of his legs and he sat down heavily in the steel chair behind him. Speaking the words out loud brought a wave of emotion to him that was too much for even him, a hardened homicide detective and FBI agent, to withstand. He put his elbows on his knees, buried his face into his open hands, and began to weep.

69

About 30 miles to the west, as the crow flies, David and Nick were walking in the front door of David's house. They had been at the gun range where, for the first time, Nick had beaten David in a shooting contest. Afterward, they had gone out for dinner, and had finally stopped to pick up a paper on the way home.

David had told Nick about his 'hobby' the day Nick arrived. He told him that he had used it to fill up some of the time between work and his martial arts training. He also told him that he enjoyed the mental focus that target shooting required. When he was focused on putting holes in the silhouette man in front of him, he wasn't thinking about how much he missed Karen and his parents.

Nick had been immediately interested, so David took him to a shooting range in Pacifica that he had been to somewhat frequently after he stopped driving down to Half Moon Bay to shoot both targets and shit with Richard and his mates. The people there knew him by face but not name, which was fine with David.

Nick had never fired a gun before, but David found that he was a natural. Nick had a mind that was much older than his years. He was able to focus on the target, to shut down the rest of his thoughts and feelings, and to squeeze the trigger deliberately enough that his shots flew straight and true. By the end of the first session, he was regularly popping holes in the center mass of his target.

The very next day, Nick had asked David if they could go back. He told David that he knew now exactly what he was saying about the focus it required to shoot. Like David, he found it to be a perfect retreat from reality. Not only that, he liked the feeling of power, and liked the competition with himself to see if he could put the holes where he wanted them. Nick, it seemed, was hooked.

By the second week, Nick had challenged David to a shooting contest. Whoever could put the most bullets in either the head or the center circle in the target's torso. Each man took turns firing a full clip. They didn't bother putting one in the chamber, so they each had seven shots. David very regularly put seven in the target area, but every once in awhile he would miss one. Nick was hitting between three and five the first week, which wasn't bad for a beginner. After another week, he was hitting five or six, and occasionally he would hit all seven. By the fourth week, Nick was popping all seven in a tight cluster in the middle of the target.

Earlier that evening, the two had battled for five rounds before David finally pushed a shot about half an inch outside the circle. Nick hit all seven, and celebrated like he had won the Superbowl. David hugged him and laughed along with him, genuinely happy that his friend was happy. David told Nick he'd take him to Tommy V's for dinner that night to celebrate, and Nick accepted the invitation gladly.

Tommy V's was a small Italian restaurant about a mile from David's house, just on the other side of the freeway from the ocean. Tommy himself was a short, hirsute Italian-American originally from Brooklyn. Gold chains, bracelets and rings dripped from his body, providing a striking contrast to the thick, wiry black hair on his chest, arms and knuckles.

Tommy V's specialized in pizza and pasta, and David had probably spent $100 a month on deliveries for the past several years. He seldom went there to eat, though, as he was self-conscious about eating alone. Now that Nick was with him, they had gone to eat there at least three nights a week. Tommy was aware of David's years of patronage via delivery, and he treated both of them like family as they began to come in regularly.

Like most nights, Tommy himself came out to greet them when they walked in. "Niko and David," he said in a thick Brooklyn accent, "How are my favorite customers tonight?"

"Great, Tommy," David said, accepting a hug and a kiss on the cheek from their enthusiastic host.

"That's wonderful. I've got a special surprise for you boys tonight. Please, sit. I'll bring two dishes right out for you."

While they waited for their surprise, David and Nick discussed what they would do the next day. Over the past four weeks, they had behaved like two kids on vacation. Both had lived in the Bay Area for some time, but, as tended to happen, neither had done many of the tourist activities the area had to offer. Since Nick had arrived, they had gone to Alcatraz, Fisherman's Wharf, Chinatown, Marin County, Santa Cruz, as well as most of the museums in the area. When they weren't doing the tourist thing, they were practicing their martial arts, shooting, eating at Tommy V's, or just relaxing. Nick was quite a chess player, and they spent a good deal of time doing that. Nick beat David every time, but David really didn't mind.

David had begun to think of Nick alternately as a surrogate son and as a good friend. For the first time in his life, David took the role of the elder, and he relished the feeling of watching Nick grow and succeed. He had forgotten what it was like to have genuine feelings for another person. He had cared shallowly about Master Chen and Richard, but there was always the true mission in the background keeping him from committing any true emotion. Now that he had completed his mission of revenge, he could allow himself to care about someone else. Nick elicited feelings from David that had not been present since Karen was killed. In a very real way, David felt that the relationship he had had with Karen had been reborn between himself and Nick.

Nick's feelings were similar, although his young heart was less guarded than David's. Nick loved David, pure and simple. He also had feelings that had been missing since Karen's death. Karen, more than his brothers or even his parents, had always rooted unconditionally for him to succeed in whatever he did. He got the exact same feeling from David. He knew his family loved him (with the possible exception of Michael), but he always had the feeling that they were jealous of his success. With David, there was none of that. David genuinely tried to teach him martial arts, and was visibly proud when he succeeded. The shooting range was the same, and he hadn't groused even a bit when Nick had finally beaten him. When they played chess, David did his best, but Nick won every time, and every time David took his loss like a gentleman and a true friend. For Nick, David was both his best friend and also his biggest fan, a role that had been vacant since Karen died and his own father had abdicated that role. Nick had loved Karen as completely as she had loved him. Now, as David moved in to take her place, Nick transferred his love for Karen unabashedly to David.

Nick was so happy spending time with David, in fact, that he hadn't even gotten started looking for Michael. He kept thinking he should get going on that, but he almost hated to ruin the great times he was having with David by bringing his sour older brother into the mix.

They finished their Osso Bucco and thanked Tommy for the meal, David paying cash and leaving a handsome gratuity. They hopped into Nick's Mustang and headed for home. They made a quick stop to grab a paper (Nick loved to read the paper but David had not gotten around to calling to have his service reinstated) and then were on their way.

As they walked in the door, Nick glanced at the headline and stopped in his tracks. "David," he breathed. Then, when David didn't stop, he managed a slightly louder whisper. "David, look at this," he said.

David turned around, his smile fading immediately to a look of concern when he saw Nick's face. "What is it?" David asked, turning and stepping back toward Nick.

Nick turned the paper around and held it up for David to see. The headline told him immediately why Nick looked like he had seen a ghost.

"Get in here," David said softly, trying to hide his own urgent need to read the article below the headline Nick had seen.

Nick got moving and stepped through the door. David shut it behind him, and they moved slowly through the living room to the kitchen. David took the paper and opened it up on the kitchen table. Nick sat down in one of the chairs and stared blankly at the page.

"Yeah, I know. I'll call him tomorrow morning and see what he can tell me, OK?"

"OK, David. I think I'm going to head off to bed now. I'll see you in the morning," Nick said.

"You sure you're all right?"

"Fine…or at least I will be in the morning."

"Let me know if you need anything, OK?"

"I will. Good night, David."

"Good night, buddy," David replied, watching Nick shuffle down the hall toward the spare bedroom.

70

About an hour after Nick went off to bed, there was a knock at David's front door.

David flipped off the TV and stood up to go answer it. He hadn't had many visitors since moving in. The only people who knew he lived here were Nick and Tommy V's delivery kids. He didn't order anything from Tommy, so who the hell could this be at 10:00 at night?

David opened the door. When he saw who was there, he felt a wave of heat swell up from his stomach into his head, making him feel for a moment as if he might faint. He took a split second to compose himself, and then manufactured a smile for his guest.

"Seamus," he managed, "How...did you know where I live?"

"I'm in the FBI, David," Seamus replied without returning David's smile.

"Oh...right. I'm sorry, come in," David said somewhat warmly, beginning to regain control.

"No thanks, David. Is Nick here?"

"Yeah, he's sleeping."

"Why don't you step out here? What I have to say won't take long."

The look on Seamus's face told David he should comply. He looked like he had just lost his best friend. And, in fact, that was not far from the truth.

David stepped out on the porch and pulled the door closed behind him. He had a strong feeling that Seamus wasn't here on a social call. He hadn't, however, slapped David immediately in handcuffs or even brought backup, as far as David could see. If he were here to arrest David, he would have done it already. Why then, was he just standing there glaring at David like he was trying to burn a hole in his forehead? David had to do something to try to break the tension. "It's good to see you again, Seamus. How's Molly doing?" he said quietly.

"Cut the crap, David. You've been lying to me since I met you. If you try to act like my friend now I'll beat you down right here on your own front porch."

I don't think you can, David thought.

"The only thing is I don't think I can. Even if you don't have your US Military issue forty-fives or your fucking knives or whatever the fuck they are, I'm still pretty sure you could kick my ass," Seamus said quietly, yet with contemptuous rage.

"Seamus, I don't know what you're…"

"David, I know you're the Reaper!" Seamus hissed.

David tried to look stunned and hurt. "What? Are you crazy? I'm not…"

Then Seamus did something that shocked both David and himself in equal measure. With a motion quick and nimble enough to get the drop on The Reaper himself, Seamus pulled his gun from his shoulder holster and pointed it at David. David raised his hands and took a step back. As he analyzed the situation and looked for either an offensive or defensive strategy that could get him out of this, he realized the irony of the situation. While Seamus was technically correct about David being The Reaper, if The Reaper really had been here right now instead of David, Seamus probably never would have gotten the drop on him.

"David, just shut up and listen to me. If you say another word a swear to god I'll blow your fucking head off."

David saw in his eyes that he wasn't bluffing, but he also saw that he didn't intend to shoot if he didn't have to. David did as he was told.

"I know you're The Reaper, David. I heard the tape you made when you killed Darius and the others. You probably didn't hear it, but Darius said on the tape that The Reaper was the one that shot the other kids."

David again felt blood rush into his face. That fucking bastard Darius had got him in the end after all. He finally let the stunned look drop from his face and allowed it to be replaced with the cold, killer's look that wanted to be there.

"I knew when you called The Reaper 'Charon' and then attacked LaShon Jackson, but you played me enough that I didn't say anything. I didn't trust my gut because you were a friend of mine. Now I know you were just using me. You came into my house and ate my wife's food and used Karen's death to make us feel sorry for you and you were just doing it to learn what I knew about you. Well, now I know the truth, and it makes me sick.

"But, unfortunately, I don't have enough evidence to prove what I know. So, the only thing I can do is what The Reaper would do, which is take the law into my own hands. Do you think I should do that, David?"

David shook his head slightly from side to side.

"No? Vigilante justice doesn't sound so good when the shoe's on the other foot, does it?"

Seamus paused. For the first time, he took his eyes off of David's. He shifted his gaze slightly down and to the left, then back to the right. Then, he shook his head as if to clear it, and looked back at David.

"I have to tell you something, though. There were times, before you started killing people anyway, that a small part of me admired what you were doing. There were a lot of other cops and agents that felt even more strongly than I did, and I know a great number of civilians saw you as some kind of superhero. I don't know if that was your intention or not, but that's what happened. Most people hate it when criminals get away with their crimes. Cops and civilians alike. What you were doing was against the law, but whether it was right or wrong is open to debate.

"Those of us sworn to uphold the law are also subject to the law. We need proof before we can legally do anything to stop a criminal, even when we know who the criminal is and that they will almost certainly strike again. It's frustrating as hell sometimes, believe me, but most of us don't cross the line because we made a promise. I'm not a man who normally breaks promises, but every man has his limits. Sometimes the only way to do the right thing is to break the law and take it into your own hands."

When he heard this, David's eyes grew to be as big as the full moon that was rising over his left shoulder. The blue light of the moon shone directly into Seamus's face. It glittered in his eyes, showing the tears that stood in them. Seamus fingered the trigger of his gun, and he had another moment of pause. David swallowed hard. His nerves were all tingling, waiting for the moment when Seamus's finger began to squeeze the trigger. When he saw that first twitch, he would have a split second to get out of the way of the bullet and close enough to Seamus to kill him before he could get off a second shot.

The two of them stood there like kings at the opposite ends of a chessboard. Seamus's eyes were glistening with tears, and his lips were trembling with either anger, sadness or fear. David's countenance was much harder...and colder. As his iron-hard gaze bore down on both Seamus's eyes and his trigger finger, he saw a single tear brim over his right eye and cut a glowing blue track down his face.

Then, to David's surprise, Seamus began to speak again. "So, I didn't come here tonight to arrest you, David. After all, I'm not on The Reaper case anymore, and even if I was I don't have enough evidence to bring you in. I came here tonight to make you a deal, and maybe to give you a chance to redeem yourself.

"You probably remember the New Dawn. They're the white supremacists that tried to blow up the Moscone Center a few years ago. When I got pulled off The Reaper case...your case...they put me back on that one.

"When I was after them before, they were an unorganized bunch of rednecks that hated minorities with enough fervor that they got pretty far out of shear will. In the end, though, they were pretty easy to figure out and stop. When I put away Luther Haines, we all figured they would fizzle out and go away. And that's almost what happened.

"About a year and a half ago, though, it appears that they had some kind of rebirth. They got some new blood from Southern California that apparently was able to reorganize the remaining members and also to recruit new ones. They've got money coming from somewhere, or maybe a lot of somewheres. They are sophisticated enough to know how to hide their sources, and they are careful enough to stay one step ahead of us. Their new leader is apparently extremely smart, and extremely dangerous. When Haines was in charge, we were able to get someone inside within a few weeks. With this guy, we haven't had any luck at all. They do thorough background checks on all new members, and apparently they're more selective than your old alma mater.

"We know where their base of operations is, and we keep track of their movements as best we can, but we haven't been able to link them to anything that's happened in the Bay Area for almost two years. I know in my gut that they are the ones who torched those synagogues in Sacramento, and I have a pretty good feeling they've been behind other crimes against both gays and blacks. You see, I know what they are doing, and I know they'll do it again, but I just can't prove it. I guess that's my theme for the night.

"What they have been up to so far is clearly no good, but they haven't approached what they tried to do at Moscone. But now their movements seem to indicate that something big is coming up. We strongly suspect that they're behind the theft of several canisters of Isopropyl methylphosphonofluoridate from a lab in Berkely a few weeks ago. Do you know what that is?"

David shook his head no.

"It's a hair's breadth away from being Sarin gas, David. And they have a chemist on staff that can easily brew it so that can be delivered in its lethal form. If they can detonate even a small amount of it in a crowd, hundreds or even thousands of people could die horrible, painful deaths. If they choose the right event and detonate a large amount, they could pull off a mass murder that would make even the furor proud.

"So I come to my deal. I know you're The Reaper, but I can't do anything about it. I know they have Sarin gas, the intent to use it, and a leader with the brains to pull it off, but I can't do anything about that either. Another thing I think I know is this: Underneath it all, David, I believe you are a good person. Misguided, maybe. Maybe even a little nuts. But I believe deep down you're a good person and you had good intentions when you became The Reaper. The New Dawn, however, is pure evil. Someone needs to stop them, and neither the FBI nor the police can do it. That's why I'm coming to you. You may be able to do what we can't. You may be the only one who can stop them.

"David, you've killed a lot of people. I know you think they've all been bad, but they all had mothers and all of their mothers cried when they were told that their baby boy was murdered. I'm offering you a chance at redemption. If you can break into their place and just call 9-1-1 from inside and tell the operator that you're with the New Dawn and you have Sarin gas that you're planning to detonate, then the cops can answer the call and come inside. Hopefully they'll find what they're looking for. I'm not asking you to kill anyone, but it will be dangerous and it honestly won't break my heart if you have to. In fact, if you do happen to meet their new boss, putting him in an early grave could save thousands of lives.

"I don't want you to answer me now, and I want you to know I was never here. I will tell you this, though. If you do this...if you get in there and help us stop these bastards before they can strike, I will keep your secret. The guys on your case are morons and they still think your attack on LaShon Jackson was a copycat. They've closed that part of the case. They believe The Reaper killed Darius Williams and the others, but I don't think they'll link that to you. So if you do this New Dawn thing and then quit, I think you'll get away with everything.

"If the New Dawn does use the Sarin, though, and you didn't do anything to stop them, I'll be forced to tell what I know. Then I'll let the chips fall where they may, but I'm pretty sure if they have you to look at they will find enough evidence to bring you to trial.

"If you decide to go after the New Dawn, their base is an estate in Mill Valley that belongs to a woman named Edith Connelly. Her husband owned half of San Francisco before he died, and she actually lives in Scottsdale now. Her grandson, Wayne Connelly, is taking care of the place. His father and grandfather had a big falling out, so Wayne grew up in Glendale, which is just outside of LA. His parents had a lot of difficulties getting by and apparently Wayne fell in with a pretty anti-social crowd. At some point the New Dawn got him on board, and he reconciled with grandma and ended up taking care of her place while she plays golf in the desert. As soon as she moved out, they moved in.

"Connelly isn't the real brains, though. We haven't be able to get anywhere with the leader. Background, where he's from, nothing. I guess that's not important, though. You just need to get in and make the call. If they stop you on the outside of the house...and there will be guards and cameras, believe me...they'll probably kill you and that won't do anyone any good. If you think you're up for this, you can find the address online. It's the only listing for Edith Connelly in Mill Valley.

"So that's it. Either way, I never want to see you again. Goodbye David."

Seamus began to back up, still holding the gun on David. When he reached his car, he holstered the weapon and opened the driver's door. He had another moment of introspection, then looked at David one more time. "If you go, David, be careful," he said. His voice cracked thinly as he said it, and David saw that, as angry and hurt as Seamus was, he still had a place in his heart for David.

David was both touched and ashamed at this fact. Seamus was right. He and Molly hadn't deserved what David had done to them, and he had every right to hate David. Seamus was a good man, there was absolutely no question about that. He would do whatever it took to do the right thing, to protect the innocent.

David had always been at odds with his alter-ego as to whether what they were doing was right or wrong. He still couldn't say for sure, but he knew at best his methods were a shade of gray somewhere in between. Seamus, however, was doing things the right way, never taking any shortcuts. David knew what it must have taken for him to ask what he did. He knew it must have torn him apart making the decision to pit one criminal against another...to offer one criminal amnesty for stopping another. What the New Dawn was planning must be very real, and very deadly, for Seamus to have made such a decision.

The last sentence that Seamus spoke, wishing him luck in the mission he had proposed for David, sealed the deal in David's mind. Seamus was right...he had used Seamus and Molly unjustly for his own dark purposes. Even worse, he again and again called upon the memory of Karen and his parents to make them feel sorry for him and thus endear himself to them. What he had done was wrong in so many ways. If there was a way to make it right, this was it.

David watched the black Yukon spin down the road toward the highway. When the taillights were out of sight, he turned and opened the door to go back inside. When he did, he was surprised to see Nick standing in the entryway. David had a second to hope that he hadn't heard what happened, but the look on Nick's face told David otherwise.

71

"How much did you hear?" David asked coolly.

"All of it," Nick replied. His voice had a dazed tone... that of someone who had awoken to find his whole world had changed while he slept. "David, it's not true, is it?"

Nick was very familiar with The Reaper. Nick was beginning the Winter quarter of his Junior year at Stanford when The Reaper first struck. By the time he finished his Junior year in June of 2002, The Reaper had struck several times and was one of the primary topics of late-night discussion in the halls of the Stanford dormitories.

The Reaper continued to be an interesting byline of life in the San Francisco Bay Area for Stanford students in the Fall Quarter of 2002, which was the beginning of Nick's Senior year. When The Reaper beat the crap out of six drunken Cal football players in late November, however, he was immediately elevated to cult-hero status on the Stanford campus.

By the beginning of 2003, The Reaper was the hottest topic on campus. Nearly everyone was behind what he was doing. At that time, he was still only working on stopping drunk drivers, and most of the students thought it was an admirable goal. There were certainly hardcore liberals who preached against the vigilante justice he was serving, and there were also those idiots who liked to take the counterpoint either because they thought it made them sound deep or because they liked to argue. The majority of the students, however, thought The Reaper was doing the public a great service by making drunken drivers think twice before getting behind the wheel.

Perhaps the most ironic manifestation of "Reapermania" was a fraternity party called "Don't Fear the Reaper," in which all attendees were required to dress as the man himself. The fact that hundreds of underaged people were drinking in honor of a man dedicated to stopping drunk drivers didn't dawn on them as being more than a little inappropriate.

When The Reaper changed tactics late in the Winter quarter of 2003, however, things began to swing back the other way. The conservative male students, who felt that a little bit of vigilante justice was just what this lawless world needed, stayed strongly on the side of The Reaper, even when he began to focus his attacks on wife-beaters, drug dealers and petty thieves. They, as did many Americans, professed to be tired of criminals being released without adequate punishment for their crimes. If The Reaper could throw a beating at some of these scumbags, it might make them think twice where the law had not been successful in doing so.

Some of the liberal students, however, began to question where The Reaper was heading. As the violence of his attacks increased, and as he began to spend more time in the inner cities as opposed to his original attacks in outlying areas, the liberal students pointed to the fact that his victims were being denied their constitutional rights. There was no proof that what the criminals were doing was what The Reaper deemed it to be, and so it was right that they continued to be released without trial. As always, the students who cried out against what The Reaper was doing to the poor inner-city people did so from the safety of the ivory tower of Stanford University. It is never so easy to espouse liberal ideals as when one is taking a four-year vacation using daddy's money, money which was more than likely made from the sweat and blood of the poor, downtrodden people that the students professed to care so much about. If any of The Reaper's victims had happened upon the Stanford campus, these same students would likely ride their $500 mountain bike across the street and out of sight.

Still, at the end of the Spring Quarter of 2003, healthy debates raged in the halls and dormitories of Stanford University, with half of the students claiming The Reaper was an American hero, the other half claiming he was either a sick demon or simply an extension of the minority-hating police.

The Reaper's first murders happened during Stanford's summer recess. By the time the students returned for the Fall Quarter of 2003, the debate had reached national prominence. As it often did, Stanford's faculty deemed it appropriate to offer a course based on a current event meant to make students think seriously about the moral, legal, and societal effects of whatever the topic du jour might be.

The course was called, "Vigilantism in America—Is the Old West Making a Comeback?" It counted toward one of Nick's final requirements…some kind of crap about modern thought and ideals that the University thought he should have under his belt before graduating. Nick had been just as interested as everyone else at Stanford in The Reaper, so he signed up for the course in order to both kill the requirement and also hear more about The Reaper.

When The Reaper first arrived on the scene, Nick was with most of the other students in thinking that what he was doing, while morally somewhat questionable, was at least admirable in purpose. If the guy was trying to stop drunk drivers, especially if he really was having some success, then more power to him. Even when he moved on to the wife-beaters and drug dealers, Nick had no real problem with what he was doing. He didn't subscribe to the theory that The Reaper was a racist just because his last few attacks had been in primarily black neighborhoods. Most of his bar attacks had been in white (or at least white trash) areas, and of course that was never mentioned. Nick thought, as did many others who felt The Reaper was in the right, that the fact he had struck a few African-Americans in a row didn't mean he was a racist.

During the summer of 2003, when The Reaper graduated to murder, Nick began to have second thoughts. It was almost universally agreed that The Reaper's intention was to punish criminals. Most of his supporters would also add protecting the innocent and deterring other criminals to that list. However, when he began to kill, the arguments for the more noble intentions began to lose water quickly in Nick's mind. He had always thought of himself as, above all, a good person. Ever since he was a little boy, he was a peacemaker. He was respectful of all people and of his elders. He believed in the good in all people and tried to set an example for others by being truly good himself. In the portrait he had painted of himself throughout his life, he should disagree strongly with The Reaper's new murderous path. However, he had spent the past year or so coming to believe that The Reaper had good intentions at heart, and it wasn't easy to suddenly throw out what had become a tentative admiration for him. More than that, though, he found that there was a place deep in the pit of his stomach, a place he had never been truly aware of, that told him that the deaths of these people were for the greater good of humanity. His conscious mind would never admit it, but subconsciously he wasn't sorry at all that the drug dealers and other scumbags were dead and gone.

By the time he entered Professor Rachel Weiss's class in September of 2003, Nick was truly torn as to how he felt about The Reaper. The lecture hall was packed on the first day. Nick scanned the room, noting approximately a fifty-fifty split between white male frat boys and Birkenstock-wearing vegans.

While the class was titled generically, the clear lynchpin was The Reaper. Professor Weiss divided the class into several discussion groups. She adeptly sprinkled the male WASP names among the others to provide the most animated and interesting discussions within each group.

During her semi-weekly lectures, she offered up for conversation examples of vigilantism throughout the ages, suggesting often that what The Reaper was now doing was not much different than what our ancestors accepted as the norm. Were farmers carrying pitchforks in the European Middle Ages different that this? What about lynch mobs and deputized posses in the American West? The ethnic gangs in major urban areas that patrolled and meted out justice in their neighborhoods throughout the nineteenth and early twentiethth centuries were also examples of vigilante justice. The real question in each of these societies was how acceptable to the law and the general public was the justice served in these ways. In most cases, if the law didn't encourage the activities of vigilantes, it at least looked the other way. The same was true for society in general.

While many in the class argued that such vigilantism was a way of the past, at least in America, Professor Weiss proposed that we might not be far from sliding back into such a society. Popular culture in America glorified the righteous villain quite liberally, so the fact that so much of the country found what The Reaper was doing acceptable was not surprising. In the crime caper movie, did we root for the thieves or the cops? When the tough guy's family was murdered, did we hope that the bad guys would be caught by the police or did we hope to see the hero get his revenge by killing the perpetrators? Our society, she argued, was not only accepting of vigilantism, it was begging for it. Whether it was Bernard Getz pulling a gun and asking questions later or The Reaper getting the criminals before they could get us, America loved to see the bad guys get what was coming to them. And everyone had seen enough stories about murderers back on the street before their victims' bodies were fully decomposed to know that the law didn't always give us satisfaction.

The debates in the discussion groups were raucous and satisfying. While Professor Weiss was able to make both sides think, most of the students left the class with the same rock-solid viewpoint either for or against what The Reaper was doing. One of the few exceptions was Nick.

The class came down to just one final essay question. The question was simply this: *Is The Reaper right or wrong?* Nick wrote a twelve-page dissertation arguing equally both sides of the question, citing sources and historical examples where appropriate. He thought he had done a fairly good job, and he had almost hoped he had taken the class for a grade instead of pass/fail. When he got his essay back, however, he was glad he had chosen the latter.

Professor Weiss had scratched in red pen on the last page of his Blue Book a "C" grade followed by a brief explanation. "Nick, your arguments here show clear thinking and an understanding of the topic greater than most of the people in the class. In the end, however, you just didn't answer the question. You say in your conclusion that you wish you could speak to The

Reaper to determine his motivation. As that is very unlikely, I had hoped you would make the leap yourself in order to complete the assignment. While I was happy that you are truly attempting to reconcile your own feelings and values with what The Reaper is doing, much more so than most of the others in the class who are generally going along with their own crowd, I'm afraid you simply didn't answer the question. I hope in the future you can come to terms with this issue to your own satisfaction."

As he had written his final essay, and as he had read Professor Weiss's comments, Nick had come to a realization. As he had always known, his nature was to believe that all people were inherently good, but sometimes circumstances made them do very bad things. When he initially thought about The Reaper's murders, he applied that thinking to The Reaper's victims, and therefore used that central tenet of his life to condemn The Reaper for his actions. What he had come to realize through Professor Weiss's course and the process of writing his final essay was that he had forgotten to apply his most basic principle to The Reaper himself. Maybe, he thought, The Reaper is really a good person who has been caught up in a whirlwind that he couldn't control. In the end, Nick found that it was impossible for him to make a judgment one way or the other about The Reaper without understanding his whole story. Of course he thought the only way that would happen would be if The Reaper were captured and then published a tell-all memoir from death row. Never did he imagine he would have a chance to personally interview The Reaper himself. Now, only five months after writing his final essay, for better or worse, he was about to get that chance.

"David?" Nick repeated. David had only stared at him when he asked his previous question. No, that wasn't quite right. David had stared near him, but he was really looking through a window to somewhere very far away.

"David? What was he…"

"Come on," David interrupted, seeming to snap out of his deep trance, "I want to show you something."

He walked down the hall toward the back bedroom. Nick followed. Neither of them spoke until they were both in the room.

David opened the closet doors and began to pull clothes from the bar that spanned its length. He lifted them gently in small groups and carried them across the room, laying them carefully on the bed. Nick stood by the door, watching with dumbfounded fascination. As near as he could tell, David had completely lost his mind.

As he set down the second group of clothes on the bed, David began to speak. "When my parents died, Karen was there for me. I wanted to kill the guy who did it. He was drugged out of his mind and he plowed right into my parents' car, and he didn't do a minute of prison time. He deserved to die. But Karen stopped me from doing it. She made me see that more violence wasn't the answer. She helped me get on with my life, and by the time we were set to get married, I had pretty much stopped dwelling on what had happened.

"Your sister was a beautiful person, Nick. One of a kind, really. I loved her...more than I can even say. I loved her before my parents died, but afterward, after she helped me so much, she had really become everything to me. She was my best friend, and really my only friend...at least on this coast.

"When they killed her...and then even your family turned your back on me...I wanted to kill myself. When I reached my lowest...I was a huge, fat slob who hadn't shaved or showered in weeks. I was eating take-out and drinking constantly. Just when I was reaching the end of my rope, I realized that there was something I could live for."

This last wasn't exactly accurate, but David thought that a little poetic license could go far in swinging Nick's feelings in his direction. A little guilt and a little pity should win the sympathy vote. David wasn't entirely sure what he wanted to happen at this point, but he did know that he wanted

Nick to understand what his true intentions had been. If he could get Nick to truly listen to him and understand him, then there was at least an outside chance things might not have to end badly. The odds of them remaining friends was pretty low, David thought, but if he could at least convince Nick to keep his secret, then he still might stay out of jail. He'd just have to do this New Dawn thing to keep Seamus quiet, and he'd be home free to go back to his staggeringly lonely life.

As that thought came to mind, he realized he did know what he wanted after all. He didn't just want Nick to keep his secret. He wanted Nick to understand and condone what he had done. If he did, then maybe their friendship didn't have to end. The sudden threat of losing Nick brought home more strongly than ever how much he had come to love him. David thought that Nick felt the same way, at least until Seamus showed up. If he was lucky, Nick's love and guilt might give David a chance.

David laid down the last armful of clothes on the bed, and then he pulled the dowel out of the closet and laid it on the floor. As he took the key, he said, "You see, Nick, when a man has nothing to live for, one of two things can happen." He paused as he inserted the key into the other side of the closet and turned it. "Either he can stop living, quickly by his own hand or slowly by wasting away." He paused again and picked up the lamp by the bed. As he felt underneath the lamp with his left index finger, he said, "Or, he can find a reason to live. If he does find a reason to live, you can be sure that he's going to throw himself into it completely. That's what I did when I found my reason to live, Nick. And my reason to live was revenge."

As he spoke the last word, he flipped the switch. The back of the closet split and opened, finally revealing his dark secret.

Nick took two steps to the left, bringing his body directly in front of the two suits of body armor on the wall. It wasn't those that caught his eye, though. He was staring at the identical, skeletal masks placed upon mannequin heads just to the left.

David placed a hand on Nick's arm. Nick shook it off and stepped back, turning his gaze directly into David's face. Nick wore a look of combined disbelief and horror. David saw that he had his work cut out for him.

"Nick, give me a chance to explain…"

"Explain what? How you killed all those people?" Nick yelled in a high, accusing voice.

"I didn't start out to kill anyone but the people who killed Karen. I know even that wasn't right, but she was my life, Nick, and they took her from me!"

"They took her from me too, David!"

"Yeah, but you still had your parents and brothers and friends. I'm not saying what I did was right, but I had no one to tell me it was wrong."

"You shouldn't need someone to tell you murder is wrong!"

"I didn't set out to kill people, I was just trying to stop drunk drivers from killing people like my parents. Then I got caught up in some kind of whirlwind. You might not believe this, but I barely remember the last year. It was like someone else was in charge, Nick. When I started doing what I was doing…it…it was like someone else was at the wheel. The kid I killed in Oakland…I don't even remember anything until he was already dead. Then I felt so bad I could barely stand it…"

Tears had filled David's eyes to the brim and now they began to slip down his cheeks. All of his crimes and all of his victims were now coming back to him…flashing before his eyes as if his life were about to end. He sat down on the bed and put his face in his hands. Without lifting his head, he said, "I know how it sounds, Nick, but I only meant to do good. It's just…hard…once you…cross a line like that. You just can't go back, and the whirlwind sweeps you forward."

"I don't expect you to stay, Nick. If you want to call the cops go ahead. I don't care anymore. I didn't tell you, but the night before you showed up, Karen came to me in a dream and said I still had a chance to redeem myself, and she said I didn't have to do it alone. I know now she sent you to help me. Since you've been here, I've been back in control of my life, and I haven't even wanted to put those on anymore. Even if you want to leave or call the cops, I owe you everything for helping me claim my life back. Other than your sister, you're the best friend I've ever had."

David stopped speaking, but he didn't lift his head. Nick wasn't speaking either. David couldn't tell if he was in the room or not, and he really didn't care either way. He could tell by Nick's reaction that he had lost him. If Nick wanted to call the police, that would be fine. Either way he would be gone, and either way David would go back to being alone. After glimpsing a normal life, remembering the duality of his life as The Reaper had taken everything out of him. He could resist no longer…it was time for fate to decide what would be next for him.

It did. David felt a tentative hand touch his shoulder and then pull away. He looked up to see Nick standing over him. He wasn't smiling, but his face had softened considerably. "David, killing people was wrong. I can't lie and tell you it wasn't. I don't even know if I believe what you're saying about your split personality or whatever it is you have. You lied to me about everything since I've been here, so I don't know if this is just another act. But I know how much you loved Karen. I loved her too. She was the best person I ever knew, and I've tried to live my life like she would be living hers right now if she were still with us."

"There was a time when I almost admired what The Reaper…what you were doing. You seemed to want to do the right thing, and you were putting yourself on the line to do it. Now that I know you intended all along to kill the people who killed Karen, your first acts don't seem quite so noble.

"Still, I wanted to kill them too, but the memory of Karen and…I guess society and my own morality too…kept me from seriously considering doing it. I think everyone feels at times like taking the law into their own hands. You did it, and people admired you for it, but killing people is just wrong, David. They are dead, and they'll never come back.

"I know that, Nick," David blurted tearily. "I don't care if you believe me, but when I killed them I...I wasn't really human. Right now I am, and I feel all of their ghosts tearing me apart."

"I don't know what to believe, David," Nick said. "You can tell me all the stories you want about not being in control, but I don't know if I'll ever believe it. The only thing you said that kept me standing here was your dream...because I had one too. The night before I came up here, she came to me out of the ocean and told me to come see you before I went to find Michael. She said you needed my help with something very important."

David looked up. "She was wearing a white dress?" This was only a question in the most rudimentary sense.

The two men looked at each other, and what passed between then was neither forgiveness nor love. It was understanding. It was as complete as it was undeniable.

"So what now?" David asked.

"You need to make one more appearance as The Reaper and then retire."

"The New Dawn?"

"Of course. If they have Sarin gas, someone has to stop them. You want to prove yourself, well, saving a few thousand lives isn't a bad way to start."

"All right. Tomorrow night. If I don't come back..."

"I'm going with you, David," Nick said firmly.

"I can't let you..."

"You can't stop me. I'd go without you if I have to. David, that's where Mike is."

"How do you know that?"

"Mike's best friend is Wayne Connelly. The two of them used to sneak around with these backpacks and all kinds of weird pamphlets and shit. This is right in line with what we always thought this Wayne would do. We all hated him, and we knew he would get Mike in trouble eventually. And I know it's the same one because he used to bitch about his rich grandparents and how he never saw any of it because his dad didn't get along with them.

And your friend Seamus said they have a chemist, right? My gut tells me that's Mike. He loved that kind of crap, that's why he majored in chemistry. David, I'm going with you so I can get Mike out of there before he gets in any deeper with these bastards."

"I can get him while I'm there, Nick. It's not going to be easy getting in there, and there may be the need to hurt or kill someone to do it. I don't think you can do it."

"Hurting I can do if the cause is right. But I'm not going to kill anyone and neither are you. You have to promise me that."

"I can't, Nick. If someone tries to kill me, I'll kill them first. I know you don't believe me, but I won't be able to stop myself. There's a haze that comes down around you and…and you don't really think any more. You just act. Maybe you'll see."

"I doubt it. Are we agreed?"

"Nick, if you got hurt or…or killed…I couldn't live with myself. Everyone I've ever loved has died. Look what I did when Karen died. If you do, what do you think is going to happen?"

"I think you're going to keep your promise to me and never put on The Reaper costume again."

"Did I promise that?"

"No, but you're about to."

"OK, I promise, but…"

"No buts, David. This is the only way. Otherwise I'll go myself and drag Mike out of there. Only I think without you I'll probably be killed for sure, don't you think?"

David thought about all of this. He saw that Nick was deadly serious about going to get Michael with or without him. David toyed for a moment with the idea of restraining Nick, but the image of Karen handcuffed to this same bed drove the thought far from his mind. At last, he came to a decision.

"OK. We'll go. But we go under my rules. I'm in charge and you do what I say. I'll agree to try to avoid killing anyone, but if it's them or us, I'll kill without hesitation. We both carry guns, and we both wear a suit of my armor. It will stop a bullet from five feet. I can attest to that personally. We'll both wear The Reaper masks too. I designed them to scare people into hesitation long enough for me to get in the first strike. It's worked great so far, and when they see two Reapers, that should make them stop even longer. And you're going to stay behind me at all times. Agreed?"

"Agreed. When do we go?"

"Tomorrow we'll drive by during the day and take some digital photos and video. Then we'll see. Maybe tomorrow night or the next night. Seamus made it sound like we don't have much time."

"Sounds good," Nick said, turning his head back to the closet. The posture of his body said that the conversation was over.

David didn't agree, though. "Nick," he said softly.

"Yes," Nick said, with only a slight edge in his voice.

"What happens when we're done?"

"I'll take Mike to LA, and you get on with your life."

"Do you think we'll stay in touch?"

"We'll see, David. After what's happened in the last half hour, I'm not in any position to promise anything."

Nick turned back to the closet, again putting an end to the discussion. After a moment, he turned back to David and said, "So are you gonna show me how to put this stuff on?"

72

Around 11:30 the following night, David parked his Honda on the hill above the New Dawn compound. He and Nick got out of the car and looked around carefully. When they were sure they were alone, they quietly opened the rear doors, pulled out their gear and began to prepare for battle.

When both were ready, they walked around to the front of the car. David held a duffel bag, which was out of character for The Reaper. This whole event, in fact, was very different than anything he had done in the past. He had learned a great deal about breaking and entering and surveillance from Richard's friends in Half Moon Bay, but he had never had to use that knowledge before. The only time he had actually been in a building as The Reaper was the time he smashed in the front door of that wife-beater in Richmond, and of course in Darius Williams's bedroom.

That wasn't the only thing that was different about this. Most of his other attacks had been ones he could call off if the opportunity wasn't there or was wrong. In this case, once inside the house, they were going to be committed to seeing it through to whatever end fate might decide appropriate. This fact made him feel claustrophobic, and he didn't like that. If he could call the whole thing off he probably would, but he didn't think another night or another week would make it any better for him and Nick. It could make it a whole lot worse for a lot of innocent people, though.

He held up the car key for Nick to see…only one so it wouldn't jingle against any others…and then dropped it into the side pocket of the bag. Nick nodded in acknowledgement. David didn't need to say anything. That movement had been part of the final instructions he had given Nick on the way over, which mostly consisted of a review of the plans they had made earlier in the day.

That morning, David and Nick had driven by the Connelly house and taken pictures of the front of the home. Nick operated the cameras by holding them just above the level of the passenger's door and aiming as best he could. The two of them then went home to view what they had on David's computer.

The pictures showed a very large ranch-style home, which was set about 100 feet back from a 12-foot tall iron gate. The gate was anchored by concrete pillars, which were connected to a 10-foot tall brick wall that stretched off in both directions. Evergreen and a few oak trees reared over the wall along its entire length. Other than that, the pictures didn't offer much useful information.

After examining them closely, David began to speak. He spoke in general terms and suppositions, almost as if he were thinking out loud as opposed to speaking to Nick.

"I don't see any guards, but I didn't expect to. This isn't the movies, and they certainly aren't looking for the kind of attention armed guards would bring. Their neighbors wouldn't take too kindly to having the western cousins of the KKK next door, especially if they were walking around inside the gate with Uzi's slung over their shoulders. If Seamus can't bust these guys and can't even figure out who's in charge, they are going to be keeping as low a profile as possible."

"You think a lot of him, don't you," Nick asked.

David started as if he had forgotten Nick was there. "Yeah. He's a helluva cop. A great person too. Not just a good person...a great person. His wife too."

David trailed off and then was silent for a few minutes, trying both to shake the guilt he had over what Seamus had said the night before and to remember where he had been. When he was able to do both, he continued.

"No guards is good, but I bet they have dogs. They might have something on top of the wall too. They'll certainly have video cameras everywhere, and probably a pretty good security system.

"I've never had to break a security system, but I know quite a bit about them from a guy I used to know. If we had more time, I could figure out what kind of system they have and then come up with a way to sneak in and bypass it. We'd need a pretty good blueprint of the house, and even that wouldn't give us an iron-clad guarantee. I got the idea from Seamus we need to move quickly, so I think we're just going to have to do our best without knowing the specifics.

"The alarm system will almost certainly be activated by sensors mounted on the doors and windows. When the sensors open up, the alarm goes off. We can get around that if we're lucky by using a glasscutter on a window, but if we break the glass they'll probably hear it. And if they also have an internal air pressure monitor, we'll almost certainly set off the alarm. Either way, we should plan for the worst. Once we're inside, I highly doubt if there is anything more extensive than a few video cameras. No photo eye beams or anything like that, you know.

"Now, which window? If the shades are down, we'll have to just choose a dark room near the back. If they are up, which I doubt they will be, we might be able to choose a room that isn't occupied and is either far from or close to your brother, depending on how much company he has with him. I'm betting they'll be down, though.

"So let's assume we get in a window, right? Odds are very good we'll set off the alarm and we'll be in a dark room in the back with no idea where to go next. Fine. Now what do we expect inside? I bet there are somewhere between six and ten guys in there. It's a week night, and I'm guessing not too many of them actually live there. Unless they have more money than Seamus is aware of, most of them probably have day jobs, and probably families and normal lives outside their little club. The leader and Wayne and your brother probably live there, along with a few others and probably half a dozen soldiers.

"Now, like I said, this isn't TV or the movies. I doubt if any of them are walking around with guns and bullet proof vests on. They'll probably be in sweats watching Leno or making plans for their big attack. The key is, they don't expect to be hit by someone like us. I don't think they probably have any real enemies outside the law, so they would have no reason to anticipate an attack like we are planning. I'm sure they have plans as to what they will do if they're raided by the cops, but I'm also sure their plan isn't to quickly grab their guns and get into a firefight. That wouldn't make sense, because they would know the cops would cut them in half if they shot back. My guess is, if they're smart enough that Seamus can't get to them, they'll hide what they have to hide and then surrender. They probably got some hot shot lawyer who is secretly behind their cause who will ride in and get them all off with a slap on the wrist, or get them off completely on an illegal search or some bullshit like that.

"So, we're in, the alarm's going off, and they don't know what the fuck just happened. I bet they will have something that will quickly tell them where we came in. Probably the same place the video camera monitors are at. If there is anyone in there, he'll send a few people or everyone down to see what just happened. If we're careful and don't break glass at least, they may even think it's a false alarm as long as we haven't been seen on camera yet.

"Now, here's the question for you, my friend. If we just call 9-1-1 and retreat, we can probably get away without killing anyone if there's a phone in the room we pick. You can call and I'll fire warning shots at them until you're done. If you want to get your brother, though, it's a whole different ballgame. I'm with you either way, but the choice is yours."

"I want to get him out of there before the cops come," Nick said flatly.

"All right then. We're going to need to wade into the house, probably over dead or injured bodies. My thought is we keep the lights off in the room we're in, wait on either side of the door, and beat the shit out of whoever comes our way. No guns...not to start with anyway. The key is to knock them unconscious as quickly as possible and move on to the next group. No fucking around trying to get them into a submission hold or break their leg or something. We want them all unconscious immediately and as quietly as possible. If we can do that without the rest of the house hearing, we'll have the drop on whoever we come across next and we can try to knock them out too. If they make noise, then we'll probably have to draw our guns and shoot everyone else we meet before they shoot us.

"How do we find Mike?" Nick asked.

"We'll have to go room by room. We'll stay quiet as long as we can, and we'll try to avoid any cameras they have inside, but eventually we'll end up in a firefight. Either way, you stay behind me. Watch my back and follow my lead. If I go down, you leave me and get the hell out of there. I'll be damned if I'll let you get killed over this.

"If we start shooting, be careful," Nick said, "I don't want Mike to get hit. Do you remember what he looks like?"

David cast his mind back to the pimply, sneering face that he last saw in court after Karen was killed. "How could I forget?" he said, trying to hide his distaste for Nick's brother.

"Just don't hit him," Nick said, sensing David's thoughts in spite of his efforts.

"I won't, Nick, but I've done this before. I'll hit what I aim at, just like I always have. I'm a little worried about you, though. Shooting at a person isn't like shooting at a target. If you find you're getting wild or scared, especially if Mike is on the other side, just stop and let me handle it. And remember, Mike isn't going to know it's you…you'll look like The Reaper to him just like I do. As soon as the smoke clears, you'll need to yell at him. Don't say your name, though, and see if you can get him to keep from saying it too. We'll steal the videotapes if we can, but who knows what recording equipment they'll have.

"What do we do when we find him?" Nick said.

"If we haven't called the cops yet, we'll do that, then we'll go out the nearest window. We'll take Mike with us…we'll drag him if we have to, but if he gives us any shit knock him out and we'll ask questions later. That decision will be up to you, OK?"

"OK," Nick said.

"I'll say it again, Nick. If I go down, you get the fuck out of there and don't look back. Take my car and come back here and then get in your car and drive to LA right away. If the shit comes down, you need to pretend like you were far away when it happened. You can worry about Mike later. Got it?"

"David, you're not going to…"

"Got it?" David repeated. The look in his eyes told Nick there was only one right answer to this question.

"Got it," Nick said.

That had been the last real discussion they had had until they got in David's car at about 10:30 that night. David had gone over everything one more time on the drive, including a few more details he had worked out in his mind since their initial talk, and then all had been as quiet as it was now as they stood on the ridge overlooking the New Dawn compound.

The two men took a step down the hill, and then David turned and placed a hand on Nick's arm. Nick looked at him, and for David it was like looking in a mirror. There was The Reaper, staring back at him in all of his terrible glory. Looking in a mirror wasn't exactly right though. It was like looking through a mirror, finally getting a glimpse into his soul. His disparate soul that had conceived the alter-ego known as The Reaper and then unleashed it to commit unspeakable and uncontrollable acts of rage. He found, as he looked into Nick's disguised face, that The Reaper was not currently present in his own person. This was the first time he had ever donned this costume without The Reaper at least partially if not completely at the controls.

Now, The Reaper was nowhere to be found. It should have pleased David to know that he was finally completely in control of himself, but it didn't.

It scared him to death.

73

"Good luck," David said through his electronic voicebox.

Nick started at the voice of The Reaper, and then nodded to David to indicate that he wished him the same. Then, they turned and walked down the hill to the back of the New Dawn compound.

When they arrived at the fence, David slung the duffel bag over his shoulder and waited for Nick to make a basket with his hands. David stepped into it and then put his hands on the wall for balance. Nick lifted up and David poked his head over the wall. He looked carefully at the top of the wall for tripwires or anything sharp. When he couldn't see any, he tentatively reached out a hand and patted the wall gently. Satisfied that there were no booby traps or alarms, he put his hands on the wall and hoisted himself up.

He sat silently on top of the wall, listening for any movement inside, either human or canine. He didn't hear anything other than a few birds and crickets. He held a hand down to motion for his duffel bag. Nick eased the zipper open and then handed it up to David. David pulled two raw T-Bone steaks from the bag and hurled them into the bushes about 15 yards to their left. He waited. Five minutes, then ten. Still no movement from inside the fence.

David could scarcely believe that they wouldn't even have dogs. If they did, though, they would be tuned enough to either respond to the noise in the bushes or the smell of the meat. David had injected the steaks with enough arsenic to kill a moose, but even at that he had been nervous about any commotion dogs would have made in responding to the meal or consuming it. Maybe this was a good omen.

David laid on his stomach and put his hand down for Nick. Nick took it, and David hoisted him to the top of the fence. Then they each dropped on the other side.

As they knew from the photos, the house was a long, narrow ranch-style dwelling. It ran from east to west, and they had come over directly opposite the east end. From their angle, they could see neither the front nor rear of the house. The end they were facing had only one window. It was small and high on the wall...probably a bathroom.

David looked carefully at the perimeter of the house. He wasn't surprised to see video cameras mounted on the roof at both corners. They were pointed diagonally out from the house so that they covered both this side and a slice of the front and back yards. He couldn't be sure, but it seemed from their angle that there was a blind spot directly in the middle of the east lawn. If they positioned themselves correctly, David thought they could make it across to the house without being seen. Once against the wall, they could move freely. The cameras were too high up to catch movement against the house itself, which would be directly below their position.

David touched Nick's shoulder and then motioned for Nick to follow behind him. They stole across the lawn quickly, coming to rest against the east wall in a few seconds. They then moved around toward the back of the house. David peaked around the corner and was able to see that the house was divided into two wings, separated by a set of sliding glass doors and an expansive patio. He now saw that the house was not actually laid out in a straight line, but it broke at the center and then angled back away from the street on the west end. This configuration allowed David a good view of the entire rear of the house. As he expected, he saw that all the windowshades were down. On their side of the patio, all the windows were dark. On the opposite side, about half of them showed dim light from behind the drawn shades.

David pointed to a low window on their side about halfway between the porch and the edge of the house. Based on its size and distance from the ground, he guessed it to be a bedroom or a den. He liked that because the room would be carpeted and the inner door possibly closed. The only problem might be if someone were asleep in the room, but that would be more of a problem for the sleeper than for them.

They moved slowly toward the window, their bodies within inches of the wall. When they arrived at the window, David pressed his ear to it, listening for any noise from within. After a minute, he set down the duffel bag and pulled a large glass cutter from within.

He placed the cutter against the upper left corner of the window. Slowly and carefully, he drew it down the left side. He pressed hard in order to make a deep, clean cut. The cutter made a squealing noise that made him pause frequently and listen for sounds from within. After about a minute, he reached the bottom left corner. He lifted the cutter and began again at the top right, moving down. He did the same along the top edge of the window, moving from right to left. David realized he was sweating and beginning to breathe heavily from concentration. He glanced at Nick, who seemed not to be breathing at all. With the mask on, it was impossible to tell Nick's mood, but David guessed from his general posture that he was second-guessing his decision to come. David himself was more nervous than he had ever been, and wished again that The Reaper could make a guest appearance just to help out.

He pressed the glasscutter into the bottom left corner of the window, and began to draw it across to the right. About a third of the way across, there was a sudden, sharp crack. The glass split halfway up the window and then broke out in a jagged star. At almost the same moment, a piercing alarm pealed out from their right. It was coming from a gray loudspeaker mounted just above the porch, and it was loud enough to make both of them jump and curse under their breaths.

His heart pounding, David dropped the glass cutter and struck the top of the window with both hands. The crack in the middle ran the rest of the way up, but the rest of the window fell inward fairly cleanly. He reached in and ripped the shade violently out through the window and cast it on the ground behind him, never taking his eyes from the gaping hole that had been the window. His red eyes scanned the room quickly. It looked like a guest bedroom that hadn't been used in some time, or, if it had, the occupant had made the bed up neatly and placed the lace pillows back in perfect order.

David turned to Nick and jerked his head toward the room in an indication that Nick should follow him in. Nick nodded, and then David placed his hands on the sill and vaulted nimbly into the room. Nick was right behind him.

David stepped across the room and opened the door wide enough to hear what was going on inside. The alarm was going in here too, but the source seemed to be at the opposite end of the house. Good…better that the people at that end shouldn't be able to hear than him and Nick.

On the other side of the door was a long hallway that led toward what appeared to be a grand, central foyer. On the other side of the foyer, a similar hallway led off down the west wing. At the moment, no one was visible in the east hallway in either direction. In the foyer, however, he saw a shadow appear on the wall, indicating at least one person coming in their direction.

David stepped back and motioned for Nick to take a position on the opposite side of the door. A moment later, they heard a mewling yell from down the hall. "I'm going," it said, "just shut that fucking thing off!"

David looked at Nick and nodded quickly. Nick nodded back just before the doorknob began to turn.

The knob turned slowly, and when the latch cleared its home in the door jamb, the door was pushed in just enough that it couldn't reseat itself. Then, the door began to move open again. When it had moved about an inch, David could see that the barrel of a gun was being used to push it.

When the door was about halfway open, a hand reached inside the doorway toward David, searching for the light switch. David seized it with his left hand and jerked its owner into the room. At the same moment, he stepped out and coiled his body away from the other man. Before the man realized what was happening, David uncoiled savagely and rocketed the base of his right hand into the man's jaw. The man's head snapped back and to the side, and for a moment it looked like it might simply keep going and tear completely away from his body. It eventually did reach its limit and sprung back toward David, the man's eyes rolled up to expose only their bloodshot whites. His knees buckled, and David held his arm long enough to lower him gently to the ground.

"Jesus," Nick said under his breath.

David snapped his head around to look at Nick and place a finger over his lips. He then pulled a pair of handcuffs from the bag and snapped the man's hands behind his back. He pulled him into the room, kicked the Uzi under the bed, and then stepped to the door to look out into the hall.

Just as he did, the alarm cut off. Another voice came from the west, requesting information of a man who was no longer conscious. "What was it, Henry?" the voice yelled down the hall.

David motioned for Nick to follow him. He stepped into the corridor and moved quickly in the direction of the foyer. There were two doors on the left between them and the foyer, and one on the right. He tried the knob on the right when he reached it. It turned freely in his hand, and he pushed the door open. Inside was another empty bedroom, although this one looked like it had been lived in very recently. Nick stepped in after him and David closed the door behind them.

"Henry, what the fuck are you doing down there?" yelled the voice again, sounding less irritated and more concerned than it had the last time.

For a moment, everyone in the house waited. Then, David heard the voice say much more quietly, "Come on." Immediately afterward, he heard the unmistakable sound of rounds being chambered.

David and Nick held their breath as what sounded like three sets of footsteps padded by their door. When they were just past, David quietly opened the door and shot his head into the hallway. The last man was disappearing into the room. David and Nick only had a few seconds to get behind them before they turned back toward the hall with their guns out in front of them. David didn't waste them.

He was out the door and back down the hall so quickly that Nick got behind several steps. David didn't hesitate or even look back to see where Nick was…he simply plunged into the room just behind the three other men. By the time Nick reached the doorway, David was delivering a violent blow to the neck of the man closest to the door. As David's hand thudded into the first man, the other two turned, bringing their guns around toward him.

David swung a looping right hand toward to the head of the man on his right, striking him in the temple and driving him back into the wall. With his left hand, he grabbed the wrist of the man on the left, preventing him from bringing the gun completely around. As the man wrestled with David to free the gun, David completed his follow through of the first blow and then quickly gathered himself again, unleashing a rising blow that crashed into the gunman's nose. There was a sickening crack as the man's nose broke and was driven up into his brain. The man's body seized violently, causing him to pull back on the trigger of his Uzi. A short burst sprayed from the end of the weapon, the flames lighting the room in like a deadly strobe light. David let the man drop, and then stood over him, seemingly stunned by what had happened.

Nick stepped into the room, looking at the man on the floor. His face was a mask of blood, and his eyes were wide open and staring dumbly up at David.

Nick had never seen a man killed before, let alone in such a horrific manner. David had killed many people, but he seemed more moved by the sight than Nick. When Nick saw that David wasn't going to move, he grabbed David's arm and shook him gently. David looked at him through his red eyes and said, "I've never killed a man with my bare hands before." He then looked back down at the man as if he had no intention of going on.

Shouts came from the hall, but Nick couldn't make out what they were saying. He reached out and shook David, harder this time. "David, we have to…shit!"

As he spoke, he pulled David down and vaulted around him, throwing his right foot up in an arc toward the gun of the man David had driven against the wall. The man had risen quietly and had drawn a bead on David's head. Nick's kick found its mark, knocking the gun to the side just as the man pulled the trigger. Nick then followed the kick with a back fist that connected with the man's right cheekbone. The man's head snapped to the left, and then came back just in time for Nick to deliver a straight kick just under his chin. The man flew backward toward the open window. He landed hard on the windowsill, sat there comically for a moment, and then tumbled out into the night.

Nick turned immediately to David, meaning to do the same to him if he hadn't snapped out of whatever daze killing the man had put him in. He saw that David was substantially back to normal, and relaxed his coiled muscles.

"Thanks," David said, "That was a helluva kick."

"You OK? Now isn't the time to grow a conscience, David. You'll get us both killed," Nick whispered harshly.

"I know. I'm sorry," David said with some indignation at the younger man's audacity. David was The Reaper, after all. This was his arena, not Nick's.

"Fine. Let's go." Nick said.

David crossed his arms and pulled his grandfather's two nickel-plated guns from beneath his armpits. He cocked each of them simultaneously, and then nodded to Nick to indicate he should do the same. Nick carried a single .45 caliber pistol that David had taken from one of The Reaper's victims to keep passing kids from picking it up before the cops arrived. Nick picked it out of a cache of nine handguns that David had collected over the past year. It matched David's grandfather's service weapon, which he had used when David was teaching him to shoot, almost exactly.

Nick pulled it from its holster and felt the weight of it in his hand. He had been nervous…maybe even scared…until he had been forced into action by David's carelessness. Now he felt energized, and the gun felt just right in the cup of his hand. He had been worried earlier about whether he would be able to fire it at a person when the time came. Now, he felt that would not be a problem at all. Kicking the guy out of the window had pumped some kind of cold adrenaline into his body, and now he was literally tingling with the urge to inflict further pain on those who had almost certainly kidnapped his brother. He thumbed back the trigger and nodded to David.

David nodded back and stepped over the bodies toward the door. He looked down the hall toward the foyer. He saw movement there, mostly in the form of shadows moving across the far wall. They had clearly determined that entering the hall was a dangerous proposition, so they seemed to be content to wait for the intruders to come to them if that was their desire.

David held up a hand to Nick and whispered, "Wait here." He looked a last time toward the foyer, and then bolted across the hall, smashing his shoulder into the first door on the other side and bursting through into the dark room. After a second, he appeared in the doorway, looked toward the foyer again, and then motioned for Nick to follow.

David watched as Nick sprung into the hallway toward him. Just as Nick moved, a shot rang out from behind him...from the east end of the hall. Nick's body contorted into a bizarre comma as it was driven past the door he was aiming for. He fell to the floor and lay motionless.

"NO!!!" David screamed as he watched Nick crash to the ground.

Panic filled David as more shots rang out from both ends of the corridor. He knew he had to get Nick out of the hall before he was hit again, but that was as far as his thoughts took him. Some sort of blind instinct drove him to fire two shots to the right and then drop to his knees and drag Nick roughly by the foot into the room with him.

He rolled Nick onto his back and felt all over him for blood. "Nick!" he whispered as he slapped his friend's face. He was wearing his armor, and David didn't see a wound on his head or neck, so the bullet should have been stopped. But there were seams in the armor, and Nick's black attire made it impossible to spot any blood.

As he crouched over his friend, trying to determine if he was alive or dead, he began to curse his own stupidity. What was the first lesson every child learned? Look both ways before you cross the street, of course. And now he, David McGuire, despite all of his experience in these matters, had allowed himself to weaken and lose focus. And what had caused this? The fact that he killed a man. Big deal…he had done it before…so what if this time he used his hand instead of a gun? And now it appeared he had killed with a new weapon…weakness and carelessness.

A familiar red pall began to seep from the depths of his mind. It spread through his entire being like an ink stain, and he welcomed it like an old friend. It might cost him dearly, but at least he had gotten his wish.

The Reaper had returned.

The Reaper shook Nick again, and this time the younger man coughed briefly and then sucked in a gasping breath. His eyes fluttered open, and then he coughed again as he tried to regain his breath.

"Nick, where are you hit?" The Reaper asked. Even though his voice was disguised by the voice-altering microphone David had worn all night, there was something in his voice that told Nick things had changed. All hesitation had left it, as well as all feeling and compassion.

"My back," Nick said weakly.

The Reaper rolled him onto his side and placed a hand on Nick's back. "Where?" He asked coldly.

"Upper left," Nick coughed. The Reaper moved his hand to Nick's shoulder blade and pressed firmly. Nick winced and tried to roll away.

"It may be broken, but there's no blood. You'll be fine. Stay here."

The Reaper didn't wait for a response. He stood up, stepped over Nick, and walked into the hall. He didn't pause or crouch. He turned immediately to the right and walked east, away from the foyer.

Shots rang out from behind him, whistling harmlessly by his ears. He paid them no more attention than he would a mosquito. He held his right arm out straight in front of him, pointing his gun directly at the only open door at that end of the hall. When he was about ten feet from that door, the man who had shot Nick in the back flashed his head and arm out of the door to see if he had a shot. He actually had a great shot, almost point blank, in fact. But before he could pull the trigger, The Reaper put a bullet in his forehead, blowing his brains out the back of his head and onto Mrs. Connelly's white carpet.

The Reaper continued into the room, stepping over the dead man who had unwittingly called the devil out of hiding and thus written his own ticket to hell. He scanned the room quickly, saw that no one was there, and turned immediately back around and began to walk swiftly toward the foyer.

He now held both guns in front of him, pointing one to each side of the hallway. There were stone pillars that stood in the foyer to either side of the entrance to the east and west corridors. He hadn't bothered to look, but he suspected the gunmen in the foyer must be hiding behind those.

A head and shoulder popped out from behind the pillar on the right. The man retreated as soon as he saw the demon that stalked down the hall toward him, but it was too late. As soon as he began to move, The Reaper's right index finger twitched and fired a round into the man's shoulder, shattering his collarbone and tearing away a huge chunk of flesh from his trapezius muscle. The man screamed and rolled backward, his gun falling from his hand and sliding across the marble floor. The scream was partially because of the pain, but mostly because of the certain death he saw in the eyes of their attacker.

The Reaper was now adjacent to the room they had first entered. He stepped in the door for a moment and calmly put a bullet in each of the two beaten men he had left alive in the room. He turned to re-enter the hall, paused, and then turned back into the room. He walked quickly to the window and poked his head out. The man Nick had stopped from killing him was laying on his back in the grass. He had begun to come around, and he opened his eyes with just enough time to scream before The Reaper shot him in the throat.

The Reaper turned and crossed the room again, pausing at the door. He looked both ways this time, and then he stepped back into the hall. He walked west, not pausing to look into the room where he had left Nick to recover.

He was now only 20 feet from the foyer, and none of the gunmen had fired or exposed themselves since the first one had been hit. The Reaper could still hear him screaming, but the man was now out of sight.

After a few more steps, three men broke cover simultaneously; two from the left and one from the right. All three fired at once, but not before The Reaper pulled the trigger on both of his guns.

The Reaper felt one of the bullets crash into his stomach, causing him to momentarily double over and clutch both of his gun-bearing hands to the impact point. He never took his eyes off his assailants, though, and he watched as one of the men on the left spun out of sight with a slug in the left side of his chest, and the man on the right flipped onto his back as a bullet tore into his skull.

The Reaper ignored the pain, cursing himself for pausing at all, and stood up and raised his guns again. The remaining gunman tried to dive for cover, but The Reaper put a bullet in his hip before he could get clear.

The Reaper stalked into the foyer. To each side was a man writhing in pain. When he came into view, both looked at him and began to scream and beg for their lives. The Reaper ignored their pleas and ended their suffering for good with one bullet from each gun.

The Reaper looked up from the last man he killed, and scanned the great room in front of him. To his left was the front door and a grand entryway. To his right was a living area centered around a majestic fireplace. The doors to the patio lay to the left of the fireplace. The room was organized into three clusters of furniture, each piece probably costing several thousand dollars.

Of course The Reaper wasn't interested in Mrs. Connelly's furniture. He saw that there was no one else in either side of the great room, but he also saw both the front and rear doors as possible entry points for his enemies.

He paused for a moment, attempting to watch both external doors as well as the corridor across the foyer. At the same time, he listened for any indication of which direction the next attack might come from.

He didn't have to wait long. He heard running footsteps from the opposite corridor. He raised both guns again, preparing to fire as soon as anyone came around the bend into sight.

The first thing he saw wasn't a person, however. Instead, a metal canister came sliding across the floor, spewing a stream of white vapor as it slid. Right behind it, three men came around the corner, each wearing a gas mask and carrying an Uzi.

Tear gas...SHIT! Thought The Reaper as the men fanned out after entering the great room.

Their intention was to blind him with the tear gas and then spray Uzi fire into the cloud until they heard a thump or they ran out of rounds. The plan might have worked, except the man in charge of tossing the first canister let go too early, and the angle was bad. All of them watched as it slid more toward the front door than The Reaper. The room was so large that, while the gas would get to where The Reaper stood in a few minutes and then become a minor irritant, it wasn't going to hinder his actions at the present at all.

There was a brief pause as all four men processed that fact and adjusted their strategies appropriately. Then, as if on cue, all of them sprung to action.

The men on the left and right depressed the triggers of their Uzis and sprayed wild fire across toward The Reaper. One of them fell dead only a second after he activated the trigger, The Reaper's bullet buried in his heart. The other would likely have died just as quickly had the man in the middle not pulled out another tear gas canister and raised his hand to throw it across the foyer at The Reaper.

When he saw this, The Reaper changed targets and fired at the man in the middle. Or, more specifically, he fired at the canister the man held in his hand.

The shot was true, and it slammed into the canister just as the man was bringing his arm forward to throw it. The canister exploded, taking the man's hand and the right side of his face with it. The Reaper had just enough time to watch the man collapse into a screaming mass before he was hit by four bullets in succession across his chest and arm.

The small caliber bullets were stopped easily by his armor, but the stinging pain was enough to cause him to collapse. He drew in a fiery breath and then raised his head. The other end of the foyer was filled with thick, white smoke. He saw the silhouette of the man who had shot him beginning to walk out of the gas toward him, no doubt to confirm his kill. The Reaper got to his feet, aimed, and waited.

When the man emerged from the gas, he hopped back and almost fell. He brought his gun up to fire again, but it was too late. The Reaper put a bullet through the right eye of his gas mask. The inside of the mask was immediately coated with thick, crimson blood. The man fell first on his butt and then flopped onto his back, one leg twitching briefly before he was finally still.

The Reaper listened for a moment to the screams of the would-be tear gas thrower, watching the gas slowly fill the foyer, and planning his next move.

74

"What the fuck is going on out there?" Wayne Connelly yelled into the corridor. The only response he got was the blood-curdling screams that had been rolling back toward them for the last three minutes. He didn't know if it was one of his guys or whoever the fuck it was that had broken in, but the lack of response from his guys was giving him a pretty bad feeling.

Wayne stood in the suite at the very west end of his grandmother's house. It was a large room that had been the gymnasium when they moved in. They had since converted the room to their "war room." The large windows on the west end that used to look out into the garden had been painted black to provide controllable light even during the day. All of the surveillance equipment was located here, as well as the bulletin boards, tables and chairs they used when planning their "activities." The Sarin was even here, stored in the crawlspace under the house and accessible by a trapdoor they had built and then covered by large storage cabinets.

With him were Mike Chavez, his childhood friend, and Duane Warren, a big hillbilly from the Sierra mountains northeast of Sacramento. Duane may look like a dumb hillbilly, but that was his secret. "Underestimated from birth," he was fond of saying.

Now, the three of them stood with their Uzis pointed into the corridor. The tear gas was seeping steadily toward them, which didn't make a damn bit of sense. They were supposed to throw the canisters across the foyer toward the other hallway and knock out the fucker in the black hood they had seen coming up the hall blowing away the other guys. They had cameras all over outside as well as two in each corridor and two in the foyer. Now, the foyer and their hallway were so clogged with gas they couldn't see a fucking thing. And now the east corridor cameras weren't showing anything and there was no movement outside. Did they get him? If they didn't, where the fuck did he go? And had he killed everyone else? If so, that made twelve dead, or maybe eleven plus whoever was still screaming out there. Wayne didn't know if the three of them could stand against this guy, whoever he was.

They waited, looking nervously from the hallway to the monitors to each other. All they could do was wait. There was no way out other than through the hallway, and they weren't going that way until they could see.

After a few minutes, shots began to ring out again from the foyer, or at least from that direction. The three of them raised their weapons, pointing them into the gas-filled corridor. Another shot rang out, and Wayne finally lost his cool. He pulled the trigger on his Uzi, spraying gunfire into the smoke. Duane put a hand on his arm, but he shook it off and kept firing until he was empty.

There were no more shots from the corridor, and the gas was finally beginning to thin. The three of them took a step closer and paused to listen. Even the screams had stopped. All was eerily silent. Maybe Wayne had hit the fucker.

The hopes that they shared came to a crashing end when one of the large windows behind them abruptly smashed inward, showering painted black glass into the room. The three of them spun around toward the window, Mike and Duane beginning to fire as they turned.

75

After he had put a bullet through the mask of the man that had shot him, The Reaper paused to plan his next move. He could pick up a gas mask and go charging down the hall, but if the smoke didn't blind him, the mask would. He didn't know how many men were at the end of the hall, but if they could see clearly they would certainly have the drop on him.

The advantage he did have, he realized, was that they could no more see into the smoke than he could. They would be so busy trying to see into it and figure out what was going on that they would forget to watch their backs.

He could use Nick's help to make sure of this. He ran back into the east corridor. When he did, he noticed the camera at the far end. He put a bullet in that one, and then turned around and did the same to the one at the near end of the hall. Then he ducked into the room where he had left Nick.

"Nick, if your brother is here he's at the other end of the hall. I believe that if you want him alive, you'll need to help me by keeping their attention this way. I'll sneak around behind them and come in a window. I'll kill everyone but Mike. I don't know if he'll shoot at me, but if he does I'll try to hide until he runs out and then I'll yell for you. You need to yell at him to beg off and let us come get him then. If he agrees, come down the hall and we'll get out of here. If he continues to try to fire..."

"Just don't shoot him. Leave if you want, but there's no reason to shoot him. If he keeps firing, head for the car and I'll call 9-1-1 and then come out the back way and meet you."

"Fine. Now listen. Come out to the edge of the hall, but stay out of the gas. Give me five minutes to get into position and then start firing shots into the opposite wall there. That should keep them focused inward and give me the drop on them."

"OK," Nick agreed.

The Reaper checked the hall—both ways this time—and then they both stepped out. The Reaper turned to exit through the window they had come in when Nick spoke. "David?" he said tentatively.

For a moment, The Reaper didn't answer. It was as if it took him a moment to register that Nick was addressing him. "Yes?" he said finally.

"How many people did you just kill?"

"Eleven. Twelve if the screaming guy doesn't make it."

"Did you really have to…" Nick began.

"You said it, Nick. Now was a bad time to grow a conscience," The Reaper said, cutting Nick off before he could finish the question.

Without waiting for another word, he stepped into the room where they had entered. He didn't look back or ask Nick if he was ready. Nick's words had given him a slight pause, as if David might come back again. He couldn't have that now, so he got out of there before any more discussion could take place.

He bent and scooped up his duffel bag and then hopped over the windowsill. He landed with both feet on the chest of the dead man on the ground, ejecting a fine spray of blood from the wound in his throat.

The Reaper skated along the back side of the building. He crossed the patio carefully, peering through the glass doors into the smoke filled foyer. He didn't see any movement, nor did he think anyone who might have ventured in there would be able to see him as he passed.

He then began to make his way along the back wall of the west wing. As he passed each darkened window, he stopped briefly to listen for voices within. He moved quickly, wanting to be ready when Nick began firing. He reached the far corner of the building in less than a minute. The last stretch had no windows, and he wondered about the room that was on the other side of the wall. He stole a glance around the West end of the house to see if there were windows there that might lead into that room. There were, but they were very dark. Black in fact.

"What the fuck is going on out there?" he heard a muffled voice yell from behind the wall. *Thank you, whoever you are*, he thought.

The Reaper stepped carefully toward the long windows. When he approached, he found that he could see small bits of clear light coming from the corners and a few other places. He stepped closer, and saw that the windows were coated with something to make them opaque. Probably simple paint, he thought. They had done a thorough but not complete job, and the places they had missed gave him a perfect line of sight into the room.

He drew close to a patch along the edge of the center window, and within he saw what he had come for. It was a large room with a bank of surveillance equipment along one wall and several storage cabinets, tables and chairs scattered throughout. Facing the corridor that led back toward the center of the house were three men carrying Uzis. Bingo.

The easiest thing would be to back up and fire through the glass, but that wasn't going to work in this case. First, he couldn't tell which was Mike, and second, even if he could, the glass might deflect his shots enough that they would run errant anyway and either miss completely or hit Mike accidentally. Moreover, he would have to step back to fire, and with the black paint he would be firing almost completely blind. It was clear he was going to have to break the glass and then come in shooting.

As he was considering how best to accomplish this, shots began to ring from the center of the house. He looked back into the window just in time to see one of the three men open up with his Uzi into the corridor. He hoped Nick had stayed under cover, but there was no use worrying about that now.

The Reaper looked around and saw that the garden had a good number of landscape rocks scattered about. He picked up a large, jagged stone, about the size and weight of a bowling ball, and moved toward the window. The gunfire from within had stopped. He waited for a second, hoping they would open up again. When they didn't, he stepped toward the window and hurled the rock through as if he were throwing a shotput.

The window crashed in under the weight of the rock. He saw the three men inside begin to turn, and he stayed in view just long enough to identify which was Mike. Then he ducked behind the brick wall that separated the windows. He knew he wouldn't have time to wait for the glass to clear, identify his targets and shoot the right ones. So, instead of standing and firing, he took cover and waited for them to blow their ammo out the open window.

He wasn't disappointed. Uzi fire rattled out the center window, clipping the hedges and bushes and slamming into the hillside. When he saw they weren't going to shoot out the other two windows, he took a quick glance through one of the open spots in the window nearest him. He saw that Mike had turned over a table and taken cover. The other two were still standing where they had been, one emptying his Uzi into the hole in the wall and the other trying to get a new clip into this own weapon. Mike wasn't firing. He seemed to be waiting for their attacker to appear before blowing his wad. Smart. The Reaper hoped he didn't have to make Mike pay for his intelligence.

The big guy's Uzi stopped spitting fire a second later, and, just as the other one finished reloading and raised his own weapon, The Reaper spun out of his hiding place into the center of the window. He pulled the triggers of each gun twice, aiming at center mass on the two uncovered targets. All four bullets were true. Both men were driven backward by the impact, blood and guts from the exit wounds spilling onto the floor just before their dying bodies landed there.

"YOU MOTHER FUCKER!!" Mike yelled as he opened fire with his own weapon. The Reaper hadn't stopped moving, and he was safely on the other side of the opening before Mike's bullets came pouring out.

Mike fired his gun empty, as The Reaper had hoped. When the echoes stopped, The Reaper sprinted into the opening toward the overturned table. Mike saw him coming and ducked down. The Reaper vaulted over the table and seized Mike by the back of his pants, pulling him away from the freshly loaded Uzi that his childhood friend had dropped as he died.

"COME NOW!" The Reaper yelled at the top of his voice. Then he lowered it to a conversational pitch and said, "Mike, I'm not here to kill you. We came to get you out."

Mike stopped struggling and turned around to face The Reaper. The coldness in his eyes surprised The Reaper. He was used to only fear when people first got a good look at his leering countenance. "Who are you?" Mike asked.

The Reaper didn't answer. He pulled Mike to a standing position and kept his gun at the ready until Nick entered the room.

Nick was coughing mildly and his eyes were watering from the residual tear gas, but he otherwise seemed to be functioning quite well in spite of his broken shoulder blade. He moved quickly toward Mike and The Reaper as soon as he entered the room.

"Mike, it's me Nicky. We came to get you out of here," he said. While his mask hid his facial expression, there was a relieved smile in his voice.

"Nicky?" Mike said, "You're The Reaper?"

"No," Nick laughed, "He is. I'm just making a guest appearance today. It's David, Mike."

Mike's face bloomed in a look of amazed wonder. He turned toward The Reaper and said, "David? You're The Reaper?"

"Yeah. Good to see you Mike. Where are the videotapes for the surveillance?" The Reaper said without emotion, still speaking through his electronic voicebox.

"Over there," Mike said, pointing toward the console. "What's with your voice, David?"

David put a finger under his chin and flipped the microphone out from beneath his mask. "Better?" he asked.

"Yeah," Nick said, almost giddy that they had actually pulled this off with all three of them in one piece. "That thing was freaking me out."

"Hear that?" David asked, cocking an ear toward the window.

The other two imitated his motion. Very faintly, they heard sirens begin to wind in the distance.

David strode to the console and began ejecting video tapes. When he had all eight, he turned to Mike and asked, "Phone?"

Mike pointed across the room. David nodded and then went to the open window and grabbed his duffel bag. He pulled it inside, dropped the video tapes in the bag and then strode to the phone.

Mike and Nick were watching him go about his business with silent wonder. As he walked toward the phone, Nick turned to Mike and said, "You OK?"

"Yeah. Thanks for coming for me. I didn't know what they had in mind until I got here, and then I was kind of trapped, you know?" Mike said with an embarrassed sincerity.

"No problem. It was just an accident I found out you were here, but I'm glad I did," Nick replied.

They paused their reunion to listen to David's end of the 9-1-1 call he made on the phone across the room. David was holding the phone in his right hand. In his left, he held the small microphone back to his mouth to disguise his voice.

"Yes, this is Henry of the New Dawn. We have a large quantity of Sarin gas stored at this location that we intend to use very soon. Please hurry before the others hide it."

He didn't wait for a response. He simply hung up the phone and waved urgently toward Nick and Mike, gesturing for them to move toward the open window.

Nick turned and walked around the overturned table. Mike followed. Nick and David came together side by side and walked toward the opening. As David reached for the duffel bag, Nick turned his head slightly and said, "Hey Mike, which of these guys was the big boss anyway?"

"I am!" Mike said with a flat hatred that made David and Nick both spin around to look at him. Mike had picked up the Uzi that Wayne had reloaded just before David had blown him to hell, and he was standing over Wayne's fallen body with his legs spread apart and a vicious sneer on his face.

David drew his weapon instinctively and raised it toward the leader of the New Dawn. Mike pressed the trigger and released a spray of bullets that cut across both Reapers, moving diagonally up and to the right. At the same moment, David pulled the trigger of his own weapon.

All three men fell. All three of them rolled in pain on the floor, struggling for breath or life or both. After about 30 seconds, one of them got up.

76

Michael Chavez found himself lying flat on his back in the war room he had built and organized. Pain screamed out of his guts, and he could barely draw breath. As near as he could tell, he had been struck in the stomach and the right side of his chest.

Michael's entire life had been a blur of hate and anger, much of it directed toward his own family, and especially his younger brother. He had finally come to a point where he was going to do something great…something that would make people remember his name for years, and his bastard little brother had even fucked that up. The wretched irony of it was so sharp it made him choke a laugh out of his bloody throat.

At least he had killed Nick and that other fucker, David, in the process. He must have hit them each four or five times, so they must be gone already. They would get to the gates of hell just ahead of him, then.

Mike opened his eyes and used all of his remaining strength to lift his head. He wanted the last thing he ever saw to be the dead bodies of the two mother fuckers who had ruined everything he and Wayne had worked for their entire lives. What he saw when he lifted his head caused a scream of rage and agony to erupt from his lips. One of them was getting up!

How in the name of hell had one of them survived that? They were dressed identically, so he couldn't tell for sure which it was that had made it. As he squinted his eyes to try to tell, he ran out of strength and his head flopped to the floor. Now all he could do was listen and wait.

His head was beginning to cloud with a cool, gray fog. He was cold…so cold he couldn't feel his hands or feet anymore. He was also dimly aware that he was thirsty. None of that mattered, though. The end was near. He focused everything he had on listening to see if either of them spoke or would give a clue as to which had survived his final, hateful strike.

One of them did speak. It was the one standing, he thought, but the voice was a whisper and he couldn't say for sure whom it belonged to.

"Come on," it said, "Let's get you to a hospital."

The one that was still on the ground responded haltingly. He managed only a few words at a time, interrupted by wet, gurgling coughs. "Too…late…go…cops…only…one…Reaper."

"No," whispered the standing voice, "I won't leave you."

"Yes…you'll…be…free…"

The wounded one's voice trailed off into a harsh gasp. Mike's vision was completely dark now. His own breathing was coming in short, uneven bursts. The last thought that ran through his head was that he hoped desperately that he would see his brother on the other side. Maybe he would have another chance there to draw a measure of revenge for the torment Nick had caused him his entire life.

With that thought echoing in his mind, the life force left the last leader the hate group known as the New Dawn ever had.

EPILOGUE

The San Francisco Chronicle held the presses for almost a full hour early that morning, waiting for the distinguished Douglas Fairchild to phone in the following article.

REAPER KILLED--FOILS PLANNED TERROR ATTACK!
FBI AGENT CALLS REAPER A HERO

MILL VALLEY—The vigilante killer known to Bay Area residents as "The Reaper" was killed early this morning in a shootout with members of the New Dawn, a white supremacist group known for its acts of violence against minorities and non-Christians.

The gun battle occurred in the Mill Valley home of Edith Connelly. The New Dawn had been using the home in the upscale neighborhood as a base of operations for several months, according to authorities. It is not clear at this time if Mrs. Connelly was aware of this fact, as she is currently living in Arizona.

According to the FBI, fifteen members of the New Dawn were killed in the attack. Many of their identities are yet to be confirmed. Likewise, the identity of The Reaper has not yet been confirmed. The names of those slain will be released when all have been identified and their families have been notified. Authorities declined to speculate how long that would take.

Seamus Molloy, the FBI agent in charge, said, "At this point, we don't know why The Reaper was here or how he learned of the location of the New Dawn. However, there was a 9-1-1 call made from inside the house after the police had already had several reports of gunfire. We believe the caller was The Reaper, although he identified himself as a member of the group. He told the operator that they had Sarin gas and were going to use it soon."

Molloy went on to say that a search of the premises turned up several canisters of Sarin gas, a deadly nerve agent that had apparently been stolen from Berkeley Labs a few weeks ago. Also found at the scene were plans detailing an attack to be carried out on Memorial Day at the "Glide for Life" concert to be held in Golden Gate Park.

According to Molloy, the New Dawn was in possession of several mortars, which can be used to deliver and detonate canisters of the gas from short distances. Plans indicate that they intended to get close to the park in four pickup trucks, and then fire the gas into the crowd on the lawn of Golden Gate Park.

The "Glide for Life" concert, sponsored in part by Glide Memorial Church, is scheduled to feature six top hip-hop and R&B artists performing for a crowd expected to be over 10,000 people. Proceeds from the concert will go to several Bay Area charitable groups, most of which focus on helping underprivileged minority youth.

"This was the perfect target for the New Dawn," said Molloy, "The crowd is expected to be around 10,000, many of whom will likely be African-American or other minorities. If they were able to use these mortars to accurately deliver the Sarin into the middle of the crowd, casualties would have been very high."

When asked to elaborate, Molloy said, "If the amount of Sarin they had loaded in these rounds were detonated in an open area, it would be expected to spread quickly over an area of several hundred square feet. It appeared that they planned to fire at least two rounds from four different vehicles. If all eight rounds struck the crowd, several thousand people would die very quickly from the gas itself. Even those who could get away from the blast area quickly enough would likely be very sick. Not to mention the deaths from the actual mortar explosions and the likely stampede that would be touched off by the attack. All in all, we would expect a casualty rate from the attack that the New Dawn had planned of 60-70%. At least half of that number would be fatalities."

It has been suggested in the past that The Reaper may have tendencies toward racism. When asked to comment, Molloy, who ironically, was assigned to The Reaper case for a period of time last year before returning to the New Dawn assignment, said, "I can't comment on his motivations tonight or in any previous attack. Since he is no longer alive for us to ask, we may never know what he was truly trying to accomplish over the past few years. I will say, however, that, if he hadn't come here tonight, the New Dawn very well could have killed several thousand people, most of whom would be minorities. I don't know if that answers the racism question or not, but in my book, what he did here today makes him a hero."

AFTERWARD

First of all, if you are one of those "read the last page first" people, please don't read this one. There are spoilers to follow.

For those of you reading in the correct order, you may be kind of pissed at not knowing who made it and who died. Well, let me answer at least one question for you. We know from the news article that one of them died, but I can tell you that the other one did live, and still lives on as I write this. When I wrote the book, I wasn't ready to choose. I knew for quite a long time, maybe even from the beginning, that this is how it would end, and that the one who lived would carry on in the sequel. What I didn't know then was what I wanted the sequel to be. By leaving both possibilities open, I could choose from many more options for my next book.

So, if that was your next question, there is your answer, there is a sequel which I am working on as of this publication. And therefore, I now know which Reaper lived, and I know what he has been up to, and I know that he hung on to his Reaper gear, should he ever need it in the future. And rest assured, dear reader, he will.

If you like this book, please tell your friends and watch for the sequel soon. If you didn't like it, well, let's just keep that between us.

Made in the USA
Columbia, SC
07 December 2022

72871984R10230